SWORD AND STARSHIP
BOOK 1: BLOOD'S FORCE

ELLIS MORNING

Blood's Force (Sword and Starship Book 1)

Published by Ellis Morning
Pittsburgh, PA
www.ellismorning.com

ISBN: 978-0-9907573-2-0

Edited by RJ Blain
Interior layout by Ellis Morning
Cover art by Chris Howard
Cover design by Ellis Morning
Printed by CreateSpace, Charleston SC

Acknowledgements

I can't thank enough everyone who helped me in some way:

- Remy Porter, for initial editing and years of unfailing support
- RJ Blain, for her wonderful editing
- Chris Howard, for his amazing cover art
- Family and friends, for their encouragement
- **YOU**, for giving this book a try!

Writing this book has proven an arduous but rewarding quest! I hope you enjoy reading it as much as I enjoyed putting it together.

-Ellis

CHAPTER 1

Eye-watering light had overtaken the void of space. Once we touched down, the ship's thrusters fell into silence. Gravity seized us again, a harsh burden after a full standard week's absence. We'd bested the gauntlet of another atmospheric entry, but relief failed to reach either my spinning head or pounding heart. Those nerves wouldn't settle until I laid eyes on Sir Branigan Cade, my friend and fellow knight errant, who remained missing. A glance at the touch-screen console before my lap confirmed it.

Disappointment made my guts plummet like they were tied to an anchor, but even that failed to keep the world from pitching about with every tilt of my head.

"I'm still not reading his ship's beacon. I was hoping, *maybe*, once we landed …" I trailed off, biting the inside of my lip.

"That beacon doesn't tell us much, Jess." I couldn't quite focus on Drea yet, but her soft voice remained patient, despite how many times she'd already reassured me on the matter. "Sir Branigan might've turned it off himself, or he might be having technical issues. Let's not assume the worst."

That was the opposite of my instincts.

"Breathe deep. Relax your shoulders," Drea encouraged.

I complied, chancing a squint through the blinding cockpit windshield. Nothing outside eased my paranoia, but nothing fed it either. A flat plane of untouched snow stretched beneath ashen sky, ending at a mountain chain along the horizon. To our right spanned a tall wooden fence, stretching out toward those mountains. Beyond that fence had to be Gules, our long-awaited destination. And Branigan.

Branigan! Our paths crossed all too infrequently; my heart fluttered like a caged butterfly at the prospect. It was his letter to Drea and my other former mentors that'd spurred us out there. He'd found a Shipbuilder artifact in Gules that he hadn't been able to move or identify. Despite the mystery, his words had betrayed great thrill over the find.

Drea had been chosen to meet with Branigan and investigate the artifact. As I'd happened to be visiting my mentors at the time, between quests, they'd asked me to serve as her escort to Gules. For weeks, Drea and I had been crossing the galaxy to reach Lord Catherwood's space, a domain new to both of us.

My gaze shifted to my traveling companion. Drea sat strapped into the copilot's chair to my right, examining our first view of Gules with an aura of gentle strength. She was two decades my senior, but silver had barely encroached upon her dark hair. The love and respect I harbored for her hit me hard then. If all went well, we'd be parting ways soon, indefinitely. After three standard weeks spending every second together, like old times, the return to solitude would leave a hole in my heart.

"Looks quiet. And cold," Drea spoke. "I don't blame everyone for staying in."

Her assessment of the void outside was more optimistic than mine. I took another deep breath in defiance of the restraints crossed over my chest, and glanced back down at the console. The limited sensors at my disposal remained quiet, while the holographic interface listed a familiar indictment of warnings. *Warnings*, at least, not *errors* — an important difference. Some demanded expert attention that had died out centuries ago. Others, I could appease myself with creative jerry-rigging. Just knowing the problems came down to natural causes, rather than the ritual I'd messed up or deity I'd riled, put me ahead of most people.

Thanks for not flying apart yet, little hellion, I thought. I raised a heavy hand to my lips, kissed the fingertips, then patted the console.

"Jess?"

Caught, red- and saliva-handed. Habit had betrayed a gesture I'd been suppressing in Drea's company. Embarrassment burned my face, even as a stubborn, senseless defense leapt from my mouth. "I promise, I don't really think my ship's alive!"

Drea shook her head with a smile. "You don't have to explain it, sweetheart. As much as we fight superstition, we all have rituals we can't let go of. It's just human nature." The smile turned devilish. "I was going to say, I've seen Sir Mayweather make that same gesture with his ship."

The name of my former master hit my ears like salt striking an open wound. I laughed, trying not to let on. "So *that's* how you'll get me to stop. 'Hey Jess, May did it.'"

"He still smokes those *wonderful* cigarillos, too."

"Don't remind me." After a full week of flying, even my eyeballs ached for a smoke.

Drea must've keyed to my discomfort, because her expression and tone turned apologetic. "He gave you a lot. You're allowed to hang on to the good things."

I only seemed capable of hanging on to terrible habits and worse memories.

Enough, I decided, glancing outside again. Why hadn't anyone approached us yet? Usually, someone arrived within seconds to extort a landing fee or offer a blessing. With mounting concern, I unfastened my restraints and pried myself out of the pilot's chair. Unfortunately, my body was still adjusting to gravity. My vision browned out and my knees buckled, forcing me to grab the headrest to maintain balance.

"Careful!" Still strapped in, Drea did her best to catch me. "I'm sorry I needled you. I'm lucky you don't shut down and refuse to speak to me the way Farid does."

I waited for my head to clear, smiling so Drea would know I wasn't annoyed. "I'm not a teenager."

"You're still young. And I still deserve it sometimes," Drea said.

"He's lucky to have you," I said, and meant it. "I'll tell him that the next time I visit, if you want, but I might botch it." I was no good with kids.

"Oh, I don't know about that," Drea said. "You're not his mother. That gives you a considerable advantage."

My second attempt at standing proved better. Drea had no difficulty herself. Navigating the narrow passage beyond the cockpit was like crawling out from our shared grave, every inch a struggle. The retrofitted handholds on every surface, so useful while cruising, became bruise-makers and clothing-snaggers on land. Our worse-than-usual torpor didn't help matters.

I was close enough to catch Drea when she tripped on a handhold. "This is why I don't usually fly more than a few days at a stretch," I said. The first two weeks of our journey had been a string of short hops with regular landings in between. After Branigan's beacon had vanished, I'd insisted on gunning it nonstop the rest of the way.

Drea was good enough not to bring up that fact. "I'm sure it won't take long to readjust."

I kept a hand on her arm and gazed longingly at the deck plating under our feet. The plates had once provided gravity outside of a planet's pull, but had malfunctioned unknown decades or centuries earlier. Long trips would've been so much easier with their cooperation. Sadly, neither I nor my friends knew how to repair them.

The cramped tunnel outside the cockpit fed into a hallway where one could stand upright, provided he didn't crest six feet. Drea and I wielded slight builds and average heights to great advantage. That hallway led to the galley, the largest section of the main deck. We pressed even further aft, through a threshold with a malfunctioning door, to enter quarters.

Both of us wore tunics, trousers, and boots, our hair woven in microgravity-minded plaits. As we donned our gear, the similarities between us eroded. Drea pulled on gloves and a hooded wool cloak. On either pale blue shoulder appeared the emblem of the Enduring Flame Beguinage, the place where Drea and many other dedicated scholars had mentored me and others in Shipbuilder disciplines, despite the risks.

Some of my gear was mundane, modern fare: wool coat, leather gloves, back baldric and belt, dagger sheath. The rest were gifts from the beguinage: actual Shipbuilder artifacts, or new items created with their ancient knowledge. For armor, I had a nanofiber brigandine, so thin as to be invisible beneath my coat. My first aid kit contained penicillin, ethyl alcohol, and topical anesthetic, supplies I couldn't find anywhere else. My side sword had been forged for me when I'd completed my studies. Its lightness was a boon given the current challenge in lugging around my own body. Even my ship was a gift, and final project as well.

Once ready, I realized again whom we were there to meet. My heart shifted from jitter to sprint. I launched into an anxious search through closets and storage units for some manner of reflective surface.

With a knowing smile, Drea halted my frantic running about and looked me over herself, smoothing stray strands of hair out of my face. "Are you planning to tell Sir Branigan how you feel this time?"

She referred to my years-long crush. Hot blood crept up my face. My legs lost some of the strength they'd regained. "Yes," I forced out.

"It's important to make yourself heard, Jess. Wherever it leads, it's better than uncertainty." Drea looked to me with encouragement, and waited for me to return eye contact. "I know this is hard for you. I'm proud of how brave you're being."

"I sure don't feel brave." And did I ever feel stupid for it. I'd fight anyone in the galaxy who posed a threat to good people, but I'd never had the nerve to stammer out a few lousy words to a long-time friend. Then again, I knew how to handle physical hurts. *Emotional* ones?

"That's when you're bravest." Drea smiled, then knelt to rummage through a knapsack on the floor. "Let's review Catherwood dogma before we go."

As a knight errant, I was permitted a ship and free travel between domains in search of quests. This meant having to comply with dozens of dogmas, all minor twists on the common theme sung throughout the galaxy. For me and Drea, this was a matter of self-preservation, not deference. We didn't believe in the theme, we just memorized its notes. Botching the song meant imprisonment or death in most places. As newcomers to Lord Catherwood's domain, we didn't want to take chances.

I pulled in a deep breath to slow my racing heart, then recited the highlights like lines from a script. "They believe the usual here, regarding the Unseen and so-called 'magic.' Cremation after death, reincarnation, broken ships treated as honored dead. No repair, no salvage."

The last struck me as especially absurd. With dogma like that, there couldn't be many working ships left in Catherwood space. Oh well. What the authorities didn't see me doing, they couldn't arrest me for.

"Correct." As I answered, Drea consulted a slim pocket-sized device: a data carrier, a centuries-old Shipbuilder artifact. Its holographic display glowed inches from her face. I longed to salvage a data carrier for myself someday. Three weeks of travel, and we'd never run short on reading material.

A possible lead sprang to mind. "Did Branigan have a carrier?" If so, there was a chance we could communicate with him.

Drea shook her head, apologetic. "I'm not detecting any signals here. He may not have one, or he may be outside of this device's range." She returned the data carrier to her knapsack, then stood, hauling the bag up with her.

We backtracked to the hallway and squeezed into the airlock. Freezing wind blasted against our exposed skin when I pushed open the hatch, making me miss the ship's canned fare. I knelt, then lowered myself into several inches of snow. Beneath the powder lay the glassy surface of a centuries-old landing pad. It was our first hint of the Shipbuilders' original settlement, the ruins from which Gules had risen.

Once I helped Drea down, she backed several steps away from the ship, well aware of what was to follow.

I grabbed the airlock hatch and leaned my full weight into it. The door bounced in and out of its threshold. A giant heave formed my next dignified attempt. When that didn't work, a flying leap slammed the door home.

"Aha!" I declared with triumph.

"That's no way to treat your 'sacred' ship." Drea shouldered her knapsack, smiling.

The smile was contagious. "Sacred" had no business being applied to my ship. She resembled a spider minus legs and chelicerae, a troublesome cuss full of venom she couldn't expel. On her hull stood my sigil: a horizontal line that started level, zigzagged up and down, then leveled out again. An arrow cut across the jagged line at a diagonal, pointing to infinity. It was an ancient symbol called a "variable resistor." Beside that, I'd painted the name I'd chosen after years of dogged restoration: *Kepler's Law*. Her namesake was a scientist even more ancient than the Shipbuilders, and his achievements had been no less stunning.

Drea hugged herself against the strengthening wind. I draped an arm over her shoulders and led her around the ship — only to halt mid-step on the other side.

Away went all the optimism Drea had tried to instill in me. An empty snowfield stretched before us; mine was the only ship in the port. A few meters away stood a flimsy signal tower, unmanned, with no fire lit. In the distance, the wooden fence I'd seen from the cockpit obscured what was allegedly a town. No footprints or animal tracks marked the snow. No one stood by to question our business.

Gules itself had vanished, right along with Branigan.

"What the hell?" I blurted amid mounting alarm. "We landed in the right place, I know it!"

Drea had long ago given up on scrubbing imaginary eternal punishments from my speech. Her voice and expression insisted on calm. "There might be some winter holiday we don't know about, or they've moved their port."

"Maybe, but ..." Every settlement had its surprises. Indeed, I *hoped* Brangian and the locals would be grinning at my worry over drinks soon. It was that worry that got me moving again, pulling Drea along as fast as our legs allowed.

Drea had no trouble keeping up. Worry most likely drove her on as well, along with the desire to figure out just what we'd landed in.

The pavement gave way to jutting cobblestones, forming a

path that wound toward the tall wooden fence stretching in either direction. Our crunching footfalls were the only sound piercing the otherwise barren winter apathy. I shielded Drea from the gusts of wind that carved into our bones and lifted swirling veils of snow into the air.

The uneven fence lacked the care and planning of a permanent fixture. It also lacked a gate. At the point where cobblestone met fence, a proclamation had been nailed up on the boards, stalwart against the wind threatening to carry it elsewhere. Flanking the parchment were two iron amulets of circular serpents gagging on their own tails, warning enough for those who couldn't read. Weathering had warped the parchment and smeared the issuing party's seal, but the message remained legible:

TURN BACK
By the Will of the UNSEEN,
by Decree of OUR LORD AND SOVEREIGN Albion Hadwin
Catherwood VII (LMHR)
and by the Might of his Magic Adepts is the Settlement once known
as Gules hereby
CURSED
for Failure to protect Assets sacred to OUR LORD and his
Dominion.
Gules is cast from the Domain of Catherwood, furnished back unto
Nature,
Her Denizens confined herein without Wish or Aid.
An any should trespass, shall the Trespasser share the Curse.
An any should render Succor to the Wretched within, shall the
Renderer share the Curse.
Such is the Will of the UNSEEN, the Powers holding Dominion
over all Dominions.

"Hell," I muttered, for once regretting my gift of literacy. I felt like I'd just read the account of a madman who'd cut off his own hand to teach the rest of his body a lesson. My ribcage tightened, but not with the primitive fear of evil forces. Drea and my other mentors had freed me from belief in curses, Unseen, and other powerless superstitions. My heart ached for the people trapped beyond the fence, who almost certainly hadn't done anything to deserve being so cruelly severed from the rest of the galaxy.

Damned magic adepts. They were the same everywhere I went. There seemed no limit to the evil they could justify as "the Will of the Unseen."

Drea separated to face me with dismay, tears welling in her eyes. "Have you ever encountered a cursed town before?"

"Sort of." I forced my answer through an uncooperative throat. "May and I ran into one in Sever space once, when I was his squire. He dragged me back to his ship without a second look. 'That town's a rabid dog now,'" I quoted, making no attempt to mimic my former master's know-it-all baritone. "'You don't reach out lest he take a piece of your arm, 'cause that's when you *really* catch hell.'" I hesitated. "I tried to get him to go back, but he wasn't having it. Maybe there was *something* we could've done."

"Probably not." Drea's eyes pleaded for understanding. "Sir Mayweather did the best thing for you both. Words on parchment can't hurt you, but the people who wrote those words can. If anyone caught you—"

"No one would've caught us. It was just as dead there as it is here." My heart burned with frustration. "May ditches his vows when they're inconvenient. I don't."

"Jess," Drea pleaded.

"It's safer for you back at the ship, Drea. I have to go in." I couldn't leave without trying to be of help to the cursed. "Besides, what if Branigan's stuck in there?" I swallowed hard. "Hell, I *hope* not, but—"

"I know." Drea glanced downward, blinking away her tears. "We may be too late, but, I know."

"We?" I repeated.

"I'm not letting you go alone." Drea faced me with sad resolve. "Steel yourself, Jess. 'Rabid dog' was putting it kindly. These people will truly believe they're cursed. They'll probably refuse our help. They might even think we're demons and attack us outright."

"We'll see." I was more determined than scared. And maybe Branigan *was* in there, also trying his damnedest to help. He'd have gotten to work keeping people alive, more focused on that than himself.

Please be all right, I urged around my wrenched heart.

In the meantime, Catherwood's magic adepts might've stolen Branigan's ship. Or, he'd hidden the ship somewhere and had silenced her beacon to avoid detection.

What about *my* ship's beacon? I decided to disable it later. Even if anyone detected it, they'd be hours or days away from putting a ship down in Gules. Better to first determine what emergencies existed beyond the fence. There was food and water aboard my ship, and though I was no great healer, I knew enough to keep people in one piece.

My attention honed in on the fence, seeking the fastest exploitable flaw. Its height made vaulting impossible, but gaps existed where the flimsy planks didn't quite fit together. I got close and crouched to peek through the largest of them.

Past the fence, the cobblestone path widened, stretching straight ahead. Single-story shacks huddled together on both sides of the path as though seeking warmth. Dozens of long snowbanks lay strewn about randomly, odd formations that wind alone couldn't have shaped. Garbage littered the ground between them. No scent emanated from the scene, for which I had the cold to thank.

My eyes settled upon a hand emerging from the nearest snowbank, mere feet from where I crouched: a human hand, palm down, reaching toward me.

CHAPTER 2

The hand jutting from the snowbank was slim and femi-nine, its fingers stretching toward me in a beseeching posture. She lay just a few feet away from me, past the fence. Maybe she'd heard my approach?

I gasped in surprise, but urgency soon took over. Someone buried in snow? I didn't stop to consider the how or why. She needed to get out into open air and under a blanket as soon as possible. Two forceful tugs on the fence planks in front of me created a passable hole. I dove through, then skidded to my knees before my discovery.

The hand's position never changed. Only after I grasped it in mine did I register the stiffness of the fingers, and the skin's bluish pallor.

Hell, too late. A sick knot formed in my gut. I glanced up with dread at the dozens of similar snowdrifts nearby, realiz-ing what lay beneath them. Too late for all of them.

It hurt, but I still wanted a look at the rest of the body beneath the snow. Lifting the hand exposed a thin arm, then a shoulder. I rolled the corpse from a prone position onto her back.

Cause of death appeared to be exposure, nothing more.

Positioning and weather had frozen the young woman's features into a grimace. Patches of thin linen clung to her skin. Her other hand clutched a roll of parchment to her chest, protecting it from the cold better than she'd protected herself.

I nudged the damp scroll loose and unfurled it to find a spell, smeared but legible. The inked calligraphy probably hadn't been the woman's work, and she probably hadn't been able to read it either. *Unseen, abide! Upon Death shall we unite, until my next Purpose comes due: Water, Fire, Breath, or Flesh anew.*

Tragedy eclipsed my disappointment. The scrap escaped my weak grip, falling to the snow. Reincarnation was part of Catherwood dogma. She'd died hoping for a better start elsewhere.

"Jess?"

Drea had slipped through the fence without me noticing. Kneeling beside me, she used one arm to hug herself and the other to brace my shoulder, her expression mournful.

"It's like she *wanted* to die, to get to reincarnation quicker," I blurted helplessly. "No blanket, no cloak, no shoes even."

"The adepts probably took them."

I faced Drea with horror.

"I've seen cursing used as an excuse for looting elsewhere. I wouldn't be surprised if it happens in this part of the galaxy as well." Drea's sorrowful gaze passed to either side of the cobblestone path. "Look at the wards on the doors. These people were evicted."

My eyes followed hers, studying the rows of thatched-roof hovels. No physical barriers rested against the doors or shuttered windows. All that had separated the townspeople from shelter were the ouroboros amulets nailed to each door.

Ignoring the knot in my stomach, I leapt up and jogged toward the nearest house. The door swung open without resistance. From my coat pocket, I retrieved my prized ancient stick lighter. Twisting the two halves of the metallic wand in opposite directions caused one end to flare with heat, and a generated bead of light that cut through the dimness.

Sure enough, the one-story structure stood empty. A pile of dirt clogged the fire pit. The straw covering the floor lay in streaks, suggesting how furniture and people might've been dragged outside.

Feudalism had been strangling the galaxy for centuries. The land, houses, residents, *everything* in Gules belonged to Lord Catherwood to do with as he pleased. It made me even sicker to imagine the "curse" being lain, whenever that might've been: no resistance, people huddling together for warmth, their heads bowed in deference to the magic adepts stealing everything they'd ever worked for.

I harbored nothing but sympathy for those townspeople. What else could they have done? Fighting back would've been terrifyingly out of the question, if defiance ever even occurred to them. Fly somewhere else? Ships were rare, knowledge of flight restricted to a few. An *ignorant* populace was easier to keep in line.

When Gules had been cursed, that fence and those wards had redefined its denizens' universe. I knew; I hadn't been so different once. Shame joined my nausea. I shook it off before I thought too closely about the things *I'd* been brought up to believe, and how dearly they'd cost me.

Drea and I followed the cobblestone path, checking every house along the way. Sadly, they all fit the same pattern as the first. I kept hoping we'd run into someone shivering in a corner, but the only evidence that anyone had ever lived in Gules lay buried beneath snow.

Eventually, the path conveyed us to a massacre at the town's center square. We both halted at its edge, horrified and reluctant to proceed. Drea covered her mouth with her hand.

The stronger winds cutting through there exposed dozens of glassy-eyed cadavers strewn about. Some seemed to have collapsed mid-step, wearing little or no clothing. Others had simply lain down, curled up, and waited.

Hypothermia did unpredictable things to a dying brain. It would've been awful to watch. Hundreds of people shivering, shambling, turning blue, tearing off their clothes, finally collapsing as their muscles and organs failed. It would've *looked* every bit like the curse Lord Catherwood had decreed.

In this weather, it wouldn't have taken long. Had it been just as cold back then? If not, their suffering might've dragged. I shoved aside another wave of nausea and grief, struggling not to think about it.

A ring of torched buildings surrounded the square, their blackened skeletons slumping against one another. Before the largest of these frameworks stood a gallows. Like the fence surrounding Gules, it served its purpose despite shoddy construction: a couple in elegant dress dangled from its nooses. The local nobility hadn't escaped the curse, but the adepts had apparently seen fit to spare them the indignity of exposure.

Drea let out a gasp, separating from me to dart toward something at the center of the square.

Her destination appeared to be a well blocked off with wooden planks. A whipping post stood nearby, with a single person tied to it. I forgot all about adjustment from microgravity and broke into a run after Drea. "Branigan!" I shouted.

He failed to glance up. Maybe he was just unconscious. Once I freed him, started cleaning up those wounds—

Stop fooling yourself.

I stumbled to a halt before the slumped, frozen form. It *was* he, or it had been; I recognized the gentle features beneath the gore. Sir Branigan Cade of Lirriven—who'd never left a settlement without teaching someone there how to read, and had out-dueled every knight errant I'd ever seen challenge him—had died friendless, stripped of weapons and armor. Someone had tied him there to bleed out where everyone could jeer and fling trash his way. Scraps of hell-if-I-knew-what refuse mingled with the blood pooled in the creases of his tunic and the ropes used to bind him. Lacerations streaked his skin. His brow sported a carving of a human eye crossed out with an X: the universal symbol denoting a heretic.

The sight smashed my heart to a lifeless, bloody pulp.

At my approach, Drea spun away from the scene, tears coursing down her cheeks.

I continued to stand there, stunned at first, then wishing that I were the one dead, not him. Everything I'd wanted to tell him formed a stone in my throat. Hot tears welled, which I fought against shedding. There was no use. Branigan was gone. Nothing I did or said would reach him.

Desperate to repel grief, my brain demanded I busy myself with something, *anything*. I separated from Drea and swept around the post, but found neither Branigan's gear nor evidence of the perpetrators. The heretic's mark meant someone had been offended on behalf of the Unseen, the same invisible forces conveniently blamed for Gules' downfall. Lord Catherwood's adepts, or someone else? Had it happened when Gules was cursed, or earlier? Was it related to the artifact he'd discovered?

"Jess? Come here, sweetheart."

Once I'd returned to Drea with leaden steps, she gathered me into an embrace, a repressed sob racking her small frame. "I'm so sorry," she whispered.

Clinging to Drea for balance, I buried my head against her shoulder. She was the only reason I hadn't collapsed to my knees.

"I wish we could take him down from there," Drea continued. "I don't think we can."

She was right, too much was frozen in place to permit it. That much didn't bother me; no part of Branigan persisted to care what his remains got up to. Still, we all had rituals we couldn't let go of. "I'd bear his sword back to Prometheion if it were here." I swallowed around the stone in my throat. "If I'd gotten us here sooner —"

"We might well have met the same fate," Drea cut me off. "This wasn't our fault."

"Knowing that doesn't help." I drew a shuddery breath. "What was Branigan doing out in this part of space before he found that artifact? Was he on a quest?"

Drea sniffled. "He might've been. I don't know."

"I don't remember him mentioning any enemies," I said.

"He had none," Drea said. "This was done out of fear or ignorance. Or both."

We risked the same persecution simply for our knowledge and skepticism. So did my other mentors, and my former master May. I'd always known it, but had never seen the point driven home so brutally.

An unmistakable whine pierced the air. We glanced skyward to find a small, sleek ship descending in the port's vicinity. Her hull was burgundy, with a gold seal on the side. The vibrant coloring meant she was part of a Lord's fleet, almost certainly Catherwood's.

Shock jolted me to full awareness. "No! No way in hell!" Even if someone, somewhere, had detected my ship's beacon approaching the planet, they couldn't have scrambled a response in *minutes*. Still, I knew this was no curse-born hallucination.

Drea sobered as well, backing away to brace my arms and arrest my gaze. "I don't have to tell you what happens if they find us."

They would, given enough time. The trail of foot-shaped confessions in our wake guaranteed it. "We can't hide and wait for them to leave, our tracks are everywhere. They're also in prime position to confiscate my ship when they go." I frowned at the desperate idea I was about to propose. "We have to sneak back and fly out of here."

Several paths branched from the morbid town square. There was no reason we had to backtrack. I pointed down a path winding east from our original route. "While they're following our trail, we'll loop back from behind." Paranoia bade me draw my dagger.

"Sounds good." Drea shrugged off her knapsack to fish out a short baton, along with a scrap of folded parchment. The latter, she pressed into my hand. "Beghard Joachim asked me to give you this upon parting ways. It seems now's the best time, just in case."

"Don't talk like that." I tucked the note beneath my collarbone, beside a chain holding a ring that had been my mother's. On impulse, I pulled Drea into another quick hug, which she returned with more force than usual.

"Love you, sweetheart." Her voice confessed her unspoken fears.

I made myself sound confident. "I love you too, Drea. Let's get the hell out of here."

The new ship had dropped from sight. Gules resumed its graveyard hush. I ushered Drea ahead of me, down another path of corpses. Speed concerned me more than discretion. Once we reached *Kepler's Law* and laid in a course, nothing else would matter. They wouldn't pursue us past their borders.

At the fence, we found a plank that yielded to our prying, and emerged along the town's eastern face. I took point as we skirted the fenced perimeter. My ears, straining for any hint of the newcomers, caught nothing.

The port inched into view. *Kepler's Law* sat closer to us, starboard side visible. The new vessel had settled next to my ship's port side, the location of her only entry hatch. A bad break, but thus far, we had no eyes or ears to evade. We hurried to my ship's starboard flank, then crouched and flattened against her hull. I stayed in the lead, inching down the aft side, until I could peek around to port.

The sleek newcomer shamed my poor wreck. Her seal, a fearsome gold griffin with a gold serpent writhing in its beak, gleamed upon her hull. A mess of footprints battered the gap between her and *Kepler's Law*. The sight implied an abundance of crew, who'd likely set out to trace our steps.

My ship's hatch sat ajar. A soldier stood beside the opening with his back to me. He wore a burgundy and gold tunic over leather armor. A loop of colorful stone wishing beads hung from his belt, a short sword in its scabbard resting beside them. He didn't appear to be adjusting from weightlessness. The pretty ship still had working gravity plating. Of course she did.

I motioned for Drea to stay put as I switched to a reverse grip on my dagger. Killing wasn't my aim, only a last resort. Planting each step carefully, I converged on the soldier, then swung my left forearm into his neck. The brachial stun knocked him off-balance. I guided him to his knees and pressed him into a sleeper hold. A few seconds of strangulation put him to sleep.

Nothing more stood between me and the open hatch. Pleasant surprise set my heart to pounding. I beckoned Drea over. "Stay out here," I whispered.

Drea positioned herself at the hatch, baton poised.

I hauled myself into the airlock, then edged up to the threshold leading into the ship. The aft view was clear, revealing open closet doors in the galley, their contents rifled through. Annoyed, I checked the cockpit, and froze. A man of flowing hair and meager build, clad in an embroidered burgundy robe, leaned past the chairs to edge up close to the console.

An adept of Catherwood. I could tell by the robe, and the many amulets dangling from the fingers of his left hand. My blood approached the boiling point. I wasn't well disposed toward adepts on a good day. So far, this had been a *rotten* day.

"Open now thine ears, O vessel!" The adept's right hand smashed down upon the interface as though clobbering a wayward insect. A chime sounded, confirming autopilot was engaged.

Did he understand what he was doing, or was he slavishly aping a ritual he'd been taught? Something in between? Whatever the case, the adept was still some ways from plotting a full course. Ignoring the sound of blood rushing through my ears, I sheathed my dagger and stood to creep up behind him. I had only to boot him out of the airlock, then we'd be leaving Gules well behind us.

The adept waved his amulets about, suspecting nothing. "Open now thy mouth—"

Drea screamed.

I stopped. The adept spun around, then jumped at the sight of me. However, his surprise quickly frosted over with malice. A dagger appeared in his right hand. His lips parted, maybe to "cast" a "spell."

Damned if I wanted to listen. Thinking only of Drea, I backpedaled and jumped outside.

A new pair of soldiers had appeared. The one closer to me recovered himself in stages, nursing his cheekbone. The other worked to pin Drea's arms behind her back. Her baton rested on the ground nearby.

"There you are, sellsword!" The one struggling with Drea glared at me. He braced her wrists in one hand, drawing his sword with the other. "Let's see what you're made of. Unless that cowardly skulking's all you've got?" He tossed his head toward the soldier lying in the snow.

"I'd rather not embarrass you in front of company, friend," I bluffed. These two had me simmering with contempt, but I preferred to avoid fights whenever possible.

"That's right, Jess. He's not worth it," Drea said. "Let us speak with whomever's in charge here."

The challenger ignored her in favor of me. "Come on! Is it worth the old woman to you?"

"You're not besting a knight, Fulton," the other soldier chided.

"Two eighths says otherwise, Boone!"

"Done." The recovered soldier, Boone, stepped past me and signaled his readiness.

Fulton, my challenger, shoved Drea toward him.

"Don't, Jess!" Drea cried, then winced as Boone clamped down on her arms.

Too late. My temper had edged out reason, and it urged me to dole out exactly what my opponent deserved. I reached over my shoulder to retrieve my side sword, letting Fulton hear every inch of steel scraping against the baldric scabbard. The sword's cross-guard swirled about my hand in helix patterns. Its coin-shaped pommel bore the stamp of my sigil. I settled into a one-handed, weapon-forward stance.

Fulton's breath-clouds misted one after the next. His free fingers hovered close to an amulet around his neck—a hand with an eye in the palm, called a khamsa—before reaching for the beads at his side, rolling one between thumb and forefinger.

When stuck with a fight, my favored strategy was to tear open an opportunity to run the hell away. There'd be no running from this fight, so my goal switched to ending things as fast as possible.

I launched at Fulton with a series of quick slashes, each strike flowing into the next. My opponent parried them, but had no room to initiate a counter. As he staggered backward, I got close enough to stomp on his foot and butt my sword's pommel into his jaw. He dropped his sword, reeling. The cord of his amulet became a garrote. I wrapped it around my left hand, then dragged him down until he ate the snow at my feet.

"Cease this fighting at once!"

Several more soldiers rounded *Kepler's Law*, followed by a woman in matching colors. Her clothing was rugged, yet suitable for a noble audience; she was probably a messenger. She straightened her beret and threw back her cloak to reveal her own scabbard, khamsa amulet, and wishing beads.

Her appearance might've been a good or bad thing. Hoping to tip the scale toward "good," I released Fulton, keeping my sword ready at my side.

The soldiers converged around me, Fulton, Boone, and Drea. The messenger stalked through the rough circle they formed, glaring at them. "Release that woman!"

Once Boone complied, Drea retrieved her baton and hastened to my side, grasping my elbow.

"This isn't the respect you show a pauper, much less a sworn knight errant," the messenger scolded. "Fall in!"

Fulton scraped himself off the ground, coughing. The other soldiers sneered at him.

Inwardly, I sneered with them. This was *surprisingly* good, so far.

The messenger faced me. "Dame Jessamine Irless of Freemont?"

She knew my name? I blinked in surprise. "Yes?"

"Apologies, Lady Knight, it seems there's been some confusion. Your restraint is appreciated." She cast another warning glance at the soldiers, then took her beret in hand to bow at the waist. "I am the herald Clarissa. In Lord Catherwood's fair capital, Spectra, the detection of your ship's beacon many days fore roused the attention of court. 'Twas feared Gules was your intended destination, and we know now our adepts' visions were correct. We timed our landing to coincide with yours, that we might steer you away and request your assistance on behalf of my master, Lord Catherwood."

A quest? From a *Lord?* Drea and I faced each other with

jaws agape.

"'Request?' Didst thou *request* of her? Nay, Clarissa, that shan't do at all!"

All eyes turned to my ship's threshold, and the breathless adept perched within. With his use of inferior "thou," he projected an air of superiority. His glare swept over the Catherwood party, making lambs of those it fell upon before settling on me.

Clarissa secured even more of my respect by protesting around the lump in her throat. "What is this, Adept Matthias? We cannot *demand* a knight errant's oath."

"She's in no state to give her consent. The curse of Gules hath consumed her," Matthais declared. "Whilst thou wert off following her path, she sneaked aboard with an assassin's katar, primed to murder me!"

Everyone aside from Drea stared at me like I'd spat in a sleeping bear's eye. Even the wind held its breath. Clarissa grasped her beads, and several soldiers mimicked the gesture.

As much as I wanted to call him a liar, I had to be more careful with my phrasing. "There really has been some confusion here." I looked toward Clarissa, pleading for understanding. "I don't even own a punching dagger."

"Let's all calm down and start over," Drea suggested. "We can start with the nature of the assistance your Lord is requesting."

"I'm afraid not!" Matthais looked to Drea for the first time, confusion flickering over his eyes as he failed to recognize the emblem on her shoulder. He masked it with a scowl. "Ye both were caught in territory the Unseen have cursed. By their will, your lives and assets are forfeit."

My heart plummeted. I cast another beseeching glance toward Clarissa, who wavered. "Friend Adept—" she began.

"Don't presume." Matthais shut her down with another glare. "Now take heed: I have sufficient magic to keep the curse confined to Dame Jessamine, but I cannot dispel it. I've breathed into her ship a course for Spectra. Some of the soldiers will take her aboard and guard her for the journey's duration. At Milord's palace, she can be healed and informed of the quest she must complete in return for Milord's mercy."

Strong-arming me into their debt? An imaginary debt at that. There was no curse aside from what those monsters had wrought with their own hands. I'd never heard of a knight errant being so roughly treated by *anyone*. If Clarissa wouldn't advocate for me and Drea, I'd have to, despite how deeply the chills of winter and horror had sunk into me.

"A knight errant can't be forced into a quest." I used a firm tone, glancing between Clarissa and Matthais. "If you attempt it, word *will* spread. It'll be a blight on Lord Catherwood's honor. Knights errant won't come here anymore, and when knights errant don't feel safe somewhere, merchants decide they aren't safe either."

Clarissa glanced downward. "I'm sorry, Lady Knight, but the curse makes this a very different matter." Before I could argue further, she addressed Matthais again. "What of the other woman?"

"Beguine Drea." My companion pronounced her title and name with defiance.

"Our orders concern Dame Jessamine only," Matthais said. "We leave the other woman here."

Clarissa nodded at her feet.

Drea remained expressionless, but the hand on my elbow tightened.

Leave her?! First Branigan, now Drea? My outrage boiled over, driving away the chill and scalding my composure. "She's in my charge. You can't separate us!"

"We *can* take precautions to prevent the curse's spread," Matthais returned.

"Lady Knight," Clarissa addressed haltingly. "I wish you

could understand."

All I understood was the dire need to get back aboard my ship. Sword in hand, I grabbed Drea and bolted toward the hatch. However, that robed parasite was still polluting my threshold. Matthais turned wide-eyed and bloodless, frozen at my approach.

I was a sword's length away, prepared to do whatever was necessary to get aboard. Then, I was falling. My arms only half-absorbed the brunt of my face and torso planting into the cold, wet pavement. I lost Drea and my blade. The weight of an anvil crushed my back just as a scuffle erupted behind me.

While Boone hauled my stunned body upright, Fulton confiscated my weapons. Melting snow sloughed off my coat and dripped down my aching forehead.

Matthais dropped to the ground, then looped an amulet around my neck from arm's length. "There's no weight-of-earths magic aboard this vessel, so take the necessary precautions," he informed the soldiers.

The scuffle behind me continued. "Jess!"

"Drea!" Her voice shocked me back into focus, reminding me of what was at stake. I thrashed against Boone and dug in my heels. Mussed hair whipped into my eyes.

With a casual wave, Matthais gestured permission to Fulton, who rammed me in the gut with my side sword's pommel.

CHAPTER 3

I doubled over, clutching at my middle and gasping through a windpipe that had collapsed to the size of a straw. In the grips of paralyzing pain, my only thought was of needing air and not getting it.

The Catherwood soldiers had no trouble hauling me aboard *Kepler's Law* and frogmarching me aft, past the galley, into quarters. Fulton pulled down one of the folded-up bunks. The bed had its own restraints built in, as I knew better than to free-float while sleeping.

Drea's still out there! Air could wait. Panic alone propelled me between the soldiers, back toward the galley.

Before I got very far, a hand clamped down on my shoulder. Fulton yanked me back, then threw me onto the bunk. The back of my skull slammed against the aft bulkhead on the way down.

"Want a little more?" Fulton taunted.

"Knock that off!" Boone cried.

While the blow reverberated through the rest of my head, stunning me out of further action, the soldiers strapped me down. There were ties for my torso, legs, and shoulders. Boone leaned down with some rope for my hands, but when he noticed Fulton had turned away from him, he tucked my arms under my back without binding them.

"Have a smoke or something. Carefully." Apology tinged Boone's voice.

The offer betrayed his unfamiliarity with zero-gee travel. There'd be nowhere for the ashes to go except everywhere, into everything.

Boone turned and left behind Fulton, who carried my blades with him.

Kick them out and save Drea! But my addled, uncoordinated thrashing proved ineffective against my restraints.

The ship's hatch slammed several times, with increasing force on each attempt. Thrusters charged, oblivious to the tension aboard. The autopilot was in command; the air had that stink about it. Framed in the broken doorway, the soldiers circled the galley, closing up the closets they'd rifled through earlier. They stowed their weapons, then buckled into chairs that flipped down from the starboard bulkhead.

Stop this! I urged myself.

Too late. The autopilot lifted us skyward, jolting *Kepler's Law* for several hour-long seconds. Through the porthole on the port bulkhead, the winter of Gules faded into the darkness of space. Somewhere far below, Drea was paying the price for my stubbornness. Sickening, painful remorse stabbed at my already sore gut.

Gravity's pull weakened, leaving my aching head stuffy and disoriented as well. Loose strands of hair floated past my face, as did the amulet Adept Matthais had given me. The clay khamsa hovered mockingly in my vision. My former master's voice reached across time again, echoing through my mind. *Side-steps, side-steps!* May snapped. *I don't care if it's a collapsing mine shaft with puppies and newborns mewling at the other end, you don't charge head-on!*

May would be devastated over Branigan and Drea. All our friends at the beguinage would be. And hell, Drea's family …

Kepler's Law jumped to faster-than-light cruising velocity. For once, I *wanted* a malfunction, but didn't get one. Artificial light flickered to life along the top deck. Green-faced, the soldiers in the galley clutched the wishing beads that sought to escape their company.

I had nothing to grasp in hopes of reassurance. The note Drea had given me from Beghard Joachim still rested under my brigandine, out of reach. Joachim was the most senior of my mentors, the one who'd sent me and Drea after Branigan. At that moment, I could only imagine his letter containing the coldest of rebukes.

In the hours that followed, a torturous churn of panic, guilt, and anxiety made sure I found no refuge in sleep. Also, the crushing grief that hadn't quite reached me in Gules had plenty of time to sink in. Branigan had never known how I felt, how much he'd meant to me. And Drea, stranded in that merciless winter graveyard … no, she wasn't lost *yet*. Somehow, I had to get back to her before she froze or starved.

Her suffering had been avoidable. It was my fault any of this was happening. I cursed myself for pushing into that town.

At all times, tears threatened to spill, which I struggled to hold back. Crying in zero-gee was a bad idea, and damned if I'd give my captors the satisfaction. There'd be time to mourn later. I just had to get through this meeting with Lord Catherwood first.

What the hell did he want with a worm like me? He hadn't sought me out by reputation; I had none out here. The "curse" had made me a convenient target for blackmail. If Lord Catherwood made a habit of kidnapping knights errant, though, Branigan and I would've heard about it and been warned away accordingly. So what was going on? As I'd argued before, Lord

Catherwood was risking a hit to his reputation *and* commerce. It had to be big enough to warrant that.

Shortly after gravity returned, the autopilot dashed us against a new atmosphere. Far from the usual shake-up, though, this was more of an earthquake. A groan creaked along the hull, prompting the soldiers' frightened cries. Only our restraints kept us from bouncing around the top deck like stones caught in a wheel well.

Terror seized me. She was coming down wrong, and the autopilot wouldn't compensate. If I failed to reach the cockpit, we were all dead.

Good thing Boone hadn't tied my hands!

Clear-headed resolve chased off the fear. I ignored the turbulence, rattles, and screams to worm out of my restraints. Once free from the last strap, I fell to a pitched and shaking deck, then pushed myself up on weak legs to stumble into the galley.

Boone remained seated, eyes shut tight over his beads. Meanwhile, Fulton's horror at my appearance lifted him out of his chair. "Where d'you think you're going?"

Without answering or slowing down, I kept stumbling toward the cockpit.

When Fulton realized my intent, an even greater panic seized him. He darted into my path, fist primed. *"Don't disrupt the flight spell!"*

I lunged sideways to dodge his swing, then straightened and threw my elbow toward his wide-open face, connecting with his jaw. Fulton staggered, landing on his backside with a satisfactory thud. I stepped over him and hurried to the cockpit.

Climbing into the pilot's chair was like threading a needle mid-earthquake. Once in, I buckled my restraints to avoid dashing my head off the ceiling. Out the windshield stretched ocean and sunny sky, disturbingly off-kilter. A khamsa had been strapped in place over the console and its blaring pleas for attention. I tore it aside and brought up the manual controls to fine-tune our yaw, roll, and pitch.

"Come on, little cuss," I murmured.

Training and experience tempered my adrenaline into delicate adjustments. Fortunately, it wasn't long before we leveled out. Unfortunately, plenty of clear air turbulence remained. Nothing for it but to endure. After maintaining a good speed and shedding altitude gradually, the unpredictable tremors wore away. I de-tensed my muscles, closing my eyes with relief.

Fulton's dim cry rose up behind me, emanating from the galley. "Thank the Unseen for saving us before you could kill us!"

I stifled a laugh. Upon reopening my eyes, I spotted an island on the horizon: a glittering gem that resolved into a massive city. Crystalline spires punctuated its skyline, bending rainbows out of sunlight. Our pre-programmed route drew us toward it.

I'd expected Catherwood's capital to dwarf Gules, but the sight stole my breath anyway. From high above, Spectra betrayed no hint of the toll paid to neglect. In the Shipbuilders' heyday, air and sea would've been thick with traffic. Radio chatter would've bounced between the ships and the city's ports. That day, *Kepler's Law* dropped alone through a silent sky.

Our coordinates placed us a short distance from the dominant tower in the skyline. We entered our final vertical descent over a bustling port, magnetic thrusters lowering us onto a vacant patch of pavement. My ship's appearance halted traffic and swiveled heads nearby.

With my conscious mind caught up in a mix of relief and dread, habit guided my hand to my lips. I kissed my fingertips and patted the plaintive console. This time, no one questioned me.

The port boasted stone walls, dozens of ships, and an ancient stupa-like structure repurposed as a warehouse. A seal of three blue flowers arranged in a triangle, set against a white field, repeated itself wherever I looked.

Was that a guild's seal? Had Lord Catherwood forced me here for *guild business?*

My dread amplified. I'd always avoided dealings with guilds. They governed trade and industry, enriching life for the privileged few by dividing the unprivileged masses among plows, hitching them up, and cracking the whip.

I studied the laborers: men, women, and children pushing crate-laden sleds, coaxing livestock aboard big freighters. Nimbler ships received fabrics dyed every color imaginable. Everyone took pains to ignore one corner of the port, where a cluster of broken-down ships lay rotting under shrouds of wilted flowers. A procession of adepts and pack animals wended toward it at that moment, towing a runabout in good repair. Those standing in their path vacated as soon as they caught on, averting their gazes.

Catherwood dogma prohibited repair. That "dead" ship might've needed just one small tweak to be flightworthy again, a tweak it would never receive. *What a waste,* I thought.

"Get moving!" Fulton barked from the galley.

Just when I'd shaken off one bad zero-gee hangover, there I was doing it again. Weak-kneed and lightheaded from low blood pressure, I boosted myself slowly out of the pilot's chair, then trudged back to the galley.

The soldiers had an even worse time adjusting. Fulton sat right where I'd left him on the deck, struggling to stand and nurse his jaw at the same time. Boone had left his chair to rummage through one of the nearby closets, leaning against said closet for balance as he did so.

I paused before the pair, focusing on Boone. "Where are we?"

"This is the home port of Linum Dominorum," Boone answered. "The largest trade guild in Catherwood space."

Hell, as I'd feared.

"Here." Boone side-stepped away from the closet to approach me, bearing my side sword and dagger. Before he reached me, they slipped from his hands, hitting the deck with a clatter.

"Sorry!" he said.

"Oh no, I'll get them." I knelt to do just that.

"What're you doing?" Fulton demanded over my shoulder.

"Worried about your hide?" Boone remained standing in front of me, folding his arms and smirking. "She's already taken a piece of it. Speaking of, where's my cred?"

Fulton muttered under his breath. A moment later, a pair of metallic slivers tumbled along the deck, stopping at my side. Boone strained to crouch beside me and pick them up.

I focused on my weapons. Dark thoughts urged me to take advantage of the weaker pair, but escape was a foolish fantasy. I was still a prisoner, bound by superstition instead of chains. I'd have to play along and watch for my opportunity.

"Are you a witch?"

I froze at the words whispered into my ear. While gathering up his money, Boone had leaned in to pose the clandestine question. He'd since pulled back, eyeing me with equal parts fear and curiosity.

A witch was one who practiced "magic" without being a

trained adept, usually because they lacked the money or influence to receive that training. In most places, witches had to keep their business private as a matter of survival. It wasn't the first time I'd been asked, but no. Nothing I did had anything to do with "magic."

My first instinct was to determine where Fulton was. Behind me, still picking himself up, paying us no mind. Good. I turned back to deliver my answer.

Boone had already thought better about hearing it. "Either way, I'm glad," he blurted. "We'd be dead otherwise."

"You were the one who left my hands free, friend. I'd say we're even." Smiling, I stood and inched my way back to quarters.

"Hey!" Fulton barked. "Where're you going?"

"Preparing for my audience with Lord Catherwood." *Come get me if you don't like it,* I added mentally.

A meeting with someone of nosebleed-inducing status was intimidating enough without worrying about what sort of carrion I resembled at the moment. Though I was more captive than honored guest, I resolved to enter Lord Catherwood's throne room with as much dignity as possible.

I swapped out my coat for a waist-length jack of plate, the closest thing I had to finery. Years ago, May had declared the blue-gray embroidery an apt match for my eyes before commissioning the jack on the spot. After weaving my hair into a single braid, I arranged the khamsa so it lay in plain sight, and slipped Beghard Joachim's note under my collar for later review. Finally, I retrieved a small tinderbox, along with my dwindling cigarillo pack, in case there was an opportunity to sate the maddening craving. My stick lighter was neater and more convenient than the tinderbox, but I had to be careful where I used it.

For a moment, I hung back in quarters, drawing deep breaths in hopes of pushing off worry.

Hang on, Drea, I thought. I'd stay alert for any chance to slip my chains and rush back to her.

By the time the soldiers funneled me toward the airlock, I felt stronger. Boone opened the hatch, and a din flooded our ears. My attention fell on the welcoming party congregated nearby. The gang of mercenaries, wearing white and blue tunics emblazoned with Linum Dominorum's seal, sported gear better than Catherwood's soldiers. A sour adept led them. Her neck hosted so many amulets, it was a wonder she walked upright. She wore a white and blue armband, but her burgundy-gold robes made it clear she was on loan from Lord Catherwood's cloister. The guild literally needed its Lord's blessing to operate.

Boone dropped to the pavement. Fulton shoved me out next. I stumbled into the intense summer heat, but kept my balance. As Fulton fought to close the hatch, the port adept folded her arms over her jewelry collection. "We run a business here, soldiers, and it's not a valet service. The public yard south of here will take this visitor's spacefaring vessel — what's left of the ailing soul."

I bit my tongue, holding back an irritated surge of defensiveness.

"Dame Jessamine's ship shall be quartered here on Lord Catherwood's authority," Boone declared, holding up a slip of parchment for the party's inspection.

The enforcers' gazes acknowledged defeat. Meanwhile, the port adept reared like a snake with an intruder in its nest. "I never received such a directive. Dame Jessamine, you said?" Her gaze shifted upward to examine my vessel's hull. "An ancient rune. Quite the potent sigil. You're favored by this Lord ... *Kepler*, is it?"

"He's not a Lord," I said.

"But there's some law attributed to him?"

"Important ones, yes. Nothing on the books today, but obeyed all the same."

She spent a moment dissecting my answer, then narrowed her eyes at the khamsas I and the soldiers were wearing. "Where have you arrived from?"

"Milord awaits her, friend Adept," Boone dismissed.

The port adept swayed on her feet, raising a hand to her temple. "I've an ill premonition! Much harm may come to you all if my questions go unanswered."

The soldiers and mercenaries froze. Nearby workers stared at the budding scene with morbid curiosity.

I was unimpressed. "Take it up with Adept Matthias, if you fear his blessings aren't good enough," I said, naming the adept on Gules.

The port adept's eyes flew open. "But of course they are," she faltered. "Off with you, then."

Fulton and Boone grabbed my elbows to pull me past the welcoming committee. I threw a parting glance over my shoulder, willing *Kepler's Law* to be safe.

Beyond the port walls, we fell in with a crush of humanity coursing like blood cells through winding arteries. Small wood and stone buildings lined the streets, many boarded up or in a state of collapse. Refuse plugged many of the missing cobblestones beneath our feet. Wagons drawn by horses and horse-hybrids spared no mercy for the slow or wayward. Aside from the occasional manure cart, the air was surprisingly tolerable, hinting at functional sewers. We dodged around charlatans who blocked traffic and pierced eardrums.

"Parasols here!"

"The day's forecast, good people! The stars suggest a general shroud of misfortune to last not more than a week ..."

Everyone had a loop of wishing beads on his belt, spilling out of a pocket, or clutched in hand. The occasional adept streamed past as well, club or knife brandished, eyes darting about. I already knew what they were looking for, but the object of their search became sickeningly obvious when we passed an adept flogging a man curled into himself on the street. "What do you think you're wearing? You offend the Unseen!"

The crowd forming around the spectacle, and the sight of the soldiers flanking me, ensured no one intervened. My heart, still burning for my friends, went out to this man as well. It filled my throat with bile to think as much, but noninterference was for the best. For all my fantasies of coming to the rescue, the reality was that I'd get him *and* myself killed.

Spectra evoked memories of Freemont, my birthplace, not in any fond way. I regressed to my teenage self from a lifetime ago: orphaned, desperate to escape. The urge to *run* hit me worst upon seeing the sick tent situated a safe distance from the moving crowds. Rows of motionless bodies lay beneath the canopy. Adepts made rounds with ewers of water, making sure everyone was well hydrated in the heat. That much was good. Not as good were the "spells" they murmured over festering wounds and other serious ailments.

My escorts kept me close between them. It was obvious where we were headed: the hulking prismatic spire rising from the tumult, the greatest of Spectra's towers. It had to be Lord Catherwood's palace. The walls blared solid colors from some angles, and became as translucent and fragile as a soap bubble from others. Although I mostly disliked Spectra and loathed the circumstances that had brought me there, this much was worth seeing. I craned my neck to take it all in, wondering what purpose the spire had served for the Shipbuilders centuries earlier.

We gained entry at a gate in the stone wall surrounding the palace. Fulton and Boone pulled me across a courtyard, past a massive sundial, into the palace itself. Heart pounding with awe and dread, I took my first official steps into a Lord's midst, a crowded rainbow of courtiers jostling one another in the hunt for fabled gold.

They made sure to march me past an open storehouse under guard of adepts and soldiers in stern dress and posture. A conspicuous open entrance provided a clear view of its contents. Inside loomed a massive collection of Shipbuilder artifacts: handheld lasers, computers, combines, holographic projectors, dozens of things unfamiliar to my eye. Some were implements of war, some were there to dazzle or make life easier. Some could free up the labor of entire planets, but that wasn't happening anytime soon.

I nearly fell to my knees. I'd heard of such Lordly hoards, but this was my first time seeing one. I wondered if any of Branigan's personal effects were in there, now just so much loot rounded up from Gules. The uncertainty, just like the uncertainty I nursed over Drea, was a deep, raw wound.

We ascended the bureaucratic obstacle course from footmen, to scribes, to a tight-faced adept in a small antechamber. He dismissed Fulton and Boone, then performed an invocation. I kept my eyes lowered and mouth shut.

After the invocation followed a long, lonely wait. I killed the time by studying my confines. On one side of the tiny chamber, lit candles huddled around a shrine containing the multi-rayed sun seal of Hegemon Zander, the first person to reunite the galaxy after the Shipbuilders' collapse. A century later, *that* empire had collapsed. Dozens of Lords had been squabbling over the territory he'd once ruled over ever since, but the galaxy still shared many things thanks to Zander: guilds, the Unseen, magic adepts, even the knights who served particular Lords and the knights errant who didn't. As much as I didn't like thinking about it, I owed my unusual degree of freedom to that legacy. At the same time, it was the legacy's fault that my freedom was so unusual.

The adept finally returned, sweeping me into an audience chamber with a wave of his arm. It was then I realized I had no idea what I was doing. However, I'd seen my former master bluff his way through everything a quest could possibly throw at him. Some of that must've rubbed off, for better or worse. I vowed to retain my wits, and not let them be carried off with the pomp and intimidation they'd surely practice there.

I expected to feel like a gnat in a nebula. Instead, I entered a cramped room robed in black drapes that made an oven of the confines. A velvet runner coursed down the floor's center, lined with brass censers, candles, and statuary of mythical beasts. Incense imbued the air with the same nose-curling sting of a cheap cigar. The furthest pair of statues depicted the familiar Catherwood griffins devouring snakes. Behind them sat two high-backed gilded chairs centered against the far wall. The one on my left propped up a wisp of a youth not long past his teenage years. Dull eyes, heavy with boredom, struggled to remain open within his lopsided face. Layers of jewel-studded finery padded his meager frame.

The chair to my right sat vacant. A graying man in a bejeweled robe stood before it: Catherwood's master adept, or so I assumed. His gaze made shrewd cuts into the image I presented, but he hid the results of his mental dissection behind a blank expression. A large circle drawn with grease marked the floor in front of his feet.

Before me stretched a path marked with bootprints of audiences past. Though dread and contempt vied for control, I refused to show either. I squared my shoulders and strode down the runner with the air of one honored at the privilege, dropping to my knee at its terminus.

The master adept raised a commanding voice. "All hail our Sovereign, Royal High Keeper of All Things Sacred, Champion Defender of his Domain, Lord Albion Hadwin Catherwood the Seventh! Long May He Reign!" He nodded to me in gesture.

"Milord, Dame Jessamine Irless of Freemont."

"Arise."

The boy's listless command deflated the dramatic intro-duction. I stood and bowed low.

"'Tis forecast to be an auspicious day," Lord Catherwood noted, working up the energy to convey annoyance with the early proceedings. "Thou art imbued with a sound sense of timing, Lady Knight, if naught else. State thy business."

He didn't know? Or was this some kind of joke? A surge of outrage almost made me blow it right there. "Your delegation retrieved me from Gules, sir," I said, fighting to keep my voice level.

"Gules?" Catherwood's eyes rolled to his left. "Master Ethan, where doth Gules lie?"

"Speak not that name, Milord," the master adept cau-tioned. "The people failed in their duty, and in Your Highness' wisdom did Your Highness order them cursed and severed."

My heart smoldered for all those dead or suffering in the wake of that "wisdom." I was sure my face matched their burgundy finery. "What failing merited a curse, Master?" I asked, unable to help myself.

"I'm quite serious in my caution, Lady Knight." Master Ethan's warning came down like a boot on a roach.

I held my breath to prevent further inquiry. *Let it go. Don't draw attention there.*

"Dame Jessamine is to quest abroad in Nidaros, Milord," Master Ethan said.

Catherwood sat up straighter. "Well! We would to know something of thy mettle first, Lady Knight. Let's hear thy finest tale."

"Milord …" Master Ethan's gaze flicked behind me. After a pause, he relented. "Dame Jessamine, recount for us a previ-ous quest." His tone insisted on brevity.

They were asking me to state my qualifications, after a fashion, but they didn't want the truth. No one *ever* wanted the truth. At my mental beck and call stood dozens of small fibs, waiting to be spun into nonsense tapestries as needed. I'd never enjoyed my bardic duty, but this was a chance to vent my frustration, couched within a dazzling lie.

"Well, my original business was to recover three legendary pearls for an adept in Lord Arceneau's realm," I began. "I ventured to the peak of a great waterfall, but found my path to the fabled cove blocked by a hydra. The beast towered and reeked of sulfur, its countless heads snapping in every direction to crush whatever fell in its jaws. It even severed some of its own heads, right there as I watched." I gestured along with the descriptions. "And if that weren't dire enough, a horde of thralls surrounded the hydra on all sides, following wherever it went!

"Vanquishing the monster was impossible. I couldn't break through the horde to sever even one head, much less dozens. I hid myself behind a rock, and watched. That was when I realized not one of the hydra's heads was directing its course! The monster trampled aimlessly, and the thralls weren't about to warn it of trouble." I clenched my fists at my sides, struggling not to betray my amusement at their expense. "All I had to do was wait. The fiend would eventually trip into the roaring falls, and — "

"Milord, I must protest!"

I turned. From the rear of the audience chamber echoed the plea of an older woman who already sounded confident of getting her way. She hastened toward the thrones, gripping her opulent skirts hard enough to wring the dye out of them, leaving a poor befuddled page in her wake. The diamonds she wore paled against her natural intensity. Her eyes spoke of urgency, but the petition rang false to me.

Turning back around revealed that Lord Catherwood had slumped with disappointment at the interruption, eyes narrowed. It was for the best that my tale went unfinished, though; Master Ethan's eye twitched with suspicion. He made the official court introduction in a level tone, though annoyance tinged his words. "Madam Eugenia Castor, Mistress of the Linum Dominorum trade guild."

I kept my hands at my sides and my mouth closed for the moment. Linum Dominorum? That was the guild whose port I'd docked at. So this really did seem to be guild business. If that were the case, why hadn't Madam Castor been present to start with? Were Lord Catherwood and Master Ethan trying to keep her out of this? Why?

Madam Castor swept past me without acknowledgement and approached Lord Catherwood's feet to dip into a graceful curtsy. "Milord," she beseeched in a sweeping, emphatic tone, "we all want *nothing* more than to end this crisis. Flax is the linchpin of my business, and of Your Highness' economy, yet flax is but a symptom of our *real* problem: those *backward* ingrates, and the disrespect they've dealt time and again to this court. Let *me* serve Your Highness in this matter! Commander Savidge stands ready with a detachment. Give the word, and my enforcers will see to *everything*."

Lord Catherwood rolled his eyes toward Master Ethan with a meaningful look.

"Ever since we detected Dame Jessamine's beacon in our space, the Unseen have bade us send her and her alone," the master adept said.

"Even now?" Madam Castor asked.

Master Ethan fished through a pouch on his belt to pull out a bundle of flat sticks, each painted red on one side. He tossed the sticks into the air, and they rained down upon the circle marked out before him. Brow furrowed, he spent a moment deliberating the pattern they formed. "The forecast hath not changed, Guildmistress."

I pretended to take the "scrying" as seriously as everyone else. It did make one thing clear: they were definitely holding

Madam Castor at bay for some reason. Master Ethan could make those sticks "forecast" whatever he wanted.

"Dame Jessamine?" the master adept prompted. "Take heed now of thy quest."

Madam Castor hesitated, then stepped aside. Her displeased gaze latched upon me for the first time, reaching uncharitable conclusions. I thought better of thanking her for hosting my ship. Instead, I gave the master adept my full attention.

"On the fringe of our territory doth lie a barony called Nidaros," Master Ethan began, "our foremost producer of flax."

"Nidaran yellow flax. You won't find better anywhere else," Madam Castor chimed in with stubborn pride. "I harvest their yield three times per standard year, and convey it to settlements abroad for retting and refinement. In return, I supply Nidaros with everything they need. They'd last all of a month without my patronage."

"A messenger from Nidaros brought word that the barony faceth certain difficulties meeting its obligations to the guild," Master Ethan continued.

"Difficulties I strain to imagine." Madam Castor's pent-up frustration leaked around her composure. "There's no better climate for yellow flax in the galaxy! They're holding out, Milord, testing Your Highness' authority!"

"That is for Dame Jessamine to determine," Master Ethan dismissed. "Lady Knight, thou art charged with identifying said 'difficulties' and correcting them. Should magics or greater force prove necessary, return and notify our court."

I frowned, bewildered by several things at once, but Madam Castor left me no room to speak. "We waste precious time!"

To hell with it, she already disliked me. I edged in before her protest gathered steam. "Didn't the messenger tell you what the difficulties were, Master?"

"We wish to know what *thou* findest," he replied.

I spotted a possible escape clause and leapt upon it, ignoring the fiery anger Madam Castor radiated my way. "Master, to be honest, I'm unknown and untested to you. Are you sure you wish to entrust me with this?"

"'Twas the Unseen who commended thee to us, and we shan't question their will."

More like they'd caught me in cursed territory and had me at their mercy. Better to throw *me* out to this Nidaros place than one of Catherwood's sworn knights. But still, would Madam Castor's people do all that worse? They knew the history and situation better. There was more to all this than they were letting on.

Madam Castor had had enough. "Even supposing the knight restores order in Nidaros, I don't trust the Baron to maintain it. I—"

To my surprise, Lord Catherwood jumped to his feet, smoldering over her. "Guildmistress! Our late father appointed Baron Tristan, and so far he's met every obligation. Question not our father's judgment lightly!"

Madam Castor rested a hand on her breast and clutched the beads at her side, collecting herself. "What I mean is, Baron Tristan is but one man. He may do everything in his power and *still* fail, owing to the miscreant attitude of Your Highness' Nidaran subjects. It's an attitude *I* am best equipped to temper. I'd be delighted to spare this weary knight errant the trip and —"

"Enough!" Catherwood faced me, pleading with a gaze too vulnerable for a Lord to be showing. "'Tis thy quest alone, Lady Knight. We care not what measures thou employ'st. If thou shouldst find Baron Tristan and Lady Amelia in peril, thou art to protect them with nothing short of thy life. Bear them back to Spectra, if they're safe nowhere else. Understand?"

Not one bit! And where was your compassion for Gules? Though frustration burned within me, those words went no further than my skull.

Lord Catherwood had a soft spot for the Baron of Nidaros, that much was certain. Madam Castor wanted to take a harsher approach than he was comfortable with. *That* was why they were sending one knight errant, rather than a whole detachment. If anything bad happened to me during this quest, no big loss. I was meaningless to them.

Dread crawled up my spine. I didn't even know what kind of problems awaited on Nidaros. Political? Agricultural? And what about Drea? How long would she suffer while this fool-ishness persisted? A potent worry gnawed at my insides, but I was desperate not to show any sign of it before these three.

"In two standard weeks, my ship will land in Nidaros for the next harvest." Madam Castor didn't wait for me to muster a diplomatic reply. "They *will* meet quota, or there *will* be problems."

"Upon thy successful return shall we remove the curse thou bearest." Master Ethan ignored her threat to address me.

I blinked with mock concern. "That's not what I was promised." Back on Gules, Adept Matthais had said the "curse" would be "lifted" once I reached Spectra.

"For the present, the curse shan't impede thee," Master Ethan replied. "If thou wert to leave Milord's space with thy duty unfulfilled, however, I shudder to imagine what horrors await."

Stringing me along. "That was never my intention," I replied with the appropriate fear, "but it sounds like I may be questing for a while. Unfortunately, I have no currency, and only enough food and water for another few days." The first claim was truth, the second not as much.

Master Ethan shut his eyes for a moment. "The Unseen permit a small purse, Milord."

"Ten cred," Lord Catherwood said, "paid from our treasury."

"*Ten*, Milord?"

"We're grateful thy hearing is sound," Catherwood snapped.

Master Ethan took slow steps around the magic circle to approach me. "Return to the Linum Dominorum port by sundown, then depart for Nidaros and meet with Baron Tristan. Swear now in word and blood to see this quest as far as the Unseen take thee." He produced a dagger and a shallow brass bowl.

Aw, hell.

The blood was no concern. They'd hold it in reserve to perform dark rituals against me in the event I broke my vow. The *vow* was what had me sweating even worse than the stifling room merited. Once given, there was no walking it back. I'd have to do what they asked, or renounce my knighthood. And if I refused to give the vow, they'd just kill me right there.

I stifled my reluctance, wanting to get it over with. Not knowing what the master adept's equipment had been used for last, I preferred my own dagger for the deed. I unrolled enough of my glove to cut my palm, then squeezed a few drops of blood into the bowl, intoning words that had to be coaxed from the back of my throat. "My honor binds me to your bidding."

"Explore Spectra in the meantime, and expend the gifted cred. There shall be little opportunity for such in Nidaros." Master Ethan lowered his head. "Fair journey, Lady Knight. May the Unseen guide thee to swift triumph."

Madam Castor held silent, but the stare she branded into my flesh warned me how closely she'd be watching the situation.

CHAPTER 4

I found myself on the wrong end of the palace walls before Lord Catherwood could yawn at his next piece of official business. The bum's rush yielded a purse teeming with eighths—ten metallic cred, cut into eight slivers apiece—and sealed papers declaring my status as Lord Catherwood's emissary for the duration of my forced quest.

A Lord's emissary. Hell. The dizzying title probably wouldn't sink in for days. I'd never before wielded such authority, or such ignorance about what I was questing for. Solve Nidaros' problems, whatever they were, and ensure a successful harvest, in *two weeks*. I sure hoped it wouldn't involve trying to raise flax from seed to mature plant on that schedule.

But I couldn't consider any of that for long without thoughts of poor Drea resurfacing, along with fresh pangs of worry and guilt. Would she really have to wait two weeks or more for me to return to Gules? Could she survive that long in the bitter winter climate alone, with only the supplies she'd been carrying on her person?

She wouldn't have to if I could help it. Sunset was still some ways off, and Spectra was a big city. There had to be a way to cover all my bases in the time allotted.

The late afternoon sun had lost none of its intensity. With no soldierly escort, I was a prime target for a pack of urchins lying in wait near Lord Catherwood's palace, who teemed around me, jumping and waving.

"Lady Knight! What's your fancy?"

"Want some food? Weapons?"

"I know where thieves and heretics are getting flogged, if you wanna watch!"

"Humomalo, please," I said. "I'd rather not pay tariffs." A minimal paper trail would be preferable.

One of the older boys grabbed my wrist and dragged me free of the rest, into the traffic-choked street. A safe distance away, he let go to spin around, walking backward without any worry of bumping into someone ahead. "Are you questing here?"

"I'm leaving for one soon." I confirmed the purse hidden under my jack was still present.

The boy knew exactly what I was doing. "My gang wouldn't steal from you, Lady Knight. Plenty of others would, though." He shrugged. "So where's your squire?"

I forced a smile. "Back at port, cleaning ogre blood off our swords."

This launched a wide-eyed, hungry interrogation into where and how "we" had fought the creatures. I fed him the requisite lies with reluctance. Still, this was better than admitting I had no squire, and having him beg to become mine. I didn't want a squire; I wasn't sure I'd ever be ready for that responsibility. Even if I *did* want one, this was awful timing. Too many other concerns demanded my attention.

My nonsense story captivated the boy, but he stayed on-task, guiding me to a market square choked with the gaudy tents of small-time cheats and wealthy guild merchants alike. A waft of roast meat cut through the air, clawing at my attention. It'd been ages since I'd eaten anything that hadn't been dried or boiled. Maybe later, time and funds permitting.

The boy skipped the legal vendors in the square, leading me to the mouth of a rancid side-street. "No tariffs here," he whispered.

I tipped him well for his trouble. "Thanks for your help."

Less colorful and decidedly quieter merchants squatted along the alley, wares spread out on blankets on the ground before them. They eyed me suspiciously from a distance. Some remained silent as I walked past, while others whispered their offerings.

One of the men sold just what I was looking for: cheap unmarked cigarillos from dozens of foreign domains. Though we didn't share enough common language to trade sentences, we got on well enough with key words and hand gestures, even with the vendor having only one hand at his disposal. The remains of his left forearm bore the scars of what looked like white phosphorus burns. Probably an old war injury. I couldn't directly relate, but I could sympathize.

Transaction complete, I lit two of my recent purchases with my tinderbox, offering one to the vendor. I took an enormous first pull from my own, holding the smoke in my mouth a while.

The extra cigarillo fell into a practiced cradle in the vendor's right hand. "Most gracious. Need quest?"

"No. Sever space?" I shook my head, then traced a line in the sky overhead with my pointer finger. I needed someone who could fly a message out to my friends at the beguinage.

"Grimes. Fulgor Port." He exhaled a smoky mouthful, then placed his hand over his chest. "Bazi."

—〰—

The vendor's tip led to a run-down port halfway across the city. Small tribes of ships huddled together for protection. A token presence of Catherwood enforcers manned the perimeter, the only burgundy-and-gold authority in sight. The workers unloaded cargo holds, bickered out their disputes, or kept wary eyes over their shoulders. Not the friendliest part of town, but I'd seen and dealt with worse before.

With resolve, I pressed my way through. My appearance garnered looks ranging the spectrum from curious to hostile, but second glances at my weaponry short-circuited any bright ideas. A good thing, as simply mentioning Grimes' name seemed to rile people. They pointed the way; I felt their eyes burning holes in my back.

The man I sought was a stout, dusty figure garrisoned amid the largest of the ragtag fleets. I found him navigating a maze of crates, comparing unfamiliar symbols painted on the corner of each box against a parchment scrap in his hand. Centered on the back of his belt was a cleaver-shaped knife.

Cautiously, I halted several feet away. "Well met, friend. Bazi sent me."

Grimes spun around and eyed me from head to foot. His raised brow relaxed, but his face was no less wrinkled as a result. "Then you're the rare knight I'm glad to help." He didn't *look* glad, rather just as guarded as I was. "What do you need?"

"I need to send a message to Sever space. I can write it myself." Whatever happened next, I wanted my friends at the beguinage to know about Branigan's murder, Drea's exile, and the quest I'd been forced into.

"Fancy." Grimes waved for me to follow him, shuffling toward a set of crates stacked chest-high. On top, an inkwell and quill weighed down a pile of rough parchment scraps.

"Help yourself. My couriers don't read," he assured me.

Even so, I wrote with the Shipbuilder alphabet for greater

security. Each parchment scrap had already been used front and back, forcing me to scratch out someone's old illegible message and write between the lines. I took a moment to sort my racing, distressed thoughts and mentally draft the message first, ensuring I got everything down as efficiently as possible.

While I worked, Grimes situated himself on the opposite side of the crate stack, frowning and scratching at his own parchment.

I handed him my finished note, along with a fistful of eighths for emphasis. "Get this to Beghard Joachim at the Enduring Flame Beguinage in Prometheion, as soon as possible." I forced the words to sound slow and calm. "There'll be some Sever florins waiting for you on the other side."

Grimes narrowed an eye — an eye made of glass, I realized. "Just how many florins are we talking about? Exchange rates are brutal lately."

I smiled. "When you arrive, name your price." The beguinage never had an issue with money.

"All right, I won't make you swear an oath. I'll have someone on it before the day's out." He relieved me of both note and currency with a pickpocket's flair.

"Good, thanks," I said. "There's something else." Something even more urgent. My heart pounded.

"Oh my, Grimes, a knight? I hope you're being nice."

A sunny voice broke in, belonging to a young woman nearly a head taller than Grimes. Half of her dark hair had been pulled into an elaborate updo, while the rest cascaded down her shoulders. Her pink dress was more of a flimsy drape. Silver jewelry and swirling henna patterns covered her exposed skin.

Smiling, the woman bounded up next to Grimes and rested a hand on his shoulder. A cloud of flowery perfume hit me a second later.

Grimes returned to his paperwork, completely uninterested in this spectacle. "This is business, Kit, but so far we understand each other."

"Business?" Kit focused on me next. Her shrewd brown eyes seemed to respect what they saw—or pretended to, at least. "That's some dangerous business you conduct, dove." She placed her arms akimbo. "Mine's not much better. But I have a real gift, and it'd be a shame to let it go to waste. *You* clearly don't let nonsense rules and expectations stand in your way, either."

Kit was a witch, I realized. The sales talk wouldn't be far behind. Sure enough, she pressed on before I could intervene. "You look like a woman on a quest, all right. Something risky, lots at stake. I can help you succeed. What blessings and curses do you need, dove? Let's be thorough. Don't worry, I'm a lot more reasonable than the adepts."

I stifled my disappointment. Grimes probably wouldn't let me get back to my true business until I gave his pet witch *something*. I resolved to make the most of it, and fished several more eighths from my purse to drop onto the crate between us. "I need the blessing of knowledge right now. I'll be questing in a place called Nidaros. What do you know about it? Have you heard of any trouble there lately?"

Kit fiddled with a lock of hair, eyeing the money as though it smelled like rotten fish. "Dove, I *am* reasonable, but I need a *little* more than that to perform a proper scrying."

I shook my head. "I don't have time for that. Whatever you have off the top of your head is fine."

"Well, that's the thing. I don't *have* much off the top of my head." Kit shrugged helplessly. "Nidaros is Linum Dominorum's concern. I've never even met anyone from there."

At the palace, Madam Castor had mentioned that her trade guild supplied Nidaros everything they needed in exchange for the flax they produced. The claim had been strengthened, slightly, but I'd been hoping for more. "Grimes? Can you add anything to that?" I chanced.

"You just heard most of what I know. My ships don't go there." Grimes remained focused on his parchment. "I met some Nidaran soldiers on a military campaign years back, though, before I took up safer work." He smirked, covering the gaps in his teeth. "Tough lot. They haven't forgotten where they come from."

"'Where they come from?'" I repeated.

"They belonged to Lord Gyllenfeld some decades ago," Grimes replied.

Not a Lord I was familiar with. But if Catherwood had conquered Nidaros in the past, maybe that was what fueled Madam Castor's claims of a "miscreant" populace, failing to meet their flax obligation out of spite. Although, *decades?* That was a long time to hold a grudge. These things would probably make more sense once I reached Nidaros.

I nodded my thanks. "There's some further business I'm looking to—"

"Hang on, dove! We're not done talking about the blessings you need." Kit pressed her hands upon the crate, leaning eagerly toward me.

Damn it, I thought, hoping the frustration wasn't plastered on my face.

"You have wits and bravery covered," Kit went on, "but even with that, you can never know for certain if your sword's going to beat your opponent's. I'll imbue your steel with a falcon's speed, give it the hardness of diamond. No trouble at all. What about—?"

"Kit! *Heat!*" a voice barked from somewhere behind me.

Both Grimes and Kit looked up with wide eyes, sending strained glances over my shoulder.

"Again?" Kit murmured. "I *told* you we need to pick a new side of town." Despite her casual tone, she paled with fear.

I wasn't thrilled with the hard sell, but whatever-this-was

didn't seem good either. I turned in time to spot a flash of burgundy amid the dense clusters of ships and cargo. A pair of adepts had entered the port, sweeping to and fro with suspicion. One carried several sets of manacles, following the other, who in turn obeyed the whims of the dowsing rod in his hands.

This was bad news for sure, especially for a witch. The port workers who'd once looked to me with uncertainty or ill will had nothing but trepidation for the adepts, who were still some distance away from me, Grimes, and Kit.

"Hide," Grimes muttered.

Turning back, I found Grimes offering Kit the knife he'd pulled from behind his back.

Kit's eyes held fear, but she grasped the weapon in a practiced and comfortable grip. She fled, disappearing behind a nearby vessel.

Grimes fixed me with a murderous stare. "Breathe one damn word about her, you won't live to leave this port. Got it?"

I tamped down my own dread. "Oh, hell no. I had no intention."

Grimes seemed doubtful, as if he regretted giving Kit his knife because it left him with nothing to wield against me. But I truly had no interest in landing anyone in trouble, especially not over nonsense. I strained to project reassurance while not letting impatience dig at me. This was cutting into my time before I'd be forced to leave for Nidaros. I still had my most urgent errand to arrange.

Silence overtook the port as the adepts, both young men, wove their way through. The people around them froze and watched helplessly. The outnumbered adepts inspired a disproportionate threat that kept everyone in line, which was typical throughout the galaxy. Few felt confident going up against "magic" or the very Unseen who created and destroyed at a whim.

The adepts passed me and Grimes without having hit upon anything, edging ever closer to Kit's hiding spot. I knew it'd be best for everyone to avoid a confrontation. A thought came to me on how to go about it.

"Trust me," I muttered to Grimes. Then, louder, "Friend Adepts! Dame Jessamine Irless of Freemont. Is there something I can help you with?" What the hell—since I had them, I produced my papers bearing Lord Catherwood's seal.

Grimes' eyes went wide, but he held his tongue.

The dowsing adept turned and lowered his device, gaping at me in shock. "Uh ... Freemont? I assume you're new to our domain, Lady Knight? Frankly, this is not the part of town anyone should be in." He waved me over to where he stood, about twenty feet away.

I obliged, walking at a sure pace. His manacle-bearing friend frowned over me as I approached.

"We'll take you to a better port once we're through here," the dowsing adept spoke under his breath. "But first, have you seen any unusual or illegal activity here?"

A knight errant was sworn to speak the truth. I could count the number who consistently did so on half a hand, but for my part, I did find a way to avoid lying in that case. "I haven't seen anything I would find objectionable."

"Ah. All right, then." The dowsing adept nodded thoughtfully.

"Get back to it," his manacle-carrying partner urged.

"No, I think we're done. In truth, I haven't sensed much of a lead anywhere." The dowsing adept glanced back to me. "Come with us. We'll help you with anything you need."

He seemed nice for his ilk, but I'd sooner rot in hell than accept help from the same people who'd plundered Gules, marooned Drea, and might've killed Branigan. I managed a disarming smile. "That's all right, thanks for your concern—

but that man is my uncle, you see." I pointed toward Grimes, who managed an admirable deadpan.

"Oh." The dowsing adept shook off his surprise and raised his voice to address Grimes. "Are these your ships, sir? Are you authorized to be here?"

Silently, Grimes removed a wad of credentials from a pocket, displaying stamps that verified either the fees he'd paid, or his skill at forging or stealing such proofs.

The dowsing adept looked to his partner. "All right, let's go."

"No no no, *not* all right. The fees have gone up since last week." The other adept looped his manacles onto his belt with a sneer, then shoved a nearby crate with his boot. Satisfied he could pick it up, he did so. "Here, this should cover it. Unseen be with you," he wished no one in particular.

Bastard, I thought.

The dowsing adept looked less than enthusiastic, but apparently had no recourse other than to follow his partner out of the port.

I held my breath until all trace of burgundy and gold had vanished. The rest of the port seemed just as tense. It was Grimes' short but genuine laugh that gave everyone permission to breathe again.

"Could've been worse. I only leave the chintzy stuff lying in the open for just that reason." Grimes shook his head at me with smirking bemusement. "A knight errant helping smugglers and witches! Now I've seen everything."

Little did he know, I wouldn't have helped the adepts in a million years. I also didn't care whether he operated illegally in Catherwood space, as long as he wasn't harming anybody. I'd run into too many stupid laws in too many places to think poorly of anyone on that basis. Besides, with all the dogma I violated every single day, I was in no position to judge.

His good cheer persisted. "Maybe Uncle Grimes won't be

asking for any florins when his courier reaches Sever space."

"Thanks." I smiled, almost glad the adepts had stopped by — not for the discount, but for the goodwill I could leverage for my even more urgent favor. With Kit still in hiding at the moment, I sobered and offered Grimes my entire purse, the remainder of my advance. "One more thing, Uncle: I need someone to make a trip to Gules. There's —"

Grimes' good humor vanished in an instant. "Sorry. No chance."

I was desperate for someone to reach Drea, and couldn't hide it anymore. "Please, a woman's life is at stake. I know what happened there, but —"

He shushed me, then closed the distance between us to mutter. "You don't go round bringing up curses unless you want someone *giving* 'em to you."

It was far too late for such caution, but I wasn't about to tell him as much.

I ignored mounting hunger and thirst to keep trying right up to the edge of sundown, combing ports ranging from decent to questionable. Everyone was willing to entertain a knight errant and her cred. At mention of Gules, however, they stared through me, pretended to deafness, or grasped their beads and retreated like I was a disease.

The day's relentless heat subsided. With the sun poised on the horizon and the sky fading from one shade to the next, I made my way back to the Linum Dominorum port, where my ship waited.

My feet carried me along more out of necessity than want. Mounting worry and frustration gave way to panic, laced with a crippling helplessness. What was I to do? I couldn't possibly proceed to Nidaros and leave Drea languishing in Gules. But

I'd given my vow, to a *Lord*. Catherwood's voice carried light-years further than mine. He could destroy my reputation in this part of the galaxy, and put a price on my hide to boot.

I halted in my tracks. *Wait. So what?* I challenged myself. None of that mattered compared to Drea. I never wanted to set foot in this domain again anyway.

These once-forbidden thoughts produced a new source of aching guilt. Never before had I even *considered* reneging on a quest ... but I'd never chosen this quest, had I? Unlike Nidaros, I knew exactly what trouble Drea faced. Ignorance didn't absolve me, but it'd be easier to live with.

It was settled. I'd return to Gules, rescue Drea, then flee Catherwood space and return to the beguinage as fast as *Kepler's Law* could stand it. Afterward, I'd seek as much justice for Branigan as was possible outside the domain that had been his ruin, and nearly mine.

The helplessness lifted, a strong sense of purpose taking its place. I felt like sprinting the millions of miles back to Gules, but my legs had to settle for a brisk walk. As I returned to the Linum Dominorum port, the guild's seal reasserted itself everywhere: a trio of blue flowers. *Flax* flowers. Madam Castor hadn't been melodramatic about the crop's importance to her business.

My ship was a welcome sight, despite the adepts chanting inside and out. One took me aside to review the provisions a crew had brought aboard earlier, then handed me a linen sack.

"Official correspondence. Deliver this to Baron Tristan's estate." Then he passed me a plate-sized wooden container sealed in delicate dyed paper. "And deliver this into Baron Tristan's hands directly. A gift from Lord Catherwood."

Suffocating doubt arose to strangle my resolve. I barely heard the adept past my fitful reverie. Once I broke my vow, I couldn't rightly call myself 'knight errant' any longer. The galaxy was full of knights who'd done worse, though. What was one more lie on top of all the others?

But now I was running off with their mail and personal gifts. Hell, they'd kill me just for that!

My heart pounded out a terrified rhythm. Though my limbs trembled, they carried me and my new burdens aboard. The adepts vacated. My escape window drew closer. A fever-ish mix of desperation and fear overwhelmed me.

Drea. Focus on Drea, I told myself. She'd scold me the whole way home, but damn it, she'd be alive to do it.

I stowed the mailbag and gift box. Once settled into the pilot's chair, I removed the new khamsa amulet lashed atop the console. That allowed me to cancel the preprogrammed course to Nidaros, then hunt through the index of galactic settlements stored in my ship's computer.

The entry for Gules was missing.

CHAPTER 5

How could Gules be missing from my ship's index?

In my pilot's chair, panic seized me, halting my breath mid-throat. I forgot the outside world to make frantic double- and triple-checks, which brought me no closer to those coordinates. What about my travel log? No, no hint of my prior landing remained there, either. The adepts had purged the data. Gules no longer existed, had never existed.

A clammy chill spread over my skin. How would I possibly get back there now? Dead-reckoning would be like plucking a grain of salt out of a sandstorm. Even if I somehow guessed the right star out of billions, *and* stumbled upon the right planet orbiting that star, I wouldn't know where to land on the planet's surface.

They'd taken away all hope of rescuing Drea. She was stuck in that cursed town. As horror gave way to despair, I collapsed against the console in front of me, arms wrapped over my head, braced for the oncoming tide of grief.

No, wait, I can't do this. Pull it together! Linum Dominorum expects you to leave!

The thought jolted me back up for one last glimpse of the trade guild port out my windshield. If I didn't hurry, I'd likely have soldiers or guild mercenaries pounding at my hull soon.

Where would I go? If not Gules, then maybe proceeding with my forced quest was the next best alternative. Nidaros was a short hop of several hours, as opposed to the weeks separating me from the beguinage. One of their ships, functional or otherwise, could still have Gules in her logs. Copying the coordinates down by hand wouldn't be fun, but I could do it.

On that dim hope, I set course and left Spectra behind.

My Dear Jessamine,

I open with the old creed: assume nothing, prepare for the worst, hope for the best. The universe operates neither for nor against human desire. Complications have a way of seeping into simple matters. If you read these words happily, I look forward to hearing more of Sir Branigan's discovery on Gules, and Beguine Drea's research. If you read them with sorrow, I grieve with you.

As you prepare to return ... I almost wrote of forewarning, but there is no threat here. You should know Sir Mayweather is en route to the beguinage, with plans to stay a while. By the time you read this, he'll be in our midst. He remembers you fondly in his letters, and hopes this might be the occasion you finally reunite.

Your feelings require no justification, but holding on to resentment only hurts you. Consider releasing it, forgiving him, and yourself.

Remember how proud we are to call you friend. Keep fighting for a more enlightened universe. May we be fortunate enough to meet again.

Much love always,
Joachim

Shock and resentment paralyzed me for a moment. The parchment nearly floated out of my fingers before I remembered to fold it back up. I stowed it inside a crack in the light fixture I huddled beside, situated on the galley ceiling. It was one of the most temperamental light sources the Shipbuilders had ever fashioned, and yet the only cooperative one aboard at the moment. Past its meager glow, the darkness of space at impossible speed permeated the ship, as did the thrum of the engine. I hugged myself against the ship's ever-present chill. At least I was no longer seeing my breath after the latest round of maintenance.

I didn't know what I'd sought from Joachim's letter, but it certainly wasn't *May*. My earlier thoughts really had summoned the bastard. Now my former master meddled everywhere, even in the most private space Joachim and I could share, expecting me to bow to his whim. No matter what, I'd be returning to the beguinage with awful news. I wasn't in any mood to face May, too.

Damn it. First Branigan, then Drea—

Hold on. I didn't know she was dead yet. In fact, why *wouldn't* she be alive?

A glimmer of Drea's optimism must've rubbed off after three weeks. I imagined her harvesting snow for water and scouring the town's ruins for supplies. She carried useful stuff in her knapsack, including a tinderbox. Fire, water, and the shelter of one of those abandoned shacks would sustain her a long time. There was still hope.

With new purpose, I shoved off from the ceiling, drifting toward the pitch-black threshold to quarters. The minute I landed, I'd hunt down a ship with coordinates for Gules, then fly right out of there.

But what about doing right by the people of Nidaros?

Another jolt of shock. I caught myself at the threshold before sailing through, grasping either side of the entryway. Inertia sent my braided hair floating past my shoulder. Following close behind was the chain around my neck, which usually stayed under my tunic, bearing a ring that had once been my mother's.

Guilt flooded me for not thinking of the people sooner. Amid all the courtly nonsense, they'd been less than an afterthought. I was supposed to be better than that. I hadn't taken up a sword to run from things within my power to fix. Drea would want me to help them first, however much I could. Joachim would expect the same. Branigan would've as well.

I took a settling deep breath. My vow to Lord Catherwood would remain intact, at least long enough to meet with the Baron of Nidaros and learn what Spectra's court had been so elusive about.

There loomed many hours to kill first. Meals and fitful sleep only vanquished so many. To stave off grief, I dove into chores, the more menial the better: exercise; checking on everything making too much or too little noise in the engine room; straightening up what Catherwood's people had rifled through; consigning the khamsa amulets to a storage bin loaded with talismans, gris-gris, and enough virulent curses to ruin me and generations of nonexistent kin. Some knights had treasure vaults, or epics written in their honor. My legacy was tangled up somewhere inside that box of wishful thinking.

I tended to my gear as well. Absent a squire to foist chores upon — by preference — I still excelled at it, in any setting. Well before I'd gotten used to weightlessness, May had stuck me, his accoutrement, and cleaning supplies in the center of his ship's cargo hold, with nothing nearby to kick off of. He'd then settled against a bulkhead, arms crossed, and ordered me to polish every last scale of his ceramic lamellar armor.

Whenever I'd faltered, or some needed object had drifted out of reach, he'd barked and taunted, just the sort of thing that pushed a grieving teenager past reason. The rage had driven me to hurl his own cuirass at his head. An equal and opposite reaction had then propelled me across the cargo bay.

I'd feared needing every inch of distance. However, the no-account braggart had merely gathered up his scattering equipment, laughing and grinning that damned rakish grin. *I knew I'd squeeze some applied physics out of you.*

I buried the recollection, and brushed out every last dirt particle from my coat as penance.

The lit crescent of my target planet teemed with water and vegetation. My ship's index reported a healthy array of settlements on the planet, but it only remembered what things were like back in the Shipbuilder days. It was possible, likely even, that several of those settlements had since disappeared for good.

As we entered atmosphere, a pale yellow sky overtook the void. Nidaros sprawled over miles of tawny, hilly meadow, but was composed mostly of empty space, like an atom. A handful of rural neighborhoods dotted the electron cloud, with long roads connecting each one to a tiny walled-in nucleus.

My ship descended toward that nucleus, presumably the barony's capital. From its center rose three formidable buildings. The tallest looked like a glossy fistful of straw. Flanking it were two identical gleaming gray structures that resembled triangular sails billowing in opposite directions. This trio was the only remnant of the Shipbuilders' original colony. They dominated here, but on Spectra, they wouldn't have prompted a second glance.

Kepler's Law touched down with a shudder just short of the walled nucleus, in the simple rectangle of black pavement comprising Nidaros' port. Its beacon tower sat unlit. Only five other ships rested there. Five chances at finding a working computer with an index that hadn't been purged recently. I still intended to hunt for those coordinates after I'd met with the Baron.

I kissed my fingers to pat a newly plaintive console. Out the windshield, altitude-obscured details lay stark and exposed. The dark rectangle had become a stretch of diseased concrete, weeds shooting from cracks large enough to swallow unwary passersby. Only two of the docked ships were visible from my vantage. A film of beaded strings, stone piles, and bent twigs littered their corroded hulls like flowers on a casket.

My restraints felt ever more constrictive, as though a looming inquisitor tightened invisible screws. Had I just found another Gules? Hell, I hoped not. I pried myself out of the pilot's chair, determination helping me past the shakiness in my limbs, and layered on armor, coat, and weapons while my head cleared.

A clean breeze rewarded my patience with the ship's hatch. Rapid footsteps followed. From around the forward portion of my ship sprinted a lone soldier, clad in familiar burgundy and gold Catherwood trappings. My heart sank at his appearance: teenaged, hollow in build, swimming in his tunic. Afternoon shadows cut into his open-mouthed stare. A short sword and wishing beads rested at his side.

What could've forced a sickly kid like this into service? Then again, the Nidarans had sent a messenger to Lord Catherwood, and would've been expecting some sort of response. Maybe they'd stationed their most pitiable specimen here to skew my expectations.

I dropped down to meet him, mailbag and fancy gift box in hand, covering up my concern. "Hail, soldier."

He shifted his weight on his feet, clearing his throat with sharp coughs. "Lady Knight, aye?" stumbled from his mouth in an unfamiliar accent. "Who sent you?"

No *hail and welcome?* For all he knew, I'd landed there on a lark in search of a new quest.

"If no one sent you, I'm afraid ye must leave," he tacked on. "Our Baron's closed the port to all but trade guild traffic."

"I have business with your Baron, friend, on behalf of Lord Catherwood and the Linum Dominorum trade guild." I put down my burdens for a moment to show him Lord Catherwood's sealed papers.

The soldier flinched at the sight of the snake-eating griffin. Odd, given it covered his own chest. "This way." He walked off at a brisk pace, not checking whether I followed.

I trailed him at a distance, looking for the ships that'd been hidden from my cockpit view earlier. *Wrecked, wrecked ...* I held my breath, fearing more of the same past the beacon tower. To my relief, the final ship was a sleek bird in good repair, most likely the Baron's own. I hoped no one had tampered with her index. I'd find out, eventually.

Hang on, Drea, I thought.

At the perimeter of the port sat a sturdy shelter for the guard's watch. The young soldier probably had friends hiding there or in the beacon tower, keeping eyes on us. We stepped from ancient pavement into knee-high grasses that crunched underfoot. Hilly brown prairie stretched in most directions, with the occasional scraggly tree to break the monotony. To our left stood the capital wall, over twice our height, built of worn masonry with patches of newer stone. Several feet removed from the wall loomed the rusting hull of the excavator that'd constructed it, ringed in garlands. A shame that so much had fallen into disrepair here.

Rounding the wall brought into view a gate tens of yards distant, flanked with weather-worn Catherwood banners fluttering in the breeze. Dozens of commoners swarmed the closed passage, exchanging heated words with the pair of sentries at watch. Everyone resembled my escort, pinched and weary, though for most in the crowd, anger exceeded all else.

"Quit holding out on us!"

"We want our fair share!"

"Skíta!" my escort cursed, placing heavy weight on the first syllable and almost forgetting the second. "Stay here." He jogged toward the scene, hand on his sword's hilt.

Considering my hands were full and my brain empty of what all this meant, I held back as requested, though I worried whether his running toward an angry crowd would end well for him.

A fist went up amid the commoners. "Gyllenfeld forever!"

"Folkvang for her fallen!" many shouted in response, raising their fists in kind.

Gyllenfeld! Grimes had mentioned that name back on Spectra, the Lord who'd ruled Nidaros in the past. So, there were still loyalists among the populace? Maybe the reigning Lord Gyllenfeld had planted or bribed agitators, hoping to eventually win Nidaros back? My stomach knotted up in anticipation of an ugly scene to follow.

The gate sentries backed up against the gate doors, fists at their sides. To my pleasant surprise, they held still, saying nothing. My own escort was the only solider in motion, but had yet to reach the crowd.

The shouting commoners tested their boundaries, drawing ever closer to the gate. The soldiers maintained their composure, but their surprising restraint couldn't possibly hold. Any further encroachment, and they'd be forced to draw.

Hoping to defuse what seemed inevitable, I pulled my burdens against myself and took off after my escort at last, racking my brain.

Before I could raise either hand or voice, the massive wooden gate doors parted, pushed along by a second pair of sentries. Behind them waited a caravan of wagons hitched to sturdy, wooly beasts of burden that resembled bison, only hairier. Driving the wagons were men and women in burgundy robes: adepts.

Surprisingly, the commoners quieted at once. Heads lowered, they stepped back to make room for the caravan, which proceeded down the dirt path leading out from the gate.

My escort had since pelted to a stop a short distance from the scene. He doubled over, hands on his knees, wheezing stronger than ever.

I ran up and halted beside him, concerned. "Are you ill, friend? I might have a—"

"I'm fine." He straightened, avoiding my gaze to watch the lingering crowd.

The protest had ceased. Chastened commoners flaked away from the gate, most of them tailing the caravan. A few noticed me and my escort, and sent fearful looks our way.

"What was all that?" I asked. "Can you tell me more about Lord Gyllenfeld, and Folkvang?" The latter term was a total mystery to me.

"Something to ask our Baron, not me," my escort answered.

I juggled my burdens until I had a hand free to withdraw two newly acquired cigarillos. "I'd rather hear it from someone close to the problem."

He glared my way. "I'm not impressed with your trashy guild coin, or the junk it buys! Try any more bribes, my captain will seek words with you."

His was not a reaction I was used to, at all. Maybe it should've been four smokes. I smiled disarmingly. "I'm just trying to be friendly. Sharing a smoke is customary in Turinger space. That's where I'm from." I hadn't been back in a standard decade, but I was fairly certain he'd never visited that distant domain, and never would. "Sorry for any offense. I'm still getting used to Catherwood customs."

My escort's scowl softened marginally. "Aye, well. Can't speak for 'Catherwood customs,' but that rot doesn't fly with this army."

"Again, sorry." I returned the cigarillos to my pocket.

Once my escort led me through the towering gate, the doors swung shut behind us. The soldiers on watch there stared after us curiously, but kept their thoughts to themselves. We started down a wide dirt path, through a cluster of abandoned dispensaries and trade posts. I wondered if business had closed for the day, or if it'd been suspended for some reason.

Beyond the ghostly commercial area lay a ring of open field, much of its brown grass flattened. We passed a long one-story building of modern construction, solid for such. Judging by the number of soldiers clustered in its vicinity, I assumed it was the army's barracks. Further into the field, tens more soldiers practiced combat drills. We cut through the field without getting in anyone's way, but my escort succeeded in alerting several of his friends to my presence. They stole glances at us, mostly grim in their assessments.

A standing army. For a tiny little place like this? It really *was* important to the trade guild, and apparently, Gyllenfeld's name still heated far too much blood. I wanted to ask if anything else justified the large garrison, but already knew my escort was in no mood to talk.

Past the barracks, an empty field separated us from the massive trio at the capital's center.

"These are beautiful buildings." This time, I couldn't help myself. "What do they house?"

"Estate, adepts' keep, storehouse." My escort swept a hand from left to right.

"What's in the storehouse?"

"Too much of what we don't need, not enough of what we do." He continued to avoid my gaze.

We approached the Baron's estate, its yawning entrance propped open. A cesspool smell shattered the illusion of beauty. Plumbing issues, most likely. At the threshold, my escort left me in the care of a footman even younger than he was. His parting words were, "Guild business."

The footman wilted and tugged at his collar.

"A quest for Lord Catherwood, actually. Dame Jessamine Irless of Freemont. May I speak with the Baron?" I flashed the sealed papers again.

"Uh … wait here a moment." The boy snatched up the mailbag and scurried away. He left me with the gift box and the responsibility of showing myself into the foyer.

I wasn't at all used to inspiring such fear, but I was completely used to long waits. Within the dim foyer, candlelit sconces lined the walls, nailed up centuries after the place had been built. Incense made a valiant but vain attempt to mask the odors seeping in from outside. Echoes of invisible conversations coursed through the chamber, insisting the building was occupied despite its deserted appearance.

My thoughts wandered. I was more accustomed to quests along the lines of "fetch this relic" or "slay that monster," wherein the relic and monster usually turned out to be anything but. Nobility and courtly maneuverings presented a new tangle. With trepidation, I realized I could be at this for five minutes or five years.

Don't worry about me, I practically heard Drea protesting. *You know Lord Catherwood is willing to curse his own settlements. Do everything possible to keep it from happening to Nidaros.*

"This way, Lady Knight." The footman returned without the mailbag, yanking me from my daydream.

Still lugging the gift box, I squared my shoulders and followed him into a squat maze of corridors lined with Catherwood regalia. The doors on either side of us were hinged wooden panels, modern replacements for malfunctioning originals. We passed the occasional adept who silently noted our movements, while servants focused a little too hard on their errands.

To my surprise, we angled for an ordinary door that

opened into a cramped room. Shelves lined the walls, stuffed with parchment scrolls. A plain wooden desk sat at its center. In front of the desk stood a trio who took up nearly all of the remaining floor space: a man in plainclothes, a woman in an ill-fitting gown, and an adept in robes almost as fancy as the master adept's in Spectra.

These were the scant details I caught before dropping to one knee to familiarize myself with the time-worn pavement, gift box clutched to my chest. On the floor, close to my knee, I noticed a posy of dried flowers inches shy of candles that would've made short work of it.

The footman promptly announced me. "Arrived on behalf of Linum Dominorum," he tacked on.

Damn it! I thought. *I'm not from the guild!* Now they'd think I was just there to nag them about their flax.

Still, I kept my mouth shut. Correction could wait until I had permission to speak.

"Arise!" commanded a male voice.

I stood. With a wave of his hand, the man in plainclothes bade the footman to close the door behind me and leave. He looked me in the eye, straight on—we stood nearly the same height—with a haunted, stern dignity. Age wasn't written into his face so much as stress was, and the stress wasn't written there so much as chiseled in.

"Tristan Foster, Baron of Nidaros." His accent matched the one prevalent on Spectra. He offered his hand, not to kneel before, but to shake.

I returned a firm handshake, hoping my persistent surprise wasn't evident. No throne room? No dragged-out pomp? I couldn't complain.

Baron Tristan straightened the golden T-shaped hammer amulet around his neck, then lowered his eyes to the woman beside him. "Lady Amelia Catherwood-Foster, my wife."

He counted on me to notice her hyphenated surname, yet

another shock. A Catherwood herself! No wonder the young Lord had insisted on me protecting this pair. Her presence further underscored Nidaros' importance. I bowed low to her, again hoping my deadpan held up.

Lady Amelia deigned to meet my gaze. "Baroness of Nidaros is but one of my titles. If we recited them all, we should be here until sundown." With a superior smile, she tilted her head toward the gift box in my hands. "Is this mine?"

"For you and the Baron, actually," I said. "From Lord Catherwood."

"Albion is a perfect angel." Lady Amelia lifted the box from my hands and hugged it close, ignoring the Baron and the adept, who both eyed it with a ravenousness they were quick to suppress.

I hadn't been curious about the contents of the box until that moment. Oh well. Even if I'd wanted to open it, the paper wrapping would've made tampering obvious.

The adept cut my musing short by sweeping up my gloved hand in his own as though he intended to kiss it. Candlelight glinted off the many rings on his fingers, the gold-threaded embroidery on the sleeve of his robe, and his eager gaze. A few silver renegades streaked through his long dark hair and boxed beard, but he carried none of the burden of age, only the distinction. The scent of cloves hung about him, overpowering the other smells crowding the Baron's estate. His wasn't quite the look of the proverbial cat, but I had a bad feeling he'd been digesting his canary for years.

"Greetings, Lady Knight. Ormyr Stirner, Master Adept of Nidaros," he spoke. "We welcome thee, and praise the Unseen for protecting thee upon thy journey."

Is this how you greet Sirs Knight too, charmer? I thought, struggling not to roll my eyes.

Ormyr kept my hand despite my attempt to free it, turning

it palm-upward. He rolled the wrist of his free hand, and a gem-encrusted medallion appeared in his fingers. An impressive bit of sleight-of-hand, but he wanted me to think he'd actually conjured it from thin air. Pressing the trinket into my palm, Ormyr muttered a spell under his breath in what sounded like the Shipbuilder language. I read it frequently, but hearing and speaking it were another matter. He pronounced it much more fluidly than I could, I gave him that.

The Baron and Baroness waited out the spell with their heads lowered in reverence. I figured it couldn't hurt to do the same.

"Thou hast traveled a long and trying course to reach us. Is it not so?" Now Ormyr was cold reading, throwing out a hook that was supposed to sound unnaturally insightful, but in reality applied to anyone in my position.

His trick would only work if I bit the hook and fed him more detail, which he could turn around and use on me as though he'd come up with it himself. To thwart his game, I summoned a pasted-on smile. "I'm pleased to be here. It's an honor."

Ormyr lowered his head, betraying no disappointment. "I shall do all I can to ensure thy sojourn with us is peaceful and rewarding." With a swipe of his hand, the medallion disappeared again. I finally got my hand back, to my relief.

"Thank you, Master." I focused on Baron Tristan with purpose. "To be clear, sir, it's Lord Catherwood who charged me with this quest."

The Baron examined my sealed papers with a careful frown. Meanwhile, hope dawned over Lady Amelia like sunlight piercing a storm cloud.

"As Milord's emissary, we grant thee every protection and cooperation," Ormyr said.

"Indeed!" seconded Lady Amelia.

You may come to regret that, I thought, fighting off a smile.

The Baron smoothed back unkempt hair, his expression strained. "Hath Milord sent any other personnel? Ships?"

"No, sir." *And you don't want to know what it took to get me out here.*

"Our pleas for help were answered *thus*?" Baron Tristan nursed his temple with a hand that soon balled into a fist.

This bewildered me. He was upset there wasn't a *larger* response? Wasn't I better than a detachment of guild thugs?

"But this is wonderful!" Lady Amelia said. "My nephew's discretion proveth his trust in us! The knight can set forth right away. Let us not impede her!"

Not just a Catherwood. She was Lord Catherwood's *aunt!* By then, I lost the battle of keeping astonishment off my face.

Ormyr said nothing, watching me with his unchanged expression as though he were merely waiting for the noble pair to exhaust themselves.

"With what art thou charged?" the Baron ignored Lady Amelia to demand of me, more challenge than inquiry.

It seemed like a challenge I was fated to lose. I tensed, hesitating, seeking the most diplomatic answer possible. "Addressing whatever difficulties you're having with your flax harvest, sir."

Baron Tristan flared, debating what cesspool I'd emerged from. "Upon my honor, Lady Knight, we've enough flax in reserve to meet quota for the next harvest. Return to Spectra and inform the court as much."

"Send her not away!" Lady Amelia cried. "'Tis a grave insult!"

"Rest assured, Milady, Dame Jessamine shall remain," Ormyr said.

Lady Amelia glared at Ormyr, then at the Baron.

Baron Tristan didn't look to either of them, or chide Ormyr for overruling him.

Damn it! I knew I should've kept the word "flax" out of it. Eager fix my mistake, I made eye contact with the Baron.

"You've got bigger problems. I see that, now that I'm here. Unrest? Lord Gyllenfeld?"

It was risky, mentioning these. It sure lit a fire in all six eyes opposing mine. Even Ormyr's self-satisfaction faltered, exposing something dark and unsettling.

"Maybe you can cover this harvest, but what about the next?" I plowed on. "If there's something I can help with, I want to."

"Help? What canst one of thy calling do for our ills?" the Baron challenged with an accusing stare. "What promises lured thee hither? For what dost thou truly quest? I assure thee there's more strife than glory to be found here. My people don't need false hopes or relic hunts. Thou *shalt not* divert them with such!"

My eyes widened at his protective fire. Could it be this Baron *cared* about his subjects, and what went on beyond his estate walls? Emboldened by the discovery, I replied without having to fake my conviction for once. "I'll be honest, it's your people I'm really worried about. The only thing I'm hunting for is the best outcome possible, for *Nidaros*. Let's talk about the barony's troubles and how to address them. Would you mind laying out exactly what's wrong, sir? Neither Lord Catherwood nor Madam Castor told me anything."

The trio exchanged startled glances.

"They told thee nothing," Baron Tristan repeated in a quiet tone that marveled even as it surrendered. "My messenger's words sailed through uncaring ears."

"But Milord doth seek to help us!" Lady Amelia objected.

Baron Tristan ignored her, lowering his head to me in assent. "Let us talk, Lady Knight. Perchance—"

"'Twould be unwise at the moment, Your Grace," Ormyr broke in, assuming command with ease. "Captain Leirfall is afield, and our visitor is likely weary from her journey. She should rest whilst I forecast for the days ahead. We can all reconvene in a few hours, at supper."

Baron Tristan wilted, his will extinguished. One hand reached for the loop of beads at his side, winding through them. "Very well, Master."

He wilted even further under the scowl Lady Amelia cast his way, just before she stormed past me and out the door. She made a point of kicking aside the posy on the floor, just miss-ing the candles. The glare Baron Tristan fastened upon the flowers was nearly enough to set them aflame.

I tamped down my discomfort and pretended to blind-ness. "I'd really rather start the discussion now, sir."

"Thy commitment is noted, Lady Knight," Ormyr butted in, "and thy patience appreciated, whilst we make all neces-sary preparations to best inform our collaboration." He stepped forward with a friendly smile. "Your Grace, I shall show Dame Jessamine to a guest room."

Behind him, the worn husk of Baron Tristan clutched at his amulet again. "Rest well, Lady Knight."

I masked my annoyance as Ormyr backed me into the corridor, one arm hovering over my shoulders. His entreaty sounded reasonable, but I could tell he was stalling, maybe to gather the rope he needed to tie me up as well as he'd tied the Baron.

Ormyr closed the door behind us and gestured me down the corridor. As I walked, he followed alongside at a respectful distance. "I do hope thy journey was pleasant." He strove hard to parrot the Spectra accent, but a few of his words sounded more like they might've come out of the mouths of my escort or the footman.

"No complaints," I said, still in the mindset of handing him as little as possible to work with.

"I shall have mine inferiors bless thy spacefaring vessel. Freemont," he mused, one of the few tidbits he *had* collected about me. "'Tis Lord Turinger's capital, is it not?"

"Yes," I said.

Ormyr's eyes lit up with a self-congratulatory light. "I do believe this is the first time we've hosted anyone from thy realm. I keep versed upon every dogma. Mine inferiors can perform Turinger rites as well as Catherwood, shouldst thou wish it."

I didn't care what his adepts did, assuming they didn't damage anything, but I had to pretend to a preference. Most people took their relationship with the Unseen more seriously than *Whatever's easiest for you*.

"I trust Catherwood rites dearly, Master." I added gravity to my words, as though I were mentally recalling the many times those spells and rites had saved me.

"Most gratifying to hear." Ormyr smiled, then ushered me into a claustrophobic staircase, where we began an upward climb. I kept a hand on the railing, still having the occasional lapse with balance after my recent flights.

"Thy spacefaring vessel doth lack weight-of-earths magic," Ormyr declared, matching my pace.

"It does," I said.

"Most unfortunate, how it defieth all attempts at restoration."

I paused at a landing, raising a brow at him. "I thought you couldn't repair ships here?"

Ormyr paused opposite me, unconcerned. "Adepts may attempt it from time to time. We're the only ones who can handle Shipbuilder relics without risk."

Right. Good to know I shouldn't use my stick lighter around company.

"I've kept our Baron's vessel in sound order for many a year," Ormyr assured me.

I wondered if he were this eager to impress every visitor to Nidaros. "It looks like you have to. No other ships in that port were flightworthy."

"Nay, indeed." Ormyr waved a jeweled hand in dismissal.

And Lord Catherwood had never replaced those ships, for some reason. Then again, who knew if he or his puppet-masters considered Nidaros worth the expense, or if they even had any ships to spare?

We climbed a few more flights, disembarking on another corridor-riddled floor. Ormyr stopped at a closed door ornamented with polished garnets strung on a cord. Out of nowhere, a dagger materialized in his hand: a long, wavy blade carved with runes.

Fear stabbed down my spine. I almost reared back and drew my own dagger in defense, but then Ormyr simply faced the door to trace out a tall rectangle, using the blade as his pen.

My nerves slowly settled. A "magic door." It was supposed to keep bad things out and let good things in. Once again, a nice bit of sleight-of-hand. With Ormyr turned away from me, I could finally see the dagger sheath strapped to his back. I believed the weapon was called a keris.

"Spell herein, Lady Knight. Supper shall commence at our local sundown. At that time shall a page arrive to bring thee to the dining hall." Ormyr smiled. "I look forward to conversing with thee again."

I gladly darted through the magic door, closing the real door behind myself. Something throat-tightening lurked under Ormyr's friendly facade. I got the feeling he wanted something from me beyond the help I was supposed to provide.

The little room dwarfed my quarters aboard *Kepler's Law*. A straw pallet took up most of the floor space, with tables situated at the head and foot. The busted artificial lighting fixtures suspended above served as hangers for several loops of wishing beads.

Everything of Shipbuilder origin seemed to have been removed from the estate. Was it all piled up in that storehouse in Spectra? Somewhere in foreign space? It was a common thing for a Lord *or* invading army to round up.

The rear wall housed a shuttered window frame, open to a view of the barony's capital. Strange, as I hadn't noticed any windows from outside. Despite the presence of an intact windowpane, a breeze blew inside. I stuck my hand toward the glass, and found it *wasn't* glass. My fingers passed through a material as substantial as fog.

I marveled at the sight. Like another magic door, only real. I'd heard of selectively permeable Shipbuilder materials; this was my first time encountering one. Curious, I tested the rest of the wall surrounding the window, but it held solid against my hand. It was easy to imagine other rooms in the estate that were windowed from top to bottom, though.

Finally, I lit a cigarillo and digested a long first draw, contemplating the low-hanging sun and the empty capital spread out beneath the window. Guilt and frustration returned to batter my conscience. I was there to help, while Drea suffered, and they wouldn't even talk to me.

Ignorance was unacceptable. I had to learn what plagued Nidaros as soon as possible. Attending the supper meeting cold echoed the prudence of entering a duel armed with nothing but fresh remarks.

But who the hell should I talk to? Where would I find them?

My first escort had been wary. All of the soldiers might mirror his attitude. Wise or not, I didn't want to approach any adepts. Recent events had me spitting mad at anyone wearing a robe. Lady Amelia's fair disposition had stood out, but there was no guarantee she'd have time to see me before supper. Seeking an audience with her would be too conspicuous, anyway. I wanted everyone to think I was resting as instructed. That obedient impression would help later, when I inevitably strayed from the path.

The estate's servants were my best short-term prospect. I'd go where the gossip was likely to gather.

I left the window to approach the chamber door. As I reached for the handle, the door seemed to open itself—or not. On the other side stood a young woman as startled at my proximity as I was at hers. Dark hair framed a triangular face that might've been heart-shaped in better days.

The shock stymied her for only a moment. "Well met, Lady Knight! I'm called Sigrid." She slipped inside with a beaming smile, nudging the door shut behind herself. "My master understands you have no squire, and sent me to serve as your handmaid."

"Oh. Hello, friend." I smiled back despite a mounting uneasiness, not just because of her uncanny timing. It was nothing I could articulate, only a gut feeling.

Sigrid approached the side of my pallet, dumping an armload of bedclothes there. "Here now, I'll help you out of your armor in a moment."

"I'm not exactly wearing full plate." I backed away from the door to tap ash into a bowl on a nearby table.

"Well, what else might I help with?" Sigrid asked. "Does your clothing need cleaned? What about your weapons?"

"I prefer seeing to those things myself, but there is something you can help me with," I said. "I need to know what kind of trouble you've been having here lately."

"You ..." Sigrid trailed off and forgot her chore, straightening to face me with confusion. Her eyes searched mine for several seconds. "You don't *know*? But, didn't Madam Castor send you? What did she tell you?"

With an inward sigh, I resigned myself to everyone believing Linum Dominorum had sent me. "Very little of a flattering nature."

"Yes, but, of the trouble here?"

"Nothing."

"Unseen!" Sigrid cried. "How fortunate we are that you're *asking* instead of trusting her!"

"How do you know what the Guildmistress thinks?" I asked.

"Oh, the people who arrive for the harvest make no secret of it," Sigrid said.

I recalled Madam Castor's throne room rant, her odd mix of pride and disdain toward Nidaros. "Harvest" was when the guild rounded up Nidaros' flax, and in return provided food, clothing, everything they needed. The next harvest was in two standard weeks, and I was to ensure it went smoothly.

Sigrid placed an arm akimbo and frowned, biting her lip. "Goodness, it's hard to know where to start."

"Tell me the worst thing happening in Nidaros right now," I said.

"The worst? Well, that's easily the drought." Her eyes pleaded for belief as she clutched the loop of beads at her side. "It's dragged on for many seasons. Our adepts haven't been able to reverse it. They tell us to stay in the capital. Things are getting bad out in the districts."

I frowned, pulling at my cigarillo. "So, you haven't seen the drought at work yourself?"

"I don't have to! We're all feeling the effects!" Sigrid cried. "We can't grow anything, not food or flax!"

Concern edged up on me. Most people I'd seen so far seemed sickly in one way or another. "Doesn't Linum Dominorum bring you food?"

"Yes, but it's never enough to last us until the next harvest. We have to supplement what they give us, except now we can't." Sigrid dropped to a seat upon the pallet she'd just made, kneading her beads in two fists. "We're rationing as best we can, but things are awful lean right now."

I sat beside her, hiding my mounting concern. "If you can't grow flax, how've you been meeting your quota?"

"We've been pulling it from a reserve our Baron created years ago."

At least he'd been smart enough to set up a reserve. That was where his confidence came from concerning the upcoming harvest. I'd have to ask later how much would be left in reserve afterward. "Are your neighbors having any problems?"

Sigrid blinked, confused.

"Aren't there other settlements on this planet?"

"No."

Hell. They must've decayed. "Do you have any idea what's causing this drought?"

"I wish I did. There are all sorts of horrible rumors." Sigrid glanced askance.

Mythical creature stories weren't of much help to me. I switched subjects. "What can you tell me about Lord Gyllenfeld?"

Sigrid froze with momentary panic before glancing to me wide-eyed. "What of him?"

"This place used to belong to Gyllenfeld, right? How long ago?"

She blinked upward, helplessly. "A century, perhaps?"

Even longer than Grimes had thought. "Does the current Lord Gyllenfeld want Nidaros back?"

"There … there is no current Lord Gyllenfeld." Sigrid stared at the floor. "His domain was conquered and divided at the same time Nidaros became Catherwood's."

Oh. Why were people rallying around a fallen Lord who must've died ages ago, if not at the time of his defeat? Amid drought and famine, maybe they were just clinging to any savior they could think up. It wasn't what I would do, but I could only imagine how much worry and uncertainty had built up while the adepts' failure dragged on.

"Do you know what Folkvang is?" I tried the foreign word the crowd outside the capital gate had shouted in protest.

"Yes, but, we shouldn't be talking about it. It's Gyllenfeld dogma." Pale, Sigrid nevertheless leaned in to whisper in my ear. "It's where the honored dead go, those who die in battle. Everyone else goes to Hel." She bolted to her feet again to straighten out the covers she'd wrinkled.

The hell of Turinger doctrine sprang to mind: a place I'd grown up fearing, often the source of paralyzing nightmares. But I doubted Hel was the same mythical realm of torment. I tapped more ash into the bowl nearby. "Thanks, Sigrid. I've bothered you enough."

"Oh no, Lady Knight, *I've* been the bother! If there's nothing else I may do for you, I'll leave you to your rest." Sigrid backed up toward the door.

"Actually, I'm not all that tired." I stood. "Who might be able to tell me more about the drought before supper? Maybe the people *making* supper?"

Sigrid deliberated thoughtfully. "I suppose so. They don't leave the capital either, but if you'd like to speak with them, I can show you where the kitchen is."

"Thanks. If anyone asks, I'm asleep in my room, all right?"

"All right," she replied without hesitation.

CHAPTER 6

Determined to learn more about Nidaros' ills, I left my chamber with Sigrid to backtrack through the estate corridors, retracing the path Master Ormyr had used to take me upstairs. Discretion was necessary since I was pretending to rest at the moment, and the handmaid delivered. Her footfalls made no noise. She even muffled the stairwell doors upon closing them. Meanwhile, other servants we encountered tended to chores without regard to noise. They frequently paused to deliver warm greetings to Sigrid, eyeing me with wariness afterward. My smile rarely assuaged anyone.

On the estate's ground floor, we entered a section that wasn't as well maintained as the rest. This was probably the space devoted to service areas that guests of the Baron were never meant to see. Sconces dotted the walls at less regular intervals, while the ever-present chatter of disembodied voices grew harsher. Sigrid hurried along without pause. I did my best to memorize the lengthy sequence of turns through the corridors.

Deep within the service area, Sigrid broke her silence to murmur to me with a strained expression. "These servants in the kitchen, they're kind people, but eager to repeat everything they hear. You and I can talk more later, if you'd like. I'll set you straight."

I frowned in confusion. "If there's some truth you haven't told me, why not just tell me now?"

Sigrid offered a sad smile. "I think you'll have an easier time believing it once you've seen a few things for yourself."

I wondered what revelations lay in store, and why Sigrid wouldn't share the rumors about the drought she'd described. Skepticism wasn't likely. Why else might she suppress a rumor? Did it involve someone or something she cared about, and she feared it or they might come to harm? I hoped to find out, whenever we talked later.

We finally ducked into a large room littered with tables, chairs, and cooking implements ready for use. The rows of clean knives and pans grated at me. Back in the kitchen at my mother's inn, tidying had been a constant losing battle, especially at full occupancy. Things had sat around dirty until we'd needed them again, which usually hadn't taken long, at which point we'd dunked them in a bucket of water and put them right back to work. This was less evidence of how neat the kitchen servants were, and more a sign that their tools hadn't seen much use lately.

Floor-to-ceiling shelves lined the far side wall. On the rear wall, an open door admitted the afternoon breeze. Close to the door, a wood-fueled fire burned within an improvised fire pit. The Shipbuilder flooring, immune to flame, held it in check. An almost certainly improvised hole in the ceiling vented smoke up to some unknown location on the second floor.

Three servants—two young women and a young man— swept the floors with brooms, each weaving a random path around tables and chairs. One of the girls was a lively blonde sunbeam. The other was muted, listening as the blonde and the equally boisterous young man bantered, frequently inter-rupting each other.

"Hello there!" my guide called from the kitchen threshold.

"Sigrid!" They forgot their work, quieted, and straightened—only to throw suspicious looks my way.

Sigrid gestured to me. "This is Dame Jessamine, the knight errant who's questing here. Dame Jessamine, this is Lif." She motioned toward the blonde. "This is Kofri—" she pointed to the young man "—and that's Alfrun." She pointed toward the quiet girl, then addressed all three servants again. "Dame Jessamine wants to ask some questions. Answer as best you can."

The servants quailed. No wonder; Sigrid had practically made me out to be an inquisitor. I had to subdue their fears quickly. "Well, what I *really*—"

"I have work waiting for me elsewhere." Sigrid glanced back at me. "Can you reach your room again?"

Was it my paranoia again, or was Sigrid setting me up to fail? Stoking her friends' mistrust, then leaving me to sink without her help? It seemed more and more like she *feared* what they might tell me. But then why bring me down here at all?

I kept the deliberation off my face. "I think so."

"Make sure to head back there before supper's ready. I'll 'rouse you' and see to your preparations." With a oddly smug look, Sigrid backed out of the kitchen and disappeared.

Awkward silence ensued. The servants smoothed wrinkles in their clothing, or stared hard at the floor. Sigrid wasn't there to mediate, but maybe that worked to my advantage. I could win them over without any threat of being undermined. My first task was doffing my sword, coat, and armor, setting them aside on the nearest table. That reduced me to tunic and trousers, clothing not much different from what they wore.

"I won't get in your way, all right? Like I told the Baron: I'm here to help, and I mean it." I glanced around, spotting a spare broom in a nearby alcove. I grabbed it, then got to work. This wasn't entirely altruistic of me. I knew they'd be more willing to help me after I'd helped them first.

Six burning eyes followed my progress for a while, then the young man Kofri piped up. "Shouldn't you be off slaying dragons and saving damsels — er, young gentlemen?"

I smiled to him, hoping to ease his confused frown. "I'd much rather be here, trust me."

"But what is it you wanted to ask us, Lady Knight?" Lif smoothed hair out of her face that'd gotten loose from the kerchief on her head.

"That can wait," I said.

Curiosity, maybe even amusement, replaced the trio's wariness as they exchanged glances. They returned to work themselves, each forging his or her own path through the kitchen. Every so often, they "accidentally" met up to trade whispers and the occasional giggle.

I navigated unobtrusively through the maze of dusty corners, pushing a growing debris pile ahead of me. It was nice to be using a broom. In too many places, "tidying up" meant throwing a clean layer of straw over who-knew-how-many filthy ones.

"One would think you were a maid in another life, Lady Knight." From over my shoulder, I heard the surprise in Lif's words.

I smiled. "That's not too far off the mark."

"*Really?*" Lif asked. "You're not an exiled princess or a widow seeking vengeance for her late husband? Not many women take up a sword, but it's usually for reasons like that."

Her authority on the matter was hilarious, but I stifled my laugh and suppressed the urge to correct her. Whatever origin story they invented for me would be more impressive than the truth, and they'd like it better. I steered toward the kitchen's back door, which revealed the shadowy clearing between the Baron's estate and adepts' keep, and swept my dirt pile through the threshold.

Outside, a well rested to my immediate left, encumbered

in a layer of charms almost as thick as some of the cobwebs I'd struck down while sweeping. Leather straps immobilized the pump, rendering it inoperative. Further out from the well stood multiple full barrels of water, with trash piles filling the spaces between them.

Hardly what came to mind when I imagined a stately courtyard, but that wasn't my main concern. A sudden realization spun me around, frowning back into the kitchen. "Those rain barrels are full!"

The servants paused mid-sweep to stare at me wide-eyed. Kofri shrugged his shoulders. "That's a *good* thing, isn't it?"

"But I heard there was a drought here," I said.

"There is," he assured me.

"Well ..." I trailed off, my confusion only worsening. "But it's been raining?"

"Yes," Lif said. "Just yesterday, in fact."

"But nobody can grow anything?" I wondered whether "drought" was the wrong word for the problem.

"No," quiet Alfrun piped up. "Because of the witch's curse."

Surprise braced me for only a moment. It melted off quickly in favor of a livid frustration, which I tamped down to avoid taking it out on the servants. "Curse? Who said it was a curse?" I asked in the most level tone I could manage, grasping the broom handle in two tightening fists.

"Our adepts are certain of it. What else could it be?" Lif asked. "We've never had trouble with our crops before."

Hell, of course. It couldn't be anything like topsoil erosion or shifting weather patterns. Yet another reason to despise the adepts, diverting everyone's attention to nonsense during a time of crisis.

My heart tensed like a third fist inside my ribcage. I was too angry to keep asking about the "curse" just then; I needed to get outside and have a good look around. Wooden buckets rested on the ground beside my feet. I rested my broom against the wall, then picked up two of them. "How about I bring you some water?"

"That's fine. We do need to start on supper, I suppose." Lif's face fell, an expression that matched her halfhearted words. "Use one of the rain barrels outside."

"The adepts have blocked off all the wells. They've been dry for a while," added Kofri. "But I hear Svana tried to use one anyway, and some weird sludge spilled everywhere—"

"Don't be disgusting!" Lif snapped.

Alfrun, the other young lady, continued to observe in silence.

I stepped out into the courtyard's breezy shade. The barrels themselves were unmarked. Unfamiliar runes surrounded each one, traced out in the mud with sticks or fingers—mud that remained soft and yielding under my feet. My anger bled off a little as confusion returned to the fore. Their wells had dried up, but it was still raining. And yet, the scant patches of grass at my feet were parched beyond revival.

Startled, I couldn't help kneeling for a closer look. At first I thought it might be an unusual variety of grass, one naturally colored that way, but no. The blades were brittle, snapping with little pressure.

I stared agape at my finding. This really wasn't a drought, it was more like the grass couldn't or wouldn't take in water for some reason. Then again, this grass was in a shaded location. Maybe lack of sunlight was the problem here. The "witch's curse" affecting their crops could've been something else entirely. I'd have to explore and examine quite a bit more, in and out of the capital, before I understood what it was.

By the time I fetched two full water buckets back to the kitchen, I'd calmed down. The three servants had since relocated to the fire pit. A chain of iron hooks dangled from the ceiling over the fire. While Kofri fed logs to the flame, Lif and

Alfrun cooperated to suspend a large iron cauldron from the hooks.

"Here, pour it in!" Lif beckoned me. "Then we'll need another round."

I complied, one bucket at a time. "Do you have a lid for this cauldron? The water'll boil faster if you cover it."

"Really?" The trio blinked at one another.

"I'll bet I can filch something off Arikur later," Kofri said.

I smiled a little, hoping I'd been helpful, then drew a deep breath. As much as I loathed resurrecting the "curse," I had to know who'd been accused and why. Just possibly, there was some glimmer of truth hiding amid the garbage. "You said a witch laid this curse. Would you mind telling me more about him or her?"

Lif leaned in with a hushed murmur just audible over the fire, eyes wide with excitement. "Her name's Thordia Naustvik, and she's from the Low North district. Many people told of strange lights and monstrous shadows inside her house. The adepts found the place *full* of dark magic. *Unspeakable* things."

"They tried to capture her, but Thordia escaped and vanished," Kofri chimed in, waving a hand.

"Her brother Verahl helped her flee," Lif resumed. "The adepts arrested him instead."

Poor things. I didn't care what the adepts had allegedly uncovered at their house. My heart ached for both of the Naustviks, especially having just lost Branigan to a similar tragedy of ignorance. Drea could well be next.

I picked up the empty water buckets and stood, burying my grief and sympathy where they wouldn't see it. "Come outside with me." A lump in my throat made speaking difficult.

The servants hurried out on my heels. Lif and Kofri flanked me, too invigorated to notice any discomfort that might've leaked past my defenses.

"So no one knows where Thordia is now, I take it?" I asked.

"No. She's eluding all the adepts' best scrying efforts," Kofri replied.

"But Verahl Naustvik's in custody. Where?"

"The adepts' dungeon, under their keep." Lif pointed toward the taller building beside the Baron's estate, the one that resembled a handful of straw.

"I take it they're … *consulting* him for Thordia's where-abouts?" My arms tensed. This almost always involved some kind of gut-wrenching torture.

"Yes, but he's yet to crack," Kofri replied with a shake of his head. "Amazing."

"No one lasts this long," Lif chimed in.

Their enthusiasm was disappointing, but hardly unusual. As my eyes riveted to the keep, my conscience picked at me. Verahl was so close at hand. I knew just what sort of horrible, unjustifiable things were happening to him, maybe even at that very moment. Was there *anything* I could do to help him? It was too soon to tell, but I'd certainly dig for that information.

I stopped at a rain barrel. Lif and Kofri stood side by side as I refilled the buckets. Meanwhile, Alfrun hovered at a distance, wringing at her apron's hem and staring downward.

Was it possible she harbored sympathy for Thordia and Verahl? Did she know something the others didn't? I had to speak with her in privacy, where her more talkative friends couldn't drown her out.

"Did any of you know the Naustviks?" I asked.

"No!" Lif shuddered. "Unseen! I've never been to the Low North, and I'm not about to go now!"

"I hear Thordia only has one arm, and she tried to steal another from her neighbor once. Poor woman got away just in time." Kofri grinned nastily. "She's coming for *yours* next, Lif!"

"Oh, don't talk like that!" Lif slapped him on the arm. "*I* heard she was a hermit and hardly ever left her house. She'd be foolish to come to the capital besides. Master Ormyr and Captain Leirfall would show her what-for!"

"I hope so," Kofri said. "A lot of the adepts are worried, given she's hidden this long."

And on it went, all the way back into the kitchen. The four of us congregated around the fire again, where Kofri and Lif seemed to compete with one another over who could dispense the most outlandish rumor. Maybe Sigrid's earlier warning had been justified. At least the names of the "witch" and her brother gave me something to ask about over dinner.

I was still curious about what troubled Alfrun, though.

As I poured out the latest round of water, an adept with a hunched back and hobbled gait slipped into the kitchen from the front entrance. His face was young, but his hair was thinning. From one of his hands dangled a chain with a teardrop-shaped green gem suspended upon it, swaying as he moved.

"Holsten!" Kofri turned and waved.

"Why, Holsten!" Lif skipped over to him. "What brings you here?"

Interesting. They were on a first-name basis with the adept — and yet, when he looked upon our gathering, he halted with a caught-red-handed look. "Master Ormyr sent me to bless the preparations," he replied in a thin voice.

"Well, you're early yet, but you're welcome to stay while we wait for our visiting knight to finish her chores." If Lif noticed Holsten's discomfort, she chose to ignore it. Grinning, she looped an arm through his, pulling him toward the nearest chair.

Holsten's gaze stuck with me even as he got towed. It wasn't just surprise. A shudder went through him, like he'd spotted the ghost of some long-dead ancestor.

CHAPTER 7

Across the kitchen, Adept Holsten's fearful stare remained on me while Lif warmly steered him toward a chair.

My hackles went up. Alarm and confusion battled for supremacy. This seemed deeper than the air of mistrust from the soldiers and servants, and it also seemed unjustified. Despite his physical limitations, Holsten was supposed to be a wielder of powerful "magic." What threat did I possibly pose to him? Were people *that* scared of what I might do in Nidaros?

Whatever the case, I supposed he wouldn't have expected to see a knight errant helping the kitchen staff. So I did what I always did when caught somewhere I shouldn't have been: pretended like I belonged, adopting a smile and casual attitude to go with. "Greetings, friend Adept," I offered after I'd finished pouring my water bucket into the cauldron.

Holsten shuddered again as Lif sat him down, his wide eyes never leaving mine.

My nerves stuck around as well. Had I done something wrong? I glanced between Lif, Kofri, and Alfrun for some sign of disapproval, but found none.

"Can- can I help with anything?" Holsten finally focused

on Lif, clutching his pendulum close to his chest.

"We have it well in hand, sweetie," Lif dismissed. "Are you all right? You look—"

"Hey, Holsten!" Kofri darted over to join them. "That wound on my hand won't go away. Any other spells you can offer?"

Meanwhile, Alfrun lingered with me by the fire pit, still pale.

Forget Holsten—this was my chance to figure out what was bothering the poor girl. "Follow me. We need to talk." I gestured toward the wall of floor-to-ceiling shelves, distant enough to place us out of earshot.

Alfrun gaped, then nodded. As we stepped away, Kofri and Lif assaulted Holsten with questions. None of them watched us. Good.

We stopped at the astonishing set of shelves. I never would've believed any noble would allow himself to feel the pinch of crop trouble, but before us stood a gaping larder, home to a few jars of dried plants, spices, and bagged staples. The sight roused my concern, and my respect.

"You've been upset ever since the Naustviks came up. Is something wrong?" I asked Alfrun under my breath.

"I …" Alfrun sneaked a glance behind us, likely reassuring herself the others remained caught up in chatter, before continuing in a plagued tone. "I think the witch Thordia is in the capital. In the estate, even."

My surprise didn't last long against my skepticism, but I gave no outward sign. I wanted to know where her suspicions might lead. "What makes you say that?"

Alfrun clutched at a string of beads nestled in her apron pocket. The stones ground against one another in her nervous fist. "Well, first, things have gone missing from the larder."

"Are you sure? I imagine lots of people are watching it carefully right now." There wasn't much to watch, either.

"It's always something easy to miss, like salt or dried thyme," Alfrun replied. "Things a witch might use for spell-craft."

That was hardly proof of an intruder, let alone a witch. "What else?" I asked, hoping she might offer something more substantial and verifiable.

"Late at night, from the stairwell, I've seen strange lights and shadows." Alfrun edged closer to me, eyes wide with trepidation. "They come from very high above, but no one's staying above the sixth floor at the moment. Every time I see them, I run back to my quarters and *hide.*"

I remained doubtful, but just maybe, she was onto something. "Do you know anyone else who's seen them?"

"No."

"Have any adepts looked into it?"

"No!" Alfrun's fear turned to horror. "They'd punish me! Saying Thordia's been here all this time, when they've been scrying *weeks* to find her? I'd catch trouble for the larder, too!"

"How long have you been seeing this?" I asked.

"A couple of weeks, I think. Ever since Verahl was arrested." Alfrun brightened. "Yes, come to think of it, I'm certain that's when it started! Thordia must be here to break her brother out of the adepts' dungeon! Perhaps *you* could go up there and stop her?"

I stifled a cringe. Alfrun's fear inspired my protective concern, but I still wasn't sure if this were a real phenomenon or something she'd imagined. That it was actually Thordia, hiding out under everyone's noses? That much I really doubted. How could she have sneaked through the capital gate, let alone into the Baron's home, without ever being spotted?

Still, I could see whether any of this existed outside Alfrun's head. If not, then I could at least put her at ease.

"I'm not prepared to do anything right this moment—I

have to be at supper soon, after all—but I'll check it out when I get a chance," I finally said. "Mind you, witches are very clever at covering their tracks. I may not find anything." Proper expectation-setting was important. I reserved the right to cover up or tell the truth later.

She nodded gratefully. "Do be careful! I'll wish hard for you."

"Thanks," I said with a reassuring smile. "Don't be afraid."

Alfrun looked relieved as we returned to the fire. Meanwhile, Adept Holsten's stare riveted upon me again—and he quivered like a mouse backed into a corner amid Kofri and Lif's cheerful banter.

With sunset approaching, I gathered up my gear and left the kitchen to return to my room. Holsten's fear stuck with me, but most of my concern remained with Thordia and Verahl Naustvik, the suspected witch and her incarcerated brother. So soon after the massacre on Gules, the thought of more suffering innocents was especially unbearable.

The Naustviks *were* innocent. Even if they self-identified as witches and *believed* they'd set a curse in motion, I knew better. If I could hide the Naustviks somewhere safe, then spin a yarn about slaying them, maybe I'd be able to steer Nidaros toward constructive action against their crop trouble, whatever the hell it was.

Muted sunlight bathed the walls by the time I stepped through my chamber door, weapons and gear bundled in my arms. The breeze coursing through the window had turned as icy as that wind on Gules.

My heart lurched. *Drea, I'm sorry.*

She'd understand. She'd want me to be there, helping as many people as possible. That didn't make the guilt any less wrenching. My mother's ring, dangling from my neck, felt like a boulder against my chest.

Then, something else occurred to me. *I'm about to attend supper? At a Baron's court?*

Throat-closing panic chased off the guilt. I'd been schooled on the motions of blue-blooded functions, but those pointers had never been field-tested. Anxiety was probably the worst emotion to start with; better to show up looking relaxed and well rested. Well aware I was neither, I took a deep breath, then launched into becoming presentable on short notice.

My brigandine went on over my tunic and trousers. The nanofiber material had a shimmery quality, mimicking satin, that made good formal wear in a pinch. I also wore my belt. It took effort not to add my dagger, back baldric, and side sword.

Don't bring silverware to a fancy party, my former master May had once cautioned, *unless you're sure one of the guests will need it.*

I had to keep reminding myself that I was Lord Catherwood's emissary. This wasn't the usual inn or boarding house. Here, they'd treat the security of my possessions as a matter of honor.

Just as I'd loosed my hair to re-braid it, the door burst open. I gave a start and nearly dove for my dagger, when I realized the intruder was Sigrid.

The handmaid swept brazenly into my room, lit candle in hand. She set it down on the table at the head of my pallet, then frowned toward my terror-stiff form. "Wouldn't you rather borrow a dress, Lady Knight?"

I laughed, which took the edge off my nerves. "No, thank you."

She approached my piled-up coat and weapons. "I'll clean these while you're away this evening."

"No, thanks." I darted into her path. It was hard enough for me to leave them, much less allow someone to carry them off.

However, there was one thing for which Sigrid wouldn't accept my refusal. She sat me down on the pallet's edge, then set to work twisting and pinning back small sections of my hair, leaving the remainder to hang freely down my back.

"Did you rest soundly, Lady Knight?" Ample amusement shaded Sigrid's question. I smelled the lavender she must've used as a perfume.

"Not bad," I deadpanned.

"What did your 'dreams' tell you?"

"A lot of wild stuff I'm not too sure about. Weren't you going to set me straight on that?" I was interested to know whether she'd ever seen Alfrun's lights, or knew anything else about the Naustviks.

"I think tonight after supper would be a better time," Sigrid mused. "What you hear from the court may be just as confusing—or illuminating."

Strange. Sigrid continued to avoid the rumors, only alluding to some truth she held at arm's length. Why was she stringing me along? Maybe it would make more sense after supper, but I doubted it.

"Adept Holsten. How well do you know him?" I tried a different line of questioning.

"Hmm? We're fairly well acquainted," Sigrid said. "He's a wonderful source of gossip from the adepts' keep. What about him?"

I shook my head, remembering too late that Sigrid was working on it. She braced my temples and pointed my face toward a corner, empty but for the jagged shadows thrown by the candle.

"He showed up in the kitchen, and he kept looking at me like I was his worst nightmare," I said.

"If Adept Holsten isn't nervous about *something*, I worry," Sigrid returned with a giggle. "We don't receive many foreign visitors. Everyone wants to make a good impression."

102 | E_LLIS_ M_ORNING_
102 | ELLIS MORNING

I was unconvinced. Still, gossip about the adepts sounded useful. I resolved to corner Holsten later. If he remained too afraid to talk, maybe Kofri and Lif could extract information for me. I'd sure have my fair share of kitchen detail in coming days, if that were the case.

"If I … oh, how foolish of me." Sigrid tapped my shoulder, allowing me to stand and face her shamed expression, framed in shadow.

"What? This?" I reached for my head.

"No, don't touch it! It looks lovely!" Sigrid batted my hands away. "I know it's unlikely, but if you think of anything *I* can do to help you, anything to hasten the drought's end …" She clutched at her beads. Only then did she seem to find her courage, meeting my gaze with determination. "I want to help."

Her helpfulness had been inconsistent thus far. Nevertheless, I nodded with a smile. "Thank you."

"I'll wish hard for you." Sigrid blinked. "Have you any charms for luck?"

"In my pockets," I lied. Every domain had a different list of favored trinkets. I couldn't possibly carry enough to satisfy everyone, so I didn't try.

"Well, here's another." Smiling, she produced a hammer-shaped charm to add to my nonexistent armament.

A page arrived to guide me through the dim corridors to the dining hall. Rising apprehension made me lose track of the twists and turns we made. To reassure myself, I went over the discussion topics I hoped to address that evening: flax reserves, food rationing, the true nature of the crop trouble. I was curious how this information would compare to what I'd gathered earlier.

If possible, I'd also find a way to request Gules' coordinates. I was desperate for them, but didn't want to give the impression that I cared more about leaving than helping Nidaros.

A resplendent jewel-studded gathering crowded the dining hall threshold. Baron Tristan, Lady Amelia, Master Ormyr … the only person who bucked the pattern was the man standing to Ormyr's right. He was lanky, about my age, wearing a simple burgundy doublet, brown trousers, and tall boots. His wishing beads were wrapped around his belt multiple times, presumably so they wouldn't catch on anything.

The page at my side vanished. For a moment, I felt the same urge to flee.

The Baron stepped forward with a smile, extending one hand toward me, and the other toward the man in the doublet. "Dame Jessamine Irless of Freemont? Ingvar Leirfall, Captain of the Guard. Our captain doth regret being unable to meet thee earlier."

It looked to me like any and all alleged regret was a figment of the Baron's imagination. The captain was clean-shaven, revealing a strong jawline set in a look of grim appraisal. Sun-bleached hair fell into his steely gaze, but made it no less incisive. Those eyes cut past all the pretense surrounding us and looked squarely at *me*.

He's dashing, I thought. Then I wondered what the hell was wrong with me, having such a thought at that moment. I pushed it aside to shake Ingvar's hand firmly. "Well met."

Ingvar remained silent, betraying nothing about the conclusions he formed.

Never mind the chill, I was about to break into a sweat. Adding to my nervousness, it seemed the rest of the room held far more interest in this introduction than was warranted.

"Lady Knight." Ormyr scooped up my hand next in a suave motion. "I do hope thy rest proved peaceful."

Not this again, I thought, but managed a polite nod.

The thin gold diadem on Lady Amelia's brow glinted as she lowered her head to me, then walked off without waiting for Baron Tristan.

"Captain, prithee show Dame Jessamine to our table," the Baron directed before hastening after her.

Ormyr broke away to follow the noble pair, sparing me the trouble of a diplomatic worm-out. Ingvar beckoned me with a tilt of his head. Like Lady Amelia before him, he seemed completely unconcerned with whether I followed him.

The dining hall contained dozens of candles packed everywhere they might fit. As I tailed Ingvar, my eyes strained to adjust to the relative brightness. Catherwood tapestries blanketed the walls. In the center of the room stretched a long table, bowls and spoons arranged for supper. Two carved chairs sat at the head, with benches stretching down the long sides.

There was no good spot to improvise a fireplace and chimney, as had been done in the kitchen. I made fists to keep my fingers warm, missing the gloves I'd left in my room.

Male and female adepts lined the left side of the table, including my old friend Holsten. He diverted his nervous expression to the floor when he detected my gaze nearing his. Was I still bothering him?

Ingvar led me down the right side of the table. Only one other man waited there, dressed similarly as he, but in every other way an opposite: shorter, older, stockier. Ingvar turned aside and gestured to him with a wave of his hand. "Lieutenant Pontus Grimsson, my second."

Pontus' graying beard exaggerated the difference in age. He was much warmer than his superior, accepting my handshake with a relaxed, confident smile. "My pleasure, Lady Knight."

Our gathering sat down together. I had Ingvar on my left, who hadn't bothered to look my way once since our introduction. To my right were Baron Tristan and Lady Amelia, in their carved chairs at the table's head. Across from me sat Ormyr and his fellow adepts. Ormyr hadn't introduced them, and didn't look like he was about to. Holsten sat at Ormyr's right hand, ostensibly a sign of his high stature within the cloister.

The meal had already been served. It appeared to be the water I'd fetched earlier, steeped with spices and grasses, with a scrap of hard bread floating on top. I wasn't sure what was in the wooden cups; my guess was some manner of alcohol. In most places, it was a safer prospect than the local water.

Ormyr raised his beads over his place setting, prompting everyone else to lower their heads. "Hear me O great Unseen, merciful guardians and guides of fate! Your generosity shall never falter. Sustain us now and forever!"

Everyone glanced up again. Had I not visited the kitchen myself, I would've wondered if this meager offering were a ruse designed to convince me of how little they truly had. Guilt braced me over the prospect of literally eating into their rations.

"Dame Jessamine haileth from Lord Turinger's domain," Baron Tristan explained to all present.

Lady Amelia stood, raising her glass to me. "To thy health and success, Dame Jessamine, and Lord Turinger's! Unseen watch over you both, and keep you well."

Everyone hastened to stand and join the toast.

Easy to be friendly when you don't share a border with him. I smiled and threw back with everyone else. The cup held a few sips of a very sweet beverage. Mead was my guess, but I had yet to see a bee anywhere. It was likely imported, along with most everything else in Nidaros. That, plus a Baroness' well wishes. It was a good thing we'd sat back down, because this treatment left me weak-kneed.

"Thank you very much. It's an honor to be here," I managed, then pulled myself up straight. "Why don't we discuss the difficulties you're facing, so that—?"

"Lady Knight?" Ormyr leaned forward with a faint smile, as though to inform me of a stain on my shirt. "Let us eat first."

"Uh, right." I killed the rest of my drink, glad that the dim lighting would hide the blush burning my face. Everyone dug in, and I was grateful for the excuse to stare downward for a few minutes.

"How is Spectra presently?" Ormyr asked. "I believe 'tis summer there at the moment. I do miss those summers."

"As do I," Lady Amelia murmured toward her lap.

"I received the majority of my training in Spectra," Ormyr continued, saying it in a way that signified this was unusual, and a testament to his talent. "I'm still quite impressed by *thy* travels, Lady Knight. How is it thou chanced upon our domain, and earned the confidence of Lord Catherwood?"

I faked a smile more relaxed than I felt, not about to shatter the illusion that I was their Lord's trusted ally. "Well, it's not the sort of thing that happens all at once." Only it had, in my case. I glanced between the noble pair and Ormyr, pretending to divide my attention when really, I was avoiding sustained eye contact with any of them. "My travels take me all over the galaxy. I try to do as much good as possible wherever I go. There's really not much more to it than that." I saw my opportunity to segue into business. "Along those lines—"

"Thou wouldst do well to pay heed, Holsten!" A sudden glare overtook Ormyr's expression, the brunt of which fell upon the adept on his right.

Holsten jumped in his seat and glanced up from the hands he'd been staring at, chastened. Still, he avoided my gaze. None of the other younger adepts were keen on looking my way, either.

That tore it. I'd be cornering Holsten at the end of supper. "As I was saying—"

"Thy travels remove thee from Spectra often, I imagine,"

Ormyr said, "but surely thou art acquainted with a fair number of people there."

His second interruption sent anger stabbing through me. Did we really have to keep playing social games while everyone went hungry? I faltered, then scraped together a last-minute smile. "I'm sure I'm not easily forgotten."

"Indeed, nay." Ormyr smiled back. "Whom mightest thou know from the cloister?"

Damn it! Frustration clamped down on my ribcage. I saw no good way of backing out of the question. "Do you know Adept Matthais?" I asked, naming the adept who'd shanghaied me and left Drea for dead in Gules. His was the only adept name I'd caught, short of Master Ethan's—but pretending to *that* acquaintance would only lead to trouble.

"Ah yes, Matthais Greene!" Ormyr brightened. "His father Samuel placed him in the cloister, as Henry is set to inherit the family business. How are they?"

"Fine." My face burned. I clenched every muscle possible so they wouldn't tremble with rage or grief, then raised my voice to address the whole table. "Ladies and gentlemen, you've all been very gracious. I'd like to return the favor by discussing the problems Nidaros faces, and how we can address them together."

Baron Tristan and Lady Amelia perked up at my words.

"There was another disturbance at the gate earlier today, Your Grace." Ingvar overstepped me, casting an imperative glance toward the Baron. "It came close to blows."

"I saw that!" I blurted. Ingvar's interruption didn't throw me. At least it was about something that mattered.

The Baron leaned forward, concerned. "No casualties, at least?"

"Nay, but given the rumors my men are picking up afield, I don't expect that to last," Ingvar replied. "People are doubting we have enough to eat 'til next harvest."

"Many are convinced we're sitting on a mountain of reserves in the capital and throwing them scraps," Holsten piped up, fidgeting with his pendulum, "no matter what we say differently."

"Then I'd say thy skills of persuasion need refinement." Ormyr turned from Holsten to fix Ingvar with a look only marginally less patronizing. "As I've said, this shall all go away once we take decisive action against the dissenting elements in our midst."

Dissent? Ormyr probably referred to those protesters who'd invoked Gyllenfeld, the Lord who'd been usurped a century earlier.

"And I've told you that's rot!" Ingvar leaned toward Baron Tristan with a pleading gaze. "We need to be out there *helping* people, not weeding for dissent or shutting ourselves in tighter! And if flaring tempers aren't enough, there're still plenty of beasts encroaching on the districts. I haven't adequate manpower out there to protect everyone!"

Pontus rested a hand on Ingvar's shoulder, pulling him back. My head swiveled to follow the soldiers. Ingvar smoldered, Pontus a few degrees cooler. While I wasn't familiar with everything the captain referred to, his heartfelt entreaty resonated with me. I respected him for trying to bring focus to reality.

"Husband? Lord Catherwood hath generously sent an esteemed knight errant to help us."

I faced Lady Amelia, who avoided looking at the man she addressed. *Esteemed? How'd that happen?* I marveled.

"Could we not dispatch *her*?" Lady Amelia suggested.

Baron Tristan wavered, glancing between Ormyr and Ingvar with a torn expression.

I tried to offer my help, but Ormyr was faster. "'Tis not the proper setting for such debate. Let us defer discussion until tomorrow. My forecasts indicate tomorrow as highly auspicious for trading information and strategy."

Tomorrow, hell! My jaw dropped. Why was Ormyr delaying business again? Given I was an "important player" from Spectra, maybe he didn't want me in harm's way. Or, maybe there were things he didn't want me to see, know about, or take back to Lord Catherwood.

Lady Amelia's fuming made me forget the chill in the room. My own heart pounded with frustration. Damned if I'd let Ormyr obstruct me for the next two weeks. "Sir," I appealed to the Baron.

"Tomorrow *morning*, Master, prithee," Baron Tristan edged in, then nodded to Ingvar. "At that time shalt thou escort Dame Jessamine to the adepts' keep."

Ingvar kept a lid on his own vexation, although said lid buckled from the pressure. On his left, Pontus didn't look much happier, but was better at masking it.

Well, this evening had been a waste. Each beat of my heart felt like another nail being driven into Drea's coffin. Gules pulled at me more than ever, but would Ormyr even let me get the whole request out?

"Dame Jessamine?" Ormyr addressed innocently. "Perchance canst thou now regale us with a tale of knightly adventure?"

I bit the inside of my lip to hold in a curse.

The noble couple softened at the suggestion. Many others also brightened. Ingvar, meanwhile, kept on smoldering in profile.

For once, my bardic duty might provide actual value by allowing my audience to escape their troubles a while. Standing with a confident smile, but still inwardly frustrated, I launched into another made-up story, this time of slaying a monster who'd stolen a Shipbuilder relic protecting a faraway city.

Everyone listened with rapt attention except for Holsten,

who stared pensively at the swaying pendulum in his hands; and Ingvar, who stared at the table, likely wishing for a crossbow bolt to the brain.

Upon noticing Ingvar's reaction, I had trouble taking my eyes away. Such unbridled resentment! It delighted me so much, I had to bite back laughter several times mid-narration.

Applause followed the end of my tale. I dropped to my seat with relief.

Baron Tristan waved over a servant carrying the gift box I'd brought from Spectra, which had since been unwrapped. Flipping back the hinged lid, he revealed a cache of small orange fruits, much to everyone's mute awe.

The Baron offered the box to Lady Amelia first, then sent it around the table. Everyone helped themselves to a single tiny fruit with an almost reverent air. Whatever it was, the excitement was entirely founded. It had a soft skin, and practically melted on the tongue.

Once the box returned to the Baron, he returned it to the servant's hands with a smile. "Prithee divide up the rest among the entire staff."

The servant almost dropped the precious cargo. "Unseen! Thanks, Your Grace!" She tore out of the dining hall.

Lady Amelia had glared at her lap while the offer had been made, but the servant's joy softened her.

"That was very generous, sir." It was refreshing to pay a genuine compliment.

When the noble pair stood to leave, everyone else stood as well. Baron Tristan exchanged meaningful glances with Ormyr and Ingvar as Lady Amelia preceded him out of the room.

The lesser adepts hurried out in a whispering cluster, foiling any chance of cornering Holsten. Before I could process my disappointment, Ormyr rounded the table, honing in on me. "A charming tale, Lady Knight. I do hope we hear more of thine exploits whilst thou art with us."

I nodded, dreading another useless conversation. *Come on, where's a page when you need one?*

"Good night, Master." To my surprise, Ingvar appeared at my side, an edge of warning in his tone.

Even more surprising, Ormyr actually yielded, bowing to us both. "I look forward to seeing you both on the morrow."

Once Ormyr left, Ingvar finally made eye contact with me: eyes narrowed, otherwise neutral. I debated thanking him for the intervention, but he spoke first. "I'd like you to join me and some of my men at the barracks this evening. Be good for us all to get acquainted."

His voice made clear he would've liked anything *but*, making the offer strange indeed. I was still so giddy over his earlier displeasure, I didn't think much of it—except I already had a date after supper, didn't I? But Ingvar's offer seemed preferable to Sigrid's. He probably traveled and met with people all over the barony on a regular basis. I could ask what he'd seen as well as heard.

"All right," I said. "Do you mind if I fetch my coat from my room first?"

"Nay. I'll walk you there."

Had someone told Ingvar where my room was? Not surprising, I supposed, if he handled security in the capital. I *hoped* he knew, because I sure didn't remember the way back there.

"I'll meet you at the barracks, sir." Pontus' tone was full of humor for no obvious reason.

"Uh, aye. See you soon." Ingvar exchanged a quick hand-shake with him.

Pontus hurried off. With less urgency, Ingvar led me out of the dining hall in stony silence.

I managed to wait until we were alone in the corridors, then darted up alongside him with a gleeful grin. "You think I'm full of it! Don't you?"

CHAPTER 8

At my strange accusation, Ingvar halted within the estate corridor as though he'd struck an invisible wall, staring at me in bloodless terror.

My glee never faltered. I stopped at his side, grinning. "What else do you think is full of it?"

He remained transfixed, probably not sure what to make of the bizarre tone accompanying my questions.

"Want me to go first? Gladly." I bounced on my toes, giddy enough to illustrate the blasphemy I hoped to hear from him. "How about Master Ormyr pushing off important business to schmooze? How about Baron Tristan knuckling under because of Ormyr's 'magic' drivel?"

"And what of knights errant, and the tripe ye peddle from one cesspool to the next?" Ingvar snapped. A scowl chased away his disconcertment. Annoyance restored the color to his face. "The only loyalty any of ye arse-head sellswords know is to your coin-purse! Ye serve no actual purpose short of bashing each other's heads in and dazzling people with lies!" An accusing finger jabbed at my nose. "Your garbage may impress the others, but I'm wise to you! Pretending like ye're the next coming of Zander. *Skíta!* If ye'd ever actually earned a *shred* of

Lord Catherwood's confidence, he'd have made you a proper knight in his service! Don't know what ye're supposed to be doing here, but damned if I'll let you make things worse!"

At this welcome display of nerve and candor, I burst out laughing. Weak knees backpedaled me against a wall, where I doubled over, laughing until every assisting muscle ached and I struggled to breathe.

Ingvar had frozen in place with a worried expression, maybe thinking he'd stepped too far.

"That was outstanding," I hurried to reassure him, pushing away from the wall and wiping at the tears my amusement had forced out.

Ingvar remained still, silent, and tense.

"I've thought all the same things about most of my ilk." I spoke with difficulty, stray giggles escaping here and there. "I have to play those games too, but, I really do try to be the good person in my stories."

Like Branigan. A second unwelcome wave of tears clouded my vision. I shoved away the thought with a sniffle and shake of my head, passing the whole thing off as further recovery from laughter.

Ingvar continued to watch me as though I were a snake coiled to strike. Confusion gradually overshadowed his anxiety. "Ye're not—?"

"Offended?" I supplied with a smile. "Hell no. The truth's *refreshing*, not offensive. Aside from the murky ill intent, you sniffed me out. Good work."

Ingvar still seemed confused, his tense posture unable to relax.

I stepped closer to him and lowered my voice to further press my luck. "Besides, I said some pretty grave things about your master adept. I notice you haven't yet hanged me for heresy."

"Not tonight. A rain's coming, poor weather for't." There were no windows nearby to lend Ingvar any guess as to the weather. His steel gaze latched onto mine, and he lowered his voice in turn. "Ormyr *is* full of rot, besides." He resumed his walk down the corridor.

I held back, staring after him in approval. A member of Baron Tristan's court who didn't jump when Ormyr found an invisible hole in the floor, and was brave enough to speak his mind. Was it just Ormyr he thought was full of it, or superstition in general?

My heart pounded. Could we be even more kindred than I suspected? Though I longed to know the answer, it was something to probe carefully. I didn't want to scare him off — and really, some caution remained warranted. This was possibly an act; Ingvar might've been earning my trust so he could draw me out and condemn me later. I didn't *believe* it, but I had to keep the idea in mind.

I caught up with Ingvar as he narrowed in on a stairwell entrance. The opening door blasted us with air even colder than the estate's interior. I resisted the urge to hug myself.

"Ormyr's so star-struck, he hath yet to realize ye're *not* some big player in Spectra." Ingvar gestured me in first with a tilt of his head, eyes narrowed.

"I'm not," I admitted as I stepped past him, approaching the stairs.

"So how'd ye get stuck with this quest?" Ingvar's voice echoed behind me. "Lose a duel to one of Milord's friends or something?"

Hell. Memories of Gules splashed over my newfound good mood like acid, painfully eroding it. I froze on the first step, digging nails into the handrail to keep from crumbling onto the landing. "N- no."

"What, then?" Ingvar closed the door and darted up beside me with a merciless, incisive gaze.

The blood drained from my face. In most cases I would've confessed instantly to avoid losing his confidence, but that, I couldn't force past my throat yet. If I acknowledged Gules in the slightest, Drea and Branigan would flood out too, and how would *that* look? A knight errant reduced to sobs by a simple question? I mustered a look of apology, then broke away to start up the stairs.

"Can't speak truth more than twice a night without it burning your tongue, aye?" Ingvar lingered behind, calling after me with a note of derision. "Sorry, Goose. I'll try to remember your limitations."

Damn it. I focused on ascending one stair at a time. Another mundane task to keep grief at bay, lest I fell apart in front of this soldier I hardly knew.

After a few moments, Ingvar bolted up after me, skipping stairs until he'd caught up. "Figured Milord didn't care enough about us to send anyone trusted." He didn't sound upset, just resigned.

The pressure had eased. Even so, I kept my eyes on my feet. "It seemed like Lord Catherwood cared quite a bit, actually."

"For his aunt, mayhap, not Nidaros," Ingvar said. "Even that's a matter of time."

Curiosity served as a mental escape hatch, helping me elude sorrow. I blinked up at him. "Why?"

Ingvar frowned, as though surprised I didn't already know. "Lady Amelia's next in line for the throne. Milord's puppet-wranglers will speak with him eventually about 'shoring up' his line of succession."

My eyes widened at that revelation. It made sense why Lord Catherwood cared about Nidaros and not, say, Gules. But he cared for different reasons than Madam Castor did: he had blood relations here, she had business.

Strange, though. Baron Tristan had sent a messenger to Spectra, who must've informed the court of the crop trouble and lack of food. Madam Castor had been skeptical, imagining a pack of disloyal holdouts. I could at least see where she'd gotten that idea, given there were some people here who still invoked Lord Gyllenfeld. But why had *Lord Catherwood* seemingly ignored the Baron's message? Why a tiny gift box for his aunt, and not a cargo hold full of emergency supplies? Had someone in court buried or altered the message? Had Master Ethan used "the Unseen" to cast doubt upon it? Had it been done to get rid of Lady Amelia and the potential threat she posed as Lord Catherwood's heir presumptive, everyone else in Nidaros be damned?

And what was I *really* supposed to be doing there? Whose interests did I serve? Who wanted me to succeed, who wanted me to fail, and why? The increasing possibilities raised my hackles even more than the frigid stairwell air.

I took a calming breath. "All I know is, it's a good thing *I'm* here, and not Madam Castor's forces."

"That harpy crowing about us again?" Ingvar darted ahead to open the door on my landing, nursing a scowl that wasn't directed at me for once. "We've kept up our obligation. Nothing's about to change."

"But, this, well …" I faltered within the next set of dim corridors. "'Drought' is the word I've heard, but I don't know if it's appropriate. It still rains here, right?"

"Aye, 'tis raining as ever. But rain faileth to abet us, beyond all sense." Ingvar raised a brow. "That what ye've come here for, Goose? Ask a few questions, run back to Spectra to be the expert on our problems?"

I'd had enough needling. I stopped, grabbed his arm, and made him face my angry conviction. "I'm here to do as much good for your people as possible. That's not strictly what Lord Catherwood wants, but maybe he shouldn't have extorted my vow at sword-point." Bitterness leaked out, defying my efforts to temper it.

Ingvar's eyes widened with shock, then softened with concern.

I'd said too much. All this stalling and misdirection and courtly intrigue — damn it, I was so done with all of it. I broke away from Ingvar and stalked the rest of the way to my room, where I darted inside and leaned against the door to shut it behind me.

Nighttime temperatures had plunged even lower, filling my room with icy air. The solitary candle beside my pallet cast just enough light to reveal my coat and weapons resting nearby. Still there, good. I was alone, also a relief. Maybe Sigrid intended to arrive later in the evening, when more people were asleep.

Grief welled, but anger kept it contained. I closed my eyes and took deep breaths, trying to rein it all in. If I kept falling apart every time Gules came to mind, I'd never get anywhere. This early line of communication with Ingvar was too promising to shut down.

Hell — but I just had, hadn't I? Slamming a door on someone was pretty final.

A shamed flush rose to my face, warming it past the chill. Was he still out in the corridor, or was he long gone by now? Could I summon the nerve to check?

Our glimmers of common thought intrigued me. I really needed a like-minded ally in this place. Hoping I hadn't driven off my only chance at one, I turned and opened the door a crack.

Ingvar stood across the hall from my room, gaze detached, possibly waiting or deliberating. When my door opened, he lowered his folded arms and looked me in the eye with that persistent concern.

My heart jumped. Relief washed over me. "I'm sorry. It's been a rough few days," I explained. "I'm not *trying* to be evasive, I just … I can't talk about how I landed this quest right now. Maybe later."

"No apology needed." He seemed sincere, which I appreciated. "Still want to come to the barracks?"

Oh, right. That was where we were ostensibly headed; we'd just come up here for my coat. Given how badly I'd faltered, it was tempting to bail and attempt a fresh start in the morning, but I was too curious about Nidaros, its problems, *and* Ingvar.

"Yes, I do." I opened the door wider. "Are you sure you want me there? You didn't sound very enthusiastic before," I tacked on for no good reason. The embarrassed flush returned to my face, which he'd fortunately have a hard time seeing in the dimness.

"Aye." His gaze dropped to his feet as he braced the back of his neck with one hand. "Only if ye want to."

Suspicion crept up on me again. His initial invitation in the dining hall had been delivered with all the joy of someone having a tooth pulled. This one was rapidly turning uncomfortable for him as well. So what were his real motives?

Studying him closer, I got a nervous vibe, not a duplicitous one. Hold on, how often did he invite *women* to his barracks? Talking with the kitchen servants earlier, it was obvious knights errant didn't show up in Nidaros often, much less female knights errant. Maybe that was it.

"Yes, I do." I offered a disarming smile, amused at our circular conversation. "It's pretty rare that I ever want to spend time with the authorities, but hell, I'm an emissary now. That makes me 'the authorities,' too."

Ingvar smirked. "Only as far as I permit, Goose, and don't forget it," he said in a half-sincere warning tone.

Thus settled, I backed away to retrieve and gratefully throw on my coat, rifling through the pockets to confirm my papers, trinkets, and cigarillos were still there. The craving rose up strong the moment I thought about it, and doubled as a nice peace offering. "Want a smoke?" I beckoned Ingvar into my room.

His eyes widened. "Sure." After a moment's hesitation, he stepped inside, leaving the door open behind us.

We both lit cigarillos using the candle by my pallet. Ingvar released his first pull with great relief, keeping his eyes on the floor. "Blood's oath. I recant every ill word I spoke of you, sellsword."

My first draw also relaxed me further. I couldn't suppress a smile. "Stick with 'Goose,' it's kind of cute. There's also Jessamine, or Jess."

Ingvar glanced up at me and snorted. "*Jess*," he sampled as though it tasted like brine. "What kind of name is that for a knight?"

I laughed, once more enjoying his candor. He pronounced the nickname as *Jayce*, which I also found myself liking.

Silence lingered between us on the way downstairs, better than resuming the depressing topic we'd nearly dredged up earlier. In the estate foyer, a footman provided Ingvar with a lantern. Ingvar gestured me outside ahead of him before following.

My breath clouded in the night air regardless of whether I took a draw from my cigarillo. The estate's chill had made me well acclimated to the cold. I kept pace with Ingvar, staying inside the spark of light he carried. Above stretched a clear sky filled with stars, an alien sight to me, but undoubtedly familiar to him.

Ingvar caught me glancing upward. Outside, he seemed more comfortable breaking the silence. "How many of those ye been to?"

"A lot." Possibly an exotic prospect to him — or not? "Have you ever left Nidaros?" I asked, flicking ash aside.

"Once." Bitterness edged Ingvar's tone, while his eyes narrowed. "This place may not seem much to you, Goose, but 'tis everything to me. Can't imagine leaving it behind, going unmoored."

"I understand that," I assured him.

Ingvar frowned. "How?"

His suspicion prompted my smile. "I haven't been hopping planets all my life. I didn't even choose this calling for myself. But once I started helping people, I haven't wanted to stop."

"How d'ye help people?" Ingvar was curious, not derisive. "Honestly? None of that bull about monsters, now."

My heart sped up at his request. I babbled with only partial awareness of the words leaving my mouth. "Well, you'd be surprised how many monster stories come about when some poor critter wanders into a settlement, or sneaks aboard a ship and ends up on a planet where no one's ever seen such a thing. So sometimes there's a kernel of truth there, but you'd better *believe* it gets blown out of proportion. Those animals become dragons and ogres and giants after the fact." I rolled my eyes.

"People lap up that tripe," Ingvar agreed. "Don't understand it."

"Me either, but, back to your question. Sometimes, I relocate those 'monsters.' I've also raised funds to pay off peoples' back taxes, and shown people how to filter their drinking water so it wouldn't make them sick anymore." I felt heady enough to add, "I can even perform minor healing, no magic involved. If you know anyone who's hurt or sick, I'd be happy to look in on them."

"No magic?" Ingvar's jaw dropped. "Ye mean no charms or potions?"

"Or spells, or wishes, or any of that," I confirmed.

"*What*, then?"

"Whatever the situation calls for."

Ingvar frowned. "Some kind of ritual depending on the injury?"

"Not ritual. *Procedure*," I corrected.

"What sort of witchery is that?"

"It's not. No magic, remember?" I grinned.

He glanced at me sidelong. "If ye insist, Goose."

Ingvar seemed interested in such a thing being possible, but also skeptical. Such a rare, enviable, admirable attitude. I was eager to find out just how far his skepticism stretched.

Fire glowed from the barracks' windows as we approached, lending an unusual coziness to what was ostensibly a military structure. Ingvar led me up to an entrance in the middle of the building.

We stepped into a smoky, pleasant warmth. Benches, tables, and hooks stood nearby; otherwise, the unobstructed entrance gave visitors ample space to remove their gear. The barracks stretched both left and right of us, almost mirror images on each side. Capping the long room at both ends were a pair of hearths, each boasting a cheery fire. Bunks lined the wooden walls. Between some of them stood doors: presumably officers' quarters, or maybe holding cells. Soldiers lounged around candles, bantering or playing card games. Some wore armor and Catherwood tunics, awaiting their next shift or fresh from returning. Everyone seemed relaxed here, in the company of friends who were more like family. That wasn't a sentiment I was used to pairing with a barracks. My surprise gave way to a pleasant appreciation.

We crushed out our cigarillos outside. Ingvar rested his extinguished lantern on a table beside the door. Still thawing out, I kept my coat on, following Ingvar as he advanced to the middle of the floor.

Young men from one end of the barracks to the other quieted and bolted to their feet. Far more eyes fixed upon me than their captain, their gazes ranging from caution to suspicion.

"As ye were, lads!" Ingvar called out, his tone more elder brother than superior officer. "Our visiting knight's seen fit to spend time with us. She'll be starting a cask of coronation ale. Want some, ye'll have to come over and introduce yourself."

Pontus emerged from the collection of bunks to approach us, smiling. In his hands were a small wooden keg and a single cone-shaped vessel, probably a drinking cup.

Many of the suspicious looks turned wide-eyed instead, riveted upon the cask Pontus bore past. None of the soldiers returned "as they were." A few exchanged murmurs. I could imagine this was a big deal, a surprise for them and me.

"What do you need me to do?" I whispered to Ingvar.

He tossed his head toward one of the hearths. "I'll explain."

One soldier worked up the nerve to jog up to Ingvar with an anxious expression. "Sir? Something I need to talk to you about. Privately."

"Rigg?" Pontus spun back with a warning look for the young man. "Come with me."

"But, sir?" Rigg's gaze pleaded with Ingvar. He really wanted his captain's ear for whatever reason.

"All right, lad, no problem. Let's talk." Ingvar threw a glance my way bearing no apology, just acknowledgement.

I didn't mind. Hell, I was glad to see him putting his men first.

"Pontus, show her a seat," Ingvar said.

"My pleasure, sir."

Ingvar put a hand on Rigg's shoulder and steered him toward one of the doors, grabbing a candle en route. The other soldiers were good enough to pretend not to notice.

Pontus beckoned me toward one of the benches surrounding the hearth. It was spaced far enough away from the fire to be warmed by it, but not painfully so. A pair of singed and dented shields flanked the hearth, Catherwood's seal just visible on their surfaces. Each looked like it'd spared several lives apiece. Little offerings rested on the floor beneath each shield, mostly grass woven into star and spiral shapes, possibly to garner luck for future battles. The absence of food and alco-holic offerings further underscored their scarcity at the moment.

Close to the hearth's base lay boots, tunics, and trousers, spread out to dry. Another young soldier weaved through the maze they created to stoke the fire.

Pontus knelt and set the cask, already tapped, on the bench beside me. In a hospitable mood, I shed my coat, then silently offered him my cigarillos and tinderbox.

"Ah! Too kind, Dame Jessamine! One moment." Pontus drew some ale into the small cup and handed it to me.

"Thanks. Am I drinking to anything in particular?" I asked.

"Whatever ye see fit to toast," Pontus explained. "Then empty it for the next to partake."

As far as I could tell, Pontus would be next. A glance over my shoulder confirmed the other soldiers had taken cover behind their bunks, peeking out toward the hearth. Ingvar's ale-bait wasn't enough to tempt them over. Even the soldier stoking the fire made every effort not to look our way.

"First into battle, last to introduce themselves to a pretty girl." Pontus smirked with the warmth of a teasing uncle. "They'll come around."

I had my doubts their hesitation had anything to do with shyness, given the way my escort had behaved toward me earlier in the day. Wariness toward foreigners most likely, maybe with sexism thrown in. After all, there wasn't a single woman within the barracks. Ingvar's and Pontus' relative age and stature had probably helped make them more enlightened than their charges, who may never have left Nidaros in their lives. I knew for certain that Ingvar had left the planet once, though he seemed not to have enjoyed the trip.

While I had no control over the soldiers' opinions, I could seek favor in small ways. Pontus had just provided one opportunity. I stood with my glass raised toward the remainder of the barracks. "To Nidaros." A few drafts killed off the ale: spicy, but pleasantly so.

Pontus refilled the cup. "I echo your toast, and add to it your safety." He clenched the beads at his side for good measure.

We both lit cigarillos. Pontus sat to my left, leaving a large gap between us.

The young soldier stoking the fire tossed in a piece of rough wood, then shook out his hand with a curse.

Here was a chance to be of actual help. I walked up to the fire with the excuse of flicking ash into it. "Splinter?"

The soldier pinched the skin under his thumb, frowning at the wound.

"May I have a look?" I gestured toward the bench.

"Drink with us, Ebbe," Pontus called.

Ebbe's head jerked back up at the sound of his superior's voice. "Aye, all right." He sounded unconvinced, but preceded me to the bench regardless.

I let him get his ale first. He gathered his beads in hand to murmur over it before throwing it back.

"Supposed to introduce yourself first, Ebbe," Pontus chided around a mouthful of smoke, amused.

"Oh, right. Ebbe Madsen. Welcome." He dropped to a seat at my left with a smile the ale had coaxed to the surface.

"Jessamine Irless. Thanks." I smiled back. "Now for your hand."

I straddled the bench to face him directly, which encouraged Ebbe to mirror my action. Over Ebbe's shoulder, Pontus observed with continued amusement.

"Oh, lots of splinters." I tilted Ebbe's calloused palm toward the firelight, squinting. "You're lucky I have tweezers with me."

I dug through the first aid kit on my belt to retrieve them. "You can have a smoke after I'm done, if you want."

"Aye, sure!" Ebbe said.

"Have ye tried one of these before, Ebbe?" Pontus' tone was loaded with doubt.

"Uh, nay, sir." Ebbe shrank at the voice behind him in an endearing fashion.

"Hold off, then, lest ye want to be joining Fasolt in hacking up a lung." Pontus rose to his feet to tap ash into the fire himself.

I lowered my voice as Pontus returned, not wanting it to carry through the barracks. "The soldier who first escorted me when I arrived here, he was coughing a lot. Was that Fasolt, by chance?"

"Aye. He's watching the port during daylight this week. Hiding back there somewhere right now with the rest of these cowering pups." Still standing, Pontus raised his voice to taunt further. "I have a five year-old at home braver than the lot of you!"

I grinned. "You don't live here, then?"

"I'd go crazy if I did." Pontus grinned back, slowly lowering himself to a seat. "My wife'd take offense besides."

"Just means more drink for us. Right, sir?" Ebbe chanced a smile my way, which melted into confusion as the tweezers appeared in my hands.

"See what our captain says. More likely we save the rest for another special occasion, though what could be more special than a visiting knight?" Pontus' grin persisted.

To build up Ebbe's confidence, I extracted the easiest splinters first. "How's that so far?"

"I've dug holes in my skin taking them out myself! Ye're a lot better at it." Ebbe dropped his voice to a near-whisper, just audible over the crackling fire. "Dumb adepts would just mumble over it and call it a day."

I smiled again. "I know this hurts, but it's a hell of a lot better than letting them sit in there."

Ebbe's blue eyes went wide enough to show whites all the way around. "Didn't expect a foreigner to invoke Hel!"

"Ebbe," Pontus warned.

"We might not be talking about the same place," I said. "The hell of Lord Turinger's doctrine is where the dead suffer forever if they've upset the Unseen."

"That's ... *awful.*" Ebbe frowned, continuing in a whisper. "Our Hel's just a void of shadow, but we shouldn't talk about it."

"Gyllenfeld doctrine?" I chanced, remembering how reluctant Sigrid had been to answer my questions along those lines.

Ebbe nodded.

We could switch to a less taboo subject. "Meanwhile, Catherwood doctrine says no one ever really dies, right?"

"There's always some next purpose." Ebbe leaned in even closer, speaking into my ear. "Have to admit, me and a bunch of the others, we'd rather die with swords in hand and go to Folkvang."

Afterlives of eternal reward did sound nice. I *wanted* something like that to be real, but I knew it wasn't. At least, not any of the dozens of realms I'd heard professed as absolute truth with nothing but conviction to back the claims.

"I understand, but no rush, all right?" I whispered back in Ebbe's ear.

Ebbe grinned, shaking his head.

"Lady Knight, welcome. Magnus Holmvik."

Ebbe and I glanced up. Another soldier had approached the bench, this one closer to my age, with a confident air that made it strange he'd hesitated this long.

"Hello, Magnus." I suspended my efforts to shake his hand.

"Well done, lad! Good to see Ebbe's not the only one here

with a spine and manners. Help yourself!" Pontus passed him the same cup to drink from.

Magnus knelt before the cask. "What's that ye're up to, Ebbe?"

"She's saving my hands here," Ebbe replied.

"You might want to wear gloves from now on when you tend the fire," I said.

"Don't ye already do that, fool?" Magnus egged. He claimed a seat between Ebbe and Pontus, one booted foot perched on the bench. "Ah well, I don't wear mine often enough for drills. My hands are all calloused."

"Like your skull," Ebbe shot back with a grin.

"Believe I said something about *manners*, gentlemen?" Pontus hovered over the younger soldiers with a smirk. "Still applies."

"Well, manners are important, but should never stand in the way of a good rejoinder," I said.

Pontus laughed. "Ye'll fit right in with this outfit."

The bravery of these young men, paired with the lure of ale and smoke-ribbons curling into the air, slowly brought around many of the remaining soldiers. Each introduced himself and secured one helping of ale; no one sought a second. Most were teenaged, maybe a little past, like Ebbe. Pontus stood out, but aside from the occasional gentle admonishment, he was one of the gang, just far more tempered.

The gathering outgrew the benches before the fireplace. Latecomers happily piled in, standing or sitting. Still, a few holdouts lingered among the shadowed bunks. I recognized my escort Fasolt out there, occasionally muffling a cough as he looked on with distrust.

It was a nice sort of attention, one that made me feel more esteemed than nervous. My cigarillos attracted a lot of attention as well, being entirely new to most of the soldiers. A few experimented with lighting and smoking one, only to go down hacking as Pontus had predicted, to the immense amusement of their brothers-in-arms.

"Takes time to acquire a tolerance," Pontus explained, throwing the stub of his cigarillo into the fire.

"And, admittedly, there are better things to spend your money on." I'd already discarded mine in the same manner.

"Cred aren't really useful here, Lady Knight," Ebbe said, still perched proudly on my left, though I'd finished with his hand some time earlier.

"No?" I asked.

"The guild brings us things every harvest," Magnus jumped in to explain. "People all get an equal share, and barter if they're looking for more or less of something."

"Trade usually takes place within capital walls, but that's suspended right now," Pontus said. "Travel between districts is too dangerous, given all the predators wandering in from the wilderness."

He didn't mention it, but I supposed they also didn't want large numbers of hungry, disgruntled people hanging around the capital. "I saw a group of adepts traveling out to the districts earlier today, though. What were they doing?" I asked.

"That must've been a disbursement of rations," Pontus replied.

So that was why the protesters had quieted upon seeing them. I couldn't remember how well the adepts had been armed, but then again, they had "magic" to defend themselves with.

"Got any questing stories, Lady Knight?" someone asked, prompting eager goading from the rest of the group.

I faltered. I *really* wasn't in the mood to spin more lies, especially not before these likable young men.

"Jackals, the lot of you!" Ingvar called out from a distance, jogging up quickly thereafter. Less conspicuous was Rigg, the soldier who'd accosted him earlier, who made a beeline for the entrance and slipped outside. Their expressions gave away no hint as to what their meeting had been about.

The soldiers jumped to their feet, calling out greetings to Ingvar. I stood with them—it would've felt awkward otherwise—and smiled as he approached. "Welcome back."

Ingvar nodded to me, working to grasp each of the many hands stretched out to him. "Expected the knight to be telling you of her adventures. Here ye're talking *her* ear off!"

"I like having a chance to listen for once." In truth, I was having a better time and feeling more comfortable than I'd ever expected to.

The toasting cup made its way into Ingvar's hands; he knelt and drew himself some ale. When he stood, the barracks went silent but for the fires at either end. "To Nidaros, and all her defenders!"

He never so much as looked at the beads on his belt. No one seemed to notice, or mind, as they echoed his sentiment with eardrum-rattling cheers. I sure noticed, though, with elation. Maybe he truly didn't care about "magic" or superstition.

The gathering settled back in. Ingvar chose a seat on my right, then leaned toward the group with interest, elbow on his knee. "How was it out there today, lads?"

"Aside from Dame Jessamine, and the gate crashers? Boring," one soldier replied.

"Must be better than all the shadow-chasing out in the districts," another soldier said. "Everything's a witch or a monster! When a *real* witch or monster shows up, it'll eat me alive 'cause I won't believe it's there."

"Handle every report seriously, lad," Ingvar said, "but if ye're too worn down, let's talk about trading your shifts with anyone who sayeth the word 'boring.'" He threw a pointed glance toward the first soldier, prompting snickers from the gathering.

"Are the adepts helping you?" Ingvar asked, settling them down.

"Mostly, sir," another said. "Sometimes they muscle us out, say we should leave things to them."

"Keep a close eye on what they're giving out to everyone, aye? Make sure 'tis really fair. Tell the adepts ye've orders to hunt down contraband, if ye must." Ingvar straightened. "Anything else?"

He waited for a short pause, filled with silence.

"If there *is* any real action, ye'll be wishing for 'boring' again right quick. Aye?" Ingvar glanced to me.

I smiled. "Definitely."

"Go on, Lady Knight. Ye must be scrapping all the time!" one of the soldiers called out.

"Wait, *does* she fight? Where's her sword?" someone else asked.

Apparently, some doubt existed as to what a *lady* knight did. I smiled in the direction the question had come from. "My side sword's back at the Baron's estate. I didn't want to scare you with it."

That prompted a laugh from the others.

"Side sword?" another soldier asked.

"It's a little shorter than a longsword, and one-handed," I explained. "That makes it good for cutting *and* thrusting. I'm all right with longsword too, though."

"Shoot with anything?" another asked.

"Oh! Fight with pistols at all?" Ebbe piped up beside me.

"No," I answered. "I don't even know anyone who can afford firearms."

"We don't have any either, but we have longswords. Show us your skill!" someone else requested.

The suggestion sent excited chatter through the crowd.

"Wee thing like that, could she even hold up the blade?" another soldier wondered, eliciting a few incredulous laughs.

"Knock it off, lads," Ingvar stepped in, eyes narrowed. "She's traveled a long way, probably tired from how late ye're keeping her up."

"But they've been so hospitable." I shrugged with a smile, pretending I hadn't heard the doubting remarks. "I'll oblige."

"*Ye* take her, sir!" someone egged Ingvar.

Whether curious to watch me fight or watch me fail at it, all of the younger soldiers erupted in vocal enthusiasm over the idea of putting their captain in the middle of the spectacle.

"Quiet down!" Pontus barked over the noise.

Ingvar glanced my way, his eyes begging apology, and leaned in close to be heard. "I'll shut them up and change the subject."

"It's all right. I still don't mind if you don't." I heard too much taunting, too regularly, to be fazed by it. And while I was no great fighter, a demonstration would be more fun than dodging requests for questing stories all night long.

"Certain? I mean, I don't doubt ye're capable," Ingvar rushed to add, "more that *no one* deserveth being put on the spot by these fools of mine."

I smiled. "As long as it's not a full-contact spar."

"Nay," he agreed, smiling back. "A few test strikes, no contact."

I nodded.

Ingvar stood, raising his voice. "All right! One exchange, then to bed with anyone not up for a shift."

An approving cheer went up in response. Most of young soldiers reoriented themselves toward the center of the barracks, while a pair of them bolted for weapons chests to dig out longswords. At least the ceiling stood high enough to accommodate the swing of that larger blade. I left my coat by the fire, but put on my gloves.

Ingvar led me to a space well away from the hearth, where we accepted our weapons and squared off for the animated crowd's benefit. Donning his own heavy leather gloves, Ingvar tilted his head toward Pontus, who shouted the gathering down to an attentive silence.

"Soundeth like some of you think there are knights errant out there who can't wield a sword for some reason, so now our visiting knight'll prove different," Ingvar addressed. "'Tis a demonstration, not a spar. *Dead slow, half strength,*" he cautioned me and our audience at the same time. "Neither of us is wearing armor."

I wore my brigandine, but it didn't look like conventional armor. The point remained valid. Nervousness didn't touch me; I was used to performing, and Ingvar's concern for safety put me even more at ease. I took the longsword grip in both hands, brought the guard up beside my head, and settled into my stance: weapon back, different from the one I used with my side sword. Longsword was more about power, reach, and leverage than speed. It'd been Branigan's favored weapon. He was the one who'd taught me what I knew about it.

"Your move." Across from me, Ingvar had stepped back into a low closed guard. The crowd held its breath, awaiting my next word or action.

I cleared my head before my wandering thoughts got me in trouble. "My master, Sir Mayweather Stark, taught me to stay on the offense," I addressed everyone in the room, "and if I should lose that edge, to get it right back." I gestured to Ingvar with a dip of my blade. "So let's say *you* have the advantage, Captain. Come at me, throw whatever strikes you want."

Ingvar obliged slowly, as promised: first with a thrust, which I stepped back and batted aside. This wasn't a strong counter on my part, more of a retreat. I countered his second thrust the same way.

From a high guard, Ingvar then swiveled his blade at my head. I blocked and backpedaled with an overwrought cry, like I was entirely out of my depth. At a distance, I dropped the tip of my sword to the ground and hunched over, further projecting an image of vulnerability.

Unlike most of the people I'd baited in that fashion over the years, whose egos had happily assured them of victory, Ingvar paused and stared me right in the eye. "There's her trap, lads." For the sake of demonstration, he nonetheless advanced and went for the obvious overhead strike to my skull.

I stepped aside, at the same time levering my blade straight up with force. My blade knocked Ingvar's askew, leaving his head open. Having captured the advantage, I brought my blade back down a few inches short of his skull.

The soldiers jumped to their feet with rowdy applause.

Ingvar straightened with a smile, offering a hand to shake. Grinning, I lowered my blade and shook firmly.

"All right, sack time! *Move!*" Pontus bellowed, herding soldiers toward the bunks as he plowed through the gathering.

Amid the chaos, Ingvar drew close to be heard. "Not bad, Goose. I want my men to be vigilant against that kind of thing." He took my longsword, and turned to stow both blades in the nearest weapons chest.

I stood still, lost in thought. May had taught me his devious ways with the one-handed weapons he'd favored. Branigan had never used tricks like that, he'd never needed to. Being shorter and weaker, however, I required every advantage I could pull from various dark crevices.

"Like strays ye fed. Ye'll never be rid of them." Ingvar returned to my side, tossing his head after his men. His amusement was hard to miss. "Sorry some of them doubted you."

I shook off my reverie. "They don't seem to doubt me anymore. They're very nice, and I was impressed by their restraint at the gate when those Gyllenfeld dissidents showed up. They're a credit to you, Captain."

"Ingvar." He gestured back toward the hearth, now empty but for the remaining ale and drying clothes. "Want to talk a while longer?" He glanced askance, almost shy. "'Course, mayhap ye *are* tired. Shouldn't keep you up."

Sitting up late talking, just the two of us? I surprised myself by liking the idea. I honestly wanted to get to know Ingvar better, having seen glimpses of his incisiveness and compassion. Even more important, this offer was *much* more sincere than the one that'd initially brought me to the barracks. It made me jittery, in a good way. I smiled around my nerves. "I'm not that tired. Let's talk."

Out of nowhere, a suffocating wave of guilt crashed down over my courage and happiness. What the *hell* was I doing? Having fun and chatting it up while Drea, the Naustviks, and everyone else suffered? Shouldn't I be trying to help them?

It must've been plastered all over my face. Ingvar's expression filled with worry. "Something wrong?"

"Actually, maybe I should get back," I muttered past knotted insides. Without another look Ingvar's way, I darted toward the bench where my coat rested, snatched it up, and hurried outside.

CHAPTER 9

Once I'd rushed out of the barracks, the cold nighttime void tore into my exposed skin like sandpaper.

Drea has it worse right now, I reminded myself. The horrible feeling in my gut persisted. I threw my coat over my shoulders, running toward the lights outlining the Baron's estate. In my haste to flee, I hadn't thought to grab a lantern, but couldn't bring myself to turn back for one. In solitude, I could use my stick lighter for navigation without anyone questioning my "magic relic."

Guilt and despair hounded me without reprieve. Messing around with Ingvar and his soldiers while Drea and Nidaros wasted away? Time to refocus on what mattered. I was *sick* of failing to reach people before it was too late to save them.

Unfortunately, there was nothing to be done for Drea at the moment. What about Thordia and Verahl Naustvik, suffering needlessly as scapegoats? Thordia's whereabouts were unknown. Verahl was supposed to be in the dungeon beneath the adepts' keep, subject to unthinkable torture.

Was there any chance of freeing him? What would it take to enter the dungeon? There had to be an entrance inside the keep, but I didn't know where, or what was required to best it.

What about a back door? Assuming the dungeon had been dug out under the keep in more recent times—the Ship-builders sure hadn't included torture and detainment facilities in their floor plans—an outside entrance might still stand wherever the excavation had been started.

I was already outside, approaching the keep. Why not see whether the hunch was valid? It was the best time to check: a rare unescorted moment. I wouldn't be plunging in yet, just sizing up my options.

Within the adepts' keep, candlelight flickered behind swelling curtains, less a sign of safe harbor and more a threat of surveillance. Upon reaching the capital buildings, I darted into the rain barrel-strewn courtyard between the keep and the Baron's estate. Lighter pointed downward, I skirted the keep wall.

Toward the rear of the building rested a pair of thick iron doors built into the ground, locked in place. A young soldier leaned against the wall, eyes narrowed like he was about to nod off, his nearby lantern outlining him clearly.

That *probably* led to the dungeon; I didn't know for certain. I also didn't know how extensive the dungeon was, where Ver-ahl was inside of it, or what obstacles stood between me and him. But if there was a soldier on watch, the soldiers probably knew. Soldiers also happened to be the ones guarding the gate that led out of the capital.

I might not have to finesse any adepts at all.

Heart pounding eagerly, I backed away before the soldier spotted me, then hastened back toward the entrance of the Baron's estate. It sure looked possible to free Verahl with just the soldiers' help, assuming I hadn't sabotaged my own good-will with Ingvar.

A new wave of guilt crashed over me. Only then did I real-ize how badly I'd behaved toward a potentially valuable ally. I resolved to apologize in the morning, hoping I hadn't driven Ingvar off completely.

I returned to the dim, silent estate and headed directly to my room. Sigrid might still show up there to compare notes. If not, there'd be ample time to think about how a jailbreak might work. Given a full mind and empty stomach, sleep would be elusive.

In the stairwell leading up to my room, Alfrun's earlier plea came to mind, her fear that Thordia practiced witchcraft late at night from high above. I paused and craned my neck upward for a good while, but saw nothing unusual.

That's what I thought.

Something held me down, and it wasn't the straps that usually kept me in my bunk. Bright light pierced my closed eyelids. Hell, what was *that?* It seemed as though the artificial lighting had gone nova.

I chanced opening my eyes a sliver. Oh, I wasn't aboard *Kepler's Law* mid-cruise. This was my room at the Baron's estate, with warm sunlight pouring through the window. Gravity held me down on my pallet, nothing else.

A strong hunger asserted itself, bringing back the full mess that'd led to Nidaros. Branigan was dead. Drea was stranded. I was millions of miles away, and couldn't go back. The terror of a nightmare paralyzed me. In solitude, my emotions threatened to spill over.

Then, Sigrid burst right into the room like she owned the place, approaching the pallet's edge. "There you are!" she half-scolded.

I gave a start. "Knock next time, all right?" I snapped, too groggy to keep the annoyance out of my tone.

"Well, I never seem to know when you're actually here," she said with false-ringing gaiety. "Come on up, I'll make your bed."

My limbs obeyed Sigrid of their own accord, dragging the rest of me off the pallet. "I'm sorry about last night. My plans often change at a moment's notice." I honestly wasn't that sorry. The barracks had been fun, up until I'd fouled that up.

"We can speak now, I suppose." Sigrid leaned past me to fuss with the bedclothes. "What've you learned since yesterday?"

I stumbled toward the chair holding my coat and piled-up weapons. My boots rested on the floor beside them. "I'm still trying to figure that out myself." Something about her eagerness nagged at me. I was reluctant to entrust her with side-chores or inside information.

Sigrid darted over to my boots first, kneeling to attack dried mud with a brush in her hand. "What will you be doing today?"

Good question. The Baron had ordered me to report to Ormyr, at his keep. Aside from looking into my chief areas of concern, I also wanted to visit my ship for food, to share my stores with everyone.

"Attending to a private matter for the Baron." I was curious to see what she'd do with this minor fib, where it might spread, and how it mutated in the process.

Sigrid masked a flash of surprise with a smile, grasping her beads. "I wish you both well!"

Once I'd stepped into my boots, Sigrid helped me into my coat, smoothing out the wrinkles. My belt and baldric went on last, weapons included. The effects of gravity adjustment had worn off, helping me feel stronger despite my plagued thoughts.

There was a knock at the door. "Dame Jessamine is decent. Come in!" Sigrid called, still fussing with me.

The door swung open, revealing Ingvar. He'd changed into work clothes as well: leather armor topped with steel pauldrons, vambraces, greaves, and a full Catherwood tabard. A longsword hung from a frog at his side. His wishing beads were still wound on his belt, out of his way.

My heart raced for no good reason. What was he doing here? Oh, right, Baron Tristan had ordered him to escort me to the adepts' keep. Remorseful, I made hesitant eye contact. Was he upset about last night? He didn't seem to be. *Concerned*, if anything. He cut an even more dashing figure in uniform.

Stop that, I scolded myself.

"Captain Leirfall!" Sigrid smiled to him, then flashed me a mischievous smile, then made herself scarce.

Ingvar admitted faint amusement in her wake before returning his attention to me. In one hand, he proffered the cigarillos and tinderbox I'd forgotten at the barracks.

"Oh. Thanks." I approached the threshold to collect and drop everything into my coat pockets. "Come in."

He stepped inside. I shut the door behind him, then turned, but guilt kept my eyes attached to my feet. "I'm sorry about last night, Captain. That was no way to act after a nice evening. Thanks again for the invitation."

"Ingvar," he corrected, as before.

I'd forgotten that too. "Right. Ingvar."

"Jayce?"

At the unusual address, my eyes jumped up of their own accord to meet his.

Ingvar's expression remained steeped in gentle concern. "'Tis plain something terrible happened afore ye came here. Want to talk about it? Not meaning to pry, just that getting it out can help you past it."

His sympathy seemed genuine, and it floored me. Why did he care? My heart's pace refused to flag. Having seen how much his men trusted him, venting to him probably wouldn't lead to trouble. Hadn't we already vented some pretty damning things to one another? Still …

"I'm not ready," I muttered. Face burning with shame, I turned and walked up to the window, the furthest extent our confines allowed, adjusting how my baldric sat on my shoulder even though it didn't need adjusting. The craving for a smoke ratcheted higher. The only thing stopping me was that I couldn't use my stick lighter with Ingvar present. I'd have to turn back around and unpack my tinderbox, and I couldn't bring myself to look him in the eye.

"Could I access the computer aboard the Baron's ship for coordinates?" I blurted. I'd just realized, maybe he'd be able to help me with Drea.

Ingvar paused at the out-of-nowhere question. "Not something I have any authority over. *I'm* not allowed aboard that vessel."

Hell. Disappointment hardened in my gut. I'd have to track down someone who *was* allowed. Ormyr, probably. Now that was a discussion I dreaded.

"Looking for the fastest way out of here, Goose?" Humor laced Ingvar's tone.

"I said I was here to help, and I meant it," I replied, more chastising myself than correcting him. It'd be nice if I actually worked toward that, wouldn't it? My eyes stuck to the window, searching for fields invisible from my vantage point. "Have you seen the crop trouble yourself?"

"Aye." He handled my segue without a hitch.

"What happens, exactly? How do the crops fail?"

Ingvar advanced until he stood at my left, arms folded, peering out the window himself. "Started with good crops drying up for no reason," he explained in a dejected tone. "Now, seeds won't take root. Began in the North and East, spread from there."

"Spread?" I glanced up at him in surprise. "Some kind of pestilence, then?"

His eyes narrowed. "Nay, our wells've dried up too. Don't know a sickness to cause that."

Right, I'd seen that yesterday in the courtyard. The disused well, the parched grass nearby … and this strange state of affairs had *spread* from one end of the barony to the other? None of this sounded familiar to me; I really needed to see those crops for myself. In the meantime, I could vet the information the kitchen servants had shared yesterday, and gauge just how closely Ingvar's thoughts aligned with mine.

"What's your best guess as to what's wrong?" I paused there, waiting to see what he'd offer without me leading him.

Ingvar faced me. Weariness aged him a decade in the space of moments. "I'm not some adept with a ready tale of curse or oblivion. Can only say what no one else will: I haven't a damned clue."

My pulse quickened again at this refreshingly honest lack of nonsense. "So you don't think Thordia and Verahl Naustvik are to blame?"

Ingvar reared back, his arms unfolding and tensing at his sides. Horror rooted him in place, as though I'd just exposed his most forbidden thoughts, and he didn't know what to brace for next.

His reaction confirmed his skepticism. Thrill coursed through me, but didn't blind me to his fear. I spoke with as much calm reassurance as possible. "It's all right. I don't think it's their fault either." I couldn't help pushing it further. "A witch hunt won't solve anything. There *are* no witches. Magic and Unseen *aren't real.*"

Ingvar unfroze just enough for a tremor to course through him. His eyes searched mine frantically. "Damned brave, or foolish, saying that to someone ye've known only a short while."

"After last night, I feel like we can be honest with each other without dying for it." I smiled a little. "Even if you *did* kill me, what would it solve? You'd wake up just as hungry tomorrow."

"Keep things like that quiet here, aye?" Ingvar leaned close to whisper, eyes darting toward the chamber door even though it stood closed. "People may like you now, but wait'll they suspect heresy."

"I'll stop talking about it. We know where we stand now." He couldn't bring himself to explicitly agree with me, but he didn't have to. "Let's focus on the Naustviks instead. Thordia's missing, and Verahl's in the dungeon below the keep. Right?"

"Aye." Ingvar frowned, confused.

"It's not fair for an innocent man to be tortured, or an innocent woman to be on the lam. Is it?" I asked.

A twinge of guilt strained Ingvar's expression before he regained his composure. "Naustvik's not my prisoner, but Ormyr's. There's naught I can do for him."

"Are you sure about that? There's an outdoor entrance to the dungeon toward the rear of the keep, isn't there?" I waited to see if he corrected me.

"Aye." Ingvar's expression turned increasingly stern.

"And doesn't one of your men guard it?"

"Only stationed there in case of emergency. We're not allowed in the dungeon otherwise."

Damn. "Does he have a key for the doors?"

Ingvar's eyes pleaded with mine. "Where in Hel is this going? Spit it out."

I did so, with conviction. "I want to break Verahl out of the dungeon. Then your men at the gate can let him out of the capital."

This was Ingvar's second great shock of the morning, but this time, a furious scowl overtook his alarm. "Ye keep saying ye want to help us. *This* is what ye mean by 'help?' *Skíta!*" He backpedaled away from the window, toward the closed door.

"Verahl did nothing wrong!" I cried, darting after him. "All he did was stand up to the adepts. If I have to explain why a brother would protect his sister, you've got more problems than this crop failure!"

Ingvar halted in his tracks, staring at me with wide-eyed reluctance.

I stopped in front of him, certain he had a conscience I could reach. "Please, just open a couple of doors and look the other way. I'll figure out the rest. If I get caught, I'll say I acted alone."

Ingvar seemed to deliberate with himself for a few moments. Then, he clamped down on my shoulders and pulled me over to the pallet we stood beside. He sat us both down sideways so our swords wouldn't catch on the edge.

"Jayce, listen." His intense stare pleaded for understanding. "Ye can be honest with me, 'tis true. I need you to be honest with yourself as well, about where this is coming from. Ye've been here a day. Ye don't know Naustvik. Wherefore would ye take on such risk? Seemeth to me like there's something ye want to atone for or absolve yourself from."

I quivered with frustration stored up since Gules. Damn it, he was good, but I couldn't admit it. Defensiveness rose up instead, tarnishing his words in my ears. "I'm *not* making this about me." My former master had been selfish like that. I wasn't.

"That's not what I mean," Ingvar said.

"Verahl is literally suffering under our feet!" I cried, uninterested in his explanation. "And it's not just him! I see so many people like him, accused of horrible things, and it's all nonsense! Most of them, I can't do a damn thing for. If there's a chance I can help Verahl, it's worth taking. He might know where Thordia is. Once I rescue them and pretend to deal with them, Ormyr and the Baron and everyone else will have to face reality!"

Ingvar glanced downward, then looked up at me again with a softened expression, speaking with quiet patience. "Your heart's in the right place. Commendable, but, 'tis not as simple as walking in and out of the dungeon with keys in hand.

We don't know where Naustvik is down there, what state he's in. He might need to be carried out. What then? I've seen him, he's bigger than two of you. Even if ye somehow get him out and find him a place to hide, he'll be forced into hiding the rest of his life, which isn't likely to be long. The rest of the barony will panic. That's fallout we're ill prepared for right now."

I wasn't used to people like him dismantling me with reason. Strong reason, at that, but it failed to chase off the worry and frustration. My gaze dropped to my hands, which had balled into involuntary fists. "I get what you're saying. But if we leave him there, we're giving our assent to whatever happens to him."

"That's rot." Ingvar's grip on my shoulders tightened. "I hate that he's trapped therein, truly, but a breakout causeth more problems than it solveth. I'm sorry."

It was some difficult bile to swallow: first Drea, now Verahl. My heart sank with despair. I kept staring at my fists, digging my fingernails into my palms to stave off any show of emotion.

"Jayce?"

Ingvar's tone prompted me to meet his gaze, full of encouragement.

"I'm trying to help people too," he said. "Would ye be willing to aid me with that?"

I blinked, intrigued. He was offering a compromise, and there was a good chance it'd be constructive. "How?"

"Want more of my lads out in the districts, for one. Not to police, just friendly faces who can intervene in case of trouble. Predators have been encroaching on homes of late, searching for food."

"You have pro-Gyllenfeld dissidents to deal with out there too, right?" I remembered his attitude on the matter from supper, but wanted to confirm it.

Ingvar glanced askance. "I'm not interested in rooting them

out. I don't care what anyone *thinketh*, so long as they do no harm. If they strike first, though, so be it."

Good for you, I thought.

He made eye contact with me again. "Our Baron feareth for anyone to think we're cracking down, so most of my lads are canned up in the capital, doing nothing useful. Ye've got influence as Milord's emissary. Would ye be willing to help me argue for increased patrols?"

"Sure." His motives were good. Admirable, even. "In return, would you be willing to take me out to the districts, show me what's going on? There's a chance that if I identify the crop trouble, I might know how to solve it."

He brightened. "Aye, certainly."

"All right. Let's do that." My heart pounded again, this time with purpose. It was refreshing to have found someone like-minded, someone willing to cooperate to find real solutions.

Ingvar looked relieved for a moment, then sobered again, finally letting go of my shoulders. "Just be careful of Ormyr, aye? He'd love nothing more than to resolve everything himself and make a name big enough to be seen back in Spectra. Doesn't need me or our Baron getting in his way."

"I caught that at supper," I said. "I really don't know what to make of someone kissing up to me, but I know I'm not letting him pull that stalling and misdirection again. We'll be part of the solution whether he likes it or not."

Ingvar jumped to his feet with a smile, offering his hand. "Imagine if *we* get crops growing again! We can force the adepts to give up on the Naustviks."

And a jailbreak would be unnecessary. "That's my hope too," I said, gladly taking Ingvar's hand.

He helped me up, and had me precede him into the hallway.

A cool morning mist had settled over the capital, thin enough to grant a view of the sun climbing through a sky tinged blue on the horizon, edging toward yellow the higher one looked. Dew beaded on the dry grasses we walked through. Occasional shouts and clanging bells pierced the air, their sources hidden. Such a promising morning to be squandering in the adepts' midst, but the prospect of collaborating with Ingvar buoyed my hopes and instilled a sense of purpose.

Ingvar announced our arrival at the keep with several fist-pounds against a featureless panel. Shipbuilder mechanics didn't shuttle it aside, rather an adept with a hood framing her face, who smiled. "Hello, Captain! Lady Knight, an honor. Master Ormyr awaits you in his calefactory. Follow me."

The tall, circular foyer she led us through was arrayed to impress. To me, it resembled the bazaar stall of a shady merchant with an overstock of silks and prosperity totems. Ahead stood four curtained archways, each labeled with letters from the Shipbuilder alphabet. Beside me, Ingvar's eyes narrowed in vexation the moment the adept wasn't looking.

The hallway we entered crushed in on us like a closed fist. Ingvar had me go first, and we followed the hooded adept in single-file. Painted invocations flowed along at eye level to either side. One of them niggled at my memory. *Unseen, abide! Upon Death shall we unite, until my next Purpose comes due: Water, Fire, Breath, or Flesh anew.*

I'd first read that spell on Gules, from the scroll in the dead woman's hand. She'd deserved better, and froze to death wishing for it, along with countless others. And now Drea—

A hand grasped my arm, pulling me backward. Painfully distracted, I'd almost collided with the hooded adept, who'd stopped before a drawn curtain. Ingvar had spared me the embarrassment. He turned me to face his questioning look.

I wasn't about to dredge Gules up any further. I shook my head, freed myself, and faced forward again.

After some silent meditation, the adept parted the curtain

in front of us. Beyond the opening lay another large circular chamber. Waist-high flames roared in a massive hearth, throwing heat all the way across the room to us. Above our heads spanned a mural of the known galaxy. Ribbons, tacked into tortured shapes, divided the stars among a multitude of domains. It didn't accurately represent three-dimensional space, but when all those borders were shifting, disappearing, and respawning on a weekly basis, there wasn't room for criticism.

A polished stone table rested a few feet away, white smoke rising from a brass censer at its center. The room smelled overwhelmingly of cloves. Closer to the fire sat a silken couch. However, no one awaited us at either location. Multiple side-rooms branched off from this one, curtains draped over each. Adepts and servants slipped in and out of them with sullen urgency, treating the calefactory like a no-man's land. A few eyes riveted our way, taking note of our arrival. The adept who'd led us there turned back with one last nod and smile before joining the flurry herself.

Glimpses of the side-rooms appeared as curtains parted. Pots full of dirt, but no plants; adepts whispering to one another in near panic; and what was probably a scrying chamber, but instead of a dowel rod, an adept somberly tracked the motion of a small robotic construct moving about the floor, seemingly of its own will.

I bit my lip hard to avoid laughing. That was no sacred Shipbuilder prognosticator, it was a device for sweeping dirt off the floor. My friends at the beguinage had restored several for use around the buildings there.

Ingvar stepped up beside me to scowl over the calefactory, scraping his heels against the rug beneath our feet. He tossed his head toward one of the curtained rooms to our right. "Come on, that's our Baron's chamber. Mayhap he's in there!" His tone echoed the adepts' haste. He bolted toward the curtain without another word.

Wait, the Baron? I'd thought we were meeting with Ormyr. But maybe Baron Tristan was also there to receive morning rites and such. He seemed a surprisingly good, reasonable person for one of his stature. If we could discuss Nidaros' problems without Ormyr stomping out the Baron's every glimmer of ambition ...

Looking back on the adepts, it seemed *everyone* was desperate to make progress in Ormyr's absence. I followed Ingvar, fully able to relate.

The captain threw back the curtain to expose a tiny chapel with bare walls. Baron Tristan sat alone inside, back in plainclothes, eyes closed over the beads wrapped around his hand. On the table before him, crystals tacked down piles of parchment bearing official paperwork and astral forecasts. Their shadows jumped in the light of the lantern on the table.

Ingvar dropped to one knee. "Your Grace! Apologies, didn't mean to interrupt."

Somehow, I doubted his sincerity. I stepped up beside him, then knelt as well.

"Captain, Dame Jessamine. Arise." The Baron sounded glad to see us. His chair scraped along the ground.

Ingvar and I sprang to our feet before him.

"Your Grace—" Ingvar addressed.

"Sir—" I began at the same time.

We stopped mid-interruption to exchange glances of apology. Hell, we'd never discussed just how we'd go about asking for more soldiers in the districts. I'd assumed it'd happen sometime after our business in the calefactory. We'd both tried to seize the initiative, only to trip over ourselves.

"How farest thou, Lady Knight?" The Baron forged through the pause created by our lack of coordination. "I realize we offer little compared to other realms thou hast visited, especially at present, but is there any lack we may correct?"

The question startled me out of my bull-rush. "Oh. No, sir.

Everything's fine, thank you very much. I'd like to—"

"Dame Jessamine?"

Lady Amelia's voice issued from behind. I turned to find her stepping out from an identical threshold on the other side of the calefactory, also in humbler raiment than the night before, beads clasped at her waist.

"I would to speak with thee," she told me.

Just then, Ormyr burst into the calefactory from the side-room beside the Baron's, bowing at the waist with a self-satisfied look. "Ah, I see everyone is present!"

Hell. So much for cornering Baron Tristan. I forced my disappointment behind my best diplomatic smile.

Ormyr ignored the aversion radiating from Ingvar and Lady Amelia, focusing on me with a hand outstretched. "Lady Knight, I trust thine evening was restful?"

"Dame Jessamine was just about to speak with me about a private concern," Lady Amelia asserted.

Deaf to her bitterness, Ormyr stopped in his tracks and lowered his head. "Understood, Milady. Please return anon, Lady Knight. We have business with thee as well."

Ingvar and I exchanged uncertain glances. I hoped to finish with the Baroness quickly so I could help push for more soldiers in the districts as promised.

"Certainly. Excuse me." I nodded to the Baron before crossing the room.

Lady Amelia preceded me into her own side-room, then hung back to draw the curtain closed. Her little chamber was the mirror image of Baron Tristan's, only loaded with candles and an incense similar to that disagreeable one in Lord Cather-wood's throne room. Several unusual snake emblems adorned the walls.

I stood with my hands clasped behind my back, wondering what this private meeting would be about.

Lady Amelia remained standing as well, picking at the

beads in her hands. She looked me dead-on, but embarrassment tinged her expression. "I apologize for the pitiful state in which we receive thee. The Unseen look down upon Nidaros with scorn of late."

I shook my head. "I've been well taken care of so far, madam."

"'Tis a kind lie, I shall forgive it." A sad smile appeared for a moment, then vanished. "Hast thou any special messages from my nephew, or anyone else?"

"No, madam."

"What of food?"

"The gift I already shared with you, that's all I was given," I said. "Aside from that, I have only my personal stores."

"By law are those thine own, immune to seizure, and rightly so. But ..." Lady Amelia's gaze fell toward her beads. Her next words were difficult to force out. "Surely thou see'st our desperation here."

I nodded with determination. "I was hoping I might bring what I have to the capital, to add to your stores. I also have some spare cred that you're welcome to."

"Nay, Lady Knight. Thou needest not go to such trouble." Her gaze leapt back to mine, beseeching. "*I* request what thou canst spare now, without difficulty. Nothing more. Dost thou understand?"

An ugly realization crawled up my spine. "You mean, just for yourself?"

She seemed glad not to have to spell it out. "There are certain deprivations one of my stature should never bear."

A stone fist clenched up inside my empty gut. I wanted to help, but *just her?* No, that wasn't happening. I racked my brain for a diplomatic way of saying as much. "Apologies, Madam, but I'd rather not limit my aid that way."

"I *could* simply take it." Resentment hardened her eyes. "I ask to avoid such ugly business."

"Seizing my cargo sets a bad precedent, madam," I returned as calmly as possible. I didn't bother mentioning legality, as she already had. What was truly illegal for the heir presumptive of Catherwood, anyway? "Besides, you'd need *someone* to help you take it. Even if they follow your orders out of sheer devotion, do you think they'll be happy knowing you have extra food that no one else does?"

Her face flushed, presumably from the indignity of it all, while she throttled her beads. "What could I offer in exchange, then? I have jewels, family heirlooms. Outside of this domain, thou couldst fetch a fair sum therefor."

"Madam ..." I was absolutely uninterested, but she wasn't having it. I reached deep down for the sweetest-smelling nonsense possible, which I prefaced with truth. "At supper last night, I really appreciated your generosity with Lord Catherwood's gift." I had no doubt the gesture had been the Baron's idea, but she'd come around once she'd seen the servant's gratitude. "Your example has inspired me to be as generous as possible in return. What I have isn't much, but it might provide another day or two of relief for everyone here while we work against our problems. Your charity in the face of adversity is sure to curry favor with the Unseen. Don't you think?"

A look of disbelief, followed by contrition, dawned on Lady Amelia's face. She whirled away from me, speechless for several moments. "Thou art the more thoughtful, Lady Knight," she finally admitted.

I stifled my sigh of relief. Annoyance and disgust came easily, but I had to respect that at present, things were hard for her in a way they'd never been hard before. Nobility bred unimaginable degrees of entitlement. With the right encouragement, though, this woman could find her empathy.

Lady Amelia sank into her chair, still not looking my way. "I would to return home. If I could only explain our trouble to

my nephew, myself, without anyone slanting the message …"
She trailed off.

"Why can't you?" I asked.

Her head swiveled toward her shoulder. She looked at me from the corner of one downturned eye. "I'd be too sorely tempted never to return here."

I bit the inside of my lip, at a loss.

Amid the ensuing silence, the notes of an argument reached us through the curtain. The voices and tones were familiar: Ingvar's frustration, Ormyr's confidence, Baron Tristan's all-too-frequent silence.

"This is far from what I once imagined for myself and my husband." Lady Amelia's profile crumpled. "And now I debase myself before a stranger."

"You can trust me, madam. Your nephew does." I was curious about what else she might divulge. At the same time, I was trying to listen in on the argument, but had trouble discerning words.

Lady Amelia stood again, her expression suggesting an eagerness to recover some of her lost dignity. She held out a charm to me: a small jeweled khamsa, much nicer than the clay ones sitting aboard my ship.

"Don't allow Ormyr to bind thee as my husband is bound," she spoke in a grave hush. "Leave the capital at once and hunt down Thordia Naustvik. Only she can reverse this blight upon us." Her eyes detached with a faraway look. "Ormyr hath not sent anyone else to search for her, as if he feareth an end to his power once she's dealt with."

He *hadn't?* Almost everyone believed Thordia was the cause of their problems, so why wouldn't Ormyr have his cloister looking for her nonstop? Maybe there was something to the lady's suspicions, and Ormyr was prolonging the witch crisis because it benefitted him somehow.

"Prithee, free us." Lady Amelia broke from her reverie, looking me straight-on.

The voices outside grew louder, more agitated. I slipped the charm into a pocket, lowering my head. "I'll do my best to set things right, madam. Excuse me, I'd better get back out there."

CHAPTER 10

I left Lady Amelia in her private room and reentered the calefactory with inquisitive haste. Baron Tristan, Ingvar, and Ormyr formed a close triangle by the fire. Ingvar smoldered at his feet, arms crossed over his chest. When I appeared, his eyes fastened upon mine with an expression that made clear the argument, whatever it was, wasn't going in his favor.

"Dame Jessamine." Baron Tristan didn't look or sound thrilled to see me, but quickly redirected his displeasure at the beads in his hands.

Meanwhile, Ormyr's gaze cautiously tracked my movements. Normally oblivious to the anger and frustration of others, *he* looked upset as well.

I started toward the gathering, still clueless about what had them so tense. They probably weren't eager to air private matters before a guest, either. I could ask Ingvar about it later. For the moment, I'd help him argue for more men in the districts, as promised. Afterward, maybe I'd help myself by obtaining coordinates for Gules, presuming I figured out a good way of bringing it up without sounding eager to fly off and leave everything unresolved.

My approach between Ingvar and Ormyr turned the triangle into a square. Unlike the barracks, the calefactory's hearth threw off a stifling, sweat-inducing heat. Not at all inviting, as hard as it tried to be.

Ormyr straightened with a determined expression. "'Tis time I blessed our visiting knight."

"Nay! This isn't over!" Ingvar clenched his fists at his sides, eyes blazing. "Ye don't bring people together by slaughtering the ones ye *think* are troublemakers! Deeds are what matter. We should never be first to strike!" This reminded me of our earlier conversation concerning the Gyllenfeld dissidents.

Ormyr bristled. Before he opened his mouth, Baron Tristan intervened, raising a hand. "Prithee let's shelve the discussion."

"Nay, Your Grace. Allow me to clarify once and for all where I stand." Ormyr's eyes narrowed scathingly toward Ingvar, then softened with a wounded look as he glanced between me and the Baron, raising his hands in a pleading gesture. "Ere another uprising should occur, we must take the initiative to track down the remaining dissidents." Genuine pain leaked from his words, as though Ingvar had reopened some personal wound. "We've been too lax in the enforcement of Catherwood dogma, and the Unseen have clearly voiced their displeasure. Nidaros can no longer survive divided against itself. We must unite as one people."

He reinforced what Madam Castor had spoken of in Lord Catherwood's throne room, about Nidaros being difficult to keep in line. Ingvar fumed, unmoved.

Indeed, however noble a frame Ormyr put on it, a second witch hunt was the last thing Nidaros needed. I normally wouldn't have butted in with my unwelcome thoughts, but I was Lord Catherwood's emissary. If Ormyr hungered for my favor, as he'd seemed to over supper the night before, my opinion might actually sway him. "I appreciate what you're saying,

Master, but speaking from experience, that sort of crackdown doesn't end well. People tend to cling even harder to their old beliefs."

Ormyr focused a pleading gaze on me. "If we do nothing, what's to stop zealots from leading good people to ruin? Violence shall follow, the last thing we want!"

"Damned if I understand this!" Ingvar snapped. "Ye won't have my men keeping an eye on things, that's going too far. But your adepts rounding up dissidents, *that* won't cause backlash?"

"Enough." Baron Tristan's strained expression and bead-grasping made plain how much he didn't want to be dwelling on the topic, possibly fearing what I'd do with the information. "I must wish and deliberate more upon these matters, but I shall say this: if my people are dissatisfied right now, I can only sympathize. I've no interest in punishing them for old traditions, or for events that occurred years ago. Understood?"

I indulged in a sliver of relief, grateful the Baron's good sense had prevailed.

"Your Grace?" Ormyr pleaded.

For once, the Baron ignored him. "In the meantime, Captain, maintain patrols as they are. Otherwise, thou hast thine orders for the day."

"Aye, Your Grace," Ingvar muttered toward the floor, still holding fists at his sides.

It was still a loss for him. He wasn't getting his increased manpower in the districts. Before I could intercede with the Baron on his behalf, Ingvar fixed me with an intense gaze. "Know where the storehouse is?"

I nodded, confused.

"Meet me there." Ingvar stalked out of the calefactory with purpose.

I stared after him, wondering what that was about.

Neither Baron Tristan nor Ormyr were fazed by Ingvar's

abrupt exit. "Captain Leirfall shall be showing thee our storehouse today," the Baron informed me, releasing his beads to straighten his amulet.

My confusion heightened. "Your storehouse?"

"We do wish for Lord Catherwood and Madam Castor to understand the full extent of our difficulty here," Ormyr explained.

Supper had done a fine enough job of that. "And after that?" I asked. "I'd like to tour the districts, if possible."

"We shall see. 'Tis very dangerous at the moment. First, do sit down." The fawning courtier was back full-force. With a smile and sweep of his arm, Ormyr ushered me toward the stone table in the middle of the room. "I shall personally confer a day's blessings upon thee."

Best not to deviate from my persona—the knight errant distinguished enough to have gotten in good with Lord Catherwood—however gag-inducing it got. I swallowed my disgust along with my dignity, and preceded Ormyr with a smile.

"Unseen keep you." Baron Tristan walked back to his private side-room, vanishing inside.

Only I and Ormyr remained in the calefactory. Frustration didn't give me a chance to feel awkward about the situation. Just have a look at the storehouse today, nothing else? Ormyr and Baron Tristan seemed eager to fence me in, for my safety, for damage control, or both. The perils of being a Lord's emissary. I intended to keep playing my part, reinforce that Ormyr was the one who had to impress me, and finesse my way into more constructive action.

Once I approached a chair, Ormyr narrowed in beside me. Half a moment later, he brandished his keris again. The wavy blade glinted with light from the fire.

Again, instinct got the better of my composure. I jumped.

Ormyr laughed, a sound less reassuring and more hackleraising. "Prithee, sit down."

I did so slowly, only somewhat assuaged. *Come on, he's trying to put you on edge so he'll have the upper hand,* I scolded myself. *Get it together and reassert yourself.*

"Captain Leirfall shall be escorting thee here every morning for these rites. They are of utmost importance." With a flick of his wrist, Ormyr went from holding the long dagger to balancing its hilt on his palm. Keeping the keris vertical proved no harder for him than standing upright. He leaned toward the table's center, pulling the brass censer there closer to himself. The rest of the room smelled like cloves, but that particular censer reeked of humomalo, the same weed I smoked.

It couldn't have been coincidental. Undoubtedly, this'd been arranged to impress me, but I couldn't remember having smoked in front of Ormyr before. How had he known? Unbeknownst to him, I wasn't the type to jump to outlandish conclusions. He must've smelled it on me yesterday, or heard about it from a soldier.

I couldn't do anything about my persistent hunger, but I could answer *that* craving. Something to settle my nerves was a welcome prospect then. "May I?" I withdrew my cigarillos and tinderbox from my coat pocket.

"I insist." Ormyr conjured a brass plate seemingly out of nowhere — it might've been sitting beneath the censer — and slid it toward me, for use as an ashtray.

While I lit a tinder and helped myself to a cigarillo, Ormyr centered his dagger-bearing hand over the censer, his eyes following the thin smoke-streams weaving through the open fingers of his palm. Spacers wrapped the bands of the many rings he wore. They were too big for him, most likely a consequence of the crop trouble.

His meditation dragged on. I wondered if he were genuinely concentrating, waiting for me to ask about the ritual, or both. Well, there was a limit to how much I'd humor him. Again, *he* had to impress *me*. That was a source of great comfort, given I was pretending to a completely unfamiliar station.

I took a pull from my cigarillo, then sighed out a mouthful of smoke, assuming a been-there attitude. "I understand there's a witch on the loose."

Ormyr lowered his head in assent. "Indeed, thou hast heard rightly. I identified her with my own divinations, as well as accounts from the Low North district. Alas, she disappeared ere she could be captured." Concern tightened his features. "I realize our stability is of great concern to Lord Catherwood and Madam Castor. The witch must be found and forced to undo her curse. Only then shall Nidaros be restored."

I raised an eyebrow, having no trouble expressing doubt. "Why do you need the witch to end this curse? Isn't there a whole cloister of talented magic-wielders right here?"

"The curse may only be undone by she who set it in motion," Ormyr explained. "Would that it weren't so, but it is. So we continue to scry for her whereabouts."

"Scry?" I repeated. "What about a physical search?"

"Prithee understand, the witch could be anywhere on the planet. This cloister doth lack the resources for such an exhaustive search, and 'tis dangerous beyond capital walls besides." Ormyr glanced askance with a distant look. "I do sense I'm narrowing in on her. The magic she employeth to remain hidden is costing her dearly. She cannot maintain it much longer."

"The things I've seen witches pull ..." I trailed off, pretending to the appropriate trepidation. "They're best left unsaid. Let's just say a physical search can be more helpful than one might think. I'd be glad to venture afield with any leads you have."

"'Tis too dangerous, and would only place undue attention on the matter. Our subjects have enough troubling them as-is." Ormyr waved a hand in dismissal. "I did take her sib-ling into custody. He shall betray to me her whereabouts. Or, she may vie for him." His eyes flashed with determination. "And if she should, I shall be ready."

"How?" I perked up. Hell, if I couldn't make headway on the crop trouble, it was back to springing Verahl, or at least figuring out how good my chances were.

Ormyr smirked. "Suffice to say, the wards I've put up around the prisoner and his cell cannot be broken without my knowledge."

Wards? Right. In other words, a stone here or there. Nothing to worry about. Still, I faked continued interest in the claim. "I don't suppose you could show me?"

"'Tis *very* dangerous," Ormyr dismissed. "We would not for anything bad to happen whilst thou art with us."

"You can't fault me for asking." I forced a smile in return. "Lord Catherwood and Madam Castor would rather hear about the prisoner I *saw* than the prisoner I was *told about*."

"If thou properly describest the danger, the court is certain to understand." Not one wrinkle appeared in Ormyr's compo-sure. The keris disappeared behind his back with the same grudgingly impressive sleight-of-hand. He slid the brass plate over to himself, making a concentrated study of my discarded ashes.

All right, so I wasn't needling him into a sneak preview. "How about showing me some affected crops? Now *that's* something they'll demand to see firsthand."

"I shall need time to prepare samples for thee," Ormyr said without looking up. "We wouldn't want to accidentally spread the curse to Spectra."

The man had an answer for everything. He was surely a master of deflection, if nothing else. Stymied, I fell back on the matter weighing heaviest on my heart. "There's something un-related I was hoping you could help me with. Space travel is risky, as I'm sure you know. My ship's index is prone to losing coordinates now and then."

"Why don't we discuss the matter in further depth at supper this evening? I would not to delay thee any longer from the storehouse." Ormyr glanced back up at me brightly. "Unless thou wouldst to hear thy forecast first?"

Frustration burned me worse than the fire. What could I do, though? If I pushed, it'd look bad. Supper it was. I took a deep breath, then shook my head in refusal. "I like being surprised."

Ormyr laughed. "Indeed, the day may hold a surprise or two for thee. Be vigilant, and if there's anything Lady Amelia bade thee attend to, I should be glad to assist whilst thou visitest the storehouse."

He wanted to know what she'd said to me. Well, I didn't mind stonewalling him right back. "Thank you, I'll keep that in mind." I jumped to my feet.

"Unseen grace upon thee, Lady Knight. I look forward to speaking with thee again tonight. Excuse me." Ormyr turned and darted across the uncomfortably warm calefactory.

I leaned over to reclaim the ashtray, mentally congratulating Nidaros' court and cloister for putting up with that *all the time*.

On the other side of the room, unaware of my lingering presence, Ormyr swept aside a curtain to reveal a whispering, giggling cluster of adepts. At their master's appearance, most of them scattered like a panicked flock of birds, leaving the rest to stare down an oncoming hurricane.

"Holsten!" Ormyr cried.

Adept Holsten stood among the brave remaining few, pendulum suspended from his fingers, scroll bunched in his free hand. His smile vanished in favor of a long-borne weariness.

"Are the forecasts ready?" Ormyr demanded.

Wordlessly, Holsten handed him the scroll.

Ormyr unfurled it for study. "What of the latest attempt?" he asked without looking up.

"Unfavorable, sir."

"Again?"

"I'm afraid so, Master."

"Scry anew, then! Ensure 'tis complete *and* fortuitous ere the mid-morning rites."

"Master," an adept standing next to Holsten piped up. "About this animation—"

"Consult Adept Elina's divinations," Ormyr said, still not looking up.

"I did, but, I can't find anything useful!"

"Try again." Ormyr rolled up the scroll and breezed past his inferiors, deeper into the side-room and out of sight. The remaining adepts scattered in Ormyr's wake.

Holsten placed a hand on the shoulder of the young man beside him, preventing from leaving. "I'll help you with that, Tarr."

I kept a silent watch over the whole exchange, sympathizing with the younger adepts. Failing to locate Thordia or torture her whereabouts from Verahl might well have left Ormyr every bit as frustrated as Ingvar and I were, only he didn't seem to mind venting upon whatever targets presented themselves.

After being jerked around all morning, I was dying to go on the offense. First order of business: consult an adept who didn't mind sharing information with people outside his circle. The kitchen servants and junior adepts seemed to favor Adept Holsten, and he was right there. I hoped he was over whatever fear I'd put in him yesterday.

I took one last pull, crushed out my cigarillo, then jumped to my feet. "Adept Holsten? If you don't mind, could you kindly show me the way out?"

Holsten nearly leapt out of his skin, then whirled to face me with a floor-focused gaze. "Uh, certainly."

He gathered himself to approach me, moving quickly despite the limp his spinal deformity gave him. We filed into to the narrow hallway, Holsten leading.

"There's nothing to worry about, friend," I said with a smile he couldn't see. "Lord Catherwood made me leave my fangs back in Spectra."

Holsten laughed without turning around, which seemed to cut through his tension. "Please, pay me no mind. The past few days have been …" He trailed off, gesturing helplessly. The green pendulum in his hand batted against the wall. "Everyone's been so afraid of what the guild might do, and, well …"

"It's all right, I promise. I'm here to help." My guess was that Ormyr created at least half of his stress.

Once we reached the foyer, I darted ahead of my guide, motioning toward an out-of-the-way spot. Holsten frowned with confusion, but understood well enough to follow me.

"You come highly recommended," I spoke under my breath, rummaging through my pockets. "How about some information, and the guarantee this conversation stays between us?" Though cigarillos hadn't gone over so well with Fasolt the day before, I wasn't deterred from offering them here, given the adepts used humomalo as incense.

If anything, the bribe seemed to calm Holsten and provide something to focus on. With deft confidence, he lifted the smokes from my fingers, concealed them up a sleeve of his robe, and made eye contact with me for once. There was a concrete, practical intelligence to his expression when fear didn't overwhelm it. "What do you need?"

"Information on getting around in the dungeon," I said.

His composure wasn't fated to last. Holsten paled, every drop of blood rushing from his face. Somehow, I'd hit upon something even more frightening. Why? It was *his* dungeon. Maybe he didn't necessarily agree with who ended up there, or what Ormyr did with them.

"Stay with me here," I rushed to explain before I lost him completely. "Where are the entrances? Who has keys? Things like that. Tell me what you know. Don't worry, I'm not asking you to do anything."

Holsten swallowed hard, his gaze focused past my shoulder. A silent debate took place in his skull. "There are entrances scattered all over the keep," he finally said. "This floor, anyway. Most are hidden and need a key. The main entrance is down that hallway—" he pointed, sending his pendulum thrashing in the process "—always under guard. And there's an entrance outdoors as well, also guarded. Keys are kept in the third sanctum. You couldn't get there yourself."

"Keys for what?" I asked.

"Doors, manacles."

So, probably a lot of locks. Great.

"There are potent wards down there as well." A shiver went through Holsten. "You'd have to get a charm for safe passage, or have someone dispel them for you."

To breach the dungeon, it was becoming clear I'd need an adept accomplice: less for the wards, more for the keys and guards. Holsten wasn't up for it, he'd faint first. Could *any* adept be trusted to that extent? My rising chagrin cast doubt on the prospect. Maybe Ingvar had been right. This was much harder than it seemed.

I'm sorry, Verahl. Guilt flooded over me.

Somewhere amid his fear, Holsten found enough nerve to frown. "What's this about? I won't tell, I'm just curious."

"I'm not sure it's about anything," I answered. "Thanks, though."

Holsten nodded, hesitated a moment, then disappeared into one of the cramped hallways.

As my prospects dwindled, frustration returned, burning away my other emotions. So much for progress today. I wanted to head to my ship for something to eat, but first the storehouse, and whatever Ingvar wanted to see me about there.

The storehouse was the mirror image of the Baron's estate, situated on the opposite side of the adepts' keep. Beside it stood a stable, most of its stalls gaping empty. The rest housed several of those wooly mounts I'd seen the day before. Adepts everywhere, and not a soldier in sight, though this was something important to guard even in the best of times. Come to think of it, I had yet to see a soldier with a mount, anywhere. Did the adepts wield control over all of them? All the time, or just during recent troubles? How much longer would they wait to slaughter them for food?

At the storehouse entrance stood a pair of soldiers I recognized from the night before: Jari and Kai.

"I'm supposed to meet Captain Leirfall here," I said, then smiled. "I think he wants a rematch."

The boys snickered.

"He's not here, but go on inside." Jari tossed his head over his shoulder.

"Thanks!" I shook their hands before stepping past.

I expected the storehouse interior to be identical to the estate's, but the first room that greeted me was enormous. They must've knocked down walls at some point. This was where the flax resided, a mountain of bushels piled to the ceiling, poised to be carted back out when representatives from Linum Dominorum arrived for harvest.

This was what Baron Tristan had wanted me to see. Then I recalled how all of this was only enough to satisfy the trade guild's quota one time. Hell. I wandered down one side of the pile, passing a few more soldiers who nodded in greeting.

The next room over was just as large, but not nearly as full. The middle of the chamber held only a few crates, which a group of adepts and soldiers inventoried together. The cavernous room amplified their whispered conversation. More surprising was what occupied the fringes of the room: firewood and metalwork on one side, munitions and unmarked ceramic jars on another. Given their placement, I supposed the jars served some martial purpose, but I had no idea what. The adepts carried wrapped bundles back the way I'd come. They might've been for another ration disbursement to the districts.

I retreated to the first room and paced slow laps around the flax, gathering my thoughts. There were many hours to kill until supper. Exploring the storehouse had slain maybe a quarter of one of them. When Ingvar appeared, I planned to ask him about about sneaking in a trip to the districts after bringing some food from my ship over to the storehouse. Since I was stuck regarding Verahl, I'd also seek leads on Thordia's whereabouts. Surely the soldiers had heard rumors that might get me started on locating and protecting her.

Then, at supper that night, I absolutely *would not* let Ormyr worm out of the subject of coordinates for Gules. If he did somehow manage the deflection, I'd consider taking my chances sneaking aboard the Baron's ship myself.

A hand seized my arm from behind. I tensed and spun around, relaxing when I found myself face-to-face with Ingvar's intent stare.

"Where've you been?" I asked, my heart still slowing.

"Arranging a few things, Goose." He dragged me into a shadowy corner, then fixed me with a determined look. "Still want to break Verahl Naustvik out of the dungeon?"

My eyes flew wide open, while my jaw fell in shock. "Yes."

"Good. Let's do it."

CHAPTER 11

"You want to break Verahl out *now?*" I struggled to keep my startled words from echoing through the cavernous store-house.

Frustration lingered in Ingvar's eyes, most likely left over from the calefactory. "Right now's the best time we'll get," he answered with conviction. "The adepts in the keep are all busy with some ritual for the next hour. Ye and I will infiltrate from the rear dungeon entrance. Already briefed Sefi, my man stationed there. He'll keep the doors open while we go in and out. Naustvik's being held in the ninth cell on our left. These unlock all the doors and manacles." He showed me a large loop of keys clutched in one hand. "We'll free Naustvik, head back out, lock up everything behind us."

I stood there stunned, my jaw still hanging loose. This was sudden, almost too sudden. It was just the sort of plan I'd hoped to execute at some point, but also exactly what Ingvar had tried to talk me out of earlier that morning.

"What's bringing this on?" I demanded under my breath. "Why the change of heart?"

"Would ye rather just look at the storehouse today?" Ingvar snapped. His gaze fell askance, letting me know I wasn't the cause of his vexation, while his other hand wrung the straps of a knapsack hanging from his grip. "I'm sick of sitting on my hands, and I've turned a blind eye toward the dungeon for too long. Ye're right, Naustvik doesn't deserve to be locked up. 'Tis not helping our crops to return. Even supposing Thordia's a witch, that doesn't make her brother one. I'm telling my men the same thing." He proffered the knapsack toward me.

I accepted, and rifled through it. Inside rested a heavy wool cloak, packed atop a canteen, candles, tinderbox, and a small amount of bread. A thoughtful assortment on short notice.

"The cloak will hide Naustvik as we walk him out of the capital," Ingvar continued. "My lads already know to have the gate open and their eyes shut." He smirked faintly. "From there, we'll escort him out to the districts. I know a few places in the East not often trafficked. He should be able to lie low for days with those supplies."

Eagerness and suspicion pulled me in different directions. This felt like a setup, but Ingvar's demeanor was sincere. He'd thoroughly covered the details that'd stymied my own planning, except he'd made no provision for the dungeon wards Ormyr and Holsten had mentioned. The omission was welcome.

"We do this quickly and quietly enough, no one in the capital will find out for a while," Ingvar said. "No one outside will learn thereof, either. Naustvik is Ormyr's responsibility, and Ormyr won't let word of his failure spread." A dark satisfaction tinged his voice at the thought.

I didn't mind the prospect of bringing Ormyr down a notch, either. But hell, was I really going along with this? My heart raced and my head spun, making it difficult to think or find words.

"This is crazy, isn't it?" I finally blurted.

"Mayhap," Ingvar admitted, looking me in the eye.

"You keep saying 'we.' Are we *both* doing this?"

"Aye. Fail or succeed together, assuming ye trust me enough to make the attempt. Otherwise, we drop the matter and never speak of it again."

This seemed too great a risk on Ingvar's part. Then again, it was riskier for him to let a stranger loose in the adepts' dungeon without supervision. Ironically, coming along and ensuring everything went smoothly was his best hope of keeping his involvement secret.

But what about the risk I faced? Well, Ingvar had played things straight with me this far. Nothing in his demeanor made me think he was lying. I'd wanted, and needed, an ally like him. And removing Verahl from the picture was the first step toward making Nidaros face their real problems.

We'd be getting something useful done that day after all. Galvanized, I swung the knapsack over my left shoulder, then rested a hand on Ingvar's arm. "Thank you. Let's go."

The clouds overhead had darkened, and an ominous breeze blew through the capital. Despite these omens, Ingvar and I ran with a purpose we'd been sorely wanting, all the way to the dungeon entrance I'd discovered the night before. A wiry sentry, Sefi, bolted away from the wall he slouched against as we approached.

"Ready, lad?" Ingvar greeted.

Sefi's gaze darted uncertainly between me and Ingvar. "Sir, I was just thinking: what about the spells down there to contain the prisoners? How will ye get past them?"

This was easy. "Nothing to worry about." I fished through my pockets for the hammer-shaped charm Sigrid had given me, then held it up for his inspection.

The sight reassured Sefi, who took a collecting breath.

"Should only take us a few minutes." Ingvar looked to me.

"Move quickly and quietly, aye? Follow my lead."

"Right." I wasn't accustomed to following leads, but Ingvar was more familiar with his home turf than I was. With rising anticipation, I re-hitched the knapsack on my shoulder.

"Good luck," Sefi whispered, producing his own loop of keys.

The younger soldier quickly took care of the lock on the heavy iron doors. Ingvar and I helped him peel them back, exposing a sloped path into darkness. After equipping himself with a lantern resting on a wrought-metal stand, Ingvar preceded me down.

Ailing wooden beams fortified the walls and ceiling of the dirt-hewn tunnel. As sunlight diminished behind us, only the lantern remained to stave off the dark. A warm waft of air rushed up, tinged with a brain-piercing foulness. I harbored no literal belief in an underworld, but it sure as hell felt like we were descending into one. My right hand strayed toward my dagger, while my left hovered ahead, primed to intercept an obstacle or threat.

Our path leveled out, transforming into a corridor with stone-lined walls. Unidentifiable muck pulled at the soles of our boots. To either side of us spanned rows of barred cells holding emaciated bodies in threadbare clothing. Lacking furniture, they sprawled motionless on the ground, making it hard to tell whether they were alive or dead. Someone was leaving them food and water—or had, ages ago, and had forgotten to retrieve the plates. The only hint of life appeared when light fell on them. At that, most of them shuddered and curled into themselves as though avoiding a lash.

If Ingvar knew their circumstances, he'd cast them aside to forge ahead without comment or reaction, keeping his gaze locked forward.

Meanwhile, pity braced me. I hurried up alongside him, fully understanding the need for haste, but my eyes and thoughts remained with the prisoners, wondering how long they'd been languishing there and why. These might've been ruthless criminals. Since the adepts held them prisoner, it was also possible they were more like poor Branigan, victims of superstition.

Curiosity gnawed at me despite our mission. I was about to ask Ingvar what he knew of them when my eyes fell upon a prisoner who wasn't just thin, but skeletal. *Melting.*

Terror jolted my heart. I gasped and halted.

Ingvar kept going. Whatever I'd seen, or thought I'd seen, disappeared into shadow.

"Come back here, please?" I forced past my constricted throat.

Ingvar turned, frowning with confusion. "We have to keep moving."

"Please?" I couldn't bring myself to describe it, or believe that I'd actually seen it. Our goal became secondary to my immediate fear.

His incredulity persisted, but something in my voice or expression must've swayed him. Ingvar returned to my side, bringing his lantern. Its light confirmed that what I'd spied had been no illusion.

"Hell," I muttered.

"Blood's oath!" Ingvar cursed and jumped back. Only some merciful quirk of gravity prevented burning lantern oil from drenching his tabard.

The man or woman who'd inhabited that cell was long gone. Their remains, propped against the rear wall, sat in grotesque defiance of reality. The flesh was shriveled dry, colored like a bruise, lips curled back to reveal a toothless grimace. Some of the missing teeth littered the floor and the corpse's lap. The eyes were missing as well. Streams of dark, shiny liquid ran from the sockets, dripping into the dirt.

Blood drained from my extremities, leaving me weak and

cold. "What is that?" I murmured, mostly referring to the discharge.

"Damned if I know." Ingvar stood transfixed, but even in duress, he made no move for his beads. "Damned if I've ever seen such a thing."

"There aren't any illnesses here that leave a body like that behind?" I asked.

"*Skíta*," Ingvar said around a lump in his throat. "Not that I know of."

I'd certainly never seen any abroad that led to such a gruesome conclusion. The lack of explanation disturbed me almost as much as the scene itself.

"The adepts must've done this, whatever it is." Ingvar couldn't take his eyes off the remains. "They're the only ones down here on a regular basis. But if there's some new disease or murderer on the loose, that's *my* concern."

"If I examine the corpse, I might be able to give you a better idea," I said. "I'm no pathologist or anything, but—"

"No one's going near it!" Ingvar declared. "I'm having it burned as soon as possible. We don't know what it's carrying!"

"Diseases can't survive in a corpse for long," I explained calmly. "The only risk is to anyone who physically handles the remains." That odd, shiny discharge could be infectious, for all I knew. "I have gear aboard my ship for safely handling things like this. If we take the corpse somewhere else for study, I might be able to tell you if disease or torture or poison were involved."

His scowl persisting, Ingvar turned away from the scene. "Something to worry about later. Let's keep going, we need to be out of here afore the adepts finish with their rites."

Fear and purpose prodded us on faster. Ingvar stared ahead, while I studied every new cell we passed. None contained another corpse like the one whose visage was burned in my memory. None of the other prisoners looked in any shape to talk about what they might've seen, either. Another disturbing mystery.

We entered a small stretch of tunnel lined with heavy iron doors, enclosures meant for those who truly deserved to be buried. Ingvar honed in on a door plastered with chalk emblems.

"I'd say that's our man," I muttered.

Ingvar knew which of the many keys on his loop to use, and had the door open quickly.

The ease with which he worked niggled at me. It seemed contrary to his earlier claim that this was strictly the adepts' domain. "You seem pretty dungeon-savvy for someone who doesn't ever step into the dungeon," I remarked.

If Ingvar recognized my suspicion, he ignored it. "While ye waited for me, I cashed in a few favors among the adepts."

"Who?" I asked.

"Not now. Come on." He stepped inside.

In fairness, I'd nearly managed the same with Holsten on short notice. Thus assuaged, I followed him inside. He pushed the door shut behind us.

Dense darkness filled the cell, along with a suffocating, unidentifiable stench. Ingvar's lantern revealed a table near the threshold littered with iron-wrought implements, all designed to elicit screams and confessions.

We advanced deeper into the room, Ingvar looking as uneasy as I felt. Manacles lined the walls. Only one set was occupied along the far wall, by a broad-shouldered young man with a good foot and hundred pounds on me. He could've ripped the whole assembly from the wall with a shrug, were he not sapped of vigor and dangling from his wrists. Blood, grime, and sweat told of a ghastly tenure. Three powdery semicircles radiated out from around his feet: wards meant to keep evil in or out, depending on the most convenient interpretation. Lit candles stood like sentries along each of the circles.

The moment Verahl fell into sight, Ingvar stopped, a haunted expression on his face. I stopped beside him, sympathy and despair constricting my ribcage. I feared whether we were too late to save the poor prisoner, who'd spared his sister from this fate.

Behind us, faint but unmistakable footsteps sounded from the corridor: a single walker, drawing closer at a measured pace.

Ingvar and I traded looks of terror. That same feeling tore down my spine.

"I thought you said the adepts were busy!" I whispered.

"They are!" Ingvar shot back in kind. "Or they're supposed to be." His eyes shifted forward and back. "Let's fetch him, quietly now. They'll probably just walk past and leave."

He'd closed the cell door behind us, thankfully. We approached Verahl together, stepping past the "magical" boundaries without a second glance downward. Ingvar kept his lantern on the scene, handing me the loop of keys with the proper key selected.

Before taking them, I probed around the charms lashed to Verahl's throat, looking for and finding a pulse. Nothing felt broken or dislocated, so I tilted his head upright. "Verahl Naustvik?"

He blinked, startled. The movement of his eyes convinced me he was responding to his name.

"My name's Jessamine," I continued. "We're getting you out of here. Just stay calm."

A full beard obscured Verahl's face, but his gaze revealed the questions filling his mind. He stared at me as though intent on finding answers by drilling through my skull.

Behind us, the footsteps rose and fell past our door, proceeding down the corridor in the opposite direction we'd walked. I bit my lip, shooting a worried look toward Ingvar.

"They'll see the open door back where Sefi is."

This didn't trouble him. "He's got his cover story."

Fair enough. Time to hurry. I took the key loop Ingvar provided and attacked the manacle around Verahl's right wrist first.

Verahl boggled at this unexpected windfall. His weight shifted to his feet as I worked, fully supporting himself. Fortunate that we wouldn't have to carry him out.

When the manacle snapped open, Verahl basked in the rush of blood returning to his arm. His free hand, almost twice the size of one of mine, flexed open and closed.

The second manacle went even quicker. I pocketed the keys, then offered Verahl the knapsack I'd been carrying. "Here, this is yours."

Verahl blinked, then threw it over his shoulder.

"We're taking you to the districts," Ingvar muttered, "but we must wait for whoever's outside to leave first."

Verahl's stare fastened upon Ingvar for the first time. His eyes narrowed with suspicion, but he said nothing.

We all held our breaths, listening for those footsteps. As far as I could tell, the intruder was indeed still out there, lingering in our path of escape. What was he or she doing? Maybe they'd stumbled upon the corpse as well? I hoped not, I wanted to examine it later.

"Come on, clear out," Ingvar muttered.

Eventually, the footsteps started back our way.

All right, good, keep going, I thought, heart rising steadily up my throat. *Go back the way you came and vanish.*

Instead, the footsteps came right up to our door and stopped. A key entered the lock.

"Hell!" Fear seized me again, along with an overdue dose of paranoia that sent my guts plummeting. My glare fastened onto my co-conspirator. "This *was* a setup!"

"What? Nay!" Ingvar's eyes flew wide open with equal

parts bafflement and dread. He backpedaled outside of the circles surrounding Verahl, but stopped there, glancing between me and the cell door at a loss.

It was a little late to be worrying about traps. I had to do *something* to assume control of the situation, put the incoming intruder on the defensive. After placing myself in front of Verahl, I turned back to him with my dagger in hand. "Here. Take me hostage."

"What?" Ingvar cried again.

"I strong-armed my way down here to question Verahl," I coached rapidly, hoping he wasn't just going to hand me over to whoever opened the door. "You're trying to stop me!"

"Are ye *mad?"* Ingvar was still too stunned to figure out what to do with himself.

Verahl, meanwhile, assumed his role with ease. He wrapped his arms around me from behind and placed the dagger to my throat just as the door shuttled open.

The intruder appeared at last: Master Ormyr himself, lantern in hand. The way the light fell on the underside of his face twisted his stern worry into something sinister.

CHAPTER 12

Master Ormyr himself! Framed in the dungeon cell's threshold, he hesitated, eyes flitting about uncertainly. Our little hostage situation was probably the last thing he'd expected to see.

Verahl kept his hold on me from behind, bracing my dagger against my throat. I fought against panic. There was no way Ormyr's convenient appearance *wasn't* a setup, but it wasn't the setup I'd feared. Standing between us and the master adept, the shock on Ingvar's face made plain that he was just as much a victim as I was. Someone must've ratted us out, maybe Holsten or the adepts Ingvar had talked to.

We're in control here, I reminded myself, tamping down dread in favor of resolve. *We got the drop on Ormyr.* I opened my mouth to bluff the master adept out of the chamber.

Sadly, the feeling of control didn't last. Verahl's powerful arms went from simply encircling me to crushing the air out of my lungs.

Pain jolted me. I gasped for breath, unable to speak, and struggled — but not too much, lest I split my own throat open. The candles resting at our feet flickered, splashing deformed shadows against the cell walls.

Ingvar's shock turned to horror. He remained transfixed.

As Ormyr's surprise wore off, he placed his lantern on the ground beside him, then stood and stared directly at Verahl. "That's no way to treat our distinguished visitor, Naustvik." His tone was conversational, friendly even, but something about him seemed to relish the prospect of an ugly outcome.

Verahl trembled against me. "Go away," he rasped, then coughed, chiseling the rust off his voice. "Go away, or I kill her!"

He sounded convincing. I hoped it was still an act, but fear was likely overwhelming whatever capacity Verahl had for subterfuge. I longed to wrest back control of the situation. Unfortunately, Verahl provided no slack to exploit. My arms couldn't even bend at the elbows.

"Naustvik, listen." Ingvar found his voice, raising it with calm control while seeking Verahl's eye contact. "That won't help you."

"Come now, we've been working so hard to correct thy stubborn streak. 'Twould be a shame to have to start anew." Meanwhile, Ormyr retrieved his keris to trace out a magic door, then entered the cell with measured steps. At his side, the curvy blade weaved and flashed through his fingers, conveying increased confidence with every unchallenged step. "Do the right thing and release her."

"She's dead. Then you are!" Verahl cried.

"Master, stay back," Ingvar cautioned, shooting him a frustrated scowl.

Ormyr did stop a few feet short of us, but certainly not at Ingvar's behest. His empty hand flicked out toward us, fingers outstretched. A sliver of steel flashed through the air.

Verahl yowled and shuddered. My dagger tumbled and fell amid the warding circles traced out on the floor, but not before glancing off my collarbone.

I winced at the near-miss. It was a throwing dart, I realized. Ormyr had conjured and winged it so seamlessly, it looked like he'd struck Verahl with pure will.

"Stop! Ye might hit her!" Ingvar snapped at Ormyr.

There was no break in Ormyr's demeanor, or even any sign that he realized Ingvar was present in the cell with us.

Verahl backed up until he hit the cell wall behind himself, dragging me with him. No more dagger to my neck—which was progress, I supposed—but the situation was still deteriorating fast. I *had* to regain control. With my arms out of commission, my feet were all I had at my disposal. I stomped on Verahl's foot, hoping he'd loosen his grip. To my chagrin, it proved as effective as kicking a tree trunk.

"Naustvik, listen to me." Ingvar resumed his calm reasoning, holding his free hand out toward us, the other still gripping his lantern. "Ye're afraid, I get that. Ye're looking for any way out possible—but that's not it. No good will come of that for anyone, aye? She doesn't mean you harm. Let her go, and —"

"Release her or die," Ormyr plowed over Ingvar's efforts to sympathize.

"Shut up!"

Verahl's shout rang in my ears. Meanwhile, my probing foot had found one of the lit candles on the floor. Self-preservation fueled a desperate idea. I kicked over the candle, then rolled it so its flame touched the innermost warding circle around me and Verahl.

The powder composing the circle lit up like dry scrub. Fire devoured the arc, sending hundreds of sparks shooting in every direction. The tallest flares cleared only a few inches in height, but to Ormyr, Verahl might as well have opened a portal to the underworld to shake hands with an arch-demon. He stood terror-welded in place, reflections of flame lighting the whites of his eyes.

Verahl froze too. I drove my heel into the marrow of his shinbone. That spurred him, but not as I'd intended. Instead of letting me go, he hauled me up such that my feet dangled above the floor, then *leapt* over the fire and barreled past Ingvar and Ormyr, out into the dungeon corridor.

I sneaked a breath past his grip. "Put me down!" I cried.

Muted sunlight glowed at the far end of the dungeon, illuminating our escape route. Verahl thumped toward this beacon of freedom with inexplicable speed, clinging to me as though I were a rag doll he wouldn't share.

"Put me down!" I squirmed in his grip to no avail.

"Naustvik, stop!" That was Ingvar, shouting a short distance behind us.

Verahl ignored us, plowing down the corridor and huffing up the ramp leading to the courtyard.

Sefi waited at the top, frowning in confusion. "Hey! What—?"

My captor's left arm shot out, delivering a stiff-arm that walloped the words out of Sefi's lungs and sent him to the ground.

"No!" I cried, still struggling. "Stop! We're trying to help you!"

Verahl spun around to face the way he'd come, his body demanding air faster than he could breathe it up. There was Ingvar, minus his lantern, tearing up the ramp after us with a vengeance.

The unrelenting grip finally loosened enough for me to slide downward. Once my feet met the ground, Verahl centered a hard shove between my shoulder blades. I hurtled down toward Ingvar and collided hard with him. He sprawled out onto his back with a grunt, with my weight heaped on top of him for added insult.

Blood filled my mouth from biting the inside of my lip. I detangled myself in a hurry and jumped to my feet, peering back down the dark dungeon path. Was Ormyr following, or still fixed with horror? I neither saw nor heard anything. Glancing over my shoulder, I found Sefi recovering. Verahl was nowhere in sight.

Ingvar bolted up to a seat on the ground, nursing the back of his head with a hand. His steel gaze stabbed into mine. "Help me with the doors!"

I had to help him stand first. Ingvar remained dazed, but powered through it. As my heart pounded with desperation and shame over our compounding failure, we lifted each heavy iron door, letting gravity slam them back down into place. At no time did Ormyr emerge. It was still smart to cut off this avenue of pursuit.

Sefi hovered behind us, rubbing his shoulder. "Sir, what happened?"

"Naustvik was more eager to leave than I thought," Ingvar explained around quick breaths. "And Master Ormyr happened along while we were freeing him."

"Master Ormyr!" Sefi repeated, stunned.

Ingvar fixed him with a deadly serious look. "Don't let anyone through here, aye? I mean *anyone!*"

"Aye, sir!" Sefi answered without hesitation.

"Did you see where he went?" I asked him.

"That way." The younger soldier pointed out of the court-yard, toward the front of the capital buildings.

"Come on!" Ingvar beckoned me.

There was no time to think, just run. We had to get our es-capee back under control before anything foolish or tragic happened.

We weaved through the ancient buildings, emerging into open field. In the distance, Verahl jogged at an impressive clip. The gate in the wall stood open, several hundred yards in the distance. A daunting chase after all that mess.

"At least he's going where we want him," I managed around short breaths.

"Aye, but my men don't realize he's dangerous. Come on!" Ingvar took off at a sprint.

One deep breath later, I hurried after him.

The sky darkened with the threat of rain. Wind stirred the sea of dry grass around us and whipped loose strands of hair into my face. Still benefitting from the incredible energy reserves at his command, Verahl blasted past the barracks, the gifted knapsack bouncing against his back. Nearby soldiers quit mid-drill to stare after the spectacle.

Running with everything he had, Ingvar managed to close to within ten yards of Verahl. Somehow, he summoned enough voice to yell after the escapee. "Naustvik! Halt!"

Verahl kept going.

I lagged behind, unable to call out, but remained in the chase. Close, yet far from stopping Verahl, whatever he thought he was doing. While I sympathized with his desperation and distrust, annoyance burned me as well. I tamped it down, remembering that this *was* what I'd wanted, after a fashion.

Once our trio passed the abandoned commercial area, nothing stood between us and the open gate. The soldiers stationed there watched our oncoming procession with wide eyes. I tensed with dread at the pending encounter, hoping it didn't turn violent.

"Stop!" Ingvar tried again, significantly more winded.

Still, Verahl pressed on without heed. I expected Ingvar to order his men to intercept, but he didn't, maybe wanting to avoid a fight as much as I did. Unchallenged, Verahl passed through the gate, banked right, and kept running.

"Sir! Do we chase him?" one of the soldiers called.

Just past the gate, Ingvar slowed to a halt, doubled over and breathing hard. "Nay," he managed over the thunder rumbling in the distance. "Close up the gate once the knight is through!"

I wasn't far behind him. His men hastened to comply.

Despite my own fatigue, I had every intention of following Verahl, until I noticed Ingvar swaying on his feet. I was sure that sort of run wouldn't have fazed him normally, but he'd taken that hit to the head earlier. No one on Nidaros had eaten properly in a while, either. I gave up pursuing Verahl to dart toward Ingvar instead, catching and steadying him.

"Get after him!" Ingvar urged me.

I couldn't. One or both of us would've planted faces in the dirt if I'd broken away then. Out of breath, I didn't worry about explaining myself. I just focused on keeping us both upright.

"Captain? Ye all right?" a soldier behind us prompted.

Ingvar broke away from me to turn and straighten. "Who can lend me a bow?"

One of the soldiers on the wall tossed down a bow and three arrows. Ingvar took the bow in his left hand, and nocked one of the arrows immediately. The other two arrows remained in his draw hand, the fletchings pinched between his right palm, ring, and pinky finger. An unusual draw, but it looked faster than constantly reaching into a quiver.

"Agni!" Ingvar called, still glancing up at the wall. "Whither did Naustvik run?"

The soldier pointed. "He broke that way, sir."

"Like Hel he did!" Ingvar replied. "He passed through the gate like it was air, then *vanished*. Ye saw nothing else. None of you did!"

A chorus of "Aye, sir!" followed.

The exchange brought a short-lived smile to my lips. Outside of a desperate chase, it would've summoned laughter.

"Keep the gate shut fast. Tell anyone seeking me or the knight that we're in the districts, organizing a search." With a final glance toward me, Ingvar resumed his chase. That time I was right beside him, hoping to catch up to Verahl before some-one else did.

Verahl ran along the capital wall, still visible some ways distant despite its curvature. Adrenaline most likely pushed him on, along with an unwillingness to trust anyone in bur-gundy and gold. The knapsack had slipped off his shoulder to dangle in the crook of his elbow.

Past the wall, the ancient shipyard slid into view. Verahl ran right in, then made a beeline for the Baron's ship, only a handful of yards away.

I gaped after him in shock. What the hell was he doing?

"Stop!" Ingvar cried.

Between us and Verahl, a soldier darted out of the build-ing at the port's edge: Fasolt. He wasted no time taking off after the trespasser. Another soldier I'd met the night before, Logmadr, popped up at the top of the port's beacon tower, nocking an arrow to his bow.

"Stand down!" Ingvar called out.

Logmadr froze as ordered, looking on fearfully as Verahl threw himself against the Baron's ship. However, the hatch held fast against his attempts to open it. Fasolt, meanwhile, ignored the order to launch himself at Verahl, wrapping arms around his neck from behind.

"Disengage!" Ingvar shouted, skidding to a halt once we entered the port.

I kept running. Only a little further, and I could break up the pile.

Fasolt's tackle would've slammed anyone else to the pave-ment. It posed a mere annoyance to Verahl, who swung around and used his weight to crush Fasolt against the ship's hull. Fasolt smacked the back of his head hard, melting off of Verahl to slump unconscious on the ground.

Horror stabbed at me as badly as fatigue. *We're trying to help you!* I was too out of breath to scream it, but pressed on, only a few yards short.

Logmadr let out an anguished cry, then his eyes narrowed with vengeful purpose. He loosed his arrow, which pierced Verahl's right shoulder.

The escapee yelped in pain and fell to his knees. At the same time, an invisible arrow lodged in my gut. This was all going to hell at a remarkable rate.

"Logmadr!" Ingvar shouted behind me. "Cease fire!"

With a shudder, Logmadr ducked out of sight.

I pelted to a stop before Fasolt and Verahl, glancing breathlessly between them as pity and frustration battled for dominance.

"Stand aside, Jayce!"

I whirled around. Back where he'd stopped, Ingvar leveled his drawn bow at me—actually Verahl, somewhere behind me—fury blazing from his eyes. Though a strong breeze coursed through the port, he exuded every confidence in striking his target.

Logmadr reappeared at the base of the beacon tower, his wide-eyed stare bolting between me and Ingvar.

We sure had let a monster loose, hadn't we? Ingvar was ready to cut his losses; I had to talk him down. Hell, staring down that arrow, I had to calm *myself* down. I searched for reason around a racing heart, sore throat, and heaving breaths.

"We did this to save Verahl from Ormyr," I began, taking slow steps toward Ingvar. "He's been through … I don't even want to think about what. I'm not trying to justify what he's done. I just don't want to add to it."

"I'm finishing what Ormyr started. That animal's past saving. Fasolt …" Grief burdened Ingvar's voice. He stared through me, shaking with anger.

I glanced back toward Fasolt—still on the ground, slumped against the ship's hull, out cold. Ingvar must've feared the worst, but I doubted he'd been killed so easily. I faced Ingvar again with reassurance. "Let me see what I can do for him, all right?"

"What *can* ye do?" Ingvar asked.

"*Procedure*," I said. "Remember?"

Ingvar blinked, recognition passing over his expression. Though a doubtful frown soon followed, he nodded his leave.

I spun around with relief, but before I could focus on Fasolt, Verahl caught my eye. He was on his knees, listing, more haggard than ever. The knapsack Ingvar had packed for him still dangled from his elbow. His left hand gripped something lodged amid his knuckles of his right: Ormyr's throwing dart. Face twisted in anticipation, he ripped it out. A shudder followed, along with a trail of fresh blood down his hand.

A fraction of sympathy surfaced past my resentment. I reached into my first aid kit to unwrap a sterile compress — not for the dart wound, but the more serious arrow wound in his shoulder. I approached him to secure it in place.

"Hold that down," I muttered. "Don't pull out the arrow, and *stay right the hell there!*"

Verahl complied with a trembling hand, avoiding my gaze. That done, I turned away to approach Fasolt, my former escort.

"What's she doing?" Logmadr demanded from behind.

"Just stay put, lad," Ingvar said.

"Don't be mad at us, sir, we had to do it." Logmadr's voice wavered with unshed tears. "If that ogre'd breached the spacefaring vessel, anything could've happened!"

"Even so, we have adepts to fix it." Ingvar's voice followed, grim. "The adepts *can't* fix you lads getting killed."

Logmadr sniffled hard.

Uneasiness braced me as I knelt before Fasolt. Some nerve he had, throwing himself at a giant like that. Blood dripped from his nose to his chin. A nosebleed from a blow to the head was usually a bad sign, but his vertebrae and vitals met my highest expectations. Could I wake him up? I hoped so. Heart pounding, I retrieved and cracked open a capsule of smelling salts, holding it under his nose.

The ammonia stench bolted him upright with sharp coughs. More blood poured from his nose to drip down his matching tunic, drowning the Catherwood griffin and its reptilian supper.

"Fasolt! Blood's oath!" The other soldiers' footsteps pounded toward us.

"I know, that's bad. I'm sorry." Relieved, I sopped up what I could, then pinched another compress into place. "Lean forward. There you go."

I studied his pupils and was checking for cranial trauma when Ingvar and Logmadr approached. Fasolt tossed the compress aside and fought to stand, using the ship's hull for balance.

"None of that 'til ye can handle it!" Ingvar chided.

Fasolt reached his feet regardless. I positioned myself at his right, facing Ingvar and Logmadr, whose astounded gratitude was difficult to miss. Ingvar had tucked his arrows away in his belt, but still clutched his bow in his left fist.

"I can handle anything, sir." Fasolt coughed, then cast a glare past his left shoulder at Verahl's slumped form. "Give me another shot at that animal. We'll see who snorts blood!"

I foisted another compress on Fasolt, watching for blood in his sputum, but didn't see any.

It was a wonder the bow clenched in Ingvar's fist didn't splinter. "Lads? He was never here."

Fasolt and Logmadr gaped at him.

"Can't have word of this spreading through the districts or the capital," Ingvar explained. "The rumor will grow a set of horns fit to gore us."

"One swing, sir. All I ask," Fasolt pleaded.

"This was my fault, lad. If I'd seen to my own business, he wouldn't have run here at all. Swing at me, an ye must." Again, Ingvar's voice hinted at the guilt plaguing him.

The younger soldiers stared as though invited to jam needles into their eyes. They would've sooner punched their mothers.

I glanced toward Verahl: pale, slumped, but still awake. Why had he run here? Why the Baron's ship? Even if he'd boarded, it wasn't like he could've hidden in there. An attempt at suicide by soldier? Or wait, had he intended to *fly* out of here? No way, that was crazy.

"Who is that bastard?" Fasolt asked.

"Pontus can brief you at the barracks," Ingvar replied. "Call in your relief, ye're done for today."

"Fasolt shouldn't be alone for the next few hours," I chimed in. He'd likely sustained some degree of concussion. "Keep him awake and talk to him every once in a while. Make sure he can tell you his name, what he's been up to today, things like that. If he forgets things or has trouble speaking, come find me or your captain." I also wanted to check his nose later to make sure it wasn't broken, but it was better to wait until after any swelling had gone down first.

"All right. Logmadr, ye're done too. Stay with Fasolt." Ingvar clapped him on the back.

"Don't know why ye care, foreigner, but … thanks," Fasolt mumbled.

Logmadr relieved me of Fasolt with his own grateful nod, then turned to walk his friend back to the capital. Ingvar stared after them, pain building on his face.

"*Procedure*, aye?" he muttered, not glancing my way. "Sure as Hel *looked* like magic."

"It wasn't," I replied.

"Aye. It *worked*."

I smiled.

Behind us, Verahl muttered something that was lost amid thunder.

Ingvar whirled on him, smoldering. "What?"

Verahl, still on his knees, forced himself up straighter. "I'm sorry," he tried again. "I—"

"Quiet!" Ingvar stormed toward him.

I grabbed the captain's arm, fearing what he might do. He stopped well short of Verahl, though, letting fly with words instead. "Powers only know what torment ye've endured of late. There'd be no sunshine beaming out my hindquarters either, in your stead, but I'd still be damned careful where my fists land!"

Verahl slumped again, making no attempt to mask his pain. "Why did you do this?"

"Because you're innocent," I spoke up, "and so's Thordia."

At mention of his sister, Verahl's gaze snapped up again, his stare reaching sun-like intensity.

Meanwhile, Ingvar's anger melted off. He faced me with a haunted look. "That arrow wound," he spoke under his breath. "He doesn't have much longer to live, does he?"

I wasn't as worried, given its placement. "There's a good chance it's not fatal, but I should tend to it quickly." Infection was my main concern. Dungeons weren't among the most hygienic of places.

Despite my earlier success with Fasolt, Ingvar's stare questioned what universe I lived in.

"Would you help me get him aboard my ship?" I asked.

Ingvar drew into himself, possibly debating whether Verahl deserved the same opportunity as Fasolt.

I lowered my voice. "Believe me, I'm not happy about what happened either. But we have no idea what he's been through lately. How clearly would *you* be thinking?" I took a deep breath. "I'm willing to grant one benefit of the doubt."

Ingvar swallowed hard. "Only 'cause Fasolt's still standing."

I nodded. There was no way I could've defended Verahl if anyone had died at his hands.

After his own composing breath, Ingvar broke free of me to approach Verahl again, leaning into his face for emphasis. "Heed well, Naustvik. This knight, and my men, are trying to help you. Don't make it any harder on us. Deal violence to anyone else, lethal or not, and there shan't be one hole ye can scurry to fast enough!"

Verahl absorbed the message in silence.

"We're taking you to get healed now," I said, stepping forward to join Ingvar.

Verahl didn't bolt or demand an adept instead. Good enough.

CHAPTER 13

The storm's opening salvo pattered down on me, Verahl, and Ingvar, all clustered beside the Baron's ship. A glance over her sleek hull sent a chill through me. What would've happened if I'd tried boarding the Baron's ship for coordinates upon first arriving in Nidaros? Would Logmadr have shot me to death?

Well, it no longer mattered. He *had* shot Verahl, and as unhappy as I was about the escapee panicking and souring our plans, I still had to get that arrow out of his shoulder. I approached Verahl's right side to bring him up with minimal movement of his injured arm. The knapsack he carried wound up slung over my shoulder again. "Just for now," I muttered.

Resentment crept back into Ingvar's narrow-eyed expression. He stepped in to haul Verahl up less carefully from the left, then steered our assemblage toward the far end of the port with all the warmth of a typical prisoner escort.

Verahl admitted no discomfort, keeping his weight to himself, for which my legs and back were grateful. My paranoia watched for the moment he recognized my intentions and flipped out again. When treating anyone unfamiliar with my methods, I knew to expect anything.

Kepler's Law rested beyond the beacon tower, a welcome sight. Not as welcome were the beads and charms festooning her hull. The adepts had dropped by to bless her, as Ormyr had promised. Past Verahl, I caught the occasional glimpse of Ingvar's mounting trepidation.

"Once we get him aboard, you don't have to stay," I said. "I'm sure there's more damage control you need to tend to elsewhere."

Ingvar shook it off, eyes narrowing. "I helped create this mess. I'm seeing it through."

Verahl's pace slowed despite Ingvar's goading, but not out of weakness. His eyes riveted to my ship with a startling reverence, as if he'd often dreamt of escaping a planet's pull to go wherever curiosity beckoned.

I softened toward him fractionally. The whole point of this had been to save him from persecution, hadn't it? I'd once felt as bad for him as for Drea. That comparison seemed insane in retrospect. Still, I had no idea what he'd been through. My judgement could take a hike.

We stopped just short of my ship's hull. I braced the arrow shaft protruding from Verahl's arm to snap it a few inches short of the wound, which would hopefully prevent it from snagging on anything, then stepped away to fight with the hatch.

Visitors. Be on your best behavior, I urged the ship.

The airlock was no place for three grown adults—more like four, the way Verahl was built—but the galley was more accommodating. I had Verahl lie prone on the deck, head pointed aft, up against the starboard bulkhead. That gave me good access to his wounded shoulder without taking up too much floorspace.

Verahl arched his back to gape in every direction anatomically possible, fascinated by scenery that'd long ago blended into the background of my existence. Meanwhile, Ingvar lin-

gered near the threshold with bow in hand, surveying the galley with the grim nervousness of someone expecting an ambush.

"She's not the prettiest, but she doesn't bite." I cast a reassuring glance Ingvar's way while shedding Verahl's knapsack,
along with my coat, armor, and side sword, into a pile on the
deck. "With any luck, she might even keep out the rain."

"She?" Ingvar repeated.

"My ship. I salvaged her myself, many years ago."

Ingvar tensed, eyes flitting about as though he expected
the bulkheads to cave in any second. "'Twas a *dead vessel* ye
raised?"

Ship repair was forbidden in Catherwood's domain! I
could've kicked myself for forgetting, but I wasn't walking anything back. Ingvar was skeptical of magic and Unseen, right?
Well, to some extent. He was still wary around ships, for whatever reason. I wanted to understand his concerns and alleviate
them.

After peeling off my brigandine, I pushed stray hair out of
my face and approached Ingvar carefully. "You wouldn't call a
broken plow 'dead,' would you? You wouldn't say it's *wrong*
to repair it. This ship's just another man-made device. It's
more complicated, but—"

"Reducing Shipbuilders to men, and their works to the
likes of a plow?" Ingvar blurted, staring at me in astonishment.

Beside us, Verahl had propped himself up on one elbow to
stare up at our exchange with intense interest.

"Who told you ship repair is bad?" I challenged. "Adepts?
You don't believe in witches or wards. Why this?"

A tremor went through Ingvar. "This is *Shipbuilder* magic,
the only magic worth a damn! How else doth a hunk of metal
like this travel between planets, aye? Ye don't go meddling
with it and expect to stay in one piece!"

"If you don't know what you're doing, it's very dangerous," I agreed, gently. "But there are people who know. I can explain once Verahl's out of danger. For now, have a seat and relax."

Frowning bemusement overtook Ingvar's fear. He remained frozen despite my offer.

Verahl was waiting. Still over-warm from recent stress, I rolled up the sleeves of my tunic and picked my way toward a closet housing surgical tools, sterile compresses, and bottled solutions upon magnetic trays. I'd restocked these supplies during my last visit to the beguinage.

"What's all that?" Instead of falling back, Ingvar shadowed me.

"For the arrow wound," I said.

"No waving something at him and *there*, done?" Ingvar pantomimed how I'd used the smelling salts earlier.

"That'd be nice, but no." Smiling, I closed up the closet, balancing two trays on my arms. "You know how I woke up Fasolt? I stuck something really foul-smelling under his nose. Someone must've pulled a prank like that in the barracks at some point."

"My lot? Nay, Goose, ye've never seen a purer flock of angels." Ingvar finally allowed a trace of amusement through, which faded as he studied the surgical implements on the trays. "How's *this* procedure work?"

"Come sit with me." The offer was unprecedented in my lifetime, but I felt comfortable making it. "I'll try to explain what I'm doing, but I may need to be quiet now and then to concentrate."

Ingvar hesitated, then laid his bow aside on the deck and followed me to Verahl's right side, where we both knelt.

Still propped up on one elbow, Verahl's awe shifted to the articles I arranged beside him. As I sanitized my hands, he paled, then grabbed my left wrist as though snatching a fly mid-air, pulling it close to his face.

I gasped in surprise.

Ingvar's hand snapped toward Verahl's neck, strangling where throat met jawbone. "Let go!"

"Hang on! He's just looking!" Even though I understood he meant no harm, I wrenched my hand free anyway. "Do you recognize that, Verahl?"

"Recognize what?" Ingvar balled his retracted hand into a fist, still ready to put it to good use.

Verahl shrank back with a cough, remaining silent otherwise.

In reply, I showed Ingvar the simple line-drawing tattoo on the inside of my wrist, usually hidden beneath my gear. "This is my sigil. It's a Shipbuilder symbol: the variable resistor."

Verahl stared at me like I'd had five generations of his kin tattooed down my forearm.

Meanwhile, the blood drained from Ingvar's face. "Procedure … 'tis Shipbuilder magic as well, isn't it?"

Despite his fears, I felt certain a proper explanation would reach him. There just wasn't time for one at the moment. "Later. Promise."

Ingvar said nothing, no less pale than before.

After donning fresh gloves and cleaning the arrow wound, I soaked another cloth with lidocaine. "I'll numb the site, but you're still going to feel pain," I told Verahl. "Hold as still as you can for me. I need to cut in deeper to see what we're dealing with."

"Injuring him further?" Ingvar clenched his fists at his sides.

"I have to create enough room to remove the arrowhead," I explained. "Leaving it in there isn't an option, it'll become infected. *Fester*. This'll prevent the festering from taking hold."

Verahl let out a shuddery sigh of relief, surprising me.

"There's no controlling a thing like that!" Ingvar's shock

gave way to nervous rambling. "Well, our adepts *try* to make potions against festering. Taste like dregs from a tanning pit, and still must ye be mumbled over like mad. Even then, 'tis rarely enough."

"Keep trusting me for now, all right?" I asked. "Verahl, is something wrong?"

"You're not just leaving it in there and wishing everything well," Verahl replied. "I'm more than fine with that."

A confused frown replaced Ingvar's trepidation. I was no less informed where Verahl's cooperation came from, but I was grateful for it.

"All right, let's start." I took a deep, calming breath. "Like I said, the first step is assessing the damage. I have to widen the opening to see what the arrow struck."

The arrow shaft, still attached, showed me where to cut. Verahl stiffened, fists clenched, but otherwise cooperated as much as I could've hoped for. Thunder reverberated along the hull every once in a while, hinting at the storm outside.

"You're doing fine," I murmured, using my forearm to wipe my brow. "Let me know if you need me to slow down or ease off."

"Just get it over with." Verahl bit back a wince.

"I'm having a look now," I said.

Ingvar darted sideways for a better vantage, eyes wide.

I probed with a tool designed for the purpose, and located the arrowhead without difficulty. "We're lucky. It didn't sever any arteries or lodge itself in bone. I'm taking it out now."

Extracting the arrowhead required steady hands to prevent further injury. With the situation less grave than I'd feared, and neither Verahl nor Ingvar presenting resistance, patience was easier to summon. Arrowhead and shaft came out together, intact. In other words, perfectly.

I let out the breath in my lungs, crumpling a moment in relief. "Now I just have to close up the wound." I wiped my hands off, then prepared a needle and thread for stitching. "This part should be a little easier, with your skin numb."

"Hasn't been bad so far," Verahl said.

"I've seen people faint over less, so good job. You too." I smiled at Ingvar.

"Please, Goose! Seen worse than that," Ingvar scoffed. As I resumed stitching, his gaze turned distant, haunted. "Can think of a few people this might've helped."

"Me too," I replied, every bit as sullen.

After disinfecting and wrapping the wound, I checked Verahl all over for other wounds requiring attention. There were far too many ugly bruises that defied treatment. Thankfully, none of the many lacerations had gotten infected, and there were no fractures to tend to. Ormyr had been dragging out his game, or Verahl was just that durable.

I was glad Verahl had withstood Ormyr's physical abuse, but he clearly hadn't had the same luck with the mental abuse. Hopefully he'd remain cooperative outside of the dungeon. I also sorely hoped he had some idea of his sister's where-abouts, now that I knew just how important it was to keep her out of the adepts' hands.

Dread hit me upon realizing I'd have to return to the capi-tal eventually and face Ormyr again. It'd take serious effort to refrain from punching him, or worse.

Cleanup came next, followed by a little water and food for Verahl. Only a little, because I worried about him throwing up after such a long period of deprivation. He dug in with pro-fuse thanks, then fell right asleep, tapped of whatever had propelled him from dungeon to port. I didn't even have time to offer him the one admittedly weak painkiller at my dis-posal.

The storm outside had eased, but the gloom persisted, making it hard to tell how late in the day it was. I fetched bottles of beer and purified water, along with dried meat and hard tack, and finally collapsed beside Ingvar, who'd long since removed himself to a seat against the port bulkhead. His eyes had tracked every crumb that'd made an appearance thus far in the galley, but he dismissed my offering with a wave of his hand, staring downward. "Sure ye haven't much to spare."

"Plenty. I'm delivering most of what I have to the capital later," I told him. "That's what I was talking about with Lady Amelia earlier."

His eyes fastened to mine, wide with surprise.

"I could use help hauling it in. You know, *after* we exhaust ourselves searching the districts for Verahl, to no avail." Smiling, I proffered the food and water once more.

"That's ... thanks." Ingvar allowed himself to accept.

"Like I told Verahl, be careful," I said. "Too much too soon, and it's coming back up again."

Ingvar cast a look toward Verahl that hinted at worried thoughts he wasn't voicing. The artificial lighting cut stark shadows into his profile.

Once again, I found myself wanting to reassure him. "We ended up close to where we wanted to, right?" I gladly helped myself to food and water as well. "Fasolt will be fine, we'll keep an eye on him. Verahl's aboard my ship instead of in the districts. No big deal."

Ingvar took a collecting breath without glancing my way. "He's looking much improved, I'll give you that."

"He can stay here as long as he needs to," I said. "Do you think we can keep the adepts away from my ship?"

"Shouldn't be a problem. Then again, adepts seem to be cropping up wherever we least expect." Ingvar's haunted look turned into a dubious frown. "'Take me hostage?' Where in Hel did that come from?"

I grinned. "If Verahl hadn't snapped, I would've talked us right out of there, easy."

"Not a chance!" Ingvar cried, sitting up away from the bulkhead. "How?"

I pushed away from the bulkhead as well and faced him, feigning a desperate expression. "Oh, Master, don't chance it! I who've vanquished many a witch now find myself out-matched! If you should test him, you may find yourself lacking! Should I ever see home again, I'd rather praise your wise discretion than mourn your foolishness!"

Ingvar fell back against the bulkhead with laughter. Upon recovering, he sent an appreciative look my way. "Think I prefer the fireworks ye set off instead."

I settled back in next to him, smiling. "Don't worry about getting caught, all right? Tell everyone you were talking to Sefi when you heard noises in the dungeon, and you came down to find us. I'll say I strong-armed my way down there with my credentials, because I wanted to question Verahl about Thordia's whereabouts." I shrugged. "That's what happens when you make an emissary sit in a storehouse all day long."

"Naustvik's absence'll fall on Ormyr's head." Ingvar looked mostly assuaged. "Just hope it doesn't worry our Baron overmuch."

"Oh no, see? Having Verahl on the loose is much better than keeping him locked up," I explained. "He's sure to lead us straight to his sister now."

Ingvar blinked. "I'm impressed. Ye put that gift of bunk to good use on occasion."

"After a while, you get used to lying for survival." I had a feeling Ingvar knew just what I meant. Emboldened by our rapport, I got up to kneel before my pile of discarded gear, digging around for my first aid kit. "How're you feeling? You took a nasty hit earlier."

"Got what I deserved," Ingvar replied behind me.

"I should make sure you're not bleeding." Or concussed, but blood was my excuse for checking.

As I returned, Ingvar felt the back of his own head. "Fine."

"Let me be the judge, all right? *Procedure's* a stubborn discipline."

His hand shifted to rubbing the back of his neck. "If ye insist."

I beckoned him away from the bulkhead, then knelt behind him. Smoothing away his hair, I found a good-sized welt on the back of his head. "Hold still while I clean this up."

Ingvar complied while sampling one of the beers. "How came a healer by a sword? If ye don't mind me asking. The *truth*, Goose, not whatever long-winded tripe ye tell people to impress them."

The request, and my reaction to it, surprised me. My real origins weren't a story I told anyone, and yet I didn't mind breaking the pattern for him. I couldn't be brief, what with all the storytelling I did, but I held to his demand for honesty.

"As it turns out, I swung a sword well before I knew anything about reversing the damage." I dabbed at the wound, removing dirt trapped under the skin. "I grew up helping my mother run the family inn in Freemont. My father died before I was old enough to know him, and I had no brothers or sisters. Mother and I were close, though, and our boarders were like extended family, especially the frequent travelers. Sir Mayweather Stark of Hale's Landing was one of them, always breezing in and out of town. Every time, he swore he'd crossed the whole galaxy just to see me." I shook my head at the once charming lie. "He'd keep me up past bedtime with one crazy story after the next, but still, I never imagined taking up his trade."

"What changed?" Ingvar flinched at the first swab of antibiotic.

"It's all right," I soothed, then gathered my thoughts.

"When I was fourteen standard, my mother took ill and died. It hurt, but, she'd prepared me to take over the inn. Except Lord Turinger's cloister challenged my inheritance." Finished, I stood to discard the used gauze. "I'd reached majority by law, but they scrounged up some flunky I'd never seen before, who swore to everything sacred that I'd agreed to marry him. Denying the 'engagement' would've proven my immaturity. The cloister would've seized my property and thrown me in an orphanage. Marrying the clod would've made my property *his*. And he'd have given the cloister a cut, I'm sure."

Ingvar turned around to blink at me. "So ye ran off with your knight friend instead, aye?"

Making eye contact was difficult while relating the story, but I had to check his pupils next. I sat myself down in front of him for that, studying one eye at a time, ignoring the rising burn in my face. "It was just damn lucky May was in Freemont at the time. He rushed in and took me as his squire. I don't know what happened to the inn, I've never wanted to find out. May and I quested together a few years, then he … left me at the Enduring Flame Beguinage in Prometheion, on the other side of the galaxy."

Ingvar raised a brow at my hesitation. "Left you there?"

I was satisfied with how his pupils looked. Desperate to hide my shame- and anger-flushed face, I spun away, knelt before my gear pile, and took to straightening and folding things that didn't really need straightening or folding. "One day, May said I was ready and knighted me. When I woke up the next morning, he was gone, and so was his ship." My teenaged self had been devastated. Friend, mentor, lover, *gone* of his own choice with no explanation.

"What'd ye do?" Ingvar asked.

His gentle, supportive tone encouraged me to continue. "I was stranded at the beguinage with only my sword and the clothes on my back. I wanted to give up, but one of the beguines there—Drea—she didn't let me." I stifled the grief and remorse that threatened to undo me. "The beguinage is a group of people who preserve knowledge and artifacts from the Shipbuilder era. They freely share what they know, despite the risks. They'd educated May in the past, and they educated me too. Drea stuck with me through everything. I learned how to read, and got a grounding in all sorts of disciplines. I had particular interest in healing, because I never again wanted to feel as helpless as when my mother had gotten sick."

I didn't know what my voice betrayed, but I managed to keep it level. "May and I weren't the only knights errant they'd helped. There were others who came back to visit on occasion, and I learned a lot from them too." Which was how I'd met Branigan. At the thought of him, my hands trembled too badly to keep up the pretense of folding.

"My mentors helped me restore this ship," I went on quietly. "Once she was ready for questing, so was I."

Silence stretched past the end of my tale. I stared down at the clenched fists in my lap, fighting against a poorly timed breakdown.

A hand braced my shoulder. Ingvar had ventured up beside me. "I mourn your loss," he said, speaking close to my ear. "But, 'tis a good thing ye're not innkeeping. Holding still, watching others come and go? Doesn't suit you. Ye would've resented it—and some right fool would be here in your stead, telling me to sit on my sword while he hunted up a magic stone for battling witches." Ingvar's voice dropped to a near-whisper. "Sitting still's been the worst, Jayce."

My pulse jumped. I trembled with relief, not fear. "I know, it's awful. I'm glad ..." I trailed off, reeling at how much I'd confided. Like with Branigan, whom I could've trusted with anything.

Then fear edged in, with a deep embarrassment right on its heels. What the hell was I doing? Using Ingvar to replace

Branigan? Ashamed, I bolted to my feet, attending to unnecessary cleanup around the galley as a whole.

"Need help?" Ingvar had stood as well, but remained in place.

I watched him from my peripherals, unable to bring myself to look his way. "No. Thanks."

We spent a little while longer resting and planning before opening the stubborn hatch into a cool, misty evening. The rain had abated, but clouds obscured any moon or stars we might've seen otherwise.

I dropped to the pavement, Ingvar following. Artificial light from the ship diffused over us, creating a glowing aura. Once Ingvar shouldered his bow, I handed him the satchel I'd packed with masks, gloves, and some food I'd sneaked in when he hadn't been looking.

"There's equipment in here for handling that corpse in the dungeon," I explained. "I think it'd be wise to bring it topside for examination as soon as you can, before it degrades any further, or the adepts realize it's there. I don't trust them to not cover it up somehow." Mostly based on Ormyr's insistence on controlling everything and everyone around him.

"Agreed." A shudder passed through Ingvar. "We must figure out if it was poison or torture or … whatever it was. And whether there's any chance of it happening again."

He seemed convinced the adepts were at fault. A strong possibility, but not the only one. "Again, I'm no pathologist," I warned. "Or chemist, or biologist, but—"

"Jayce?" Ingvar frowned.

I offered a faint, self-deprecating smile. "Sorry, forget all that. I'll try to figure it out."

"I trust you more than the adepts." He glanced at me curiously. "Sure ye'd rather remain here tonight?"

Despite what we'd discussed, I still felt torn on that point. "It's not that I don't want to help out. It's just better that I stay in case Verahl needs something."

Ingvar gave a nod. "I'll tell the court ye're still out in the districts searching for him. At sun-up, I'll return here so we can report to the keep together. And I'll bring men to offload your stores, if the offer standeth yet."

"Absolutely." I smiled again.

"I'll also send some men to stand watch over Naustvik, so ye can rest." Ingvar tilted his head toward *Kepler's Law.* "In case ye need them, there are also two men stationed within the port. They'll have orders not to let anyone approach your vessel, not even adepts."

I hesitated, then voiced a niggling thought that'd resurfaced. "Is there any chance your men could look the other way while I climb aboard the Baron's ship for a few minutes?"

Ingvar shook his head. "The hatch is sealed. Only Ormyr possesseth the key." From there, his frown softened into a look of concern. "Second time ye've asked me, Jayce. What's this about?"

"Beguine Drea, the woman who mentored me ..." I clenched a fist, swallowing around the painful knot in my throat. "I'll spare you the details. Right now, she's stranded on a cursed planet without supplies. Its location was removed from my ship's index while I was in Spectra, so I have no way of returning. I'm hoping the Baron's ship has that location still. I *really* need to get back to her."

He'd already known something bad had happened before I'd reached Nidaros. By his sympathetic look, I could tell Ingvar was adding things up. "We'll try asking Ormyr tomorrow, all right? First thing."

I smiled, relieved and grateful. "Thank you, Ingvar."

"Thank you too, Jayce. My offer standeth yet—talking about what happened, I mean. Ye needn't keep the details bottled. Ye have my ear should ye need it." Ingvar held my gaze another moment, then jogged off and vanished behind the beacon tower.

I watched him leave, mixed up with heady feelings I'd only ever harbored for Branigan and May before him—but guilt choked them out almost instantly. They were just a knee-jerk reaction given our like-mindedness. Otherwise, what kind of horrible person was I? Wasn't it an insult to Branigan's memory?

The sooner I forgot about it, the better. Ingvar was a good person, but I had work to do here, and then I'd be racing off to Gules.

Unfortunately, my heavy heart struggled with being so rational. I climbed back into the airlock, pulled the hatch shut, and trudged back to the galley.

Verahl had pressed up against the starboard bulkhead, sleeping on his side, fortunately not the side I'd operated on. I would've repositioned him like that anyway if I'd had the requisite strength. It was a better posture, and opened up the airways. Nothing interrupted his sleep, not even my footsteps or the mysteries unfolding around him.

Welcome aboard, I thought. *Like Ingvar said, don't hurt anyone else.*

Whatever consequences awaited me and Ingvar the next morning, they'd be better than whatever Ormyr had been doing to Verahl. I was more than fine with that tradeoff. As for Verahl himself, why had he gunned for a spacefaring vessel? How had he recognized my sigil? Might he have seen or heard anything in the dungeon that would account for the disturbing corpse Ingvar and I had found?

Though I yearned to ask these questions, I resigned myself to mystery. Verahl needed the rest.

CHAPTER 14

Waking up aboard *Kepler's Law* was much less jarring than at the Baron's estate, even with sunlight streaming through a porthole accustomed to displaying darkness. Verahl remained unconscious. Concerned, I geared up quickly, then knelt beside him to check his pulse and breathing. Everything felt normal; this seemed to be heavy sleep. I wouldn't worry any further unless he still hadn't awakened by the next time I returned to my ship, whenever that might be.

After I'd eaten something, faint voices became audible outside. Ingvar had returned to *Kepler's Law* as promised, he and a small group of soldiers towing a sled with heavy ropes attached. I headed outside to meet them.

As the sun rose in a clear yellow sky, we all threw in with unloading supplies from my cargo bay. I gave them most of what Linum Dominorum had given me, but retained a fair amount for Verahl and myself. And Drea eventually, I hoped.

The thought of her mired my brain in worry and guilt again. How was she holding up? What was she doing at present? It'd only been two days. *Twelve* to go before the trade guild arrived in Nidaros.

I tried to keep it off my face. If I'd learned anything from

Drea during my time at the beguinage, it was that people could be surprisingly tough under duress. Drea would keep trying, and so would I. At least Ingvar and the soldiers offered some hope of progress toward solving Nidaros' problems. It was nice to see them again, and provide what material help I could.

"How's Fasolt?" I asked Pontus, sliding a box onto the sled.

"The lad's fine." Pontus stacked a different box into place. "We're resting him all the same today. Logmadr's fussing over him like his own mother."

"I'll follow up with him as soon as I get a chance," I promised.

Pontus waved me off. "Ye've done enough for now, lass. They'll be wanting you in the capital. Same with you, Captain."

"Aye, thanks." Ingvar approached my side. "See the rest of you later!"

"Later, Captain! Lady Knight!" Farewells rose up throughout the cargo bay and around the sled.

Pontus made eye contact with Ingvar, his smile vanishing in favor of wariness. Ingvar acknowledged his second with a nod and nothing more. I wondered at the contents of the secret message, but wasn't about to pry into it.

Ingvar and I started across the worn pavement at a brisk pace. For once, I felt no worry about leaving my ship in the hands of others. I'd geared up fully, including my side sword and a new dagger to replace the one lost in the dungeon. Ingvar, likewise, was equipped for a fight. Our pending meeting at Ormyr's calefactory sure seemed to merit our arsenal.

"Are we in any trouble for yesterday?" I asked out of earshot of his men.

"Nay," Ingvar replied. "Your line worked well for us both. Everyone's more worried than angry."

"Good." Being an emissary was a wonderful thing. Anywhere else, I'd have been in for such hell. But relief failed to reach me past one stubborn, unanswered question. "Do you have any idea how Ormyr sniffed us out just as we were retrieving Verahl?"

Ingvar blinked as though the thought hadn't occurred to him. "Can't say for certain."

"The adepts who helped you with keys and directions, might they have ratted you out?" I'd decided it probably hadn't been Holsten. Though I'd asked him about infiltrating the dungeon, he couldn't have known I'd be trying it right when I had.

"Wouldn't expect them to." Ingvar's surprise turned into a skeptical frown. "We've traded secrets back and forth a long time. Be foolish of any of us to betray the others."

There was that. People who stayed in one place for years, or a lifetime, had to cooperate to get anywhere long-term. Stabbing paranoia urged me to reconsider the possibility right in front of my face: that Ingvar and Ormyr had collaborated to stage the whole thing, and that I was walking into a trap back at the capital.

I could've pressed Ingvar about it, but after yesterday and all I'd learned about him thus far, I decided I trusted him. Still, that brought me no closer to understanding how Ormyr had known not only *of* the plot, but also *when* to foil it. There had to be more to it than I'd managed to glean in two days.

"How's Naustvik?" Ingvar asked. If he noticed my internal deliberation, he didn't show it.

"Still resting," I said. "He's fine as far as I can tell, just exhausted. Were you able to retrieve that corpse last night?"

"Nay." Ingvar's eyes narrowed. "Adepts were posted at every dungeon entrance, saying all the broken wards had to be repaired first."

"Damn." Hiding something? Or had they been honestly tending to their wards, unaware of anything else amiss? "Did you try appealing to the Baron?"

"Nay," Ingvar said again. "Was waiting for you to back me first. Otherwise, Ormyr'd just dismiss me as seeing things."

"So you want to bring it up this morning?" I delayed his answer by raising my hand. "We should figure out *everything* we want to talk about today, I think. We tripped over ourselves yesterday and lost our opportunity with the Baron."

"Fair enough," Ingvar said. "Securing your mentor's location, that can be first."

Reinforcing his promise from the night before. Gratitude warmed me. "All right."

"Permission to retrieve the corpse can be next."

"If we corner the Baron, then yes," I said. "I'm not sure I want to bring it up in front of Ormyr. I don't know if he knows what happened to that prisoner, let alone was responsible for it, but just like with everything else, he'll hold us at arm's reach while he either looks into the mystery himself or destroys the evidence."

"He's *responsible* no matter how that prisoner died," Ingvar stated flatly, then settled into a familiar frustration. "But aye, ye're right. He'd just talk our Baron into leaving it in his hands."

If we didn't get a moment alone with Baron Tristan, we could well end up sneaking into the dungeon again—but that wasn't the moment to worry about it. "We can also push for more soldiers in the districts, if you still want that," I offered.

"Aye!" Ingvar's gaze lit up with determination. "Now with Naustvik 'out there,' we have more leverage."

"And we'll push to keep 'looking for him,' of course. I'd still like a chance to actually see the districts myself." The pavement had since given way to the endless brown grasses. I reached down to break off and study one of the long, dry stems. "Is it like this out there as well? Dried-up plants every-where despite the rain?"

"Aye, mostly."

I frowned, puzzled. "It's still worth a look, but like with the corpse, I can't promise I'll know what's wrong."

Ingvar frowned himself, staring downward a moment, then glanced my way again with a shot. "What of your mentor, then? Drea?"

Her name knifed through my heart. "What about her?" I managed.

"Would *she* know what the trouble is?" Ingvar asked. "Don't just ask for her location. Ask to fly off and bring her back here to help us."

"I ..." My jaw fell as I trailed off, stupefied. Hell, that was perfect. Why hadn't I thought of that? Both of my most pressing concerns solved at once. Drea's data carrier was a treasure trove of Shipbuilder knowledge, and she knew a lot about navigating computers and huge data structures to get what she wanted.

I looked to Ingvar with elation. "That's brilliant! We could work together to identify the problem and cure it!"

Ingvar cheered up along with me, his pace quickening. "How far away's this cursed territory she's at?"

I struggled to keep up with him and think around my giddiness. "I don't know for sure, but it can't be more than a couple days standard, based on—"

"Goose! Wrong answer!" Ingvar chided with a grin. "Ye say, '*What* cursed territory? My friend's in a peaceful settlement close by, and would be glad to help us.'"

I laughed. "She really would!" I was primed to jump out of my skin from excitement, until a sobering realization struck. "I still need to convince Ormyr to give me the coordinates for the planet she's on."

"Ye'll make it happen." Ingvar placed a reassuring hand on my shoulder. "Ye know just the sort of lies needed to get your way, Jayce. What're ye afraid of?"

My goodness, he was right. I could rationalize this. To save Drea, I could rationalize zero-gee horse racing. A huge smile broke out on my face. "I promise, I'll get her and come right back here and fix everything!"

Though Ingvar laughed at my enthusiasm, the light in his eyes was no less bright.

Before we'd fully crossed the threshold into the stifling calefactory, Baron Tristan, Ormyr, and Lady Amelia flew in on us from different angles. We weren't allowed to kneel to the nobility. The Baron insisted upon bracing my hands, not a trace of anger in his expression. "What a relief to find thee unscathed after that terrible ordeal! It should never have happened! We apologize, deeply."

It was a big relief to me as well. Yes, being an emissary was better than I'd ever imagined. "Thank you, sir. What happened wasn't anyone's fault."

Ormyr picked up my hand next, raising it toward his cryptic smile. "I did foresee thy successful return. Unseen be praised for their protection."

My hackles jumped to attention. After what I'd seen of him in the dungeon yesterday, even his friendliest gestures seemed full of disturbing intent. Everything about him looked gratified, but I couldn't tell how genuine it was. It took effort to lower my head in greeting, and not yank my hand out of his and shove him backward for good measure.

Ormyr flicked his wrist. Two identical amulets on leather cords appeared in his once empty hand; he'd probably had them hidden up a sleeve. Each amulet resembled a blue human eye, free of its socket. Ormyr hung one of them around my neck. "May this mati surveil and protect thee from here on."

"Thank you," I managed past my disgust.

"And thee, Captain." Ormyr passed the second amulet to Ingvar.

Ingvar's eyes had narrowed distastefully. Without a word, he looped the amulet on his belt, right next to his unused beads.

Ormyr waved an arm toward the stone table nearby. Everyone slipped into a seat: Ingvar and Lady Amelia on the left side of the circle, Ormyr and Baron Tristan on the right, I at the "head" of the gathering. It wouldn't be easy in the presence of nobility, but I intended to steer the day's conversation the way Ingvar and I had agreed upon earlier. The prospect of rescuing Drea ahead of schedule, with official sanction, imbued me with courage I might've lacked otherwise.

"We're all grateful for thy return, Lady Knight," Lady Amelia said, strained. "But truly, what shall we do now?"

"This is actually a blessing in disguise, madam," I assured her. "Verahl's alone, scared, and will make mistakes. I'm sure he'll lead us to Thordia."

Pleasant surprise lit up the Baron's expression. "Perchance. I do wish it so."

"Thou shouldst return to the field at once!" Lady Amelia leaned toward me with purpose.

"After the events of yesterday, Dame Jessamine needeth time to recover." Ormyr observed me carefully as he spoke.

Typical. "I wasn't sent here to sit idle, Master."

"There's truly no need to take on further risk," he pressed. "I shall scry for the Naustviks from here, as ever. As thou said, it shall be easier to find them with two on the loose. Once they are found, I would be most grateful for your help in apprehending them."

You won't be too busy killing more prisoners? I thought in spite of myself. There was every chance Ormyr was innocent of the prisoner's demise, but he'd likely contributed to it, in much the same way he'd *encouraged* Verahl the day before.

"All right then." Time for my main proposal. My heart pounded with anticipation. "If I can't help with the Naustviks right now, I'd like to help with the curse instead."

"How, pray tell?" Baron Tristan asked.

"Well, first, with your soldiers' help—" I nodded toward Ingvar "—and at Lady Amelia's request, the majority of supplies aboard my vessel are being brought to your storehouse. They're not much, but I hope they prove useful." I hadn't wanted to be conspicuous about it, but the goodwill was probably necessary for the favor I was working up to.

Ormyr blinked my way with naked surprise. "How very generous."

Lady Amelia clutched her beads to her chest.

The Baron cast warm appreciation on me and his wife equally, and had trouble finding words. "Prithee accept our thanks, Dame Jessamine."

I smiled and continued. "Second, a few days' flight from here resides a wise woman of some renown, greatly attuned to nature. I've seen her reverse many a blight once thought irreversible."

"Truly?" the Baron marveled.

"With her help, we may not need to wait on the Naustviks' capture for relief," I continued. "By your leave, sir, I want to retrieve her so she can put her talents to work against this curse."

Ormyr raised an eyebrow. "Space-flight?"

"Go to!" Lady Amelia snapped, souring. "Two witches now infest our realm, and thou wouldst to *fly?*"

I leaned toward the Baron. "You said yourself, sir: officially, my quest is making sure your harvest goes smoothly in two weeks, and it will, because you have enough flax for quota. That's great and all, but you don't really want me sitting here for two weeks doing nothing when I can be of help. Do you?"

Ormyr's head tilted at an inquisitive angle. "This wise woman, is she an adept? Perchance I know her."

"It's unlikely you do," I said. "She's native to distant realms, but arrived in Catherwood space recently. Her knowledge and skills are greatly trusted, and she's helped a lot of communities in need." All true. I steeled myself for the big question. "I do need your help with one thing, Master: obtaining the coordinates for where this wise woman resides. Remember yesterday, I mentioned my ship's index isn't what it used to be? It lacks a number of locations in Catherwood space."

"Which settlement dost thou seek?" Ormyr asked.

Hell. He may or may not have known Gules was cursed. I wasn't taking any chances. Despite my pounding heart, I managed a casual shrug. "I've been traveling through so many foreign domains of late, the names escape me. I have it written down somewhere."

"Ah. Thou hast a gift for letters?" Ormyr asked.

"Yes." Not unheard of for a knight errant, especially a knight errant who allegedly ran in higher circles.

Baron Tristan clutched at his hammer-shaped amulet, then looked to Ormyr as though seeking his approval.

Ormyr stared off into space, deliberating for several moments, then lowered his head to the Baron.

Finally, the Baron turned back to me. "Very well, Dame Jessamine. I give thee my leave to travel."

The triumph was overwhelming. Somehow, I managed not to fall out of my chair.

"By your leave, Your Grace." Ingvar, who'd remained quiet the entire time, finally spoke up. He clenched a fist upon the stone table, looking to Baron Tristan with determination. "I would to accompany the knight on her journey."

His request shocked everyone, me most of all. He'd only ever flown once before, and my ship had frightened him.

Paranoia emerged to hunt down some shady motive, but had trouble finding or even inventing one. It made sense as a precautionary measure, to ensure I made it back with the wise woman safely. I also liked to think there was some element of friendly concern.

"I'd welcome Captain Leirfall's help," I declared. Now those were words I never thought I'd say about any court official and mean it.

"Pontus can manage things whilst I'm abroad," Ingvar added, "*and* send more men to the districts."

That item had been accidentally lost amid my excitement. "I think it's a good idea, sir," I seconded. "Your subjects will welcome more protection right now."

Baron Tristan blinked toward Ormyr, once more seemingly awaiting his verdict.

I feared the resurrection of yesterday's debate, or a change of subject. Instead, Ormyr glanced around the table with affirmation. "We'd need to scry on the matter of increased patrols to see if it would pose any unforeseen problem. As for our Captain of the Guard accompanying Dame Jessamine on her journey, I consider it a wise precaution."

He finally agreed with us on something. Were it not for a niggling suspicion, I could've jumped from my chair with glee. Oh well, maybe Ormyr welcomed the chance to have us out of his way for a little while.

The Baron nodded to Ingvar. "I grant thee leave conditionally, Captain, pending discussion of Dame Jessamine's destination and how long the journey shall take."

Ingvar nodded back, his deadpan concealing whatever he felt about the prospect.

"Neither of thee must tarry abroad," Lady Amelia said, clutching her beads tighter. "I fear what ground the witches may gain in your absence."

"There's nothing to fear, Milady," Ormyr assured her. "I've

everything well in hand."

Lady Amelia's narrowed-eyed expression conveyed a lack of faith, but the master adept was blind to her skepticism.

"Thank you, sir." I faced the Baron, struggling to keep my voice level. "On my honor, we'll return as soon as possible."

"'Tis upon thine honor as a knight errant that I entertain the notion at all. Prithee do not forget," the Baron replied. "Master, assist Dame Jessamine now with those coordinates, then return here for for my final determination."

"Certainly, Your Grace—though I would to perform additional rites over Dame Jessamine first, to remove the corrupting influences she encountered within the dungeon," Ormyr said.

"Very well," the Baron said. "Captain, make thy preparations, then report back here as well. However, I reserve the right to keep thee in Nidaros if the journey should prove too long or perilous."

"Understood, Your Grace." Ingvar stood, bowed, and saw himself out, sneaking a tiny glance my way before leaving. When our eyes met, my heart jumped. I couldn't wait to speak to him again, hopefully when we were *on our way to rescue Drea*.

"Holsten!" Ormyr called.

A few moments later, the hunched adept peeked out from behind one of the curtains along the perimeter, pendulum in hand. His eyes passed over our high-ranking assembly without fear, but stopped before meeting my gaze. "Yes, Master?"

"Is the libation chamber ready?"

Holsten bowed his head. "Gaermar and Botvi saw to it this morning."

Ormyr immediately forgot him to rise and approach my chair, smiling all the way. "A full forecast shall follow thy blessings today, Lady Knight. No more hidden surprises shall confound us!"

I somehow rose to my feet without leaping to them. The thought of leaving for Gules, in fine company no less, elated me to the point where I forgot to be annoyed at the skullduggery soon to follow.

Ormyr led me into a cramped hallway. I shivered against the change in temperature, and tried not to bounce on the balls of my feet. Gules was only a few bureaucratic motions away. We'd save Drea, and she'd surely be of help. Once Nidaros was well, we could return to the beguinage. Then I'd seek justice for Branigan.

The contents of Beghard Joachim's letter returned to mind. According to that, my former master May would be at the beguinage for certain. Hell, it didn't matter. With Drea out of danger, I could overlook a lot of things.

We navigated a long, snakelike path. From branches and side rooms, adepts called out questions and flagged Ormyr down for help. He rarely stopped, usually just barking out answers, as his mind was on other things. I was only paying half-attention myself.

Then, a crash of wood and shattering glass erupted in the hallway ahead of us.

"Master!" a thin voice choked out. "I'm so sorry!"

"Stay back!" Ormyr shouted, hastening toward the commotion.

I was about to follow him, but at that moment, the floor under my feet inexplicably gave way. Terror seized me. With a surprised yelp, I fell backward into a darkness of uncertain depth.

CHAPTER 15

Before I could brace for impact, my shoulder slammed into an unforgiving dirt surface. The rest of me hit the ground in short order, knocking the air out of my lungs. As I lay there struggling to draw breath, I registered the nostril-burning reek of the dungeon.

Pain and dread racked me. A trap door? I glanced back up at the blazing rectangle of light, but failed to spot anything other than a patch of ceiling high above. Several adepts, including Ormyr, bickered in the distance—presumably over whatever had been dropped in the corridor—as though nothing unusual had happened.

With the wind knocked out of me, I had no voice to call out with. I'd have to help myself out of there. But just as I wondered whether I could reach the ledge with a solid jump, the opening above narrowed, seemingly of its own volition. All too quickly, the last sliver of light disappeared, plunging me into dark, uncertain silence.

Stuck in the dungeon. My heart and head pounded in desperate unison. What in hell was going on? Was this the adepts' way of detaining me without a fuss—over Verahl? Had the Baron ordered this? Would Ormyr happen by to "ask" about what had really happened yesterday? Was that why he'd been so willing to grant me and Ingvar permission to travel, *and* so insistent on performing blessings first?

At the same time, Ormyr had sounded distracted by whatever mishap had occurred in the corridor. Did he even know I was in the dungeon? Did Ingvar? My stomach lurched. I'd wondered earlier whether a trap awaited at the keep.

I shoved it all aside. The who and why, I could worry about after I'd gotten myself to a good hiding spot.

Adrenaline allowed me to ignore pain and push myself up to my knees. Whatever was going on, I had to reach my feet, take measures to defend myself. They'd left me with my weapons, after all. I'd also take stock of my surroundings. Maybe there was still some way out.

My confines remained plunged in darkness. Straining my ears brought me no closer to abandoning the heavy silence. I retrieved my stick lighter from my pocket; the tiny bead of light revealed dungeon floor and nothing else. No immediate danger, at least. I resolved to scout the room, or cell, more likely.

Something flashed in my peripherals: the glow of lantern light, newly revealed by a door sliding open about ten feet away. Soon after, a burgundy-robed arm lobbed a hand-sized ceramic pot with a lit fuse into the cell.

Grenade!

Without another thought, I threw myself in the opposite direction. Unfortunately, the cell's dimensions were stingy. I hit a wall well before I wanted to.

A boom like thunder rattled my eardrums. Tongues of fire splattered around my feet. Turning, I found knee-high flames covering the floor behind me, surviving on the fuel from the grenade. Some version of Greek fire, it looked like. Radiant heat seared my exposed skin, while a thick smoke stung my eyes and clawed at my throat.

Forget questioning or detaining. Someone was trying to kill me. Either fire or smoke would finish the job in minutes. Ironically, my pockets held plenty of fire-making implements and things to burn, but nothing for smothering flames. Escape was my only hope. I knew of only one option: the door on the other side of the room, the one the grenade had been launched from.

I'd long forgotten my hurts and all notions of fear. My first move was to duck low to the ground, where the eye- and lung-stinging smoke would be least prevalent. I had to navigate around the flames to reach that door. If I followed the perimeter of the room, I'd make it there eventually. My stick lighter would allow me to avoid further surprises.

With my free hand on the wall, I started crawling. Furniture blocked my path occasionally, which I dodged or pulled out of my way. Keeping my eyes open became more difficult by the second. On occasion, I had to lie prone just to catch half of an acceptable breath. Finally, my hand sank into that welcome depression in the wall that marked the threshold.

Triumph lifted me to my feet, until my lighter fell upon a keyhole. Relief quickly turned to horror.

Locked! Of course it was. *I'm dead. I'm—*

Wait! I still had the dungeon keyring I'd used to free Verahl. Ingvar had never reclaimed it from me!

Frantically, I dug the loop out of my pocket. The only trouble was, I didn't know which of the many keys would work, if any. Nothing for it but to brute-force through them.

One key after the next failed to coax open the lock. Meanwhile, the flame's heat became ever more oppressive. I couldn't hold my breath forever, especially as fear crept in. The overpowering need for oxygen forced me to let in ever more smoke that my lungs harshly rejected. A lightheaded haze settled over me. Carbon monoxide, probably. How much longer could I keep this up?

Just when I feared passing out, the key in my hand turned over. My celebration consisted of collapsing face-first into the hallway beyond the door, gasping and coughing—keys in one hand, stick lighter in the other. For a few moments, the dungeon bouquet was the most blissful air I'd ever sampled.

As my brain cleared, I realized my surroundings were familiar. I'd escaped into the muck-riddled dungeon hallway. Verahl's former cell door loomed directly across from mine, still heavily decorated. I saw it by virtue of a lantern in the hands of an unknown adept wearing several amulets around his neck. He darted toward me, wrath smoldering in his eyes.

This had to be the person who'd locked me in with a grenade. It looked *personal*. When and how had I inspired such anger?

I was in no shape to fight, but circumstances left me little choice. Forcing back coughs and tears, I hastened to right myself in time to defend against whatever was coming next.

The adept stopped short of me, then threw a hand out toward my face. A red flash leapt from his fingers. Pure agony set upon my eyes, like the acid from a bushel of cut onions. The pain forced them shut as I cried out, momentarily overcome.

That was all it took to end up tackled, lying prone. A pair of hands seized my throat, pushing knuckles into the arteries.

From coughing to strangled. Not a good transition. My eyes felt like they were melting on top of it, but the lack of blood to my head became the more urgent matter.

Desperation forced my eyes open. Though my vision was blurry, I made out the outline of my would-be killer, half-lit by the lantern resting nearby. The adept was dedicated to finishing me off, but he wasn't a good grappler. He hadn't pinned any of my limbs. Instead of sitting and using his weight to hold me in place, he knelt over me. That left plenty of room for me to raise a knee and strike him in the groin.

He winced and stiffened. I grabbed his arms, threw him aside, then pulled myself to my knees, ignoring protest from my lungs and eyes. As the young adept lay stunned before me, I shoved the dungeon keys into my pocket, took my stick lighter into my left hand, and removed my dagger from its sheath with my right. "Who put you up to this?" I managed.

Upon recovering, the adept's only answer was to lunge at me for another tackle.

I held up my left forearm to block, right hand poised to strike with the dagger if needed. However, it seemed the stick lighter, this inexplicable spark of fire I commanded, was what really threw him. He let out a startled cry and fell aside, crash-ing into his own lantern.

Some of that Greek fire must've gotten on the adept's hands and clothing. Flames tore over his robe as though it were tinder. He leapt to his feet, screaming, and bolted down the dungeon hallway like a wraith.

Stop! Lie down! I couldn't chase after him, couldn't manage more than a rasp in my throat. I could only watch, horrified, as the fire intensified.

Eventually, the adept slowed and collapsed, writhing. More smoke, thick with the stench of burned flesh, filled the hallway and coaxed bile to my mouth.

Hell. That was what he'd tried to subject me to, but still, unwelcome tears of sympathy joined the ones I was already shedding thanks to whatever he'd thrown in my eyes, not to mention the smoke. I had to reach fresh air, or I was dead as well.

The dungeon entrance Ingvar and I had used yesterday was closed; that end of the dungeon sat in darkness. In the other direction, the same way my attacker had run in from, a faint light issued from another open cell.

Let's see what that's about, I thought. My stick lighter and dagger remained in my hands. I forced myself to my feet and staggered toward the light, limiting my breaths, forcing my eyes open through the smoke and stinging.

Inside the chamber, the first thing to catch my eye was a second lit lantern resting on the floor. Did the adept have an accomplice somewhere? My frantic searching, both in and out of the cell, failed to uncover one. The lantern sat next to what looked like a door cut into the wall of the cell. Past the opening, a ramp led upward into darkness.

Another secret passage? Odd that it wasn't vertical, like the trap door had been. Then again, the dungeon was a single long hallway, while the keep above had a much larger footprint. Secret entrances would plunge underground at all different angles.

I approached the door. The lantern revealed a short ascent ending at a closed panel. No keyhole, handle, or latch. Still no sign of additional adepts, either. I walked up the ramp, then paused to listen at the door at the summit. Silence met my ears.

Please open, I thought, hoping like hell that there weren't more murderous adepts on the other side.

CHAPTER 16

The secret dungeon exit yielded to a push. Heart and lungs aching with desperation, still blinking back stinging tears, I nudged it open a crack and peeked out through it.

Beyond sat a tiny circular room, empty aside from a magic circle in its center. To my burning eyes, the candles poised along its circumference looked more like blurry halos. A curtain hung over the only exit, situated across the room from me.

Compared to the smoke, fire, and corpses in the dungeon behind me, this little room was the threshold to paradise. I put away my stick lighter, keeping my dagger as a precaution, then pushed the secret door fully open. Once I'd fallen inside, a hinged mechanism swung shut the door shut again, hiding it seamlessly in the wall.

The room's sour incense would've been offensive, had I not just emerged from worse. I remained kneeling for a while, doubled over with coughs and dry retches. My heart pounded in time with my aching head. Dark, unidentifiable splotches marked my clothing. Burns? Mud?

That one small speculation brought back every other unanswered question regarding the hell I'd just endured, paired with an unsettling chill. Had Ormyr arranged for my murder?

Had the whole court been in on it? Ingvar as well?

I had no proof of anything yet. Ormyr had never provided those coordinates for Gules, either. Poor Drea, she didn't deserve this. My nausea worsened.

Worry about surviving for now, I told myself, pushing it all back again.

Whatever trap I'd just escaped, whoever had set it, one thing was certain: the adepts' keep wasn't safe. Hell, until I knew who'd orchestrated this, my ship was the only safe place around. I had to leave the keep, then the capital. From there, I could hole up in *Kepler's Law* and take stock of my options. Or, if I found myself *very* unwelcome, I could take off for some other port in Catherwood space, where someone else might have Gules' coordinates in their index. I'd be reneging on my quest, but what other choice would I have if everyone wanted me dead?

What would happen to Verahl and Thordia, and the other innocents on Nidaros? I didn't know. Something to think about later.

Until I knew more, it was best to assume every adept in the keep was an enemy. That meant I was heavily outnumbered at the moment. Stealth would be my friend. I hoped to sneak to an open window, or the front foyer, and slip outside without being seen. After that, I wanted to just tear off to the capital gate, but wasn't in any shape to repeat yesterday's run. Besides, the soldiers at the gate might also have turned hostile.

I'd have to figure it out on the fly. Time was no ally; eventually, someone would miss that adept who'd tried to kill me. As much as I loathed the idea of moving another step, I had to get going.

Placing my free hand on the wall for balance, I slowly took to my feet, then rounded the wall to reach the curtained threshold and glance past it. A narrow corridor stretched beyond, leading directly to a second curtained threshold. It looked and sounded clear enough. With my left hand on the wall and my dagger in my right, I advanced, stifling coughs at the same time.

No signs of life appeared past the next curtain either. Rows of shelves loomed between big windows open to the sunny day. Those giant panels of light reduced me to squinting at first, but my heart raced with gratitude. Maybe I'd make my escape right there. I inched my way toward the windows, left hand outstretched. Unfortunately, unlike the window in my estate room, each one of these held solid against my touch.

Footsteps surfaced, approaching my location rapidly. Heart in my mouth, I dove back behind the curtain through which I'd entered.

The footsteps entered the room, halted, then slid about with painful slowness. A peek past the curtain revealed an adept scanning the scrolls on the shelves with a deliberating frown.

Had he just looked the way I'd come? Was he waiting for the killer to report in? I doubled over with my breath held, struggling not to let the slightest cough escape. *Leave already!* I pleaded silently.

The adept plucked a magnetic contraption from a shelf. As he held one magnet in his hand, its twin obediently levitated over it. He fiddled with it absently a while, then froze, frowning toward my curtain.

I leaned out of sight, tensing every muscle, and prepped my dagger for action. While I didn't care to strike first, I'd have to stop him if he moved to attack or announce my escape to the world at large.

Seconds dragged past. Breath held, I strained to listen for any clue of what was coming next. At last, unhurried footsteps. *Retreating.*

Relief fell over me. A series of revenge-coughs sputtered out past my caution. Upon recovering, I got back to pursuing escape.

Each room in the keep had one or more corridors branching to further rooms. I traversed the convoluted network as carefully as possible. Occasionally, I was forced to back up and detour to avoid passersby or groups of adepts gossiping or studying scrolls. None of them looked like bloodthirsty schemers awaiting word of my demise, but assuming anyone's innocence would be a mistake.

It dragged out far longer than I'd hoped. There were two problems: every window I came across was solid, and none of the corridors I chose led back to the foyer. On my best day, I would've had trouble navigating. The fierce headache joining my other symptoms made it even more difficult to concentrate on building a mental map of the layout.

After an exhausting, mind-bending journey, the foyer finally revealed itself in all its bazaar-stall glory. My triumph was short-lived, though. An adept watched the door there. At least there was plenty of cover in the form of all those trinkets. I dropped behind an iron cauldron to think, still holding back coughs.

By then, my patience had worn thin. I just wanted to get past the final adept and outside. Maybe a diversion would suffice? Having a convenient lack of qualms about such things, I decided to shove my cauldron into a glass totem sitting nearby.

The crash was terrific. Glass shards scattered in all directions. I scrambled away from the crime scene and hid behind a silk drape, expecting the adept to hone in on the source of the noise. Instead, I heard her gasp. Footsteps pattered down another hallway.

I peeked out, confirming that indeed, she was gone. She'd run off looking for backup, or a charm for banishing ghosts. Even better. I darted toward the front door, pulled it open, then slipped outside and shut it behind myself. Finally free, I fell back against the keep's front door, doubled over with a coughing fit that would be denied no longer.

Back to the ship, I urged myself.

How would I flee the capital without anyone being the wiser? I lacked anything that'd help me scale the tall capital wall. I had no recourse but the gate, and there was no way I wouldn't be recognized there. Would the soldiers gladly let me through, or shoot me to death?

Reaching the gate presented its own problems. A lot of empty ground stretched between me and it. What if a hostile spotted me before I even got that far?

Cover would help. It wouldn't be foolproof, but it might buy me a few precious seconds when I needed them. Where to find it? Well, I wasn't about to backtrack through the keep for something to mask my appearance. The storehouse was also well guarded, potentially crawling with soldiers and adepts.

The Baron's estate, then? I'd made some friends there. Were they still friends? Well, the kitchen was easy to reach from there. If they had turned on me, I could bolt when they raised the alarm. It was worth a try.

Following the keep wall, I hurried into the rain barrel-filled courtyard. There, I found the back door to the estate's kitchen propped open. I put away my dagger and approached the threshold.

The kitchen was in much the same state as when I'd left the day before. Lif, Kofri, and Alfrun sat a short distance away, Lif chattering while the other two listened. All held steaming cups of what might've been tea.

Here goes nothing. I braced the threshold and leaned inside. "Hail, friends."

The trio jumped to their feet with startled looks at my half-entrance, half-collapse.

"Pretend I'm not here." Though I struggled noisily to catch my breath, I put a finger to my lips. "I've hit a rough patch in my quest. I need help reaching the capital gate without anyone seeing me."

"Are the Naustviks after you?" Kofri asked, his eyes wide.

"The Naustviks are *here?*" Lif shrieked.

Kofri and Alfrun hushed her with glares.

"No. I promise I'll explain later," I said. "Could you lend me a cloak or something?"

"Hang on, I know what might work," Kofri said. "Come on, Lif!"

As they darted off, Alfrun retrieved a ladle and rag, dunked both in a nearby water bucket, then hurried to my side. "Does this have to do with the lights upstairs at night?" she asked in a hush. *"Is* Thordia here?"

Several swigs of water calmed my throat. "Thank you. I'm sorry, I don't know. With Verahl's escape, I haven't had a chance to find out."

Alfrun bit her lip, glancing downward, then looked up again to swab around my eyes with the damp rag. Bright red streaks leeched through the fabric. "All this blood ..."

I froze with panic for a moment, then took the rag and unfurled it for a closer look. "No, this stuff was thrown into my eyes," I explained around a relieved sigh. My tears had mixed with a fine red powder, some ground-up plant or seed maybe, like pepper. A good thing I hadn't been rubbing at my eyes. Aboard *Kepler's Law*, I'd be able to flush them out better.

Before Alfrun could react, Kofri and Lif hurried back with linen cloaks and bundles of kindling in their arms, radiant with anticipation. "We'll go with you, Lady Knight!" Lif gushed. "We deliver wood to the barracks on occasion. No one will think anything of it. Once we reach the gate, the soldiers can help you from there."

My innards knotted up with apprehension. "I appreciate this, but I honestly don't know what's going to happen at the gate. It may be dangerous. It's better if I go alone."

"Nonsense! They wouldn't hurt us," Lif protested.

"And you must be daft if you think we'll miss out on this," Kofri said.

I plainly wasn't talking them out of what might've been the most exciting thing to happen all week, month, or year. I hoped Lif was right.

While my friends donned their cloaks—Kofri and Lif bouncing with excitement, Alfrun more reserved—I first shed my baldric, then concealed my side sword and scabbard among the kindling. The sword's hilt would've poked up over my shoulder in a conspicuous fashion otherwise. The cloak might still look fishy given the sunny weather, but at least no one would identify me on sight until we reached the gate.

Dread crept up on me. I hoped like hell I wouldn't need my sword against the soldiers I'd befriended.

Off we went, Kofri and Lif in front, Alfrun and I bringing up the rear. We walked at a casual pace that allowed me to catch my breath. The lightweight cloaks posed no burden. One could even make a plausible argument for donning one's hood to keep the midday sun off.

"What if the Naustviks *are* loose here?" Kofri turned to Lif. "It's the only place the adepts aren't looking!"

"Stop it!" Lif snapped.

They babbled on, acting just as naturally as I could've hoped. Alfrun stuck to my side, casting nervous looks my way. I summoned a smile in return, but had trouble putting reassurance behind it.

We strolled past the barracks, our presumptive destination. Soldiers practicing outside looked our way, but didn't stop us.

Was Ingvar there? Or had he returned to the keep, anticipating a flight to Gules? Nausea hit me again. Ingvar had seemed genuinely serious, even excited, about rescuing Drea. It couldn't have been an act. Could it?

Despite the relaxed pace and banter, my nervousness ratcheted higher as we neared the gate. The soldiers who spotted us held position, presumably waiting for us to reach them. No doubt the archers on the wall had us in their sights as well. Every second we weren't attacked, my heart sped up, daring to hope that the murder plot was confined to the adepts, or at least *some* adepts. But I was a long way off from knowing for certain.

Closer to the gate, the soldiers' curious gazes locked onto ours. I saw signs of recognition, along with the blinks and faltering of confusion. My hand closed around the sword-hilt amid the pile of twigs I carried, just in case.

"Lady Knight?" Finally, two soldiers stepped out in front of our party, hands at their sides. "'Tis too dangerous to leave the capital right now."

"Dame Jessamine needs our help to escape the witches!" Lif declared.

"It's a little more complicated than that, but yes, I'm leaving the capital," I said. "These three are covering my escape."

The soldiers traded surprised looks. "Where're ye headed?" one asked.

A lie wouldn't get me far. "My ship." I promptly held my breath.

The soldiers shared another glance. At no point did their hands stray near their weaponry. Finally, one nodded toward me. "All right, go ahead. The rest of you better head back."

Somehow, I refrained from crumpling onto the field in weak relief. At least *these* soldiers were friendly.

Alfrun lifted the kindling from my hands. "Will you be all right to keep questing?"

"I think so." I kept my side sword and baldric in hand. "I won't leave things unfinished here, but I may have to bring help from abroad to defeat the witches."

"Those lights. Don't forget," she urged me.

"I won't." I glanced between the servants. "Thanks for your help, all of you."

Kofri wound a hand around his beads with a mischievous smile. "Come back soon. This has got to be worth a few stories, or some pot-scrubbing at the least!"

The trio turned around with their burdens. One soldier from the gate went sprinting ahead of them toward the barracks, presumably to notify Ingvar or Pontus.

Hell. Maybe I wasn't in the clear at all. Well, I'd best hurry to my ship in any case.

Shaking off dread, I ran to the port as fast as my aching hide allowed. The soldiers on watch there remained silent and invisible at my entrance. Once again, *Kepler's Law* was a welcome sight. I wrested her hatch open, and was about to step aboard, when two soldiers rushed in from the galley to pile up in the airlock before me.

I stumbled backward with a gasp.

The pair would've had me dead to rights, but they didn't draw weapons, just stared at me wide-eyed.

"Lady Knight," they both greeted, their surprise turning to concerned frowns. However, they were good enough to refrain from asking what hole I'd crawled out of.

It was only then that I recalled Ingvar's desire to maintain a watch over Verahl at all times. They were stationed aboard my ship to keep an eye on him, not to ambush me.

"Sorry, I forgot you'd be here." I forced a smile, swallowing my heart back down. "Thanks for your help, but I'd appreciate it if you returned to the barracks."

"We're not allowed to leave," one of the young men informed me, "but I guess we can stand outside. Let us know if you need us."

"Thanks." I let them step out, then jumped into the airlock and closed up the hatch with a deep, shuddering sigh.

Away from scrutiny, pain and fatigue surged to prominence. A fearful tremor overtook my limbs, so bad that I wondered how I'd leave the airlock. Things sure seemed to have gone irredeemably hellward.

After a few collecting breaths, and several looks around to remind myself where I was, I mustered the strength to press into the galley. There, the table and bench normally folded into the deck had been propped up. Verahl lay on the deck as before, his head just inches from the furniture. At my appearance, he bolted up to a seat, tracking my tentative movements.

It was good to see him awake. I looked forward to some civilized discussion, as well as some mystery-solving. "Hello again." I knelt in front of him and placed my sword aside, speaking around a residual cough. "How're you feeling?"

"Fine. Thanks." He slumped against the starboard bulkhead, eyeing me up and down. "What happened to you?"

"I almost took your place in the dungeon. For good." I dragged myself toward the nearest closet, gathering first aid supplies for myself, along with food. Eating on Nidaros' schedule for just a few days already had me starving.

"Because of me?" Verahl's voice wafted from behind the closet door.

"I don't know." It was possible, but there was no reason to put that on his conscience.

He hesitated. "I'm sorry about yesterday."

"It's all right. Let's put it behind us." I backed out of the closet and plunked down beside him, much as I'd done the day before.

Verahl said nothing more, focusing on the items I'd brought over.

"Eat something, if you want." I had to remove my gear first. The cloak was easy. Pulling my coat sleeve off my left arm proved a far more painful chore, given how I'd landed on my shoulder after falling into the dungeon, but at least the joint hadn't left its socket. It'd stop complaining soon enough.

My left hip and thigh still smarted as well, and would surely develop a rainbow of new bruises in coming days, but there was nothing dislocated or broken there either. The stains on my clothing continued to defy identification.

Something wedged against my neck tumbled down my front: the mati amulet Ormyr had given me. It must've gotten trapped in my coat amid the excitement. I slipped it under my tunic, alongside the chain bearing my mother's ring.

"What is it you're supposed to be doing here?" Verahl tracked my every movement, eyes narrowed. "I doubt you fly around the galaxy just pulling people out of dungeons."

"You'd be surprised." I checked myself for open wounds. "Ignoring the political mess, I'm trying to figure out the crop trouble here. I know it has nothing to do with you or your sister."

My reassurance plunged Verahl into silence. He focused an ashen look down at his hands.

Strange. What was this, guilt? Over what? I raised a brow at him. "Am I wrong about that?"

"No, just ..." Verahl fumbled with his hands in his lap. "My sister. Thordia. I have to find her."

I understood the sentiment, but hell. Verahl running around loose again: the worst possible ending to an already miserable day. I paused my self-ministrations to lean toward him, speaking gently. "You've been tortured, and shot. You need time to recover. I'm sure the last thing Thordia wants is for you to get hurt worse, or recaptured."

Verahl's head remained lowered. He ran a shaking hand over his scalp.

At least he wasn't arguing with me. I reached for a nearby stoppered bottle. "Do you know what aspirin is?"

His astonished stare riveted to me in a second.

I offered him the bottle with pleasant vindication. "It may not be strong enough, but you're welcome to it. I suggest four pills spaced out through the day. Take them with food and water."

Verahl uncorked the bottle and dumped a few pills into his hand, frowning over them. I took the bottle back, fished out my own pill, and downed it with a swig of water. Only after he'd witnessed me doing that did he seem comfortable with doing the same.

First ships, then my sigil, then medicine. Where in hell had he come by knowledge that I'd only been able to obtain through the beguinage? I was dying to ask, but there were a few other things I had to understand better first.

"Why was Thordia blamed for everything?" I recalled Kofi and Lif talking about the strange sights and sounds coming from the Naustvik house. They'd also painted Thordia as a one-armed recluse. True or not, it certainly added to the "witch" lore. I wanted to hear what Verahl would offer.

Verahl stared hard at his lap, silent for a long while. "People have been suspicious for as long as I can remember. This was their chance to actually blame her for something."

"Because you both have Shipbuilder knowledge? Is that why?" I asked.

Verahl neither moved nor answered.

"It's nothing you have to hide from me, all right?" I soothed. "Maybe you've been made to feel ashamed of it, or guilty, but—"

"I'm *not*." But the glare he fastened on me sure melted fast, revealing plenty of pain.

"Can you tell me what happened?" I asked.

Verahl continued to stare at his lap. One of his legs shook nervously. "Thordia always told me nothing could *ever* justify exposing what we know. When the crops began dying, she hadn't wanted to get involved. I begged her to reconsider. People were going to die."

Thordia had refused to put her knowledge to good use?

Having learned from some of the most generous souls imaginable, I couldn't fathom that attitude. But I hadn't spent my entire life in a remote, superstitious community, either.

"I convinced her, finally," Verahl continued. "It didn't take long for her to isolate something in the soil. It's causing the trouble. But before she could do anything about it, the adepts showed up at our house."

I leaned in even closer, heart pounding. "What's in the soil? Some kind of microbe, disease?"

Verahl took a long, shuddering breath. "I don't know, but there's proof back home. Thordia can show you."

My eyes went wide. "Thordia's at your house still?"

"When the adepts came …" He trailed off, hesitating. "There's a crawl space in our cellar. She ran down there and hid while I held them off. I imagine she's still hiding there."

"That was good of you." Verahl seemed a good enough sort in general, just rattled after who-knew-what torture he'd received in the dungeon. I struggled to maintain calm amid mounting excitement. "Is anyone else at home? Parents, siblings?"

"Our parents are dead. We live alone."

I nodded. "Listen, I don't want to see anyone tortured or killed over nonsense. That's why I pulled you out of the dungeon, and why I hope to go looking for Thordia as soon as I have the chance. If she can also help identify the crop trouble, that'd be great too. You should stay here and recover, like I said. I'll bring Thordia here if I find her."

Verahl didn't look up or acknowledge me.

Part of me remained paranoid of a well intentioned but dangerous tag-along. It seemed wise to give him more reasons to stay put. I glanced about the galley. "I couldn't help noticing you like my ship."

His head shot back up finally, eyes gleaming. "Starship mechanics have always fascinated me. All theory until now."

I resonated with that passion. It coaxed a smile to my face. "Where'd you learn about things like that?"

He glanced askance a moment, then back. "Our parents taught us."

"Who taught them?" I asked.

"I don't know."

Interesting. Maybe they'd learned from mentors, or the knowledge had passed down through his family over centuries. The latter was unlikely, but intriguing to think about. "Would you like to have a look through the engine room when you're feeling up to it?" I offered.

He boggled at me. "Can I?"

"Sure, but I'll thank you not to disturb anything," I said. "I'd like to keep our options for egress wide open."

Verahl nodded. "I'll—"

Several knocks reverberated along the hull, cutting him short.

We exchanged worried frowns. What was that? More likely, *who?* The soldiers I'd placed outside? Or someone with more sinister intentions?

"Stay here, all right?" Ignoring the trepidation I'd earned, I hauled myself up to my feet with a grunt. Instead of the airlock, I hurried to my quarters and had a look out the porthole.

Outside stood Ingvar, pounding against the hatch with his fist.

CHAPTER 17

Through the porthole, I watched Ingvar pounding a fist against my ship's hatch. Though he frowned, he had no weapons drawn, and his free hand hung loose at his side. He looked more worried than aggressive.

A weird mix of relief and anxiety left me tense. It seemed the soldiers were still friendly to me. Still, as much as I didn't want to believe it, was it possible Ingvar been in on the murder attempt?

Yes, it was. But here he knocked on my ship's hull. *Requesting* entry, not barging his way aboard. If anyone deserved the benefit of a doubt, it was Ingvar.

I crossed into the galley again, making my way to the airlock. Verahl, slumped up against the galley's starboard bulkhead, fixed me with a stare of burning curiosity.

"Captain Leirfall," I explained as I walked past.

At the revelation, Verahl dropped his head toward his lap without comment.

Once I'd opened the hatch, Ingvar sprang up into the airlock, eyes fastening upon me with concern. "Heard ye fled the capital for some reason," he spoke around short breaths, like he'd sprinted there from the barracks. "*Skíta*, your eyes. What happened?"

His apprehension and sympathy further disarmed my paranoia. "I barely know myself. At least one adept tried to kill me. He's dead. I couldn't—"

"*What?*" Ingvar braced my arms, eyes wide.

I stifled a wince at the unintentional jolt to my shoulder. "An adept tried to kill me."

"At the keep?"

"Yes. You didn't know?" I asked with more hope than was likely appropriate.

Ingvar stared at me for a few moments, stricken. "Was Ormyr—?"

"No. I don't know. I mean, we were separated, he wasn't there. But he might've arranged the whole thing. *I don't know,*" I half-rambled, half-begged.

"Blood's oath," Ingvar muttered. Then his gaze softened with encouragement. "Come with me to the barracks, Jayce. We need to talk."

Tempting, but I still feared trouble at the capital—if not from the soldiers, then elsewhere. "I'm not sure it's safe to leave my ship." My voice quavered more than I would've liked.

Ingvar's eyes remained on me as he spoke reassuringly. "I understand. Hel, going back to the capital must seem insane after what happened." He paused. "I want to help you figure this out, and punish whoever did this. Afore we can get anywhere with that, I need you to tell me what happened. Prefer we don't talk where Naustvik can hear." His eyes narrowed with distrust, which he directed over my shoulder. I assumed his men had told him Verahl was awake.

I longed to believe him. Between tense heartbeats, my paranoia resurfaced. What if he were just coaxing me into a peaceful arrest? There was a dead adept in the dungeon, after all.

Never mind who tried to kill whom, charging me with the adept's murder would be much simpler than an actual investigation. Besides, wasn't this the *second time* Ingvar appeared to be involved in a setup against me?

"Still suspicious, aye? Ye've earned that." Ingvar let go of my arms, holding me in place with his friendly, supportive expression instead. "Jayce, I swear I haven't the faintest what happened at the keep. Last I knew, we were preparing to rescue your mentor."

That failure hit me again like a shot to the gut. I dropped my head before my face betrayed too much.

"Whatever happened, I'm sorry," Ingvar continued. "The last thing I'd do is add to it. Ye have my word, I'm not marching you back to one of my holding cells, or the dungeon." He leaned in closer, dropping his voice to a near-whisper. "I think we can trust each other. We *are* jointly sheltering an escaped prisoner."

Between that, our earlier interactions, and our shared understanding, I did trust him, paranoia be damned. Together, we stood a real chance of unraveling the motive behind the murder attempt. Besides, lingering aboard *Kepler's Law* gave my opposition time to spin their own story, arrange their own evidence. The last thing I wanted was for the murderous adept's cohorts to transform me from victim to suspect.

I took a deep, steadying breath. "I'll go with you. Let me grab my gear first."

Ingvar looked relieved. "I'll be waiting right here." He dropped to the ground from the airlock.

I hurried back to the galley with purpose, ignoring my thoughts and pain. Verahl remained sitting where I'd left him. The gaze he directed toward me was every bit as distrustful as Ingvar's had been toward him. "What did he want?" he half-whispered.

"To help," I murmured back, gathering up my coat, armor,

and weapons with slow movements. "Stay here and make yourself at home, all right? Enjoy looking around the engine room. I'll arrange to look for Thordia soon as soon as I can." I would've liked to ask more about Thordia's investigation into the crop trouble, and how she and Verahl happened to possess so much "dangerous" knowledge between them, but—much like the dungeon prisoner's corpse, whose cause of death remained unknown—those things would be easier to focus on once my disposition was sorted out.

"Sounds like you're in as much trouble as I am," Verahl said. "If the worst happens, how will I know? At what point can I assume you're not coming back?"

I faced him, torn. Any estimate I gave was sure to bite me later. On the other hand, the promise of my return might keep Verahl rooted aboard the ship, where he'd be safer. "It's hard for me to know. How about three days?"

"*One* day."

"Why'd you ask if you planned on dictating?" I smiled faintly.

"It's still a lot of time," Verahl said, deadly serious. "More time than Thordia might have."

I completely understood his concerns. At the same time, I wanted him to lie low and let me handle it. "All right. Within a day's time, I'll be back with some kind of update."

"I'll take that."

Verahl went back to staring at his lap, one leg fidgeting up and down. After gearing up, I gave him an encouraging pat on the knee, then left.

Outside, Ingvar braced me upon noticing how slowly I lowered myself to the ground from the airlock. "Ye all right?"

My heart jumped. "Nothing I won't walk off."

Ingvar sent the two soldiers who'd been standing watch over Verahl back aboard my ship before we crossed the port again, en route to the capital gate.

"Naustvik behaving himself?" Ingvar asked.

"So far so good," I replied. "He believes Thordia's still hiding at their house."

Ingvar waved a hand in dismissal. "Adepts tore the place apart looking for her. He might not have seen that."

"He says Thordia hid in a crawl space in their cellar, and that she found something in the soil that's causing the crops to fail."

Surprise flashed over Ingvar's expression. He quickly faced forward again, frowning in thought.

"Whenever we visit the districts, we may as well go to the district where their house is. Right?" I asked.

Ingvar let out a humorless laugh. "Let's worry about this murder attempt first, aye? I still need to hear what happened."

At the barracks, we walked past multiple curious gazes as Ingvar led me to one of the side rooms. "Have a seat," he offered. "I'll return soon."

Three chairs surrounded a simple wooden desk. Behind the furniture, a small window admitted plenty of sunlight. Despite its sparse profile, I could tell this was Ingvar's office, not an interrogation chamber. A stack of parchment sat at one corner of the desk, marked with his initials in a stylized pattern. The same initials repeated several more times across an erasable slate nearby. Penmanship practice, literacy practice, maybe both.

Though Ingvar had kept his word thus far, my frayed nerves made me less than eager to recount what had happened at the keep. I wished to return to that comfortable hearth of a few nights ago, but at the moment, any hint of fire would be more than I could handle. Instead, I dropped myself into one of the chairs and waited, hands fidgeting in my lap.

When Ingvar returned, he carried two cups in his hands. Pontus shadowed him, breaking away to take the empty chair to my right.

"Uh, hello." I forced myself to sit up straighter, jolted by the unexpected audience.

"Lass," Pontus said by way of greeting. His neutral expression softened with concern. "Just here to listen, so our captain needn't repeat himself later."

Ingvar set one of the water-filled cups down near me, keeping the other for himself as he rounded the desk and claimed the chair opposing us with a relaxed posture and reassuring expression. "All right, let's hear every detail as best as ye can remember it, starting with you and Ormyr leaving the calefactory."

I obliged with as much coherence as my brain permitted, reaching for the water frequently. The mere recollection of the burning-flesh smell sufficed to make me gag again. The soldiers listened without interruption or skepticism. Amazing, given I still had trouble believing some of the crazier details myself.

Once I'd finished, they asked questions—curious, clarifying, not accusatory. Worry clouded their expressions, convincing me they were more interested in saving my hide than burning it. I felt secure that my answers wouldn't be used to incriminate me later.

Ingvar finally leaned Pontus' way with a concerned frown. "Report to our Baron and Master Ormyr what happened, gather as much evidence as ye can. Also grab a few men, along with those supplies I brought in last night. See if ye can't bring up that prisoner's corpse now."

"Aye, sir." Pontus stood, nodding my way. "Glad ye're still with us."

"Thanks," I said, relieved and impressed.

Pontus showed himself out. Once we were alone, Ingvar

leaned across the desk toward me, waiting for me to return eye contact. "Your word as a knight errant should stand on its own, but the more evidence we find in your favor — afore anyone has a chance to meddle with it — will be valuable not just for you, but also for figuring out who did this and wherefore."

"I know. Thanks. I'm *glad* you're doing that." I took another swig of water.

"Still have those dungeon keys on you?" Ingvar asked.

"Oh. I should." I sat up straight to dig through my pockets. Having limited patience for a prolonged search, I took to dumping out fistfuls of items onto the edge of his desk. Cigarillos, tinderbox, stick lighter, coin purse, Lord Catherwood's seal —

"What's that now?" Ingvar prompted.

I paused mid-excavation. "What?"

Ingvar leaned forward, using a finger to drag something free from the rest of the pile. A flat, polished green stone several inches across, with an open hand carved into it. Not a charm I remembered picking up anywhere.

I frowned in confusion. "I have no idea. I've never seen that before."

Ingvar stared at the charm with trepidation, then focused that look on me.

My pulse quickened. "Seriously, I haven't. What is it?"

His gaze carefully probed mine. "'Tis Lord Gyllenfeld's seal."

The conquered Lord of the past whose adherents caused friction now? Horrifying realization struck, rattling my newfound security. Did Ingvar think it was mine? Or that I intended to plant it somewhere and stir up more trouble?

"On my word, Ingvar, I've never seen it before!" I pleaded. "See, I got this one from Sigrid. And Lady Amelia gave me this one." I pointed out the hammer charm and jeweled khamsa respectively, both resting on the desk. "I have *no idea* where the

Gyllenfeld one came from. Someone must've planted it on me!"

To get me in trouble, most likely. While my face burned, sweat broke out over the rest of my skin. Over the past several days, there'd been plenty of opportunity for someone to drop it in my pocket. I'd taken off my coat at the estate, the barracks … it was even possible some adept had slipped it in there with a sleight-of-hand trick.

Ingvar seemed to deliberate. The silence between us stretched ever more painfully, bringing despair with it. My head dropped. Apparently, someone really had it in for me that day.

"Carry any charms ye actually believe in?" Ingvar asked quietly.

I glanced up, meeting his inquisitive gaze with surprise. "No!" Then I realized, "Well, that's not entirely true." I pulled out the chain around my neck, the one with the amethyst ring strung upon it, ignoring the mati amulet Ormyr had given me.

"This was my mother's," I explained. "I don't really believe it helps me or anything, but, it'd feel wrong not to have it with me. Does that make sense?"

Ingvar gave a nod, softening further. "Ye'd be surprised. Charms *can* actually work."

"No, they can't." Only a few days ago, this objection would never have left my mouth, except within the company of Drea, Branigan, or my other friends at the beguinage. I knew I could debate the point with Ingvar, though. There was a good chance of getting through to him.

"It dependeth on the situation," Ingvar replied, undaunted. "If there's an important task at hand, they can provide one confidence, help him relax and perform better. Nothing magic about it, just a trick of thought."

Oh! Like a placebo effect! I realized with pleasant surprise, but didn't say it out loud. "All right, I can see that."

246 | ELLIS MORNING

"But if we're talking about coaxing flax out of the ground, forget it." Ingvar's eyes re-fastened upon the Gyllenfeld charm. "Guess that's supposed to make me think ye're an agitator. Well, ye *are*, just not that way."

A relieved laugh escaped me. We understood each other, and yet another plot against me had been thwarted. I fell back against my chair, tucking my mother's ring back under my tunic.

Ingvar reached across the desk, retrieving the dungeon keys from the pile between us. After gathering myself, I pocketed the remaining items more carefully than I'd taken them out, looking for any other stowaways. I found none. My thoughts shifted to motives for the planting, as well as the murder attempt.

"When I first got here, everyone assumed Madam Castor had sent me," I said, thinking out loud. "Ironic, because she hadn't wanted me involved at all. *She'd* wanted to send a detachment here, but Lord Catherwood wouldn't hear of it."

"As if sellswords could pull flax out of the ground!" Ingvar slumped against his chair, folding his arms and scowling at a distant corner. "I wonder ..."

"What?" I prompted.

"Well, even if people here are confused about who sent you, I still can't think of anyone who'd want to kill you."

"Really? Ormyr led me right to that trap door." I held in a shudder. "Is he angrier about losing Verahl than he lets on? Is Baron Tristan, or Lady Amelia?"

"Ye're more valuable to Ormyr alive," Ingvar said, his gaze returning to mine. "Solving this crisis and earning your favor is his best prospect of returning to Spectra. As for our Baron, and Lady Amelia? I don't see either of them resorting to murder for any reason. Killing you can't help either of them, only hurt." He leaned closer to me again. "Ye're Lord Catherwood's emissary. Should ye be killed here, ye know who'll be punished, regardless of who actually performed the killing? Baron Tristan. He beareth the ultimate responsibility."

I sat up straighter, sucking in a breath. "So you think this might actually be a plot against the Baron?"

"There are plenty who'd want to unseat him," Ingvar replied. "Gyllenfeld dissidents, mayhap even Madam Castor."

A recollection made me gasp. I leaned toward him, narrowing the gap between us to inches. "I did hear Madam Castor say that she didn't trust the Baron to keep order here."

Ingvar's eyes lit up with confirmation. "So she might seek to replace him somehow, aye?" he posed, speaking faster.

"But she'd need him to screw up big first," I said, speeding up with him. "Lord Catherwood really likes the Baron."

"Aye, exactly. An emissary dying here would suit her well."

"It'd certainly help paint you as the 'miscreants' she claims you to be." My heart raced. At that point, I would've been shocked to find out Madam Castor *wasn't* involved in some way. But one thing still seriously confused me. "How the hell does that lead to the adepts' keep, though? At least one adept arranged to kill me. Assuming it was Madam Castor's idea, how'd she get them to carry it out?"

"The order probably came through the mail ye brought with you," Ingvar said.

A sick feeling braced me. "Hell, that's possible. It would've given the adept or adepts a couple of weeks to come up with a plan and execute it, but just a day or two would've been enough time to learn that I'd been ordered to visit Ormyr at the keep every morning. That kind of regularity makes a great opportunity for laying a trap."

Ingvar nodded, also sobering. "Surely Madam Castor hath her informants here, but I don't know whom. I've never had success rooting them out before. Whatever messages they may trade are coded to oblivion."

"But what's the motive?" I asked. "Why would anyone here help Madam Castor get rid of the Baron?"

Ingvar tilted his head toward the Gyllenfeld charm on the desk between us, the only item I hadn't re-pocketed.

Putting two and two together sent my jaw dropping. "Gyllenfeld dissidents among the *adepts?!*" I cried. "They're all sworn to uphold Catherwood dogma!"

"That's just one possible reason. 'Tis not the only grudge people may have against Baron Tristan." Ingvar frowned downward at the desk.

"What else is there?" I asked.

"It'd take time to explain."

"I'm listening."

Ingvar assumed a ramrod-straight posture and remained silent for a few moments, gathering his thoughts. "Seven years ago, afore Baron Tristan's ascension ... back then, our army and cloister were run by high-born men of Spectra, dismissed from the capital for whatever it is blue-bloods get heated about. Master Ormyr was still Adept Ormyr, a trainee in Spectra. I was one of the few low-birth officers here, owing to a battlefield commission." He hesitated. "Received that commission when we were all ordered out to a foreign campaign in Lord Lagana's realm. It claimed both mine elder brothers and countless others. Only time I ever traversed space." His voice stayed level, but he clenched a fist upon his desk. Pain edged his expression.

My sympathy welled up. No wonder ships made him nervous. "I'm sorry."

He forged ahead with his original explanation. "Our erstwhile Baron Nolan died without an heir. Lord Catherwood— Lady Amelia's brother, still alive seven years back—bestowed the title of Nidaros upon an official from one of the trade guilds."

"Linum Dominorum?" I asked. Madam Castor's guild, the one leaning on Nidaros?

"Nay, one of the others," Ingvar said. "The official had distinguished himself and won Lady Amelia's affections. They were wed to seal his claim to the title. 'Twas how Journeyman Foster became Baron Tristan."

So the Baron wasn't noble by birth, *and* he and Madam Castor had come up through rival trade guilds. No wonder the Guildmistress resented him. I killed off my water, waiting for Ingvar to continue.

"When news reached us, it enraged the high-born men here, all of whom believed they had a stronger claim to the barony," Ingvar continued. "They declared Nidaros independent and planned to murder Baron Tristan's retinue upon arrival, Lady Amelia and Master Ormyr among them."

My jaw dropped again. "Independent?" *That* was the most shocking of his words. The prospect was a fever-dream.

"They dragged up the specter of Gyllenfeld, and swayed a majority to their cause thereby. But I and a few other officers resolved in secret to defend Baron Tristan, however outnumbered." Ingvar's gaze pleaded with mine. "What's 'independence' when Nidaros can't survive without patronage? With our Baron dead, were Lord Catherwood and Madam Castor to forget us? Were the rebels to share a united Nidaros? Never. They'd have staked claims and ground us down until the victor ruled over ashes."

"You're right," I said.

Ingvar's gaze, still pained, dropped to the desk. "Milord and Madam Castor expected trouble; Baron Tristan arrived with large detachments at his behest. Battle lasted not more than a day. The purge of court and cloister took longer. Some of those prisoners in the dungeon, now ye know how they came to rot therein. Our Baron appointed me to replace the Captain of the Guard."

He let out a weary breath. "Plenty in Nidaros bear grudges over lost friends and kin. And plenty more ache to throw off Catherwood rule, never mind there's no living Gyllenfeld to defect to. They died out ages ago, afore any of us were born. Still, my own grandparents bled green from crib to grave, as do my parents, who forswore me for continuing to wear these colors."

Sick with grief over two sons, they'd rejected a third. Maybe this was part of the reason Ingvar argued against Ormyr's calls for a crackdown against the dissidents. He was right to resist, but at the same time, he was also protecting the family who'd cast him out.

"Goodness, Ingvar," I managed past a tight throat. "I'm sorry."

He gave small nod. "I did what was best for them and Nidaros. I'll never regret that."

I didn't doubt his confidence, but the haunted look on his face made an equally convincing case. It was a wound he still carried close. In that moment, the longing to comfort out-weighed the mixed-up feelings that would've kept me distant. I rested my hand on his right forearm. "You have a really good family at the barracks."

"All natives of Nidaros, now." His eyes latched to mine with appreciation. Pride leaked through his voice. "Told our Baron this was no dumping ground for spoiled fops who'd squandered their privilege in Spectra, and he agreed. Meant losing many veterans, but we're not poorer for't."

"Not at all." I smiled with a new admiration for him, one that quickened my pulse.

Ingvar had brightened at my reassurance, and lingered on that little moment of happiness before circumstances forced him to sober again. "Mayhap that adept who attacked you was one of the grudge-holders who'd see us fall. Mayhap Madam Castor promised him something in turn. Hope Pontus is able to find some proof—and that Ormyr doesn't throw up any obstacles."

"I hope that adept was acting alone, but I'm not going to assume it," I said.

"Nay, me either. We won't be blindsided like that again."

Ingvar rested his left hand over mine, which I'd forgotten was still resting on his forearm. My heart pounded, electrified, while a flush crept up my face. His touch was so much more meaningful now that I understood the breadth and depth of concern behind it.

"I'm sorry this happened," he continued quietly. "Also sorry it delayed us from reaching Drea."

The flush intensified, bearing off my brains with it. "I … I'm really surprised you wanted to go with me to rescue her."

Ingvar didn't seem to notice, meeting my gaze with a look of conviction. "Still do. Hoping she can help us. Regardless, she's important to you. And ye're …" He faltered.

"Yes?" The prompt shot out of my mouth with half-longing, half-dread.

It seemed like Ingvar knew what came next, but just couldn't get it out. Eventually he gave up, lowering his gaze in defeat.

CHAPTER 18

I didn't know what I'd been hoping to hear Ingvar say, but those hopes had been dashed. In their ruins, I felt foolish for ever hoping in the first place. Guilt and grief surged back stronger than ever. My forehead dropped against the arm I'd stretched across the office desk toward Ingvar. Tears leaked out past my defenses, and for once, I didn't resist them.

"Drea's like a mother to me, you know?" Since Ingvar had brought her up, she wasn't easily forgotten. "I couldn't save my first mother, or my second."

Ingvar's hand lifted away from mine. The abandonment might've spurred me to deeper mourning, had he not tapped on said hand a few moments later. I lifted my head to find him proffering a handkerchief and an open, receptive expression.

I sat up straight again and accepted with a grateful nod, finally letting go of his forearm. This time, an explanation felt earned, and safe. From my mouth tumbled the details I'd avoided telling him before.

"A friend of ours, Sir Branigan Cade, found a Shipbuilder artifact in Gules and needed help to identify it. I happened to be visiting the beguinage, between quests, when his message arrived." I dabbed at my eyes. "Drea and I flew out to meet up with Branigan. It meant crossing the galaxy, making frequent stops so the lack of gravity wouldn't get to us, but I was glad to do it. It was like old times with Drea.

"By the time we got to Gules, though, it'd been cursed. It was awful, Ingvar. The whole town ransacked, people left to freeze to death in the streets, and Branigan executed. I don't know who killed him or why. He was the *last* person who deserved to go out like that."

I paused a long while, handkerchief glued to my face as I fought back a sob. The words concerning my feelings for Branigan refused to leave my throat. A cowardly betrayal, but I'd have a hard enough time just continuing the story. I took a shuddery deep breath and pushed on. "Lord Catherwood's forces showed up. They forced me into this quest, and made Drea remain in Gules." I shook my head. "Like you said when we first met: coming here was a punishment. I'm not some great trusted knight errant. I just landed in the wrong damn town."

Grief got the better of me. I slumped over the desk again, pressing my face into my forearm, and succumbed to a fit of racking sobs.

Eventually the urge fell out of me, leaving me weak and sniffling. I left my face buried in my arm, feeling ashamed after such an inexcusable display. I *never* broke down in front of strangers like this. Well, I supposed Ingvar was no stranger anymore, but I feared him thinking less of me.

Just as I was about to straighten and apologize, Ingvar's hand braced my elbow. "I mourn with you, Jayce," he spoke with quiet reassurance. "I'm even more committed than ever to helping you reach Drea. But we can't leave Nidaros afore the murder attempt's resolved."

"I understand," I muttered shakily, hastening to wipe away my tears with my sleeve.

"We'll stay at the barracks 'til Pontus returneth with whatever he's able to gather," Ingvar continued. "After that, we'll decide our best course of action."

"Fair enough." I sat up, sniffling hard and clenching the handkerchief in my fist, still too embarrassed to face him. "I'm sorry. I can only imagine what kind of child you take me for—and you're probably right."

"Not what I'm thinking at all, Jayce." His tone was warm. "What ye described, 'tis a lot for anyone to endure in a lifetime, never mind a matter of days. Surprised ye're at all interested in helping us."

Ingvar ended on an appreciative note. By the time I looked his way, he'd left his chair to round the desk toward me.

I really could tell him anything without being mocked or thrown in a dungeon. That sort of security and trust was so rare. It meant so much to me. I craned my neck to follow Ingvar's progress. Relief, and a glimmer of honest-to-goodness love, had me waiting in breathless anticipation.

Then foolishness crashed over my head. This wasn't right, or convenient. Hadn't I supposedly loved Branigan? What if *these* feelings proved equally shallow?

Fear stabbed me. Maybe I was more like my former master than I wanted to think about. Maybe *all* my so-called "love" was that weak. Wasn't Drea's continued suffering proof of that? Wouldn't I just end up hurting Ingvar too?

I tamped it all down and forced myself to my feet, sticking out a hand for Ingvar to shake. He accepted, betraying no sign of what his original purpose had been or what he thought of the gesture. In vain, I tried to ignore the warmth of his calloused hand, and the shape of the joints and scars that gave it character.

"I'm planning to drop by the afternoon drills," Ingvar said. "Ye can come outside with me or stay here. Up to you."

I recalled something more pressing. "Actually, where's Fasolt? I should follow up with him."

Ingvar's eyes brightened like I'd jogged his memory. He nodded his appreciation. "This way."

We stepped out into the barracks proper, angling for the bunks. A few soldiers rested or prepared for duty between the two hearths. I was glad to find Fasolt playing cards with his friend Logmadr across a storage chest-turned-table.

Logmadr dropped his cards and stood to wave us over. "Welcome back! Fasolt slept well last night, but that damned cough—"

"*Skíta!* I'm no invalid!" Fasolt slammed his cards down.

This brought Logmadr up short. "I know. Just worry sometimes is all."

"With good reason," Ingvar said, drawing up beside the interrupted game and folding his arms. "The knight would check you over, Fasolt."

Fasolt tracked my approach warily. "What for?"

"Just to confirm there's no lingering trouble from yesterday," I said, slipping to a seat on the bunk beside him.

He stiffened, but a look up toward Ingvar confirmed he wasn't about to worm out of this.

Logmadr sat back down again and leaned toward his friend, speaking in a hush. "Fasolt, she raised you from the dead! I saw it!"

"We talked about that, lad," Ingvar half-whispered. "Fasolt wasn't dead, but passed out."

Logmadr seemed unconvinced. "What do ye remember?" he asked his friend, wide-eyed. "Did ye see Folkvang?"

"Don't remember a thing," Fasolt said, making no secret of his confusion.

For that moment, he forgot his suspicion as well. I gently turned his face toward me. "You look much better. Any headaches, dizziness?"

"Nay." Fasolt remained tense, but tolerated my probing fingers. "Still don't know why ye care, foreigner."

"Fasolt," Ingvar chided.

I smiled a little. "Some of us are *trying* to do good. We don't always get it right. I'm sorry this happened."

"It would've been worse without her," Logmadr assured him.

Fasolt said nothing, content to wait out the rest of my examination in silence. His nose didn't appear to be broken, and his pupils still looked normal. I was grateful on both counts.

"What about that cough?" I asked. "How long has that hung around?"

"A few weeks," Logmadr answered for him.

Fasolt's immune system was probably weak while he and everyone else struggled to keep fed. I was surprised more of the soldiers didn't have the same symptoms.

"Is your throat bothering you?" I asked Fasolt.

He waved me off.

I was willing to bet otherwise, but didn't press the point. "Well, if it ever starts, try mixing some salt into warm water and gargling with it. That should help. I'd also recommend taking it easy until that cough goes away."

"Lady Knight?"

I glanced toward Logmadr, who'd clasped his hands in front of himself nervously. "Don't want you to think I'm not grateful, 'cause I am, but ..." He hesitated. "Were ye an adept at some point, mayhap?"

It was a very polite way of phrasing the real question on his mind. Namely, *was I a witch?*

"What's it matter, lad?" Ingvar challenged from above before I could answer.

"Well, I ..." Logmadr trailed off, his shoulders tensing.

I leaned across the card table with a smile for the younger soldier. "I have really smart friends who taught me a lot of things. That's all," I whispered. "I'm no witch."

A flush rose to Logmadr's face. "I wasn't calling you one, swear it!"

"Do you see this here?" Undaunted, I ran a finger along a scar on my forehead, several inches above my right eye.

Logmadr frowned his confusion. "What of it?"

I mirrored his frown, as though surprised my lead-in wasn't obvious. "Well, witches don't have scars. They heal themselves with magic that never leaves a trace of injury. I'd get rid of this if I could, but I can't."

"Now that's enough grilling, aye?" Ingvar cut in under his breath. "I'd never let a witch anywhere near you lads."

"Aye, sir, I know!" Logmadr replied, chastised.

"Don't be angry," Fasolt intervened, glancing between me and Ingvar. "He's a worrier."

"He's a good friend." I smiled, bearing no offense. "Keep taking it easy."

Ingvar beckoned me away with a wave of his hand. I left Fasolt's side and followed him as he cut a path toward the barracks front entrance.

"Heading out to the drills now," he told me. "If ye're feeling up for it, come with. I think everyone'll be glad to see you."

I'd been ignoring Ingvar while focusing on Fasolt. His offer forced me to return to my mixed feelings. The irrational part of me longed to stay with him. The rational part urged me to refuse, keep my distance. Then the irrational side pointed to the way Ingvar had framed his request. If I declined, I'd be letting the other soldiers down, wouldn't I?

"Sure," I said.

Ingvar smiled. At the barracks entrance, we threw on the weapons we'd doffed earlier.

"Again, my thanks for helping Fasolt," Ingvar said.

I smiled back and shook my head, muttering to avoid being overheard. "I'm glad he's all right, but I wish I hadn't had to lie to them like that."

"But ye *did* have to," Ingvar replied in kind without batting an eye.

"It's harder with people I like. If I had time to explain, really explain …" I trailed off, tugging my baldric into place on my shoulder.

Ingvar opened the entrance to a sunny afternoon, and waved me outside ahead of himself. "For some, there'd never be time enough." Remorse tinged his expression at that thought. "Right now, with everyone worrying about witches, best to stop that speculation cold."

I nodded, somberly recalling all too many examples of needless suffering brought on by such rumors. It was an accusation leveled at me constantly, but I never stuck around long enough to land in serious trouble. Here, though, there was a much higher risk of being grouped in with the Naustviks. I doubted even Ormyr's ambitions would spare me if he believed I were a witch.

We walked side by side along the open field, approaching a group of practicing soldiers in the distance. The capital buildings loomed far off past our left shoulders, ominous despite the cheerful weather.

As much as I feared getting too close, I couldn't help myself. "How did *you* stop believing in witches and things like that?"

Ingvar frowned toward the horizon for a long while. "Don't know." He sounded perplexed at first. "Suppose it never took hold in the first place. Tried to be convinced of Unseen and mysticism, seemed so much easier than always doubting, but it never happened."

"I envy you," I said, and truly meant it. "I was so taken in as a child that it still haunts me sometimes. I wish I'd been smarter."

"That's no fault of yours. What's a child to do but listen to her elders?" Ingvar gave me a reassuring look. "Later, ye faced down those lies and bested them. Be proud. That's something most people never manage."

His approval warmed me all over, and I was helpless to ignore it. I glanced downward, hoping he wouldn't see me flush.

"All right, now I'm curious," Ingvar said with amusement. "Where *did* that scar come from?"

I laughed with sudden self-consciousness, but telling Ingvar the truth posed no challenge, even with the rest of my emotional difficulty. It was a novelty I cherished. "When I was still a squire to Sir Mayweather, flying through Kamori space, some old smuggler friends of his tried to settle a grudge by sending six mercenaries after us."

Ingvar's eyes went wide.

"We escaped the trap, but we were pretty torn up. May never apologized so many times before or since. He was used to traveling alone, getting himself in trouble. That was when he realized his actions fell on both our heads." I tapped at the scar: still bumpy, but less prominent than it had been years earlier. "He called it '*his* reminder.'" A prime example of May's self-centered worldview. I rolled my eyes in contempt.

"When ye talked about getting rid of it, was that a lie too?" Ingvar asked. "I hope so. Scars usually have good stories to them. They're signs of experience, not failure."

"I hadn't thought of it like that before." Heart pounding, face burning, I still had trouble meeting his gaze.

The drilling soldiers had divided into two teams, one standing their ground against a wave of rushing attackers. They were equally kitted out on both sides: longsword, sword and shield, polearms, even some shooting with bows and blunted practice arrows. Many had charms lashed to their arms or belts in addition to their ever-present beads.

Focusing on the combatants helped me bury my emotions. "I suppose you can't run these drills for long," I remarked to Ingvar. It had to be tough to exert oneself while hungry.

"Everyone's still putting time in unless he's sick," Ingvar said. "Can't afford to be caught unprepared. If the crop trouble doesn't ease, something will give." He clutched the sword-hilt at his side. "When the next harvest arriveth, that will help a while, but even with the strictest rationing, we always run out of food afore the guild returneth. Our reserves in the storehouse will be spent soon, *and* we'll be out of flax. No telling what will happen then."

I nodded. It had to be tough managing a perpetually uneasy population during the best of times. As more people turned desperate, an attack on the capital became ever more likely. His pessimism was sad, but realistic.

"Look lively, boys! Captain's here!" Ebbe called out, waving his arm over his head. His eyes widened upon spotting me. "Lady Knight! Good to see you again!"

The young men quit their practice to hurry toward us, throwing out enthusiastic greetings. I recognized Magnus from my first visit to the barracks, as well as Rigg, the soldier who'd sought a private audience with Ingvar. I hoped he'd resolved whatever he'd been worried about.

"What're ye breaking ranks for?" Ingvar waved them off. "Trying to teach you lads to be focused, act without thought! Ye must maintain your sense of control!"

"Sorry, sir," Ebbe apologized.

"Ye're forgiven this time." Ingvar smirked at him. "While we're here, any questions?"

Ebbe immediately turned doe eyes upon me. "Lady Knight, d'ye want to fight on our side this round?"

"After she fights with us!" Magnus countered.

The group erupted into goodnatured bickering. Only Rigg held to silence, leaning against his sword, expressionless. He didn't seem upset, rather simply waiting for practice to resume.

Being so highly sought after—for a fight, of all things—

brought a smile to my face. "I'm sitting this one out, friends. Sorry." After the morning I'd had, I doubted I'd be much good to anyone, even in practice. Better to conserve my energy for whatever challenges lay ahead.

Ingvar called for silence, and quickly received it. "Afore stopping for the day, I want all of you lads to 'breach' the gate. The next drill group will defend against you. Tomorrow, ye'll switch, then ye'll practice safety and defenses for the predators out there."

Affirmations followed. Judging by the looks in the crowd, this was nothing new to them.

"'Tis unpleasant, but I also need you lads thinking about who it is ye might be fighting one day," Ingvar continued earnestly, his eyes passing over every member of the group. "Could be Lord Lagana's forces, could be faithless mercenaries, or, could be your very own kinsmen. That's the worst case. We should be defending them, not engaging them. Even so, another uprising's more likely than anything else. Your brothers *here*, around you, will need you to step up, just as ye'll be counting on them to step up for you. Some of you, like Magnus here—ye've been through it, ye know we'll pull through again. We'll do everything possible to avoid a fight, but if that's our only recourse, we'll be better prepared than anyone who faceth us." Ingvar tossed his head over his shoulder. "All right, lads, so much for preaching. Get back to it."

He strove to prepare them for everything he possibly could. That was admirable. At the same time, I irrationally hoped that training would never be needed.

The gathering responded with affirmatives before fractioning into two opposing forces again. "All right, lads! Let's show those old men a thing or two!" Ebbe shouted to his group.

"Let's show that pup where he can stick his attitude!" Magnus challenged his side.

"Keep it friendly!" Ingvar cautioned, then faced me and

lowered his voice. "Ye'll be a good distraction for them to work against." A trace of a smile tugged at his mouth.

"I won't get in the way," I promised.

Ingvar waved a hand in dismissal. "See anything off, I'd rather ye tell me. 'Tis usually Pontus I rely on for that, but it'd be good to have a different perspective. No pressure, though."

"Sure," I said, though I didn't expect to be pointing out anything wrong.

The drill resumed. I tailed Ingvar as he paced along its fringes, mostly observing, only slipping in to interject when he spotted a costly error.

"Here, lad. From *there*, your best angle of attack is right here. Simple." Standing beside the longsword-bearing soldier, Ingvar took his arms and slowly guided his hands and wrists through the intended strike on his adversary, who remained frozen in place for the demonstration. "What ye were doing isn't wrong, it just taketh more time. That's time your opponent can use to retaliate or get away."

He was always friendly and encouraging. Every interruption was about improvement, not about making anyone feel inadequate for their mistakes. Branigan's teaching style had been very similar. I'd much preferred it over May's showboating and provocation.

Ingvar wasn't Branigan, but he was wonderful in his own way. Dashing, supportive, intelligent, a perfect confidant—I wished I could stop seeing it. Too many other problems demanded attention at the moment. Even with everything resolved, I'd have to leave Nidaros eventually, and he couldn't come with me.

Whatever happened over the next few weeks, it was already too late for our eventual parting *not* to hurt. I could only hope to mitigate the pain. I wouldn't be able to erase it.

-ᐞᐞ-

The afternoon passed quickly. I was helping Ingvar correct Ebbe's longsword technique when Pontus and two soldiers emerged in the distance, hurrying toward the barracks. They carried no corpse, no piles of evidence. Nervously, I wondered whether Pontus had gotten anywhere at all with his investigation.

"Ingvar?" I pointed toward the approaching soldiers.

He followed my gaze with a difficult-to-read stare. After signaling to Pontus and the drilling soldiers with a big wave, he gestured me back toward the barracks.

Soon after, we stood in Ingvar's office. Pontus barged in moments later, glaring, but not at either of us. He closed off our triangle and folded his arms.

Ingvar folded his arms in turn. "Fared that well, aye?"

"Captain." Pontus then greeted me with a nod. "Everyone's been worried since ye 'disappeared,' Lady Knight, and are glad ye're well."

Well, that sounded promising so far. I nodded back.

"Did Master Ormyr permit you a look at *anything?*" Ingvar asked.

"Surprising enough, Master Ormyr let me into the dungeon himself," Pontus continued. "Our Baron insisted on being there as well."

"What'd ye find?" Ingvar asked.

"Plenty of smoke at first." Pontus shuddered in disgust. "Then the attacker's remains, the tipped-over lantern, and the cell where the grenade had been cast. In the ceiling there, we found a trap door mechanism—right where ye were walking 'fore ye dropped." His gaze shifted to mine. "According to Master Ormyr, the mechanism is triggered by a Shipbuilder relic that only an adept would be able to use. Asked him to show it to me." He shook his head. "Wasn't able to find it. Said he'd keep searching."

"So, someone would've had to command that door to

open while she was standing on it?" Ingvar tilted his head in my direction.

"Aye, sir," Pontus said.

"Is there any way the attacker in the dungeon could've seen or heard where she was to open it at the right time?" Ingvar asked.

"Nay," Pontus said. "Whoever set it in motion had to have been upstairs to get the timing right."

"Then the attacker in the dungeon had an accomplice for certain," Ingvar mused.

The blood drained from my face. "Maybe more than one. Just before it happened, someone in the hallway dropped something, which is what stopped us and drew Ormyr's attention away."

Pontus nodded. I'd mentioned this when he and Ingvar had questioned me jointly. "Asked to talk to the person responsible for that, but Master Ormyr refused to even furnish a name. Said they couldn't possibly be involved, and to leave it at that."

Ingvar scowled, but said nothing.

Pontus lowered his head to me. "'Tis clear to everyone ye were ambushed, and defended yourself against your attacker. Our Baron wishes me to assure you he'll seek justice in your name."

Before I could bask in vindication, something niggled at me. "The Baron doesn't want to see me right now?"

"Didn't mention it," Pontus said.

Strange. I would've thought he'd be eager to beg me not to bring up this unfortunate incident with Lord Catherwood.

"What about that prisoner's corpse? The one dead of ... Hel only knoweth what?" Ingvar asked.

"Had no chance to find or secure it, sir," Pontus said. "Master Ormyr rounded us right back upstairs, assuring us

he'd figure out what drove Dame Jessamine's would-be murderer to his crime."

"*Skíta*," Ingvar cursed. "Get the attacker's name, at least?"

Knorr Lindgren. Trying to find out who his friends were,
but damned if all the adepts aren't cagey and more clueless
than cattle right now." Pontus scowled. "Damned if I know
how he got a grenade, either!"

"Must've filched it from the storehouse," Ingvar said. "Did
ye talk to our lads on shift?"

"That's the devil of it, sir. No one on shift for the past several days saw anything strange," Pontus replied. "All our
inventory counts reckon properly. Adept Knorr must've conjured the thing through arcane means."

"Or, he or someone else might've stolen it a long time ago,"
I said, trying to offer a rational possibility.

"I'm sure we'll figure it out." Ingvar nodded. "Thanks,
Pontus. Appreciate your help."

"Not done yet, sir." Pontus' distaste persisted. "Master
Ormyr was rather … numb over Adept Knorr. Plain to me he's
hiding something, but we'll have to get at it indirectly. I'll keep
trying for Adept Knorr's work areas and sleeping quarters,
and for that corpse ye saw. See if I can't find an adept who
wants 'help' cleaning up the dungeon."

"Do so." Ingvar threw a glance my way. "And if Adept
Knorr received any mail in the last shipment, I want it."

Pontus blinked. "Why's that?"

"A hunch right now. We'll see if it leadeth anywhere." Still
looking my way, Ingvar nodded. "Time to discuss our next
moves, aye? Ye're in the clear, so options are open."

"Sort of," I said. "We were supposed to be retrieving Drea,
but now I doubt the Baron or Ormyr will let me out of the capital, much less off-planet."

When I brought up the failed trip, Pontus' eyes narrowed
as distastefully as ever. Did he not want me leaving? Did he

not want me taking Ingvar? I continued as if I hadn't noticed. "Until we have more evidence, we can't piece together this murder plot." Or determine who'd masterminded it. Master Ormyr? Madam Castor? All of the above? "I'm back to wanting a look at your crops and soil, and visiting the Naustviks' house to see what's there." Thordia herself, along with the cause of the crop trouble, according to Verahl. "Now's as good a time as any."

Pontus' disapproval vanished in favor of mute, wide-eyed horror.

Ingvar deliberated with a frown. "The wilderness between districts isn't safe, and the districts themselves get worse all the time." After a few moments, he faced me with a decisive nod. "I don't let my men travel unaccompanied. I'll go with you now."

It was my turn to be wide-eyed, more out of surprise and dread. What motivated this offer? He truly cared about Nidaros. Was he trying to make up for Drea as well? While I'd welcome his help, would it be wise to remain in close company?

Before I could figure myself out enough to reply, Pontus intervened to plead with both of us. "If ye insist on such a horrible destination, Lady Knight, Rigg knows the Low North best. Captain, send him with her. Your place is here."

Honestly, it was Ingvar's help I wanted. We'd make uninhibited progress without regard toward superstition. Anyone else, I'd be lying to and evading half the time.

"What for?" Ingvar asked calmly. "What's happening in the next few hours?"

"Sir?" Pontus glanced between us with the same wariness he'd shown in the port that morning. "What we talked about earlier ... think it applies here."

"Got a problem? Don't be bashful," Ingvar returned.

Pontus soured, likely unhappy with Ingvar calling him

out. When he glanced my way, he tried to filter out as much of that negativity as possible, but a trace lingered. "With all due respect, Lady Knight, ye're just out of the fire, literally. There's no need to leap back in—nor must *ye* plunge in after her," he added, turning a loaded frown on Ingvar.

"We're narrowing in on the real problems that plague us," Ingvar replied.

"That so?" Pontus challenged. "In a matter of days, ye two are putting together what a whole cloister of adepts haven't?"

"The adepts have a lot to worry about," I intervened delicately. "Sometimes they're stretched thin, and good leads get overlooked."

"Never mind we don't know which of those adepts we can trust," Ingvar said.

"Aye! Just what I'm saying!" Pontus cried. "We may have more murderers loose in the capital, and ye want to chase after witches in the districts!"

His response brought me up short. Maybe Ingvar should remain, if only to keep order. Moreover, I didn't want to be responsible for spawning a rift between these two. I glanced Ingvar's way. "Maybe I should just—"

Ingvar held up a hand to stop me, then made eye contact with Pontus. "Tell me what ye're really nervous about."

Pontus scowled, annoyed. "I'm nervous about your reasoning. I'm nervous about both of you disappearing without a trace!"

Ingvar nodded, still calm. "I appreciate your concern. Just trust me, 'tis not as foolish as ye fear. Put more men on watch in the capital, and keep pressure on the adepts. We'll head to the Low North and return as soon as we can."

"Lad." Pontus shook his head with a sternly set jaw, winding his hand through the beads hanging at his side. "I can only hope that with your good intentions, the Unseen'll take pity on you."

"I hope *ye'll* take pity as well." Lowering his head, Ingvar fell back toward the door, gesturing me out with him.

Outside his office, Ingvar approached a bank of storage chests with quiet resolve. He already bore a longsword; he strapped a quiver of arrows to his open hip, then worked on stringing a bow.

I hovered at his side, nervously tugging and re-tugging my baldric into place. "I feel really bad about all that," I blurted.

Ingvar paused to blink at me. "About what?"

"About what just happened with Pontus."

Ingvar's surprise persisted. "Expect us to agree on everything, Goose? 'Tis for the best that we don't."

"He has a point, though," I struggled to explain around my guilt and a pulse that gathered steam. "I mean, I really want your help, but your men should come first."

"They do, but they don't need me staring over their shoulders day and night. 'Tis a disservice to them." Ingvar's expression turned to concern. "Something else bothering you?"

"No. I just …" I lied, then trailed off. Was I being a distraction? Screwing up Ingvar's priorities, driving wedges between him and his men? And his insistence on accompanying me — was it only about saving Nidaros, or, was it possible *he felt the same way about me?*

An embarrassed flush rose to my face, while a stabbing self-contempt plunged into my heart. *Please!* I chided mentally. *Don't flatter yourself.*

"Just?" Ingvar prompted.

I pretended to great interest in my own feet. "Nothing."

Ingvar leaned in to whisper. "The Naustvik house, then? I'm not convinced we'll find Thordia, much less the true cause of our ills, but I prefer not to leave the place unchecked."

Having seen Verahl's conviction, I felt more optimistic. I nodded, then gestured to Ingvar's armament. "Exactly what kind of trouble are you expecting?"

"On the way there? Predators that're hungry and desperate as anything. At the Naustviks' house? Neither of us can say." He shouldered his bow. "Still insisting on that waistcoat, yourself? Ye might wish for proper armor."

"My brigandine's stronger than it looks," I said.

"Any good at shooting?" he asked.

"No."

His eyes narrowed. "Best fix that when ye can. Ye should threaten from every range. Fortunate that hasn't cost you earlier."

I shrugged. "My quests aren't usually that exciting."

"Aye, Goose, I'm falling asleep on my feet here."

Despite my mixed feelings, I couldn't help laughing.

With a faint smile, Ingvar picked up an unlit lantern and procured two canteens on long leather straps. From there, we headed back outside toward the gate.

CHAPTER 19

Well equipped for our journey, Ingvar and I headed for the capital gate under a cheery afternoon sun. The soldiers' drills continued behind us. Ahead lay potential progress, and potential danger. I still smarted from the dungeon fight, but was more than ready to keep fighting if that was what it took to rescue Thordia and learn what plagued Nidaros.

Still, part of me wondered whether the real danger wasn't the captain at my side, walking along with silent resolve. The more time I spent with Ingvar, the more I found to admire—and despair, given our partnership would be short-lived.

"The Low North district is a decent walk from here." Ingvar's voice cut through my thoughts, catching me off-guard. "I know where the Naustviks' house lieth. Unfortunately, 'tis nestled deep amid the district. However we approach, we'll be in line of sight of several houses. Still have your papers from Lord Catherwood?"

"Uh, yes," I said, studying my feet. Hell, this wasn't the time to be thinking about this. Put it aside, don't give any sign.

"Might help if anyone taketh issue with our presence," Ingvar continued. "Your weapons might as well, but no lethal force except as a last resort."

"I—no." I could hide it. I had all too much practice with hiding my true feelings from Branigan.

"Also have a few men patrolling the district. Don't know where they might be at any moment, but we could call for them if needed."

But I felt *terrible* about hiding things now that Branigan was gone, didn't I?

It took a while to tamp down that remorse again. Afterward, I became aware of a lengthening silence. My gaze snapped up to Ingvar, who glanced back at me with concern.

"Supposing we do find Thordia," he started up again, "how will we get her to trust us?"

Face burning with embarrassment, I forced myself to cast all that aside and focus on the matter at hand. "Good question. We can tell her the truth, that we rescued Verahl and he's safe with us. We'll have to play it by ear after that, depending on her reaction. If we both have Shipbuilder knowledge as a common language, so to speak, that might help."

Ingvar blinked at me. "Ye ever *plan* anything, Goose?"

"This *is* a plan, in broad strokes," I returned with amusement. "We won't know the details until we're living them."

And that was my strength: thinking on my feet. Ingvar's meticulous preparation was commendable, and no doubt served him well. He probably didn't deal often with the sort of situations I did, situations that had a nasty habit of going straight to hell. Rescuing Verahl from the dungeon was a prime example. Being able to adapt and compensate was just as valuable as thorough pre-planning.

Ingvar's narrowed eyes conveyed his lack of conviction on that count. "Better think about where to hide her, also."

It was my turn to frown, with confusion. "On my ship, with Verahl." That seemed the obvious answer.

"Keep in mind: I convinced my men that her brother shared no blame, but there's no chance of me talking them out of believing Thordia's a witch," Ingvar said.

Good point. "So dismiss the men you stationed aboard my ship."

"That's no problem, but I can't dismiss the men standing watch in the port," Ingvar replied. "The Baron's vessel must be protected at all times."

"You could order them to look in a different direction for a while," I said, smiling a little. "The same way you ordered them not to see Verahl, remember?"

I won that point. Ingvar shook his head, a smirk spreading over his features. He pressed no further, likely still skeptical that Thordia was at home. I held more optimism on that count. While Ormyr and his adepts had no doubt torn up the house in search of her, they obviously hadn't located the crawl space Verahl had told me about. Thordia could still be there, lying low in the one place no one expected to find her.

We passed through the capital gate, waving to the soldiers stationed there, then followed the wagon path meandering through the hilly fields. A clean breeze stirred grasses to either side of us.

"We'll want to stay quiet out here, keep alert." Ingvar pulled his bow off his shoulder, holding it at his side for the moment. "Lots of dangerous animals wandering out of place in search of food and water. The sverma are most likely along this path. They seem as shadows, darting low to the ground. Alone they're not so bad, but they'll call out to their friends when they find something, and 'tis the swarm that's deadly. They leap high and have a nasty bite. Backs are plated, your blade won't get through. Flip them over and stab them."

"Understood." A lot to take in at once, but these wouldn't be the first unusual local fauna I'd tangled with. I drew my side sword.

"'Tis ideal to move quickly, but ye did fight in a smoke-filled dungeon not long ago," Ingvar continued. "If ye need rest, let me know and we'll stop."

I nodded, appreciative of the offer, but not expecting to cash it in. My rising anticipation of what we might find in the Low North distracted me from the fatigue and injuries I'd earned earlier that day.

We walked on in brisk silence, scanning the terrain for trouble. After the recent bout with smoke, my lungs welcomed the abundant fresh air around us. The capital disappeared, leaving nothing but rustling grass, sky, and Ingvar's ever-vigilant company. Despite his warnings, it felt safe out there, and free—free of the capital and its politics, obligations, and hazards. Our potential for making progress seemed just as boundless as the rolling landscape.

For the longest time, we were the only living beings in sight. Then, Ingvar froze at the crest of a small hill, pointing to a spot several yards downhill.

I stopped beside him and followed his gesture to a tangled, writhing knot of knee-high creatures. They were squat and dog-sized, shaped like inverted arrowheads, with mandibles I could see all the way back from our vantage point.

"Sverma?" I whispered, clenching my side sword's hilt tighter.

Ingvar nodded.

They reminded me of some group predators I'd seen before on other planets, but I knew better than to compare those experiences with this one. The sverma were sure to be different in many important respects. They looked to be swarming over a horse-sized animal, now reduced to a carcass. "Do you think they're distracted enough for us to sneak past?" I asked.

"Hope so," Ingvar spoke under his breath. "Standing still's a mistake. They'll catch us for certain." He hitched the handle of his unlit lantern to his sword-belt and pulled multiple arrows into his hand, nocking one of them to his bow. "We'll circle around. Follow my lead."

I let him slip ahead of me. Keeping our eyes locked on the swarm, we traced out a slow, wide arc around it. Despite all his gear, Ingvar moved through the knee-high grasses without making a sound. Not as experienced with stealth in landscapes like this, I placed my feet wherever Ingvar had, ensuring I mostly stepped on grasses that'd already been stepped on.

To my relief, we reached the bottom of the hill without attracting attention. Unfortunately, three of the sverma had no share of the kill, and were far more alert as a result. They broke away from the swarm, bounding through the grasses in our direction.

With dread, I hastened to recall everything Ingvar had told me earlier. Most critically, we had to kill them before they summoned more. Side sword at the ready, I darted out to engage them.

A hand clamped down on my shoulder, hauling me back. "Don't run out!" Ingvar said. "We'll pick 'em off from back here!"

"I trust you not to shoot me!" I said.

The sverma capitalized on our lack of coordination, melting beneath the grasses like sharks below water. They were even better at moving through the grasses than Ingvar was. It was impossible to get a bead on them.

"*Skíta!*" Ingvar dropped his bow and drew his longsword. "Put your back to mine! Listen!"

He was used to issuing orders. I was used to following my own instincts. But there was no wounded pride here, just the desire to escape this trap alive. I placed my back to his accordingly, holding my blade out in front of me in a defensive guard. We each covered 180 degrees of terrain. My sweeping eyes detected no movement in our vicinity. The wind had died down, aiding my search, but for several moments, not even a single grass-blade twitched.

"Hell, where'd they go?" I muttered, heart pounding.

"They'll leap right in front of you," Ingvar muttered back. "Won't give you much chance to—"

He fell silent. Soon after followed the sound of a blade encountering a hard object, followed by a metallic crash.

I wasn't able to turn around and assist. A single sverma sprang out of the grass ahead of me, hurtling toward my face.

As Ingvar had been trying to say, I barely had room to swing, but swing I did. I slashed in a downward arc with the intention of batting the sverma to the ground, setting up a finishing strike. To my surprise, my blade cleaved the thing into convulsing halves.

"Blood's oath, Goose! Nicely done!" Ingvar stepped up beside me with a look of incredulous triumph. In one hand was his longsword, a single dead sverma stuck to the end of it. In the other was his lantern, now dented beyond use.

Heart still pounding, I whirled around, confirming the third dead sverma lay curled up on the ground behind us. Not only were we in the clear, but my side sword also lent me an unanticipated edge against these creatures. Victory fueled the grin I returned to Ingvar once I faced him again. "Let's get going."

He was about to give his assent when an ear-piercing shriek erupted in the distance, its source invisible. Nearly a dozen non-feeding sverma, lapping at the edges of the carcass, bolted toward us at the prospect of a fresh kill.

All our happy relief plummeted into frozen dread. "Aw, hell," I muttered.

"We have to fight. They'll chase us to oblivion." Unable to quickly dislodge the sverma from his sword, Ingvar dropped it and the busted lantern in favor of his bow on the ground. "Stay there, cut down as many as ye can. I'll cover you!" While gathering multiple arrows into his draw hand, he fell back and partially ascended the hill we'd walked down, gaining both distance and higher ground.

"Right." I shook off my nerves and faced the newcomers, sword chambered for the first strike.

Ingvar got to work right away on thinning the swarm's numbers. With calm resolve, he loaded and fired the arrows in his draw hand faster than I'd ever seen anyone do before. He only raised the bow to chest height without sighting down it with one eye, which helped with his speed. Untold years of practice aided his accuracy. His arrows struck sverma on their weak sides, sending them rolling through the grasses, twitching and curled into themselves.

The sverma he didn't pick off leapt at me, mostly targeting my head. Single strikes, wherever I managed to place them, went right through them. Between that and Ingvar, I mostly kept from being overwhelmed — until pain shot up my leg.

I yelped and staggered. One sverma had sneaked in beneath my awareness, latching its mandibles onto my right ankle. I switched my sword-grip and thrust downward, skewering the attacker before its mandibles cracked bone.

The few remaining sverma disappeared into the grasses. Silence returned to the rolling countryside, hard to trust at first, but it persisted. Ingvar and I were alone again, aside from the large animal carcass some distance away, picked clean.

Ingvar shouldered his bow, ran back over, and retrieved his longsword. He knocked the blade against the ground until the sverma's remains jolted off, then whirled on me.

Still nerve-racked and fight-primed, I gave a start.

"Hold still, Jayce." Ingvar knelt at my side, where the sverma I'd stabbed through held on to my ankle with undiminished ferocity. Carefully, Ingvar wedged his blade between my ankle and one of the mandibles. "This might take some time. Don't worry, ye'll be fine."

His soothing concern swept aside my adrenaline, replacing it with that longing I'd been trying to ignore. Forcing calming breaths upon myself, I dislodged my side sword from the sverma's middle. While Ingvar worked at prying off one of the mandibles, I used my own blade on the other.

"Never seen a blade go *through* one of these things, like that plating wasn't there." Ingvar's voice conveyed his astonishment. "What's that little fencing stick of yours made of?"

"I'm not sure," I said. "My friends at the beguinage forged it for me."

"Shipbuilder magic?" Ingvar stopped and stared up at me with trepidation, apparently more afraid of *that* than the sverma.

It was possible my friends had employed some ancient forging technique to infuse my blade with extra strength or density, but this was the first time I'd ever learned of its special resilience. Now how to explain that to my friend without startling him further? "Remember procedure? It's not *magic*, but —"

"*Skíta*. I know." Ingvar scowled back down at the stubborn predator's remains. "Prefer a bow anyway."

"I can see why. I've never seen anyone shoot so naturally," I praised. "Does everyone here handle a bow like that?"

"How many other ways are there?" Ingvar frowned up at me for a second. "Never mind, I'm sure ye've seen plenty."

"None that fast or accurate," I assured him. "Now that's some bow-handling I wouldn't mind learning."

He smirked. "Bring me a few dozen swords like yours, I'll teach you."

I smiled back. "Deal." We spoke in light tones, but I found myself seriously wondering how hard it would be to arrange that deal whenever I returned to the beguinage.

Our combined leverage finally snapped the sverma's mandibles away. With relief, I gave my ankle a test-rotation, and found it accommodating. No new holes in my leather boot, either.

"Not much further." Ingvar stood, sheathing his sword. "All right to run?"

"Yes," I said.

He threw a grim look toward the horizon. "More are coming. Let's not be here when they arrive."

We kept quiet to conserve our breath and avoid detection. An occasional straggling sverma emerged during the last leg of the journey. I fended them off whenever possible, allowing Ingvar to conserve arrows. Fortunately, they dropped without summoning friends. Still, I fully understood why Ingvar didn't allow his soldiers to travel alone.

The late afternoon sun lost some of its warmth. Beneath our racing feet, the grasses thinned, then gave out. The Low North district emerged, sprawling and barren. Little wooden houses stood at irregular intervals, capped with thatched roofs reaching nearly to the ground. A typical rural village from a distance — but, as with Spectra, the close-up reality was likely to be very different.

Our haste didn't subside until we reached the edge of the neighborhood. There, we pelted to a stop beside a section of worn, waist-high wooden fence that no longer seemed to serve any particular purpose.

We remained alone for the moment. As we caught our breaths and took swigs of water from our canteens, Ingvar's eyes darted about in search of some break in our solitude. "Been encroaching on the districts as well," he muttered once he could speak again. "Got most of the livestock people were saving."

The relief I'd embraced upon our arrival quickly evaporated. "Sverma?" I asked.

"Aye, and worse."

"*Worse?* Like what?" I demanded.

"If I tried explaining everything we might find, we'll be here all night," Ingvar said. "Our best bet is not to be detected, by anything or anyone." He shouldered his bow, freeing up his hands. "Follow my lead. I'll keep an eye up ahead, ye watch our backs. See anything ye're not sure about, let me know."

I nodded, sheathing my side sword. While potentially useful against predators, I was more concerned with not scaring any people we came across — people who, between lack of food and abundance of witches, were likely on their last nerve. "I'm right behind you."

The wagon path that'd led us to the district branched out like a clutch of indecisive serpents, but Ingvar guided me along without hesitation. Our pace was much slower, not just for avoiding detection; Ingvar seemed to need more time recovering from our run than I did. A heart-aching reminder that no matter how tough the Nidarans were, the lack of food affected them. The thought reawakened my own gnawing hunger, which I found difficult to dismiss.

Empty plots sat beside the houses we walked past, fenced in with more crooked waist-high wood frames. Polished rocks, animal bones, shaped twigs, and the occasional metal emblem adorned the barren fields, each one a silent, unanswered plea. Tool sheds sat untouched, animal coops and stalls stood empty. Trash lay between the plots, wafting smells that coaxed the bile up the back of my throat.

Scythes, sickles, and hammers leaned beside every door. They were probably there so residents could arm themselves whenever they stepped outside, assuming there *were* any residents. The place remained as empty of human presence as when we'd first arrived.

A chill crawled along my skin, worsening as our solitude lengthened. I'd hoped to keep Nidaros from becoming another Gules, but it was already well on its way. Those corpses in the streets returned to my mind's eye, Drea and Branigan among them. I had to physically shake off the worry and dread.

"Where is everybody?" I muttered.

Ingvar glanced over his shoulder at me. "Inside, conserving strength. Toward nightfall, many of them join my men in patrolling for predators, and for the Naustviks. Guarantee they'll be drawn to any odd sight or noise."

I nodded, then fell quiet again.

Our path took us through the district commons, where rain barrels stood amid the foot-worn expanse. A shroud blanketed the well at the center. Dry, allegedly. But wait—when I'd first talked to the kitchen servants, hadn't Kofri mentioned something about some weird sludge? Was there any truth to that rumor?

"Have you seen what comes out of the wells?" I whispered to Ingvar.

He frowned back at me. "They're dry."

"When was the last time you tried one?"

Ingvar halted, thinking about it. "A while ago. The adepts closed them off."

"Could I try?" I stopped too, gesturing toward the well.

His eyes went wide before he gathered himself and waved a hand in strict dismissal. "That may be the one thing that landeth us in trouble faster than being sighted at the Naustviks' house."

I assumed he feared the fallout from getting caught, not breaking wards or disobeying the adepts. "All right, not here. But could I try one in the capital later?" Maybe the one near the kitchen, if I could find an opportunity when no one was around.

"Mayhap, if we're careful about it. Now let's focus on what

we came for." Ingvar resumed course.

I followed, satisfied for the moment.

A short while later, Ingvar stopped and pointed to a house that had just come into view in the distance. It wasn't really necessary for him to point out the Naustviks' plot, though. The little house sat by itself at the end of a lonely path, buried in pendants and adept graffiti. It reminded me of "witch houses" I'd seen elsewhere. What must it have taken for Thordia to survive trapped in there alone for so long, assuming she had? Although, the isolation might not have been anything new. If she and Verahl really were the heirs to some mysterious fount of Shipbuilder knowledge, they may've felt alienated from their neighbors long before the crop trouble had struck.

Ingvar helped me over the fence around an adjoining property, then vaulted over himself. Keeping half-crouched, we sneaked up to the fence at the rear of the Naustviks' plot. There, baubles covered every inch of dirt, with no trace of plant life among them. Once we scaled the fence, Ingvar sneaked up on the back of the forbidden house. I knelt and sifted through the mess at our feet, trying to get a look at the soil beneath. What might Thordia have found within it?

A hand settled on my shoulder. I glanced up with a start. It was Ingvar, who'd doubled back to point me toward the house with a scowl.

He had every reason to prefer haste. Still, I had no intention of leaving the Low North before I at least had a look at the soil, maybe collected some samples. For the time being, I followed Ingvar, picking a careful path through the charms to avoid breaking or slipping on them. Shrouds flanked the house's back door: an ouroboros painted on one, and on the other, the crossed-out-eye "heretic" symbol that'd been carved into Branigan's forehead.

The sight simmered my blood. I bit my sore lip, and somehow managed to keep an angry cry from escaping.

Weather-worn planks lay in a haphazard pile by the rear of the house. Maybe someone had intended to nail them up over the entrances, or use them as kindling for a major arson project. We finally converged upon the back door, almost invisible behind beads, stones, and other protective devices.

Ingvar turned to me with a somber look. "The adepts were the last to venture inside. Expect nothing pretty."

I nodded, more determined than ever to get Thordia out of the prison that'd been built up around her. "Actually, let me go first. No offense, but if she's watching the door, your colors might frighten her."

"Fair enough." Ingvar stepped back to wait behind me.

With a steadying breath, I took hold of the handle and pushed slowly.

The door creaked open into a cramped single-room abode, each wall about twenty feet long. I froze at the threshold, stunned by what spread out before us.

Inside, the Naustviks' home might've ranked with Elysium or Eden weeks earlier, but that comparison was now a distant memory. The sunlight at our backs cut through the dimness, revealing a thick web of dead vines and shriveled flowers that coated the ceiling and poured down the walls. On the floor, the carnage took the form of overturned furniture: beds, chairs, cupboards, and a table, all suspended at unusable angles. An inexplicable warmth poured outside, carrying the powerful sting of decay. No *human* decay though, thankfully.

Footsteps sounded behind me. I whirled around to find Ingvar reeling backward, choking back a retch.

Worried, I lunged after him and braced his arms to keep him from collapsing. "Are you all right?" Disappointment, combined with all too much experience around similar smells, had shielded me from a similar reaction.

Ingvar held on to me for balance with one hand, burying

his face in the crook of his opposite elbow. "Aye, just, what in Hel *died* in there?"

"Dead plants can smell like that," I said. "Rotten ones."

After a moment, Ingvar eased away to stand straight, his confusion plain. "Nothing rotting around here lately, but drying out."

True, that was confusing. Less confusing was that this creepy, witchy abode only looked the way it did because of what Master Ormyr and his cohorts had done days or weeks earlier, when they'd come to arrest Thordia. Those plants must've looked amazing in the peak of health — and they must've scared the adepts clear out of their skins. How *had* Verahl and Thordia maintained a lush indoor garden while dry grass covered the rest of Nidaros?

"Where'd ye say that crawl space was?" Ingvar asked.

"The cellar," I said, struggling to pull myself away from the past tragedy and focus on the present. "I'm guessing there's an entrance somewhere inside, built into the floor."

Ingvar gave a nod. "Let's get in and find it. Keep alert, Thordia might not be the only one living in there."

"Verahl told me they don't have any other family members," I said.

"Thinking more of predators." Ingvar's gaze darted about nervously.

"Good point." In close quarters, my dagger was preferable to my side sword. Both remained sheathed for the moment, though, as I preferred to keep my hands free. It'd also make a better impression on Thordia, were she hiding somewhere amid her ruined garden.

"Lost our lantern to one of those sverma back there. Had nothing else to fend it off with," Ingvar continued, his voice containing a note of apology. "Let's work fast so we're not stuck trying to get home after sundown."

"It's all right. This is no lantern, but it'll help." I felt comfortable enough with Ingvar to retrieve my stick lighter.

He blinked at it, dubious. "What's that?"

"A Shipbuilder artifact," I whispered. "It's like a candle that never burns away. Watch."

When the small bead of light surged on, Ingvar jumped.

I placed a hand on his arm to steady him. "It's not so different from matches, or a flint and steel, when you think about it. Just more convenient. I can explain how it works."

"Not now." Ingvar took a deep breath, forcing his fright down to nervous doubt. "Go on, I'm right behind you."

I nodded my thanks, took my own deep breath outside, then crossed the threshold with slow caution. Ingvar shadowed me at first as promised, gradually separating to follow his own curiosity.

My small bead of light, sweeping from one side of the room to the other, expanded upon the mess we'd first viewed from outside. The straw-covered dirt floor was almost invisible beneath rags, pottery shards, and other remnants of two simple, innocent lives. To clear a path, I nudged things aside with my foot, or lifted them to check underneath. Sometimes, all I found were insects clouded around overripe fruits. Surrounding us was the unmistakable scratching and skittering of small animals.

Damn it, Ormyr, was this really necessary? I choked back my resentment. With every passing moment, I felt increasingly worse for, and kindred to, the Naustviks. I'd always feared something like this happening to my friends at the beguinage. Lord Sever had never bothered them before, but that didn't mean he wouldn't.

"We may only plant what the guild alloweth."

I faced Ingvar when he spoke, standing a few feet behind me. His expression was difficult to read, as it was craned toward the vine-coated ceiling.

"This place is cause enough for *me* to arrest them," he continued.

"Over house plants?" I asked, incredulous. "Haven't they been through enough?"

Ingvar's stern stare fastened on me. "Never seen such flora. Can't imagine where they came from. Did the Naustviks know what they were doing with them? Imagine if they're invasive, and some seeds get loose?" He threw out his left arm, pantomiming a breeze coming through the window. "Could jeopardize everyone's crops!"

Hell, I hadn't thought of that. He was right. Upon thinking a little further, a terrifying realization jolted me from head to foot. "Ingvar!"

He stared back at me with equal horror, pale at his own implication. "Blood's oath, Jayce. What if the Naustviks *did* destroy our crops?"

Ormyr right all along? My brain and stomach reeled at the thought, as though finally succumbing to the death all around us. It was possible, it was absolutely possible their lovely garden had been more full of poison than perfume. They might not have even realized.

"We can't be certain yet," I spoke around the lump in my throat. "Besides, an invasive species wouldn't explain the wells and flax drying up."

"Mayhap not. But if they're capable of *that*—" Ingvar pointed at the withered canopy above "—what else d'ye suppose we'll find here?"

Dread entered my heart, spreading through my limbs. Still, what we found here might not be all bad. "Verahl said Thordia isolated the cause," I forced out. "Let's keep looking for—"

Ingvar put a hushing finger to his lips.

Having learned my lesson with the sverma, I held still and

shut up as ordered, listening hard for whatever he might've heard.

Amid the tense silence that followed, Ingvar leaned down and retrieved a candle from the floor, resting near his left foot. He held it out toward me for my inspection. A thin stream of smoke rose from the blackened wick.

Snuffed out recently. *Someone* had to be nearby, or had recently fled. I nodded my understanding, my heart beginning to pound.

Ingvar then pointed at a blanketed, misshapen lump on the floor close to where the candle had lain, propped up against the room's right wall. He stood beside it, while I was a few feet away, closer to the center of the room. The hidden form looked big enough to be a small person curled up in hiding. Thordia?

My instinct was to call to her. Ingvar, however, motioned for continued silence. He then pointed to the front and back of the house, as though to suggest covering the entrances.

I shook my head vehemently. Thordia wasn't about to run outside; if anyone spotted her, she'd be in grave danger. Where was the cellar entrance? I would've preferred to cover that.

The blanketed form decided not to wait for us to work out our logistics. It shot upward, sprouting short legs that sprinted toward the left side of the room.

Ingvar lunged after it, but missed. As it rushed past me, I reached out with my left hand and gripped something solid under the blanket. A shoulder or elbow, maybe. *Child-sized.*

The child yelped—a boy. My grip was weak against the momentum he'd built up. He shook me off and changed course, bolting for the front door instead. One of his bare feet came down on something that broke with a loud crack.

Before my disbelieving eyes, a dead vine along the ceiling unfurled itself, shot down, and wound around the boy's waist.

CHAPTER 20

Late afternoon sunlight and my stick lighter conspired to reveal a scene that made no sense. Before me, an animated vine as thick as a snake hefted a shrouded boy toward the ceiling of the Naustviks' house. The boy thrashed in mid-air, yelping obscenities in a voice on the cusp of adolescence. Several more vines unfurled from the ceiling, dropping down to help lift him higher.

I gasped and gave a start. Ingvar fell back toward the rear of the house and the open back door, readying his bow while silhouetted in sunlight.

Once we rescued the boy, we'd sort out who he was, what this creature was, and what they were doing in this house. With angry resolve, I pocketed my stick lighter and drew my side sword, then darted toward the ensnared boy to slash through the nearest vine.

My blade passed through with satisfying ease, dropping a length of fleshy innards to the floor. The remainder of the vine snapped back into the ceiling with a hail of dead leaves in its wake. Before I could reach the boy, even more vines shot down at me from multiple directions. I dodged and slashed, fending off each one as fast as I could. Fortunately, none got past my side sword.

When the flurry ended, I refocused on the boy, hovering above my head only a few feet shy of the ruined garden covering the ceiling. There was no safe angle at which to slash at the vines holding him; I risked hitting him.

"Take my hand!" I reached up with my free hand instead, hoping to pull him free, or at least anchor him while Ingvar spent a few arrows on his attackers.

The boy thrashed without a glance my way or any sign he'd even heard me. Probably too caught up in his own struggle, or he trusted me as far as he trusted his attackers.

A large, shadowy mass emerged from the decaying canopy, lowering toward me and the boy. That was when I realized the "vines" were actually part of one single creature: a massive tumbleweed, with dozens of appendages flailing around the core toward which it pulled its prize.

"Oh, hell!" I blurted, frozen in shock.

An arrow pierced that core, sinking in up to the fletching. A second arrow followed. A third.

The thing hissed and shuddered. Several vines receded, dropping their prey, but my triumph was brief. The boy crash-landed atop my head, flattening me on my back.

"*Skíta!*" Ingvar cursed from the threshold.

A pained grunt escaped my lungs. My back took the brunt, with my head just slightly behind. It was a lucky thing we fell on dirt and not overturned furniture, but the impact with the floor jolted the side sword out of my hand.

Whether considerate of me or just thinking of his own hide, the boy hauled himself up, bolting off to an unknown destination. His weight lifting away was a relief; the sight of the creature looming directly overhead was not. However, its flailing had slowed. No vines shot down to capitalize on my weakness. It appeared to be as stunned as I was for the moment.

"Jayce! Can ye move?" Ingvar called.

"I think so." I forced myself onto my stomach, wincing at sharp new hurts all over.

Ingvar stood calm under pressure in the threshold, about ten or fifteen feet off, holding several more arrows in his draw-hand. "This way, quickly." A flicker of worry crossed his expression. "I'd come over there, but if it snareth us both, we're dead."

A quick look around revealed no sign of the boy. I hoped he was safe, wherever the hell he'd escaped to. It was time to attend to my own safety and get myself out from under the thing's shadow before it regained its senses, and I learned firsthand what happened once it reeled in its prey. Back and head still smarting, I dragged myself toward the threshold past chairs, pottery, and the rest of the mess we'd sifted through earlier.

Ingvar waited until I'd reached the halfway point to fire more arrows at the beast in rapid succession, covering my getaway. Some deflected off furniture or walls instead of sinking home, possibly batted away by the vines.

I kept going. Once I was close to the threshold, Ingvar chanced a step forward, offering me a hand off the floor—only to freeze in horror.

A great weight crashed to the floor behind me a half-second later, shaking the ground and the flimsy house perched on top. Vines lashed around my legs and torso, pulling backward with force.

I cried out and grabbed the leg of an upturned chair with my left hand. My right hand dug into the straw-and-dirt floor. It wasn't perfect rigging, but it held for the moment. The vines' pull intensified, popping joints in my back. How much ground could I lose before it had me? I held fast, fear chilling me all over.

"Jayce!" Ingvar lunged after me, eyes wide. He seemed to have forgotten, or actively disregarded, the danger of getting too close to the thing.

More vines flew out over my head. One lashed around Ingvar's left arm, the other his neck. The bow dropped from his hands. With his free hand, he seized the choking vine, struggling to breathe around it.

"Ingvar!" My heart screamed at me to do something even louder than my brain did, but I was powerless. Or was I? My dagger was pretty well buried between me and the floor. What about my stick lighter, in my right pocket? It'd be easier to reach, provided I could hold on long enough one-handed.

Nervous about how well the chair would hold, I clawed the fingers of my left hand deep into the dirt floor instead, then reached for my pocket with my right, stirring around inside with my fingertips.

Every moment I held my ground, it seemed another vine arrived to coax me out of my stubborn ways. I only had seconds before the creature's strength won out. Ahead of me, Ingvar dropped to his knees, doubled over and silent.

Oh hell, he's not breathing, I thought. Dread set my heart to racing. *Come on come on it's not ending like this!*

Finally, my fingers closed around the lighter. With triumph and determination, I twisted it on, then stabbed its business end into one of the vines bracing me. It unwound and fell away with a hiss.

Encouraged, I burned as many as I could reach. As the creature's grip weakened, I rolled onto my back to finish the process. A glint of light caught my eye, bouncing off a metallic object: my side sword. The hilt and part of the blade jutted out from beneath the writhing mass.

Soon. Once I'd finished freeing myself, I scrambled to my feet and burned the vines holding Ingvar. His loud gasp for air was equal parts reassurance and morale boost. Turning back, I closed the remaining distance between me and the creature, closing my left hand around my sword-hilt and pulling backward with all my might. Even with that, I only freed a few inches of the blade. New vines snapped at me, which I fended off with my lighter.

Several tugs of increasing leverage and desperation freed my sword entirely. I staggered backward a few feet, then regained my balance. With one last collecting breath, I darted in and thrusted the blade deep into the dark core.

Warm, foul-smelling gore sprayed against my chest and face. The creature went into wild convulsions, whipping vines at me that didn't latch on. I backed away, shielding my face with my left arm. Eventually, those vines grew listless and fell to the floor, never to move again.

Relief was short-lived. A new sickness, one of worry, sent me stumbling back toward the threshold. "Ingvar?"

He knelt, facing outside in hopes of fresh air, coughing hard with his face buried in the crook of his arm. At least he was still breathing. I knelt beside him, dropping my side sword to brace his shoulder.

"I'm fine," he sputtered. "Give me a moment."

Only then did I realize how much of the creature's syrupy insides had settled on me. I'd left a handprint on his tabard. "Oh hell, sorry. Hang on." I darted back inside, sword in tow, to pick up the nearest scrap of linen and clean off my skin, hair, clothing, and blade.

Ingvar glanced over his shoulder at me, then turned back around, waving out a hand in dismissal.

Ormyr's mati amulet had tumbled out of my coat; I wiped gunk off the eye-shaped pendant as well. My own eyes strayed toward the sprawling, leaking remains, studded with arrows. The sight, added to the smell, brought on a choking retch. Nasty and dangerous, the sort of creature that an eager storyteller elsewhere in the galaxy might label a hydra or demon. "What is this thing, do you know?" I asked.

"A vinrake." Ingvar faced me, still kneeling at the threshold. The waning sun outlined his furrowed brow. "Few miles out from here are some forests, that's where they come from. Hard to believe one wandered all the way here, even with things drying up."

It was my turn to frown. "Do you think the Naustviks were keeping it as a pet or guardian?"

"Nay!" Ingvar scoffed at the thought. "No way anyone could tame such a thing, teach it who's food and who isn't."

"And Master Ormyr *probably* would've found it earlier." I threw the linen scrap aside, stood, and walked back toward the threshold with sword in hand. "I wonder how that boy got in here without attracting its attention."

"If he moved quietly enough, he would've avoided it. Same as we did afore we startled him."

True. It'd only emerged after the boy had stepped on something fragile in his haste to escape from us. I offered Ingvar my free hand. "Did you see what happened to him?"

Ingvar accepted my hand and reached his feet. "Saw him run for the left wall. Lost track of him from there."

"Do you have any idea who he was?" I asked.

"Mayhap. We'll see." He picked up and shouldered his discarded bow nearby, then headed for that wall.

I was curious what he meant, but a more urgent thought pulled my attention aside. Holding my breath, I circled the vinrake's remains, just to be sure. Fortunately, as far as I could tell, the boy wasn't trapped beneath.

"Here!" Ingvar waved me over.

I approached his side. At his feet gaped a rectangular hole in the floor, its hinged trap door thrown aside. A ladder propped on one side descended into silent darkness.

My pulse quickened. "That must be the cellar. I'll bet our friend's down there." Along with the crawl space, and maybe Thordia.

Ingvar dropped beside the opening, studying it with narrowed eyes. "This reeketh of ambush."

For once, my paranoia was absent. "I think he just ran down there to hide." I sheathed my sword, knelt next to Ingvar, then raised my voice to call down to the boy, to Thordia, whomever else lay within earshot. "Hello? Don't be afraid, we're here to help you."

No reply, but that didn't faze me. "I'll have a look," I offered, eager to get down there.

Ingvar held out a checking hand. "Have only that wee light of yours between us. Hold on." He stepped away, then returned with the candle that'd initially tipped him off to the boy's presence.

"Good thought," I said.

Once I lit the wick for him, Ingvar reached down into the darkness with the flame for a few moments, an intent look on his face. Finally, he retracted it and frowned toward me with confusion. "Some cellar. 'Tis practically another house down there! Can't tell how large it is, or if there're any traps set up."

"So we have to put boots on the ground for a proper recon. Sounds good to me, Captain." My smile returned in a bid to soothe his nerves.

He allowed a trace of a smirk. "Fine, Goose, away with you first. Unless there's some immediate threat, hold position at the base of the ladder 'til I get there."

Stick lighter active, I descended the ladder. At its base, the air cooled, blissfully clear of the stench above. To my surprise, my feet touched down upon wood. A finished floor? Sure enough, a sweep of my lighter confirmed it. Smooth wooden planks, at that. The ceiling was finished with the same.

"This is some expensive hole in the ground," I murmured. Not to mention the time and effort involved, and everything required to keep groundwater from seeping in and rotting those planks.

How big *was* this hole? I couldn't tell. In every direction, my lighter faded into darkness.

Ingvar hurried down next. Just as he turned away from the ladder, an unearthly blue glow erupted all around us.

I gasped; my knees buckled. It was almost surprising how I stumbled. I should've floated, as I did aboard my ship between planets. This was no cellar, but another universe, stretching forever in all directions. In place of of stars and galaxies, the void teemed with glowing blue symbols. Molecules, fractals, isosceles triangles, even my sigil, the variable resistor. They floated everywhere: above, below, far off, right in front of my face.

Despite weakened knees and shortened breath, I kept my footing. "What the hell?"

Ingvar gave a startled cry. The candle fell from his hand with a clatter, sputtering out. He tried to backpedal, but immediately tripped against the ladder behind him.

I grabbed his arm, sparing him from what could've been a bad fall.

This *was* an ambush, a successful one. However, no one arrived to redeem his advantage. As the symbols surrounding us performed the slow dance of dust trapped in a sunbeam, Ingvar clung to my steadying hand like it was the last shred of sanity, trembling in horror.

"It's all right!" I soothed. "We're still in the cellar, we're fine."

His reaction reminded me of my own first weeks at the beguinage. He was already so much sharper than I'd been back then. I ached to help him understand.

"I think I know what's going on here." How to explain? I spent a moment gathering my thoughts, keeping vigilant for trouble. "Think of sunlight. It's usually invisible, but there are times when you can see it, like when it passes through a cloud, or treetops. These symbols are like that. Beams of light we can see. There must be a Shipbuilder artifact down here that's generating the light."

It was my best guess, anyway. I'd seen holographic emitters before at the beguinage.

Ingvar stopped trembling, but remained frozen beside me. "The Shipbuilders could *forge light* into whatever shape they wanted? Blood's oath."

"It does seem like magic at first, I know, but think of what the adepts pass off as 'magic,'" I said. "When you look a little harder, you can see the string they're using to make things jump or float. It's no different with Shipbuilder artifacts. Strings everywhere, just … different kinds of strings."

Ingvar was silent a long while, eyes darting from one symbol to the next. "Looketh more like starlight," he finally said. "The light of a thousand stars at once."

I heard the awe edging out over fear. The smile on my face didn't convey a tenth of my foolish joy.

Ingvar eased away from me, still wary, but no longer panicked. "How do the Naustviks have such power at their disposal? This shameth anything I've ever seen in the adepts' keep."

My grin faded as I sobered. "Verahl said his parents taught him and Thordia. The knowledge and artifacts may've passed down through their family over time. And they'd been careful, and damn lucky, until recently."

Ingvar made eye contact with me, his expression strained. "'Tis some secret to have to keep all one's life."

I nodded. "We can sympathize, can't we?"

His gaze lowered to the floor, conceding the point.

"I'm glad I don't have to lie or tiptoe my way around you," I said, and meant it.

"I'm grateful ye want to help me understand," Ingvar replied. "Not sure I ever will, but I'll try, if only to avoid panic like that again. That could've cost us."

"Strings. Remember." I smiled, heart pounding.

Ingvar returned a bashful smile and rubbed at the back of his neck, but recalled our mission quicker than I did, glancing about the cellar. "Where in Hel do we find a crawl space here?"

"The walls might be a good start," I suggested, yanking my head down from giddy heights.

"*What* walls?"

He had a point. Were there mirrors on the walls? I saw no obvious reflections, but wasn't sure how else the cellar seemed so endless.

"If we walk far enough in one direction, we're bound to find one." I took the initiative, turning left.

The proposal seemed reasonable enough to Ingvar, who followed alongside. Though he tried to avoid the floating holograms, the effort proved as futile as dodging raindrops. The first time he disturbed one, he flinched.

"Sunbeams, remember?" Curiosity got the better of me; I reached for a simplified atomic diagram floating at eye level. The electrons whizzing around their nucleus detoured around my fingers. I blinked my surprise.

Ingvar watched me carefully, then gave a nod.

We resumed our walk with more confidence. Deeper into the cellar, glass crunched underfoot, the remains of smashed bottles. Dark stains soaked into the wood beneath.

"I think the adepts were down here," I murmured. Hunting for something useful or incriminating, like the adepts and soldiers who'd raided my ship's closets on Gules.

"Not while these lights burned, I promise you that," Ingvar said. "If Ormyr had seen this, 'tis all we would've heard about when he returned with Naustvik."

He took my elbow, guiding me around the trail of glass. A few paces later, the hand he held out in front of himself touched against a solid wall. Said wall was covered in luminescent paintings of symbols mimicking the holograms, only motionless. The symbol directly in front of us was a collection of ever larger circles spiraling outward, like the petals of a rosebud: a representation of the golden ratio. One of Johannes Kepler's favorites, I realized. My breath caught in my throat.

I approached and traced the pattern with my pointer finger. The "paint" — soap, most likely — smudged my glove. There had to be ultraviolet light in the cellar as well, making it glow like that.

"There's grooves here!" Examining another part of the wall, Ingvar fit his fingers into a shadowy depression, then pulled. Out came a set of floor-to-ceiling shelves several feet long, stacked with glass jars.

"Look at this!" Ingvar cried.

I gaped, equally stunned. Under my stick lighter, the jars appeared to contain preserves of some kind.

Ingvar eyed them ravenously before studying the wall again. "There's more of these shelves here, in both directions. If they're all loaded with food like this ..."

"Amazing," I breathed. "Thordia could hold out a long time down here, supposing she has access to water."

"Mayhap one of these leadeth to the crawl space," Ingvar said.

A solid idea. I helped him examine multiple preserve-laden shelves, one by one. No luck for a while, until Ingvar pulled out a shelf that was full on top, empty on bottom, breaking the pattern. Suspicious, he knelt and rapped a knuckle against the bottom shelf's back panel, then looked to me excitedly. "Hollow!"

I dropped to my knees beside him. Grooves carved along the empty panel proved ideal for gripping. I tugged at the back panel, which dislodged and slid out into my hands.

A moment later, the cellar exploded with eyeball-scarring light. I screwed my eyes shut. Something barreled into me, knocking me flat on my back.

"Hold!" Ingvar shouted.

Unheeding footsteps hurried back the way we came, gunning for the ladder. Another set of even faster footsteps followed. Feet scuffling up the ladder, then a wince.

I forced my eyes open a painful sliver, turning toward the commotion. Across the room, now revealed as a plain wood-paneled chamber, Ingvar had peeled someone off the ladder. He spun around, pulling with him the boy we'd saved from the vinrake, who struggled as if Death itself had him.

Trails of caked blood ran from a cut on the boy's forehead, with strands of long hair stuck to the scabs. Bruises lined his jaw. He hadn't sustained these injuries during the fight upstairs; they were all too old for that. His clothing was ratty, his feet barefoot. It was hard to guess his age. I feared the number was terrifyingly lower than my best estimate.

"Ye deserve the same scare ye put on us, lad!" Ingvar marched him deeper into the cellar. "Lucky the knight and I don't have it in us."

The boy sank his teeth into Ingvar's forearm, a desperate measure that Ingvar's armor allowed him to ignore. Ingvar shook himself free, pushed the boy to his knees, and pinned his arms behind his back.

"Hel with you both! I'm not afraid!" the boy shouted, no less resistant.

"Jayce?" Ingvar prompted with a concerned glance my way.

Time to get up, however much my abused hide disliked the idea. I shoved the false panel aside, recovered my stick lighter, and crossed the cellar to drop to a crouch before the boy. Flanking him reduced the odds of his escape, in case he managed to break free of Ingvar.

The boy appraised me with a seen-it-all-twice glare, still struggling. "Not afraid of you! Hear me?"

His panicky behavior gave lie to his words. Though I rarely dealt with children, it wasn't hard to understand the reason for his fear. He was the one who'd set up this elaborate light trap, and neither of us had run off screaming. How was he so comfortable with manipulating artificial light? Who'd taught him? I was dying to know.

"Ye shouldn't be afraid, lad," Ingvar said. "*Calm down.* I'll let you go, and we'll talk."

The boy's struggling continued. His glare was also undiminished as it raked up and down my person.

Ingvar's burgundy and gold tabard marked him as an authority figure. So far, the boy had shown him nothing but disdain. Maybe I could differentiate myself, get him talking that way. I threw a quick glance back toward the shelf—no change, no Thordia. All right. My focus returned to the boy. "My name's Jess. What's yours?" Best to start off simple, omitting titles and other trifles.

Our young mystery finally stopped squirming, but his muscles remained tensed. "Dag," he said.

"Dagfin Nyvind!" Ingvar cried. "Thought ye might've been Rigg's brother!"

The boy's eyes widened unmistakably at the sound of his full name. Having met Rigg a few times, I spotted the family resemblance.

"He's been sweeping the barony for you, lad." Ingvar released him, a flicker of apology in his expression that Dag didn't see. "I've been helping him."

So *that* was what Rigg had been worried about when I'd first visited the barracks.

Dag's freed hands came around front. In his left hand rested a slim, glassy black tile: Shipbuilder, but of unknown function. Beads covered his right hand, the better to secure a hammer charm to the palm. The middle and ring fingers of that hand were fused together, and the first knuckle of the pointer finger was missing. Some of that might've been congenital, some earned later in life through various misadventures.

Surprise overcame Dag. He faced Ingvar, placing his back to me. "*Skíta*, he has? Didn't mean to worry him. Had to lie low a while."

Lie low? What kind of heat was on a boy that young? Bullies? Broken home? Hell. My stomach knotted with sympathy.

"*Here?*" Ingvar asked, incredulous about Dag's chosen hiding spot.

"Lots of places, but aye, here too." The boy's voice hardened. "The Naustviks are my friends. Don't care who knows it!"

"Really?" I seized upon this piece of common ground. "They're our friends too!"

Dag whirled on me with another glare. "Bull."

"We rescued Verahl from the adepts' dungeon," I said.

"*Bull!*" he repeated, but his eyes widened with interest.

"Did Verahl and Thordia teach you how to operate all these lights?" I asked, unable to help myself.

Dag's pale silence suggested I'd stumbled upon a forbidden topic.

"Need a place to stay, ye can come back with us to the capital," Ingvar said. "Rigg's at the barracks, he'll want to see you. But first, we mean to help Thordia if we can. Is she here, lad?"

Dag spun toward him again. "Nay. Don't know where she is, that's truth."

Over the boy's head, Ingvar lowered his eyes in resignation.

I stifled my disappointment. After all, it could've been a lie. I'd check the rest of the cellar before leaving. "When's the last time you saw her?" I asked Dag.

"Not since the adepts took Verahl." The boy's shoulders slumped.

What about the cause of the crop failure Verahl had mentioned? Was it still there? Once again, I glanced back toward the shelf, peering into the space where the false panel had once rested.

"Ingvar, there's a whole passage back there," I said, pulse rising. "I want to have a look before we leave."

"Don't!" Dag whirled toward me, swiping a finger across the thin tile in his hand.

The room went pitch dark. A struggle erupted, punctuated with shouts of pain. I activated my stick lighter. There was Ingvar, pinning Dag's arms and legs to the floor in self-defense. Otherwise, the thrashing boy stood to tear him apart.

"Calm down, lad!" Ingvar said. "No one's trying to hurt you!"

"Let go! Get out of here!" Dag shouted.

"Ye'll draw the neighborhood here with that screaming! Is that what ye want?"

I hovered at Ingvar's side, feeling useless. The kid seemed more of a wild animal than the vinrake. Guilt immediately gnawed at me for having such a thought. Dag was *afraid*, not feral. Maybe life had handed him plenty of good reason to be wary. But in calmer, safer moments, he was capable of grasp-ing Shipbuilder technology. No mean feat for a boy in this rural farming community. Once he calmed down, I hoped to learn how that had happened. For the time being, I leaned in close to him. "It's all right. I promise we're here to help."

"Check out the crawl space. Quickly now," Ingvar im-plored me.

He was right. Best I sate my curiosity as fast as possible.

As I stood to leave, Dag's wide eyes latched onto my stick lighter. He followed the light's progress with astonishment, forgetting to struggle against Ingvar in the meantime.

I knelt and crawled into the cramped passage hidden be-hind the shelf. Not far down the tunnel was the glow of more artificial light, the start of another room.

Another cellar? Another tunnel leading to more cellars? Ever grander speculation sent me flying toward the light on trembling limbs.

Once I reached the new threshold, I froze, stunned. The little room was about ten feet on all sides, and no less remarkable than the cellar. Inside, potted vines flourished: climbing up corners; spilling down the bookshelves lining the walls; curling around a water clock, an astrolabe, and a wooden model of an Archimedean screw. Bafflingly, these more fortunate houseplants didn't seem to mind the lack of sunlight.

On the floor nearby lay rumpled blankets. Half-consumed jars of preserves stood sentry around what appeared to be a device condensing water out of the air.

Was it possible? Breath held, I crawled closer for a better look, pressing my hand up against the domed glass enclosure. Inside, a condenser coil cooled the air in its vicinity. The reservoir beneath it collected the droplets that formed.

My jaw dropped. What I would've given for such devices in settlements where the water supply had dried up or been contaminated! This was far better than the filtering methods the beguinage taught, but those methods, while far from perfect, didn't require anything fancier than cloths and sieves. This device needed an intact condenser to cool the air, something an adept or Lord would snatch up the moment they learned of it.

Only then did I remember Thordia. There was no sign of her, but it was easy to imagine her hiding undetected in that small room for as long as she needed to. The food and blankets suggested she had, at least for a while. When had she fled, and why? What had forced her to leave these wonders behind?

Curiosity was the only thing that put enough strength in my limbs. Otherwise, I never would've reached my feet. The bookshelves housed bottles of oil, powders, dried leaves, nothing identifiable on sight. A botanical catalogue of bound parchment lay open, displaying dried samples and meticulous notes.

The far end of the room finally caught my eye: sterile, with the exacting cleanliness of a proper chemistry lab. To one side rested several black square tiles like the one Dag had used, and a small leather-wrapped chest. To the other, a set of experiments. Soil samples in glass tubes, soil spread out on parchment ...

Verahl had said she'd found something in the soil. Heart pounding, I approached and sifted through the dried sample. The dirt seemed unremarkable, but something had soaked into the parchment it sat upon. Something dark, purplish. Was *that* what Thordia believed to be causing the crop trouble? I had no idea what it was.

My eyes strayed toward the leather-bound box with eagerness and dread. I flipped it open. Inside sat two more small, unmistakable Shipbuilder devices.

"Data carriers!" I cried aloud in amazement.

Beside them lay two stoppered vials full of the same dark purplish substance. All of these rested atop a clean, folded piece of parchment.

I retrieved the note and unfurled it with trembling fingers. Across the page ran lines of neatly handwritten Shipbuilder, prefaced by something that looked like a date, but I wasn't familiar with the calendar. A short letter followed:

> *VERAHL—*
> *Though there's little chance of you reading this, a faint hope spurs me to write. That same hope now bids me depart for the Harbinger. There's no other way I might find a means of dispelling this poison stealing our water.*
> *That I can't help you without killing both of us is more than my heart can stand, but you sacrificed everything to buy me more time. I owe it to you to stay this course.*
> *If you read this, I hope all danger is past. If it isn't, I hope you'll join me, and forgive me. I love you always.*
> *—THORDIA*

CHAPTER 21

I stood rooted before the laboratory table in Thordia's small sanctuary, ignoring an encroaching sickness in the pit of my stomach as I processed her note. The "Harbinger" reference wasn't familiar, but Thordia *had* found something in the soil. I picked up one of the vials of purplish liquid, then glanced to the parchment soaked through with the same material. She'd called it "poison stealing our water."

Stealing? I'd never heard of such a thing. And yet, my brain insisted the substance was familiar. I thought back carefully over the days I'd spent in Nidaros. When had I seen it before?

The answer struck me like lightning: the corpse Ingvar and I had found in the dungeon. This substance had been leaking out of its eyes.

The breath in my lungs froze. Human bodies held a lot of water. The prisoner might've been exposed to the substance through the dirt walls and floor of the dungeon. Whether he'd ingested it, or it'd gotten in through mucous membranes in his eyes or nose, it might've "stolen" the water in his tissues and blood. And if the substance had spread through his digestive system or bloodstream, the way the crop trouble had supposedly spread from one end of Nidaros to the other, he would've slowly dried out all over.

I stared at the vial in my hand with a new feeling of menace, as though it were an acid about to burn through the glass and then my skin—but, I reminded myself, this was no more than speculation, the claims of a woman I'd never met before. Was there a way to test the substance's alleged deadliness without exposing anyone to it or contaminating more soil?

The canteen Ingvar had provided me was still slung over my shoulder. For experiment's sake, I uncorked the vial, poured the purplish substance into the half-full container, then closed it up. Once we got back to the capital, we'd have a look at the results.

One more vial of the substance remained. It found a new home in my coat pocket, as did one of the slim black tiles that Dag had been using to control artificial lights within the cellar. Finally, with a strange mix of excitement and chagrin, I pocketed one of the two data carriers from the leather-bound box. I wasn't in the habit of helping myself to Shipbuilder artifacts with clear ownership, but there was a very slight chance of contacting Drea with it, provided enough of the right technology had survived between Nidaros and Gules to facilitate a connection between our devices. I didn't want to risk Verahl's refusal to lend it to me. I'd try messaging her as soon as I had the chance.

In Thordia's box, I packed up the other data carrier, along with every remaining parchment, sample, and experiment to be found on the table. I couldn't help rereading Thordia's note, imagining her grief, the aching doubt that Verahl would ever escape the adepts' dungeon to see it. It'd bring me great satisfaction to deliver her note to Verahl, but how long would that triumph last if there really were a water-stealing substance spreading throughout the barony, killing people and crops? My heart pounded with worried urgency. Where in the galaxy had such a thing come from?

Again, I pulled myself back from speculation. Nestled away in this hidden crawl space, Thordia's note had been meant for Verahl's eyes only. It wasn't there to throw adepts, or anyone else, off her trail. So she really was gunning for this Harbinger, whatever it was, in the hope of finding something to neutralize the substance. I'd have to get back out into the cellar and ask Ingvar about it—and Dag, if Ingvar shared my ignorance. Dag had known about the crawl space and the artificial lighting within the cellar. The Naustviks might've entrusted him with a lot of things.

With purpose, I turned to leave the wondrous little room, but reluctance braced me upon looking over the flora and Shipbuilder material preserved there. My friends at the beguinage would be interested to hear about the Naustviks and their cache. Drea included, assuming I could still save her.

I ducked into the cramped tunnel, carrying Thordia's box in one hand. At the other end lay the cellar, still plunged in darkness. Faint scuffling was audible. It seemed Dag's resistance had resumed while I'd been exploring.

My instinct was to reach for my stick lighter, but then I recalled I could do one better. I pulled out my newly acquired light tile instead, swiping a finger across it the way I'd seen Dag do earlier.

The cellar lit up brightly in response. Dag cried out in surprise.

"That was me!" I called down the tunnel. "I'm coming back."

Ingvar still pinned Dag to the floor. As I emerged from the tunnel, the fight went out of the boy, who once again stared at me with wide-eyed amazement. I supposed he too had decided I was a witch.

"There now, lad. Let's sit up, aye?" Ingvar shot me a relieved look, easing away from Dag.

Instead of sitting, Dag scrambled to his feet and ran from

us to the furthest corner of the cellar, wedging himself in there to glance between me and Ingvar with narrow-eyed suspicion.

Ingvar backed up toward the ladder, most likely covering it to prevent Dag from escaping. Slowly, I returned to legs that were weaker than before, as though my new knowledge and artifacts weighed me down.

"What's that ye found, Jayce?" Ingvar glanced my way with concern, nodding toward the box.

"It's more what Thordia found." I approached him, withdrawing the vial of purplish fluid from my pocket. "She claims this stuff is in your soil, 'stealing' water."

"What?" Ingvar eyed the vial like it was a snarling beast, making no move to take it from me. "What sort of Hel-born ichor is that?"

"I don't know," I admitted, "but I think we saw it on the corpse in the dungeon." And on my clothing, I realized with a chill. The splotches I hadn't been able to identify before, earned from various misadventures in dungeon. I finally had an idea of what they were.

Ingvar's eyes widened. After a moment of frozen shock, he craned his neck for a better look at the substance — *ichor*, as he called it, seemed more appropriate — turning pale and clenching his fists at his sides. "Blood's oath, I think ye're right," he muttered with dread.

I continued, trying to be calm for us both. "I poured some of this into my water. I'm curious to see what happens to it." I shrugged the shoulder where my canteen was slung. "I'll also take some soil from here and the capital, see if I can isolate this stuff myself." Best that I replicated everything Thordia had done so I wouldn't be operating under any assumptions. Apparently, the ichor would leech out onto parchment placed beneath it. That'd be enough to confirm its presence.

Ingvar regained enough composure to eye me with confusion. "If Thordia's not here, how d'ye know these things?"

"She left a note for Verahl." I pocketed the vial, then removed the folded parchment from the box.

Ingvar snapped it up to hold close to his face, eyes narrowed with a concentration that soured into a frustrated frown. "Only learned my letters a few years back, but, most of these look wrong."

"It's the Shipbuilder language." I reclaimed the note, paraphrasing its contents out loud.

To my chagrin, the message rendered Ingvar entirely ashen.

"Unseen. The Harbinger?" Those words jarred Dag out of his silence as well. From across the cellar, he regarded us with wide-eyed dread.

"Not content to be ruined alone, lass?" Ingvar muttered, staring off at nothingness. "Bringing it on all of us?"

He'd never called me "lass" before. He had to be referring to Thordia. "Ingvar?" I prompted.

He failed to respond.

Concerned, I rested my hand on his arm.

Ingvar gave a start then, refocusing on me with pleading eyes. "Nothing we can do anything about right now."

"What do you mean?" I asked.

"The Harbinger." With the same imploring gaze, Ingvar reached up and placed his hand over mine. "'Tis days distant on foot. Approach is forbidden upon penalty of death."

His touch made my heart leap a mile into the air. I had to shake it off to focus on his words. "Wait, *death?*" I repeated, taken aback. "Just what the hell is this thing?"

"We'll talk more at the capital." Ingvar lowered his hand and straightened, glancing to Dag. "Come with us, lad. We've room for you at the barracks."

How good of him. I forgot the Harbinger for a moment in warm appreciation of Ingvar's gesture.

Dag hesitated, nervous. "Don't want to get Rigg in trouble."

"Rigg's not in any trouble, neither are you. Promise," Ingvar said.

Dag's gaze volleyed between us again. Finally, he straightened with resolve. "If ye really rescued Verahl, I want to see him."

My instinct was to refuse. I longed to return to the barracks and talk things out with Ingvar in private. But Verahl deserved to know what we'd found, and there was food aboard my ship that I'd gladly partake of and share with everyone else. Plus, I could completely empathize with the longing to reunite with a friend who'd been in danger.

"All right," I relented. "I'll take you to him once we're through here."

Dag had already queued up his snarling retort. At my unexpected consent, it stalled in his throat, but his wide-eyed surprise came through with no trouble.

Ingvar grabbed one of the ladder's side rails, glancing to me. "Anything else ye want to look for here?"

"I don't think so." I could've hunted for more Shipbuilder relics, but figuring out the ichor and the Harbinger was more urgent. My eyes strayed to the open shelves. "But maybe we could take some of these preserves back with us."

Ingvar laughed bitterly. "Can ye imagine explaining where they came from?"

"I'll take some," Dag declared with a scowl. "Thordia shared with anyone who asked."

"Mayhap that's how she got away with breeding those illegal plants upstairs." Ingvar glanced up toward the entrance into the house proper, then back at me. "Wait down here with the lad. I'll make sure the coast is clear afore we head out."

I nodded.

Ingvar turned and ascended the ladder silently, one rung at a time. Near the top, he paused to scout the ground floor.

Meanwhile, Dag used the opportunity to dart over and vanish into the crawl space.

Damn it, so much for keeping an eye on him. I was terrible with kids.

I hurried over to the crawl space entrance and knelt beside it. The tunnel was empty, implying Dag had ducked into the secret room. Did he have any intention of returning? If not, I'd have to go get him. There was food and water here, but what else might be lurking like the vinrake, waiting for its chance to strike? What if the neighbors found him? What about whoever it was that Dag had been hiding from to begin with?

My sympathy and concern welled up again. It was great that Ingvar was taking him in, but I also had to protect Dag, the same way I sought to protect the Naustviks, and hopefully learn more about the depth of his Shipbuilder knowledge in the process.

Fortunately, Dag didn't stay out of sight for long. He crawled back down the tunnel with a blanket in hand, ignoring me as he returned to the cellar and loaded the blanket with several jars from the nearest open shelf. Come to think of it, Dag was beat up, but not hollow like so many other people in the barony. The Naustviks' foresight, combined with his lack of fear, seemed to have kept him better fed than most of Nidaros.

I returned to the ladder's base and watched him wrap the jars in a tight, practiced bundle, not yet brave enough to bring up my many questions. At a gentle tap on my shoulder, I turned around. Ingvar had lowered himself back down to the cellar floor, eyeing me with concern. "Company," he muttered.

I froze. "In the house?" I whispered.

"Nay. People gathering at the fence. Spied them out the back door. I'll head out and send them home afore things get out of hand." Ingvar's gaze passed between me and Dag.

"Best ye both stay down here, aye? I'll come back for you when 'tis safe."

"What if you need help?" I asked. "They might panic when they see something emerge from the house. It doesn't matter who or what."

Ingvar waved a hand in dismissal. "I'll tell them I chased the vinrake here. Nothing more to see."

I wasn't fully convinced. "You should wear some kind of visible charm to convince people you were able to pass through the adepts' wards without issue." The mati amulet I wore, and that he had a copy of, never occurred to me. I thought only of the chain bearing my mother's ring, which I retrieved and dropped around his neck.

He gaped, at a loss. "Are ye sure?"

Willingly parting with that ring? In most circumstances, I would've parted with my hand first. But with Ingvar …

"Keep it for now, all right? I want you to have it." The words were difficult to speak around my jittery heart, but they were honest.

Ingvar brightened with a smile. For a few giddy moments, I forgot what we were doing in the first place. Eventually his smile faded, but the appreciation lingered in his eyes. "Thanks, Jayce." He turned and climbed the ladder back up.

I sobered too, pushing back that elation in a hurry in case something went wrong. However, Ingvar reached the ground floor and departed in uneventful silence. Still I lingered at the foot of the ladder, staring after him like a fool.

"How're ye not afraid?"

Startled, I jumped at the question posed calmly behind me, then spun around. Dag lingered near the shelves, shiny black tile in hand, stony curiosity outshining his wariness for once.

I reluctantly forgot Ingvar, forcing myself to breathe deep. *Don't screw this up,* I thought, certain Dag wouldn't give me another chance. "What do you mean?"

With no change in demeanor, Dag swiped a finger along the tile. We promptly returned to the mysterious universe of glowing blue symbols.

"How're ye not afraid?" In the light of several floating holograms, the boy's determined glare fastened upon me.

In other words, why hadn't I gone running when the symbols had appeared? Why didn't I cower at his adept-like talent with Shipbuilder artifacts? I scrutinized every word before it left my mouth. "I've seen lights like these before. Even if I hadn't, I know there's a rational explanation for everything. There always is. Besides, I think they're beautiful, not scary." I reached for a nearby dodecahedron, sending it tumbling away.

Dag's brow furrowed in confusion. "But ye must've learned the magic from *somewhere*, aye?"

So, he lacked the scientific background. He thought he was casting spells. Was that what the Naustviks had told him?

"Here and there, lots of places," I answered. I couldn't go into full detail just yet, it'd only confuse him. "What about you?"

Dread nipped at Dag's resolve. "From here. But don't tell, all right?" he pleaded. "Verahl and Thordia never let me near the cellar. I knew they were hiding something big. Couldn't help myself."

My jaw dropped. "Wait. You taught *yourself?*"

Dag nodded, tensing all over. He clutched the food-bundle and light tile closer to his chest.

Though my surprise added to his anxiety, there was no way I could mitigate it. Sure, his knowledge was all show and no substance, but to intuit as much as he had? If he weren't just lying to impress me, then this was some clever kid.

"How did you teach yourself? Can you show me what you did?" I gestured toward the tile in his hands, then beckoned him closer.

Dag held up his tile, but remained where he was. "Found

these, didn't know what they were. When I picked them up, *magic* happened. Different ways I touch, they're all different spells." A defiant pride lit up his eyes as he demonstrated with the tile, turning the different light fixtures within the cellar on and off. There was one trick I hadn't seen, though: with one of his gestures, he made the light tile itself glow brightly, a little star in his hand. Finally, he returned us to the universe of blue holograms.

Trial and error? Completely different from my training. Every new device had been introduced to me in a careful and gradual manner, explained by patient, loving guides. It'd been necessary, otherwise I wouldn't have strayed within a hundred yards of those artifacts. It hadn't just been operation, either. Beguine Drea and the others had taught me all the background principles, *why* things worked. While I hadn't gone on to study computers or mechanics in depth, I still had a solid enough understanding of the Shipbuilder devices I used every day.

The Naustviks had denied Dag those things. Shameful, but they'd probably sought to protect him, keep him completely ignorant for his own good. Hadn't Verahl told me that Thordia declared nothing would ever justify sharing what they knew? Until the crop trouble had arrived, and the only other option had been slow starvation.

I was stunned, almost appalled, at Dag's bravery. Most people wouldn't go near a Shipbuilder device, they'd seek an adept to safely bear it off. Maybe Dag had observed Verahl and Thordia using the light tiles, and had either purposely or unintentionally omitted that.

"Weren't you afraid to try?" I asked, curious to know where his courage came from.

Dag's expression hardened into a scowl. "I'm not afraid of anything."

Oh. It was more bravado than real courage. "Not even the very first time?"

"I wanted the power."

The poor boy. His battered face and deformed fingers told me why the idea of power appealed to him.

"He called you a knight." Dag tossed his head toward the ladder, referencing Ingvar.

I nodded. "I'm a knight errant, yes."

"What's the difference?"

"I'm not beholden to anybody. I can quest wherever, for whomever I want." Technically.

"What's your quest here?"

"It's a long story," I said, "but I want to help you and your friends."

"Going to the Harbinger, then?"

"We'll see." I definitely wanted to if Thordia had gone there looking for a cure for the substance, but Dag and Ingvar were terrified at its mere mention. And this death penalty, what was *that* about? "What do you know about it?"

Dag's hand tightened over the hammer charm in his palm. "Not much. Heard tell it destroyed whole districts once. Horrible things happen to people who go near it. Like Frodi Fuldarr. Him and his brothers tried once, been haunting the forests outside the districts ever since."

I frowned at the unenlightening ghost story. "But Thordia thinks she might find a cure for this water-stealing substance there. Why is that?"

Dag shrugged again and glanced askance, unable or unwilling to offer a clue. Worry tightened his expression.

It seemed that was all I'd get from him on the topic. Hopefully, Ingvar or Verahl would be able to fill in the gaps.

"If you think of anything else, let me know." I threw a quick glance upstairs, wondering about Ingvar's progress. No sight or sound reached me; I hoped that was a good sign. My attention returned to Dag, whose old wounds still stood out in the blue light. I reached for the first aid kit on my belt. "Here.

While we're waiting, there's some blood on your face."

He frowned in confusion. When I advanced toward him with compress in hand, he skittered back like a spider avoiding sunlight.

I stopped. "Don't you want to clean up?"

Dag waved me off, his expression fiercely set against the idea.

"All right." Again, I cursed my weakness with children. That was when alarm stabbed at me, followed by a sickening fear: Dag's bare feet. How long might he have been innocently traipsing through soil containing that water-stealing substance? I seemed to be unharmed, but all the ichor I might've come in contact with had ended up on my clothes and boots, not my skin.

"This'll sound strange, but, may I see your feet real quick?" I demonstrated by lifting my own foot, exposing the sole of my boot.

Dag scowled. "Why?"

Unlike the Naustviks, I'd gladly fill in any 'whys' he had for me. His curiosity was the only way we reliably connected, and deserved positive reinforcement. "You know that ichor Thordia found in the soil? I just want to make sure it's not on your feet."

After a moment's deliberation, he complied, maintaining his distance. In the light of the holograms, his feet looked dirty and calloused as anything, but otherwise fine.

"You look all right," I confirmed with relief.

Dag focused a narrow-eyed look on the cellar exit above my head—not retreating to his corner, not coming any closer either.

I hoped physical contact with the ichor was indeed harmless, and that the only danger was in ingesting it, but there was no guarantee Dag had been in contact with it. All the same, I made a mental note to ask Ingvar about finding shoes for the boy.

Awash in a sea of holograms, we waited. Above, the sun-light pouring into the house had waned considerably. I watched and listened for any change, any indication that Ing-var might need help.

CHAPTER 22

From the cellar, the view above changed little aside from the darkness of night settling over the Naustviks' rotting garden. Muffled, agitated voices arose at the fringe of my hearing, presumably in response to Ingvar steering concerned neighbors away from the property.

Were they giving him a hard time? Nervousness sent me pacing around the ladder's base, fidgeting with my baldric. Amid the sea of floating blue holograms, Dag kept narrowed eyes on the cellar entrance.

The grim urgency of our findings, and our need to act upon them, only eroded my patience further. I debated when to say *to hell with it* and head outside to help Ingvar. Sure, I'd scare people, but maybe it was for the best if they ran home and never came back here.

Eventually, the voices died down. A single set of footsteps drew closer, bringing with it the strengthening glow of fire.

I waited with tense hope, breath held. Finally, Ingvar appeared, kneeling at the edge of the cellar entrance with a lantern in hand. "All right, come on up," he called down in a hush.

Relieved, I turned and waved Dag ahead of me.

Dag shut off the cellar holograms and slipped his light tile into a pocket. Neither the darkness nor his bundle full of preserves proved a hindrance. He raced up the ladder like he was climbing stairs.

Once he'd ascended, I followed with Thordia's leatherbound box in hand. The garden's warm stink returned; given time to air out, it wasn't as awful. In the center sat the vinrake corpse in its early stages of decay. The tumbleweed now looked more like a mound of dead vines, mirroring the canopy overhead.

Ingvar offered a hand to help me off the ladder, which I accepted with a small smile. My mother's ring, still strung around his neck, glinted in the lantern light. But I'd thought he'd lost his lantern on our way to the district? My confusion lasted until he tossed his head toward the back door, still yawning open. Outside, a pair of soldiers corralled the spare wood lying about. They were alone; the rest of the property lay bare.

"My men on patrol showed up while I was defusing the situation," Ingvar muttered. "We'll be boarding up the doors and windows. Don't need anything else sneaking in."

Or anyone. "I'll help." For once, I saw a real need to cordon off a witch house. I hoped to return sometime after the crop trouble had passed, though. The Naustviks were entitled to their Shipbuilder belongings. It'd be criminal to leave them buried in the cellar.

"What about Verahl?" Dag demanded, scowling at this change in plans.

"We'll go to him once we're done, lad," Ingvar assured him. "Come, let's not linger in here." He ushered me and Dag ahead of him, out the back door, into the cool evening air.

A starry night sky stretched overhead. Closer to the ground, the occasional distant, lonely light bobbed in and out of view. Most likely, some brave torch-bearers were out keeping watch for all the varied monsters on the loose. Meanwhile, the soldiers hefted wooden planks through the Naustviks' backyard with cautious movements, shoulders hunched and eyes darting about. They straightened at Ingvar's reappearance, a measure of relief dawning on their faces.

Ingvar and I exchanged whispered greetings with them. Dag found a shadow against the side of the house to stick to, fidgeting impatiently with his beads and hammer charm.

He was concealed, but also defenseless. Before assisting the soldiers, I slipped over to offer him my dagger. "Here. Just in case you need a weapon on the way to the capital."

Dag silently grasped the hilt in his disfigured right hand. Judging from the look on his face, it seemed he'd decided I wasn't so horrible after all.

We boarded up the house as Ingvar had described. Afterward, I knelt amid the barren plot to unearth two handfuls of dirt—some topsoil, some a bit deeper—which I wrapped in compresses from my first aid kit and shoved into my already full pockets. If the ichor really were present in the soil, I expected it to soak into the compresses the way it'd seeped into that parchment in Thordia's secret room. These samples, and the ongoing ichor/water experiment in my canteen, would go a long way toward testing her claims. It would've been nice to collect soil from multiple locations in the Low North district, but I feared someone spotting me and getting the wrong idea. I'd aim for some soil from the capital instead. The dungeon would be ideal, assuming Master Ormyr ever granted me passage.

The patrolling soldiers returned to duty. Ingvar, Dag, and I left the district in watchful silence. I stuck to Ingvar's side, safely within the glow of his lantern. Dag hovered all around us, clinging to fences and shadows, moving with enviable stealth despite the bundle in his non-dagger hand.

Once we'd covered some distance outside the district undisturbed, Dag put away my dagger and brought out his light tile instead. One swipe of his finger, and the glassy surface lit up like a torch.

"*Skíta!*" Ingvar jumped, but quickly recovered himself with a frown. "More of that light-forging!"

"Right." Having seen Dag demonstrate this earlier, I could afford Ingvar a reassuring smile. I hoped the tile in my own pocket was just as versatile.

"Better than a lantern, aye?" Dag swept the ground ahead of us with a bounce in his step, seemingly glad for a chance to show off.

"Quiet now," Ingvar urged in a hush. "We'll see better, but so will predators."

Our brisk pace, and my much-abused coat, kept me warm. For a while, my brain churned over all the amazing and horrible things we'd found at the Naustviks' house, especially the ichor. Supposing we confirmed it was as prevalent and dangerous as the corpse in the dungeon implied, how the hell would we even begin to remove it from the barony's soil?

My mentors at the beguinage, many of whom were well traveled, had never described such a substance. Neither had my former master. Maybe Drea knew what it was, or had the answer on her data carrier. With the data carrier in my pocket, maybe I could ask her. But the chances that enough technology had survived between Nidaros and Gules to facilitate a connection were very slim. As for the chances of Drea still being alive ...

I bit the inside of my lip, shoving the thought away to instead focus on Thordia's response to the crisis. Was this "Harbinger," whatever it was, our only recourse? Why had Thordia thought so?

Sadly, the worry and unanswered questions would have to remain mine for a while yet. In the interests of staying alert for predators — not that I was terribly alert, given my thoughts — I couldn't talk to Ingvar about our next steps. He was better focused on our surroundings, but it was clear by the occasional longing look my way that he was just as eager to talk.

Each time our eyes met, it sent everything from yearning to sorrow coursing through me. There was no kidding myself about how I felt about him, but that was yet another thing I couldn't voice, no matter how much I wanted to. Better to remain focused on problem-solving. I really hoped I could be of help to Nidaros like I kept promising I would be.

One step at a time. First, we'd get Dag to my ship, reunite him with Verahl for a short while, then take him to the barracks. After that, I'd check on my various experiments, try messaging Drea, and coax Ingvar into explaining the Harbinger.

Fortunately, no ravenous creatures tried their luck during the remainder of our trek. Upon sighting the capital wall in the distance, Ingvar glanced back at Dag, who trailed behind at the moment. "Quench that light and keep it hidden, aye? Or the adepts will take it away and toss you in the dungeon for good measure."

Dag cast a sour glare at him, but complied. The bright artificial glow vanished, leaving just Ingvar's lantern between us. Shadows fell across the boy's face, now with a questioning look to it. "Ye'll let me keep it, though?"

"Ye know what ye're doing with it better than I, lad. Like the knight here." Ingvar tilted his head my way. "Mayhap she'll teach you more someday."

Dag's eyes widened, refocusing on me.

"We'll see," I said uncertainly. "We've got a lot of work to do first." And who knew how things would pan out.

"Agreed," Ingvar said, focusing forward again.

I did the same, not wanting to see if I'd disappointed Dag.

We banked for the port first. As we converged upon the silhouettes of ruined ships, Dag's footsteps grew slower and more distant until they stopped entirely.

Ingvar halted and faced him; I turned as well. Dag had halted, frowning at his surroundings. However, the way his shoulders tensed made me think he was more anxious than angry.

"Like sneaking through a memorial, isn't it?" Ingvar addressed gently.

"I'm not afraid!" Dag spat.

"No one said you were," I intervened. Normally I would've left this to Ingvar, but my earlier interaction with Dag had bolstered my confidence. I pointed toward the outline of *Kepler's Law,* sparks of artificial light glowing out of her portholes. "See there? That's my ship, still functional. Verahl's aboard, and I have some food and water there too."

Dag focused on the ship, deliberating, then stalked toward it with purpose.

I followed him, Ingvar a few steps behind. "Here, I'll open the hatch," I offered.

Instead, the hatch opened of its own volition, swinging out inches shy of Dag. The boy yelped and stumbled backward, colliding with me.

Equally startled, I worked to prevent us from falling. While we recovered our balance, the pair of soldiers standing watch aboard my ship, Hals and Ragni, exited the airlock and dropped to the pavement.

Dag went stiff. I tried to place a reassuring hand on his shoulder, but he shrugged it off as though it were a branding iron, glaring daggers up at me.

Damn it, I hadn't meant to upset him. That scare had wounded his pride. Maybe his shoulder was wounded, too. He looked away to smolder privately, preventing me from apologizing.

"Captain, Lady Knight!" Ragni greeted. He and Hals glanced over our trio curiously.

"Lads," Ingvar acknowledged, stopping behind me and Dag. "Naustvik been giving you any trouble?"

"Nay, sir," Hals answered. "Holed himself away in the lower deck, quiet."

Dag straightened at this evidence that his friend was actually aboard my ship.

"Thanks, good to hear. Ye two wait outside a moment." Ingvar waved me on.

Once inside the airlock, I turned back to help Dag aboard next. He ignored my hand to boost himself up without assistance.

Before he could dart into the ship proper, I blocked his path. I had to set expectations. "Dag? Keep in mind, Verahl's hurt from being in the dungeon," I half-whispered. "He'll be fine, he just needs some rest."

The boy sent several nervous looks between me and Ingvar, who still waited outside. "Don't tell him I was in the cellar."

"We won't," I said.

Ingvar nodded his assent.

Dag nodded to me. At my direction, he advanced through the hallway and into the galley. That fearlessness of his seemed rewarding in some ways, dangerous in others. I was just glad the ship's hatch hadn't clobbered him.

Meanwhile, the engine room hatch gaped open, with Verahl nowhere in sight. Otherwise, the galley looked just as I'd left it. Dag halted in the middle of the deck, squinting about, while Ingvar left his lantern in a safe corner and resumed his old cautious perch at the threshold.

It was a relief to be "home" again after a long, perilous day. Though tired and sore all over, anticipation lent me the strength to approach the engine room hatch, not so different from the passage into the Naustviks' cellar. "Verahl?" I called down. "We're back. We've got a friend of yours here."

"Hey, mate!" Dag belted out, taking a few tentative steps in my direction. "Ye really down there?"

At first, silence met our greetings.

"*Dag?!*" Verahl's voice boomed upward, disbelieving and overjoyed at once. He thudded over to the ladder, hauling himself up two rungs at a time until he emerged on the main deck, towering over the rest of us with a grin. Despite his injuries, he moved without difficulty.

"*Skíta!* Never thought I'd see you again, mate!" Dag's eyes and voice made plain his elation. However, not one hint of a smile appeared on his face. He didn't move in for a hug or handshake, and Verahl offered no affection either. Strange, but the reunion was still heartwarming. I was glad for my part in making it possible.

Verahl's gaze darted between all of us. "Captain?" He settled on Ingvar first, contrite. "I … I'm sorry about yesterday."

Ingvar continued to hang back with wariness, one hand clutching his longsword's hilt while the other waved off the apology. "Save that for Fasolt, should ye see him again."

"Fasolt's fine, at least," I said, hoping Ingvar could get past his misgivings. He and I would almost certainly have to cooperate with Verahl, and later Thordia, in coming days.

Verahl looked to Dag, his happy surprise returning. "What are you doing here?"

"I was hiding out at your house when the knight and the captain showed up. And a vinrake," Dag explained.

"A vinrake! At—? You went to …? *Where is she?*" Verahl's demanding gaze narrowed in on me, then the box in my hands.

At that, his shoulders slumped, and the light in him extinguished.

My brief triumph crashed into remorse. I surrendered the box to him.

Verahl flipped it open and ignored all else in favor of Thordia's note, which he froze over, dumbfounded for several moments.

"Uh, Jayce?" Verahl sampled the moniker, glancing my way with pleading eyes. "We should talk, down below."

"In the bowels of this thing?" The blood left Ingvar's face.

"We won't be long," Verahl said.

Ingvar squared his shoulders, then crossed the galley toward us. "I'm part of this discussion also, Naustvik."

Verahl really wanted to talk alone, but I had no intention of humoring his mistrust of the man who'd made his escape possible. "We can talk wherever you like, but Captain Leirfall stays with us," I said.

Verahl couldn't fully mask his disappointment as he faced Dag. "Can you do me a favor and wait outside?"

Dag frowned his surprise. "What for?"

"It's not easy to explain. The same things that got me and Thordia in trouble …" Verahl trailed off. "I don't want you catching trouble too. All right?"

"Too late for that, mate," Dag dismissed.

"Please?" Verahl pressed.

The boy hesitated with a glance my way, maybe hoping I'd intervene on his behalf.

Unfortunately for him, I shared Verahl's protective sentiment. "Go outside the same way we came in and close the hatch behind yourself," I directed in a gentle tone. "I'll come get you when we're ready to eat."

Dag coldly narrowed his eyes, then trudged back out of the galley as ordered.

I regretted that my stock had fallen in his books yet again.

Still, I wasn't about to compromise his safety just so he'd like me better.

Ingvar, Verahl, and I waited to hear the airlock hatch open and close behind Dag. Once it had, Verahl took the lead back down into the engine room, clutching Thordia's belongings to his chest.

I took off my baldric and side sword, the better to keep from getting caught on anything, then looked to Ingvar with reassurance. "There's nothing dangerous down there. It's just cramped."

Ingvar followed my cue, doffing his own weapons. "I'll go next."

He descended gingerly, but at no point lost his nerve over the "Shipbuilder magic" below. I followed close behind.

The core of *Kepler's Law* was a windowless mishmash of components harvested from less fortunate wrecks. Around the boxy engine sprawled mazes of conduits, scorched in places. Filters and generators jutted from every available niche. The odor of some misbehaving system occasionally stung one's nostrils, but that night, the air was blessedly clear.

It all looked more precarious than it actually was. The ship's systems were hardy, with few to no moving parts. They didn't call them "Shipbuilders" for nothing. The occasional swap-out, I could handle myself; my friends at the beguinage saw to more complicated maintenance. With our combined vigilance, I'd never been stranded mid-space with a problem.

Verahl squeezed himself into a far corner. It was impossible to miss the awed light in his eyes, the tremble in his hands, as things he'd only ever read about sprang to life around him once more. I hung back by the ladder, leaning against it. Ingvar positioned himself in a gap between us, with fists clenched and eyes narrowed in determination. For facing his fears, I admired him more than ever.

"Thank you for bringing this. I know what it must've

taken." Verahl held up the leather-bound box, staring my way with a burning look. He probably wanted to talk more about our mutual Shipbuilder knowledge, hence the original request to speak alone.

I wanted to discuss that as well at some point, but we had more urgent matters to worry about. "I'm sorry Thordia wasn't there. I'm glad we found her research, at least."

"I know why she wasn't home." Verahl took a deep breath. "I'm leaving, as soon as I can, to go search for her."

"Search?" Ingvar scoffed. "Ye know damn well where she went. What in Hel is Thordia doing, endangering us all by approaching the Harbinger?"

Verahl gaped at him in shock.

"We read the note she left for you," I explained.

Verahl's shock doubled. Despite everything else he'd seen, he'd still assumed I couldn't read Shipbuilder.

"We also found a weird substance in your cellar," I continued. "This is what Thordia believes to be causing the crop trouble, right?" I removed the remaining vial of ichor from my pocket and held it up. "What do you know about it?"

Verahl sent a death-glare toward the vial. "I don't know any more than you do."

"Come on, Naustvik!" Ingvar scowled.

"I'm telling the truth!" Verahl pleaded. "Agriculture is Thordia's specialty, but even she was stuck. She's gone to the Harbinger seeking answers. She thinks that's what I want!"

"Isn't it?" I wished I knew what the Harbinger was, aside from a ghost story setting.

Verahl lowered his gaze. A tremor went through him. "I just want Thordia back. Do what you want after that, if you feel you owe these people something. I don't, anymore."

Ingvar smoldered. "Not even Dag?"

"Don't you use him against me!" Verahl met Ingvar's ire with plenty of his own.

"Verahl, that's not his point," I intervened. "You told me you were the one who convinced Thordia to investigate the crop trouble in the first place. You had compassion once. Don't let a handful of people scare you into losing it."

Verahl was silent for several moments, gaze dropping to the floor again. Ingvar glared at him in silence.

After the way he'd been treated, I understood why Verahl wanted to turn his back, but I hoped he was better than that. I wanted to *help* him be better than that. I took a step toward him, making eye contact and speaking with conviction. "Listen, we can work together to bring Thordia *and* the cure back safely. I think that's what we all want."

"You've shouldered enough risk for my sake. I'll always be grateful." Verahl shook his head. "I'm leaving tomorrow. The only thing I ask is that you *don't* send Dag back home."

"He can stay at the barracks with his brother," Ingvar said.

For a brief moment, Verahl looked to Ingvar with real thanks.

At least he cared about Dag. Even if he couldn't bring himself to care about the rest of Nidaros, I still didn't want Verahl striking out on his own. He risked aggravating his wounds, not to mention getting captured again. Besides, whenever we did find Thordia, she'd be more likely to trust us if we had Verahl in tow. I tried a different tack. "Isn't the Harbinger days away by foot? If you're willing to wait a little longer, we could fly there, together." He really liked spacefaring vessels, after all, and it'd be a much faster and easier trip.

The proposal gave Verahl pause. "When would we leave?"

"Well, I don't know yet." I had way too much to sort out before I could answer that. Thordia, the Harbinger, the ichor, Drea … not to mention, it'd be wise to check back in with Baron Tristan and Master Ormyr at some point, just to soothe their nerves. I needed to talk these things out with Ingvar, at minimum.

"That's no good," Verahl said.

"Stay here, Naustvik," Ingvar spoke, calmer. "Ye're in no immediate danger, everyone thinks ye're running loose in the districts. Jayce and I need to rest tonight, show our faces at court in the morning. We'll have a better idea thereafter." He raised a brow. "After what we just risked for you, ye ought to be able to stand waiting 'til midday tomorrow for an update."

Verahl sighed. "All right. I'll wait for you."

I hid my relief. I had no idea how we'd convince Verahl to wait several more *days* if needed, but that was something to worry about later. "Good. Thanks. Come on, let's grab something to eat."

I scaled the ladder and returned topside just in time to catch a flash of Dag's foot disappearing into the airlock.

Someone had been listening in. Nothing for it, I supposed, and returned to the airlock myself. There, the hatch rested in its threshold, but was still ajar.

Sloppy, Dag. Then again, slamming it shut would've been a dead giveaway. Pretending to ignorance, I peeked outside to address Dag and the soldiers. "Come in. I have food if you want some."

At the offer, Dag leapt back into the airlock, eyes wide open, and shadowed me as I returned to the galley to raid the closets. While Verahl took a seat at the table, Ingvar stepped over to silently assist me.

"Ye really fly this thing between planets?" Dag asked.

I smiled. "It doesn't look like she'd go anywhere, but she does."

"She?" he repeated.

"Ships are female," I said.

"Oh." Dag blinked. "So they really *are* alive?"

"Not like you and I are alive." I paused to rebalance the packages piled up in my arms. "She's a machine, but she still deserves respect for all the good she does, so I call her 'she' instead of 'it.'" In honesty, it was a habit I'd acquired from May, but that'd been his rationale. I wondered who might've taught it to him.

Ingvar leaned toward me with a smile. "Not just a sign of respect, but of your kindness," he spoke under his breath.

My heart leapt, sending blood rushing to my face. Before my brain caught up, he was off, taking water bottles to the table as his soldiers reemerged to follow him.

"Does she fly better when ye show her more respect?" Dag asked, deadly serious.

My head plummeted out of the clouds. Smiling, I shut the closets with my foot. "Probably not, but I like to think so."

Dag and I approached the table, where the soldiers seated themselves opposite from a detached and thoughtful Verahl.

"Glad ye're all right mate, really." Dag made a beeline toward his friend. "Stay on this ship, aye? An army of adepts couldn't breach her! Ye could use the rest besides."

This concern stemmed from the conversation Verahl hadn't wanted Dag eavesdropping upon. Nevertheless, Verahl offered him a faint smile. "I won't run off anywhere if you don't."

We gathered up our weapons and left Verahl aboard my ship with Hals and Ragni, reentering the capital with Dag to approach the barracks. Within its warm confines, Ingvar left me and Dag at the door to find Rigg.

The wait was short. Rigg fairly sprinted toward his brother, his once reserved demeanor crumbling with relief.

Dag had a rare glimmer of cheer in his eyes as well. Still, the pair stopped several feet short of one another. No smiles or affectionate gestures from either of them. More evidence of a less-than-ideal upbringing. I struggled to push aside that depressing thought.

"Where in Hel've ye been?" Rigg demanded.

"Just lying low is all." Dag pushed hair out of his eyes with a forearm.

"Where?" Rigg pressed.

"Near home."

"In some cesspool I don't know of?" Rigg rolled his eyes. "Now, what do we do with you?"

"He'll stay here for now, lad." Ingvar had strayed up behind Rigg, lantern still in hand.

Rigg flashed his captain a grateful look.

"Hath Pontus gone home?" Ingvar asked.

"Don't think so, sir," Rigg said. "Still at the keep, stirring up trouble there."

Good. I hoped that meant he was getting somewhere with his search for evidence.

"I'll get Dag billeted, then." Ingvar nodded to the boy. "Looks like ye could use boots too, lad."

Also good. Ingvar had noticed without me having to say anything.

"Thank you, sir. Lady Knight." Rigg glanced to me, then beckoned Dag with a toss of his head. "C'mon, let's clean you up."

Dag spun back to me first, proffering my dagger. "This is yours."

I shook my head. "Keep it, all right? Take care."

Dag's eyes widened a moment. At Rigg's further beckoning, he turned away to follow his brother and Ingvar deeper into the barracks.

I hung back and waited, feeling more at ease about this reunion than the one aboard my ship. With Ingvar and the other soldiers, I *knew* Dag was in good hands.

So much for the boy's short-term fate. Long-term? If he learned to temper that angry, something-to-prove streak, he'd have mountains of potential with minimal risk of getting himself killed. He seemed far too promising to have to be a farmer — but would soldiering be any better? Had he already learned too much for his own good? His self-taught "magic" was a liability, just as it had been for the Naustviks. He might also need protection, or a new home, once my quest was over. But how could I separate him from Rigg?

I'd have to talk about it with Ingvar later. So much to talk about. Most pressingly, the little experiments littered all over my person.

Ingvar returned after some time with his lantern, waving me toward one of the spare rooms. "After what happened today, don't blame you if ye still don't feel safe in the capital. Welcome to stay here if ye want."

I nodded. "I'd like to — thanks. But right now, I've got too much on my mind to sleep. We really need to talk."

"Aye, figured." Ingvar looked alert and worried himself.

"First, let's check on this — " I hefted my canteen " — and the soil I picked up. Can you bring me a bucket or some other container?"

Ingvar nodded. "Hold on."

He stepped away to fetch an empty bucket, then led me to a small room with only a bare table inside. A holding cell, maybe; I was too concerned with the tasks at hand to pay much attention. First, I removed the soil samples from my pockets, unwrapping each one carefully in the light of Ingvar's lantern. The compresses had both soaked up traces of ichor like blood from a wound. The deeper soil had given up more of the substance than the topsoil.

Ingvar leaned in beside me, surveying the evidence with a stricken expression. *"Skíta."*

I shook my head grimly. "I bet if I fetch soil from right outside here, it'll look like this too. Something to try in the morning. For now, let's see if this ichor's done anything to my water yet."

Poised over the bucket, I opened the canteen, then poured.

We both jumped, then peeked into the bucket to make sure we weren't seeing things. Sure enough, that small amount looked nothing like water anymore, having changed over completely into purplish ichor. Heart in my throat, I poured out the rest. It seemed about the same amount of fluid as before, but all trace of water had vanished.

"It seems to … change water into more of itself," I murmured. "That's why your crops aren't growing. That must also be how it spreads." A gut-wrenching realization struck me. "And if it's in the soil, I'll just bet it's in your groundwater too. *That's* why the adepts closed off your wells!"

Ingvar's eyes latched onto mine, frightened. Without a word, he hooked me by the elbow, then stalked back toward the barracks entrance.

"Where're we going?" I asked.

He was too distracted to answer or even look my way. Near the door, he released me to pick up another bucket sitting nearby, then darted outside.

I trailed Ingvar and the lantern flame that flickered precariously as he hastened to a well just outside the barracks, bound up like all the others. In the absence of a smaller blade between us, he set aside his lantern and used his longsword to sever the mess of charms and leather ties. Ingvar then placed his bucket beneath the spigot to work the freed pump. It was dry for a while at first before sputtering to life — pouring out a ghastly, familiar sludge.

Ingvar sank to his knees, agape in horror. After a moment, he released the pump to sit back hard on the ground, drawing his knees toward his chest and bracing his head in his hands.

"No wonder everything's dead," he mourned. "If it weren't raining, we'd be dead too."

It was just as Kofri had described in the kitchen days earlier, but that didn't make the discovery any less of a gut-punch. I stood frozen in place at first, eyes stuck upon the ichor-filled bucket. I longed to comfort Ingvar, and felt like an idiot for it. All the trouble surrounding us, and *that* was where my brain went. What could I do, though? I had no answers; that was what I really wanted to offer. No, I just had more worrying thoughts. According to Ingvar, the problem had originated in the North and East, spreading from there. As long as the ichor kept coming in contact with water, it'd keep spreading. Hell, where would it end? If nothing stopped it, could it threaten the whole planet?

"The adepts have known of this ichor for some time, and yet, never a *word* of it." Ingvar's head shot up, his furious and questioning gaze locking onto mine. "Was it *their* doing? The prisoner in the dungeon … what if this is some poison of theirs that got out of hand?"

It was a frightening, real possibility, but it wasn't the only possibility. "Maybe. Or maybe they found this stuff, but didn't know what it was. So they kept it a secret, warned people away from it. It wouldn't be the first time adepts have covered up something they couldn't explain."

Ingvar shook his head. "Even if we take these buckets to Baron Tristan and shove them under his nose, Ormyr will have a deflection ready!"

"I know," I said quietly.

"What do we do?"

I summoned the nerve to sit on the ground beside him and rest my hand on his back. Surprise flickered over Ingvar's expression, but he didn't flinch or push me away. Though my heart pounded, I kept my voice level. "We need to find out what this stuff is and how to get rid of it. Why does Thordia think she'll find answers at the Harbinger? What *is* the Harbinger?"

Ingvar's head dropped, hanging between his shoulders. Silence stretched between us. Just as I was about to try asking again, he faced me, eyes full of trepidation. "The old ones say it presaged the fall of Lord Gyllenfeld. 'Tis how it got its name. Truth is, Gyllenfeld had fallen afore it struck."

"Struck?" I repeated.

"Ages afore any of us were born, this great *thing* fell out of the sky and drove into the ground like a tent spike." Ingvar swallowed around a lump in his throat. "The earth shook, forests fell, entire districts burnt up. Sky full of light one moment, ash the next. Hundreds died in the chaos."

Sympathy strained my ribcage. My free hand rose to my mouth. "That must've been awful."

"The Baron at that time decreed that anyone who approacheth the thing should be put to death," Ingvar continued. "Every Baron since hath upheld the decree, not wishing to risk stirring up its wrath again."

"What was it? Some kind of rock from space?" A meteorite was all I could think of. It must've been *massive* to cause such turmoil.

"Nay. 'Tis something Shipbuilder for certain, some manner of relic long dead. When ye look from the right places, ye can see it towering in the distance still, miles of ruin spread out around it." Ingvar glanced off into the nighttime void, sizing up a nemesis across an invisible battlefield. "My family's farm lieth in the East, in a district spared its violence. I faced down the beast every day there wasn't a fog or storm. Always felt like it was watching us, waiting for the right moment to finish what it began."

Something Shipbuilder? Something huge that'd fallen out of the sky, driving into the ground like a tent spike? I could only think of one thing that fit the profile. My already fast heart raced with astonishment. I searched my feverish thoughts for the right words to explain, and labored to speak them with a measure of coherence.

"A long time ago, the Shipbuilders built hundreds of stations in space," I began. "Like spacefaring vessels, only much larger, and not faring anywhere. I won't know for sure until I see it, but it sounds to me like the Harbinger's one of those giant stations. Without the Shipbuilders there to take care of it, it might've drifted out of its proper position in space and crashed on Nidaros." I skipped the discussion of Lagrangian points and orbital decay. "That crash would've been very violent, like you said. Think of a stone sending ripples through a pond, only through air and land instead."

Was the Harbinger truly the ruins of a former space station? I'd never *dared* imagine stumbling upon such a find. Was it possible that anything aboard the station had survived impact? Just trying to conceive of the incredible things that might lie in wait sent chills of anticipation through me.

Ingvar stared deep into my eyes, struggling to process my explanation. His uneasiness killed my excitement, replacing it with dread.

"Thordia must be seeking more powerful Shipbuilder magic to use against the ichor," he murmured. "But if she's not careful, she might unleash something even worse."

CONTINUED IN BOOK 2: HARBINGERS

The Quest Continues!

Jessamine and Ingvar are about to run headlong into a real witch, and don't know it yet! Will they save Nidaros from the ichor, or is it already too late? And what secrets lie within the mysterious Harbinger?

Harbingers, Book 2 of the Sword and Starship series, is now available!

If you liked this book, I'd appreciate you revisiting the product page where you purchased it and leaving your honest review there. Your feedback means a lot!

You can also visit my website to sign up for updates and giveaways: http://www.ellismorning.com

Thanks for joining me on this adventure!

-Ellis

About Ellis

Ellis has always loved staging adventures in her head before going to sleep each night. When she was twelve, she started putting these adventures on paper.

For the next twenty years, she wrote with varying degrees of seriousness, but always as a hobby. In that time, she fell in love with Mark Twain and Kurt Vonnegut, the original *Star Trek* series, and *Mystery Science Theater 3000*. Science fiction became her favorite domain to work in, but she also enjoyed reading fantasy, horror, Western, and detective stories, and incorporating their elements into her work. One of her favorite things to do was make people laugh.

Ellis denied being a writer for decades. But then she sold articles to The Daily WTF, and a short story to Analog Science Fiction and Fact. After quitting her full-time job to finish her first novel, it was time to own up to writing as her calling. She's currently having the time of her life penning the *Sword and Starship* series, and has ideas for many more stories and books to come.

Website: www.ellismorning.com
Email: contact@ellismorning.com
Google Plus: +Ellis Morning
Twitter: @EllisMorning

www.ingramcontent.com/pod-product-compliance
Lightning Source LLC
Chambersburg PA
CBHW030558180626
46816CB00005B/1598